Strange Matings:

Science Fiction, Feminism, African American

Voices, and Octavia E. Butler

D1596814

❖ *Photo by Leslie Howle*

Strange Matings:

Science Fiction, Feminism, African American

Voices, and Octavia E. Butler

◕ edited by

Rebecca J. Holden and Nisi Shawl

Aqueduct Press
PO Box 95787
Seattle WA 99145-2787
www.aqueductpress.com

Strange Matings: Science Fiction, Feminism, African American
Voices, and Octavia E. Butler

ISBN: 978-1-61976-037-0
Library of Congress Control Number: 2013934568

10 9 8 7 6 5 4 3 2 1
First Printing, July 2013

Cover painting: "Call for Strange Matings" courtesy Luisah Teish,
photographed by Gail Williams

Octavia E. Butler letters courtesy Merrilee Heifetz

Book design by Kathryn Wilham
Interior photographs courtesy Leslie Howle, David Findlay,
and M. Asli Dukan

Printed in the United States of America
by Thompson-Shore, Inc.

Acknowledgments

This project has been a true labor of love for both of us, and took more time and effort than either of us imagined. Rebecca would like to thank both Catherine Prendergast and Lisa Yaszek for encouraging her to pursue this project despite early setbacks, as well as her husband Christian and two children, Clara and Soren, for supporting her work. We both want to thank Nalo Hopkinson for suggesting that the two of us work together on it. In addition, we would like to acknowledge the role that WisCon played by providing a forum for our collaboration and a source for contributors. We appreciate the work and effort that both Timmi Duchamp and Kath Wilham at Aqueduct have put into the manuscript. We know that the book is better because of their work.

The excerpts of Nisi's interview with Octavia come from an unreleased film made by M. Asli Dukan that was recorded during the Black to the Future Black Science Fiction Festival, which took place in Seattle in 2004. We're very grateful to the Central District Forum for Arts and Ideas for organizing the festival, and particularly to Denee McCloud, who did much of the work of putting together that gala weekend. We also thank Asli for making the interview soundtrack available to us.

We thank the Carl Brandon Society for paying the cost of transcribing the interview. The Carl Brandon Society is a nonprofit organization dedicated to supporting the presence of people of color in the fantastic genres. Octavia was an early member, and the Octavia E. Butler Scholarship Fund created in her memory is administered by the Carl Brandon Society. If you'd like to learn more about the Carl Brandon Society, read the entire interview, and find out how to support the Scholarship Fund and other wonderful programs administered by the Society, visit www.carlbrandon.org.

Finally, we want to thank all of our contributors for being patient as we navigated the rather slow process of putting out this anthology.

for Octavia,
and all those who knew and loved her,
and all those who wish they had

Contents

Clarion West class of 2005 with Octavia E. Butler and other teachers at a party during Octavia's last year of instruction. After they had posed for a number of photos somebody called out "Zombies!" and the whole group turned into a shambling, moaning mob. Octavia joined in with glee.

❧ *Photo by Leslie Howle*

Strange Matings and Their Progeny: A Legacy of Conversations, Thoughts, Writings, and Actions

Rebecca J. Holden and Nisi Shawl

> She realized she did not mind his attention. She had avoided animal matings in the past. She was a woman. Intercourse with an animal was abomination. She would feel unclean reverting to her human form with the seed of a male animal insider her.
>
> But now...it was as though the dolphins were not animals.
>
> She performed a kind of dance with the male, moving and touching, certain that no human ceremony had ever drawn her in so quickly. She felt both eager and restrained, both willing and hesitant. She would accept him, had already accepted him. He was surely no more strange than the ogbanje, Doro. Now seemed to be a time for strange matings. (*Wild Seed* 1980, 84–85)

A mating between a human and a dolphin is far from the strangest of the strange matings in the fiction of Octavia E. Butler. Butler writes about matings between humans and a large variety of other beings, such as blue-furred aliens, tentacled aliens of three different sexes, insect-like aliens whose eggs hatch inside human hosts, and perhaps strangest of all, matings between all the varied categories of humans that we have divided ourselves into.

What is most significant about all of the matings in Butler's work, however, is not their strangeness, but what such matings produce or lead to—and the necessity of those matings. For Butler's characters, the inevitable crossing and blurring of boundaries such matings entail often bring with them physical and emotional pain. Still, Butler shows us that these matings are key to her characters' survival, both for the individual and for the group. Sometimes that survival is raw, as in *Dawn*, when Butler's human protagonists mate with aliens in order to avoid extinction, and in *Kindred*, when slaves mate with their masters in order to preserve their own lives. And sometimes it is much more, as in the celebration of survival that Anyanwu engages in with her dolphin mate above.

Butler herself crossed many boundaries—perhaps to ensure a certain kind of survival for herself and her ideas of what we might become. In the most obvious of these boundary crossings, she, an African-American woman, crossed into the then mostly white, male arena of science fiction in the 1970s, demonstrating that women of color could successfully inhabit the worlds of science fiction. At the same time, she refused to let either herself or her writing be solely defined by her race or her gender—though both affected her subject matter and overall themes. In this way, she also crossed into the mostly white, middle class arena of 1970s feminism.

➥ ⬳

NISI: By the time I met Octavia in 1999, she was doing more than crossing the barriers of race, gender, and genre. She was rising above them, partly by refusing to be contained within them. She was using what she had achieved to reveal such categories as imperfect and incomplete, and, I think, deliberately making herself into the sort of person who would be picked as a model by those of us who, like her, sought to confound such categories. The last Christmas card Octavia sent me had a photo of Mt. Rainier on the front. Not only did she love that mountain, she resembled it. She towered over everything ordinary; she made her own weather. Speaking at a memorial gathering in New York, Octavia's publisher Dan Simon spoke of her in the same vein: "Does it ever seem to you that there are people among us who hold up the sky and make the rivers flow.... Octavia comes to my mind as first among that group of people" (personal communication).

Certainly her work has influenced many people, many communities, many genres, many fields, many schools of thought. She also lived her life in a way that made her mere presence a strong influence on anyone she came in contact with.

Octavia did her best to encourage other people of color to write science fiction. I, like the other fiction writers in this anthology, am among those she encouraged. She spoke with me about writing as if I were her equal, and that helped. She listened, and that helped too. And she taught—several times at Clarion and Clarion West. One of my published stories, "Momi Watu," is a response to an exercise I received from Octavia secondhand, through a student of hers: "Write about what scares you."

Within the sf (science fiction) community we expect our writers, even those at the top of the professional heap, to be approachable, but it isn't always so. And Octavia had a reasonably good excuse for secluding herself from fans and emulators: she was painfully shy. By teaching beginners, by giving us her phone number, by supporting our work in the most basic ways—with her own money and time—Octavia levitated over boundaries others might have found insuperable and that she herself might have clung to, if all she cared about was her own comfort.

❧

REBECCA: It was this levitation over boundaries in both her writing and her life that led me as well as the other scholars collected here to her. I was initially drawn to Butler because of the ways in which she was a part of many differing worlds and the ways in which she influenced those worlds—the worlds of science fiction (including the fans, the writers, and the readers), feminism, African American writing, and now, even the "academy." As an academic, who also happened to be an ardent feminist and a science fiction fan, I could see into a number of these worlds and how much she had changed them.

❧

This anthology seeks to present a unique take on an author. Rather than restricting its contents to only memoirs or only tribute stories or only academic investigations, we have drawn on all of these and on other genres as well, in an effort to demonstrate both the wide range of Butler's appeal and its influence in multiple worlds.

As the editors of this anthology—one of us an academic scholar and the other a science fiction author—we ourselves are a strange mating. Our partnership, bringing together differing approaches to the task of putting together this book is emblematic of the strength Butler's protagonists find by embracing diversity. It's our belief that *Strange Matings* as a whole will be more interesting for the general reader than would an anthology that was purely academic, or one that was strictly personal, or one that concerned itself only with literature. We've included poems; letters; footnoted essays from scholars of science fiction, popular culture, and women's studies; wistful reminiscences from friends and on-line journal entries posted by a former student; an interview transcript and an exchange of emails; a memorial speech; and many, many personal testimonies to her influence on the lives, careers, and work of contributors coming from fields as diverse as priest of a West African spiritual tradition and Hollywood scriptwriter. Our goal is to create in this text "Bridges, not walls," as a labor-organizer friend always says.

⇒ ⇐

With *Strange Matings* we intend to continue the conversations that Butler began. She was never one to let herself or her audience off easy. Reading her books—the violence, the trauma, and the reminders of what we humans could do, not only to an alien other, but also to each other—was never a Disney-like feel-good experience. She wanted us to confront who we are and what we are capable of—both good and bad. As the essays in this book demonstrate, her work provokes not only discomfort but also new questions and concerns. *Strange Matings* seeks to continue Butler's uncomfortable insights about humanity, and also to instigate new conversations about Butler and her work—conversations that encourage academic voices to "talk" to the private voices, the poetic voices to answer the analytic. In initiating these additional conversations, we set out to explore numerous questions about Butler and her fiction. How did her work affect conceptions of what science fiction is and could be? How did her portrayals of African Americans challenge accepted assumptions and affect others writing in the field? In what ways did her commitment to issues of race and gender express itself? How did this dual commitment affect the emerging field of overtly feminist science fiction? How did it affect the perception of her work? In what ways did Butler inspire other writers and change the "face" of science fiction? How did she "queer" science fiction? In what ways did she inspire us and motivate us take up difficult subjects and tasks? In other words, what is her legacy?

⇒ ⇐

No single essay or even book can fully answer all of these questions, but here we have brought together voices from a diverse group in order to begin this effort. The voices of *Strange Matings* include women and men, African Americans and European Americans, academics and writers, sf fans and sf professionals, the relatively famous and the relatively obscure. And Butler herself speaks, from a 2004 interview interspersed throughout the anthology.

Part One, "Patterns of Kinship" examines Butler's 1970s fiction from numerous perspectives. Rebecca begins the section with a discussion about the Patternist series as a progressive development of feminist cyborg fiction. Then, doris davenport imagines poetic sequels to *Mind of My Mind,* as she gives voices to "Mary's Children" in her poem. Butler explains the difficulties of her research trip for *Kindred* in an excerpt from the above-mentioned interview, while Wendy Gay Pearson and Susan Knabe investigate issues of kinship and "gambling against history" in this most widely-read of Butler's books, through the lens of queer theory. JT Stewart's poem, inspired by *Kindred,* provides us with another insight into Butler's revision of slave histories, one filtered through the writer's own history. Next, we learn how *Wild Seed* provided a model of fiction writing for a novelist seeking to write anti-establishment feminist fiction in L. Timmel Duchamp's piece, and finally Luisah Teish writes about this novel as "the spirit in the seed" that influenced and inspired her, a black feminist making traditional African religious practices accessible to the West.

Part Two, "Tendencies toward Hierarchicalism and the Breakdown of Society," moves into the 1980s—the time of Reagan and political apathy, and Butler's move into post-apocalyptic sf. Writer Steven Barnes reminisces about how Octavia "took him to school ruthlessly" regarding his naïve views about trickle-down economics and shared her views on humanity's tendency towards hierarchicalism—a tendency she believed might destroy us if we let it. Our contributors probe Butler's exploration of that thesis in this section. However, their essays demonstrate that this exploration is far from the depressing one it might be. Sandra Govan highlights how personal resonances between herself and Octavia, both growing up as black women in the 1950s, brought Govan even closer to Butler's fiction, while Candra K. Gill talks about growing up as a black woman in the 1980s, raised on *Star Trek* and Butler—happy that Butler made black women visible in the science fiction world. Thomas Foster's essay highlights how Butler herself came back again and again to issues of identity (including race, gender, and humanness) as they relate to tolerance and survival. He reads the Xenogenesis trilogy against her 2003 short story "Amnesty," which he sees as a narrative corrective to overly utopic or dystopic misreadings of the alien rescue/invasion of the destroyed Earth.

Part Three, "The *Parables*" brings us back from the far-flung future of stories like Xenogenesis and "Bloodchild" to the very near future of Butler's Parable stories, a future whose bleakness is almost paralyzing. However, Butler herself explains that these are "cautionary tales"—warnings, not predictions. Butler's pessimism could sometimes get the better of her, as we see in the exchanges Butler's literary agent Merrilee Heifetz shares. However, Butler's grim tales had far-ranging, powerful effects. Kate Schaefer remembers fondly the hope of the journey and the payoff for the preparation in *Parable of the Sower*. Lisbeth Gant-Britton highlights the ways in which these novels fit into the tradition of activist, utopian literature and have inspired real life groups to embrace "new mutually empowering forms of social interaction and to reconceptualize currently divisive notions such as race, class, and gender." Finally, Nisi writes about the never-completed third parable, *The Parable of the Trickster*, a book that displayed its true trickster nature in never showing its face fully, either to us or to Butler.

The final section of the book, "New Media, New Generations, and a New Take on Vampires," brings Butler into the twenty-first century. African American novelists Nnedi Okorafor and Tananarive Due share with us pieces of their personal connection with Butler—connections enhanced via email and shared politics for Okorafor, and the fullness of what remained unsaid for Due. Scholars Steven Shaviro and Shari Evans provide us with incisive readings of *Fledgling*, Butler's vampire story that, despite her deprecation of its escapist nature, turns out not to be escapist at all and in fact, continues Butler's questioning of the categories we put ourselves into and the ways in which we use power (or race, gender, class, and culture) to create divisions among ourselves. We end the book with a beginning, or more precisely, two beginnings: Octavia's reminiscences on the start of what was to become her lifelong career as an sf author and Benjamin Rosenbaum's essay—which incorporates his blog and thus another new kind of conversation—about how Octavia's advice as his instructor at Clarion West gave him his start on a similar path.

⇒ ⇐

Throughout the book's different sections, illustrations reflect Octavia-as-she-appeared-to-us: her public face at readings and interviews and signings and conferences, and also, happily, more personal moments shared with longtime friend Leslie Howle on the beaches and mountain paths of the Pacific Northwest. Howle and all *Strange Matings*'s diverse contributors have one thing in common: we were changed irrevocably by our interactions with Octavia. A chant in honor of the Yoruba goddess Oya for whom Parable heroine Lauren Oya Olamina is named says: "She changes everything she touches, and everything she touches changes." This is certainly true of Octavia, as anyone who had some sort of relationship with her, no matter how distant or fleeting, can testify.

⇒ ⇐

REBECCA: Our relationships with Octavia Butler were not and are not the same; some of us never met her, never had a personal relationship with her, but still felt the power of her words and her life in our work and life. To some of us, she is mostly "Butler," and to others of us she will always be Octavia, and to others yet, she is both. I love the way Sandra Govan writes about the "Octavia" she shared stories of her childhood with and the "Butler" whose "deft, economic prose" she analyzed. When I started this project, she was definitely "Butler" to me, but now I feel as if I have come to know her better, to know her as both Octavia and Butler.

🌿

NISI: The process of putting this book together has taught me to accept that I will continue to miss Octavia, to miss her always. I'm no longer surprised or ashamed to find myself crying when I write or read or talk about her, and sorrow hasn't stopped me from sharing what I remember.

Our relationships with Octavia have not ended with her life, any more than the changes she engendered have come to an end.

Since 2007, students of color who demonstrate talent and a commitment to Octavia's ideals have been selected as Octavia E. Butler Scholars and receive full scholarships for the Clarion or

Clarion West Writing Workshops, which usually cost thousands of dollars to attend. Octavia attended the Clarion Workshop in its first incarnation in Pennsylvania, and she taught several times at both current versions of this six-week intensive class. She credited the workshop with providing the education she needed to become a professional author. These scholar awards provide the means for a new generation of writers to follow in her footsteps. These new writers and other people are forming new relationships with Octavia: Butler Scholars; donors to the scholarship fund; members and officers of the Carl Brandon Society, which administers the fund; those who read the fiction written by those inspired by Butler. More relationships. More change.

⇒ ⇐

We hope that the essays, poems, and photos here will help all of our readers come to know the multiple faces and names of Octavia E. Butler—to relate to her as a writer, a teacher, a friend, a mentor, a feminist, an African American, a full human not afraid of the inhuman in all of us. The voices and conversations we've included here do not represent all there is to say about Butler and her work. Instead, we conceptualize the texts within as several opening gambits in more than one discussion about Octavia that we hope will continue outside of these pages. We want to motivate our readers to investigate what is not explored in these pages—to interrogate what her fiction ignores or perhaps glosses over, to uncover new aspects of her stories that our contributors do not investigate here; in other words, we want our readers to take part in the dance, the strange matings called forth by Octavia E. Butler's work and life.

One of the reasons Octavia moved to Seattle was her love of mountains, especially Mt. Rainier. Leslie Howle took her on an expedition to explore the glories of Mt. Baker and Mt. Shuksan. Though Rainier remained her favorite, her pleasure is obvious in this photo taken near Mt. Shuksan's reflection in Picture Lake.

❧ *Photo by Leslie Howle*

Editor Nisi Shawl conducts a live interview of Octavia E. Butler for the 2004 Black to the Future Black Science Fiction Festival. Portions of the interview are reproduced in this book.

❧ *Photo by M. Asli Dukan*

Excerpt 1 from "A Conversation with Octavia E. Butler"

Nisi Shawl

(Interview Conducted at The "Black to the Future Conference:
A Black Science Fiction Festival," Seattle, June 12, 2004)

Nisi: The woman seated next to me is perhaps best known for *Kindred*, a book used as a teaching text in colleges and universities across the country, around the world. *Kindred* tells of a twentieth-century Black woman compelled to travel through time to rescue a white ancestor, and its harrowing pages have hooked many a reader. But *Kindred*'s author has also written some simply amazing short stories. In addition to *Kindred*, her novels include the five book Patternist series, beginning with her first published novel *Patternmaster* and continuing with *Mind of My Mind*, *Wild Seed*, *Survivor*, and *Clay's Ark*. Then there's her latest two-book series, *The Parable of the Talents* and the predecessor *The Parable of the Sower*. They focus on this messianic empath named Lauren Oya Olamina—a heroine almost as formidable as the woman who created her. Ladies and gentlemen, and just plain folks, it is with great pleasure that I ask you to join me in this conversation with Octavia Estelle Butler.

[AUD: Applause]

Octavia: Okay, now before you say anything, I have to say one thing that somehow didn't get said in the book. When my publisher was thinking about putting the three Xenogenesis novels together, she didn't want to entitle them *Xenogenesis*, because the Science Fiction Book Club had already done that, and she wanted me to come up with a new title. And I was shopping around for titles. And I had gotten to the point of "Lilith's Children" or something like that. I didn't like it and who should call up but Nisi. And I put my question to her and she said, "Well, Lilith's Brood?" And there it is. Now you have the story of at least one title.

Nisi: So, we're going to assume that most of the audience is as familiar as I am with your work. But we're going to pretend there's someone here who's never read anything by you. So how would you describe your writing to someone who's never read it?

Octavia: Well, I'm essentially a storyteller, and I think things like titles and beginnings are advertisements for the stories I write. So I guess I think of myself hopefully as a good storyteller.

Nisi: A good storyteller, all right. A fan that I spoke to about you insisted that you were not a science fiction writer.

Octavia: It's one of those things. I used to wonder. I went through a couple of tours for the Parable books—and I don't mind tours at all because they help sell the books—but in this case I couldn't figure out why everywhere I went someone was saying, "Well now are you a science fiction writer? Or do you dislike that term and you want to be called...?" It's like, who cares? I want you to read the book. My goodness, and the problem turned out to be, my editor had written a publicity release that said, "She doesn't want to be called a science fiction writer." So of course everyone had to ask about it or call me one, in the hope of getting a rise out of me. But I really don't care. I want you to read my stuff. The only problem I have with the word science fiction is sometimes it stops people from reading, as in "Oh I don't like science fiction."

I was doing a mall signing one time—just for the record, authors hate mall signings. I mean, unless they're Anne Rice. Normally—[AUD: laughter]— normally in a mall signing you're sitting in a place where a lot of people are rushing past you. They have no idea why you're there, even though you're sitting next to a pile of your own books and a big sign. They'll stop and turn a page or something or ask you where the Anne Rice books are. Ask you where the restroom is. And after a while I started collaring people. You know how people are a little bit too polite to walk by when you speak to them. They don't really know whether they want to talk to you or not, but they will stop. And this one woman stopped. I said, "Ma'am?" She stopped. And I said "Would you like to read a good book?" I had no modesty, and she picked up the book and was reading it, it was *Kindred* by the way, and she looked interested. And I said stupidly, "Do you like science fiction?" She put the book down; "No, I don't like science fiction." And I said, "Well it's not like *Star Wars*." She literally looked down her nose at me and said "I know what science fiction is," and walked away. So in that sense I really, I don't care what you call it, but I do want you to take a look at it before you turn it down.

Nisi: As a reader yourself, do you differentiate between science fiction and fantasy?

Octavia: [to audience] She keeps doing this.

Nisi: Okay, so you don't care. Got it.

Octavia: If I'm using science, I hope I'm using it accurately. If I'm writing something that has no science in it, like *Kindred* by the way, then all I have to do is follow the rules I've set up.

A photo from one of the many journeys through natural
surroundings Octavia and Leslie Howle enjoyed together.
 Photo by Leslie Howle

Part One

Patterns of Kinship:

On Butler's Patternist Series and *Kindred*

"I began writing about power because I had so little": The Impact of Octavia Butler's Early Work on Feminist Science Fiction as a Whole (and on One Feminist Science Fiction Scholar in Particular)

Rebecca J. Holden

When I first encountered Octavia E. Butler's science fiction in the mid-90s, I was trying to find a way to be feminist in my varying lives as a woman, scholar, teacher, graduate student, and person with insulin-dependent diabetes.[1] I had recently decided to write my dissertation on feminist science fiction (sf). While I had read numerous science fiction books by women—feminist and otherwise—graduate school had left me little time for any leisure reading, so I felt out of touch with what was out there in the category of feminist sf. I headed to a local used book store and bought every science fiction book by a woman on the shelves. Then I started to read.

The second book I picked up from my stack was Butler's *Wild Seed*. In the notes I took at the time, I referred to it as "my first Octavia Butler," as if reading a Butler novel was some sort of initiation—which indeed it turned out to be. I wrote that the struggle between the two main characters—a man and a woman—sounded "like a typical love plot in some ways," but that the female protagonist's "power and her will and the circumstances [of the story] add many new twists and dimensions which make me say that although this reminds me of [Chinua] Achebe and some other texts, it was [*sic*] also like nothing else I have ever read. I wanted it to continue and continue." While the book itself did come to an end, I found that Butler's unique narrative perspective continued in her nine other novels available at that time, books that I immediately acquired and read.

My reading of Butler's early work alongside other feminist sf written in the 1970s led me to believe that Octavia Butler's fiction, in spite of or sometimes because of the ways she drew on the traditions of African mythology and slave narrative, *was* like nothing else being published at that time. Not only was her work novel, but as I argue in my history of feminist sf (aka my dissertation), it had major ramifications on the science fiction genre as a whole, and most directly on the evolution of the emerging sub-genre of feminist sf. For this reason, Butler ended up as the only writer with a chapter to herself in my dissertation. Butler's choice of black female protagonists, emphasis on biological technologies and disease, and incorporation of African-American history, forces readers and writers of feminist sf to step back and acknowledge historical, cultural, and socio-economic differences among women. Her refusal to reduce her complex characters with their multiple narratives of identity to simple, more recognizable heroines reveals true alternatives for imagining feminist stories of the past and future. The power in her work, even decades after it was first published, significantly affected not only the direction of my doctoral research, but also my perceptions of myself as a feminist.

Clearly, my history does not match that of Butler's protagonists—I am white, middle class, and highly educated. Still, my body and perspective on the world have been (and continue to be) transformed by disease and technology as well as the current politics of gender and race. Perhaps that was why the powerful voices of Butler's hybrid protagonists spoke to me as I struggled to develop my own feminist voice. My students at the time seemed to think that sexism and racism were problems of the past—sometimes in spite of their personal experiences. "Feminism," if not exactly a dirty word, smacked of a rigid political correctness that they wanted nothing to do with. My professors, many of them academic feminists, supported and validated feminist literary critique but saw my desire to apply such critique to science fiction as suspect.[2] I was not interested in becoming an apolitical, opinion-free, and thus supposedly value-free instructor or scholar who simply followed past models of research and writing for academic feminism. At the same time, I did not want to turn students off from developing critical and social awareness by stuffing "Feminism" with a capital "F" down their throats, nor give up my academic career because my research interests didn't fit into accepted categories.[3]

Eventually, I discovered that like Butler and her protagonists, I needed to embrace what I now call—using Donna Haraway's cyborg myth—a cyborg multiplicity to give weight to my voice and my goals. In the classroom, that meant willingly identifying myself as a feminist, acutely aware that I could not speak for all women or feminists while at the same time acknowledging the different places my students might be coming from. It also meant posing those uncomfortable questions about sex, race, class, and politics, and encouraging students to discuss and analyze their discomfort. As a scholar, it meant using an academically acceptable topic—that of utopian literature—as a lead-in to what I saw as the more exciting, open, and relevant one of science fiction as well as finding alternative outlets, such as the non-academic feminist science fiction convention WisCon, for my work.[4]

In this essay, I return to my initial fascination with Butler's early work and focus on three books from Butler's Patternist series, *Patternmaster* (1976), *Mind of My Mind* (1978), and *Wild Seed* (1980), to demonstrate how Butler experimented with varying hybrid or "cyborg" identities in order to make women of color both visible and powerful within the futures or pasts that she imagined.[5] Reading Butler's science fiction in conjunction with Haraway's "Cyborg Manifesto" (1991), I argue, can show us how feminist sf can critique patriarchal society and maintain its critical edge without erasing differences among women, thus pointing the way for future feminist sf as well as for feminists, such as myself, who read this fiction.

Monsters: African-American Women and Feminist Cyborgs

In the late 1960s and early 1970s, feminist sf, like the women's movement, exploded onto the scene.[6] The feminist sf of this era was dominated by stories of future utopias in which women came together as women—despite their differences—to create societies where gender discrimination no longer existed. Race and class discrimination were also absent, but gender equity was the driving force behind these utopias. Because gender identity was primary in these stories, black women—marked socially by both gender and race—were not fully represented. Women of color appear in Suzy McKee Charnas's *Motherlines* and in Marge Piercy's *Woman on the Edge of Time,* but as Michele Erica Green notes, all women are seen as "interchangeable" and their racial and ethnic differences "seem only skin-deep" (1994, 168).

This failure to make African-American women visible is not found solely in 1970s feminist sf. In fact, mainstream feminism has often been regarded as the territory of white women while the civil rights movement has been viewed as championing black men. In multiple instances—including the fight for suffrage of the late nineteenth and early twentieth centuries, the civil rights and women's liberation movements of the sixties and seventies, and the more recent Anita Hill/Clarence Thomas controversy—African-American men and feminists have been set in opposition. The pitting of two disenfranchised groups against each other was not accidental nor, given the difference between these groups, difficult to engineer.[7] Those in power know that the best way to maintain power is to keep the oppressed from unifying. In these struggles, black women were expected to take on, at least metaphorically, the guise of white women or black men.[8] As Nellie McKay explains: "For in all of their lives in America, whatever the issue, black women have felt torn between the loyalties that bind them to race on the one hand, and sex on the other. Choosing one or the other, of course, means taking sides against the self" (1992, 277-78).[9] Such a choice leads once again to the invisibility of black women.

Octavia Butler, however, refused to make this self-abnegating choice. In a 1991 interview, she explains: "I thought it was just as important to have equal rights for women as it was to have equal rights for black people and so I felt myself to be very much a feminist" (Kenan 1991, 501). Her refusal to choose one narrative of identity or oppression over another allows Butler to give not only life, but also power to her African-American women, a power that appealed to me as a reader, scholar, and feminist even in my first reading of her work. The strength of her characters, however, does not arise *in spite* of their sometimes conflicting narratives of identity or lack of unified self, but rather *because* of how these women learn to draw on their multiple narratives of identity—their race, gender, class, and "alien-ness."

Transformed by mutation, genetic engineering, "breeding" practices, and disease, Butler's protagonists provide fictional representations of the post-gender, boundary-breaking cyborg "monsters" first proposed by Donna Haraway in her oft-cited "Cyborg Manifesto." Haraway's essay, first published in 1985, marks the beginning of the feminist takeover of a mythic cyborg, a being that incorporates the biological and technological within itself. Haraway claims that the "Manifesto" is

> an argument for *pleasure* in the confusion of boundaries and
> for *responsibility* in their construction. It is also an effort
> to contribute to socialist-feminist culture and theory in a

postmodernist, non-naturalist mode and in the utopian tradition of imaging a world without gender, which is perhaps
a world without genesis, but maybe also a world without
end. (1991, 150)

Haraway acknowledges the dystopic aspect of a cyborg world, which "is
about the final imposition of a grid of control on the planet,…about the
final appropriation of women's bodies in a masculinist orgy of war" (154)
but also points significantly to this world's utopian side, which "might be
about lived social and bodily realities in which people are not afraid of
their joint kinship with animals and machines, not afraid of permanently
partial identities and contradictory standpoints" (ibid.). She tells us that
while we must not forget about the negative consequences of embracing
technology, neither should we engage in a futile attempt to refuse it—
something that has only become clearer in the decades since she wrote
the essay.

Haraway's take on the cyborg and advanced technologies was in
many ways designed to provoke her contemporaries and perhaps oppose
the views presented in some feminist utopias from the late 1970s. In a
2006 interview, Haraway notes that she wrote the "Cyborg Manifesto" as
a response to the prevailing negative views of the cyborg:

> My feminist friends and others in 1980 thought the cyborg
> was all bad. That's a simplification, but that was the reign-
> ing view towards science and technology among my buddies.
> It was either a kind of unsustainable realist, quasi-positivist
> point of view about science that believes that you actually
> can say what you mean non-tropically, or an anti-science
> back-to-nature program. The "Cyborg Manifesto" was a re-
> fusal of both these approaches, but without a refusal of an
> ongoing alliance. The "Manifesto" argued that you can, even
> must, inhabit the despised place. (Gane 2006, 156)

Haraway dared feminists in 1985 to inhabit the cyborg and thus acknowledge the possibilities located within this technologically-mediated
identity. The difficulty, Haraway points out, is to negotiate between the
negative and positive possibilities in a way that allows for productive and
subversive uses of technology that do not naïvely ignore how technology

has been and can be used to dominate various groups of people. The hybrid nature of the cyborg's identity, Haraway asserts, allows it to incorporate both sides of cyborg existence without suffering paralysis. Haraway sets up her cyborg as both a metaphor and literal mode of identity that allows feminists of all types to take advantage of scientific technologies to make partial but potent connections with each other—what she calls "potent fusions and dangerous possibilities" (1991, 154). Haraway, I argue, correctly asserts that "By the late twentieth century,... a mythic time, we are all chimeras, theorized and fabricated hybrids of machine and organism; in short, we are all cyborgs" (150). Thus, while embracing the cyborg does not promise salvation, Haraway argues that we must learn how to successfully negotiate and construct own our cyborg identities in order to act within our postmodern world.

Haraway identifies Octavia Butler as one of "our storytellers exploring what it means to be embodied in high-tech worlds" (173). As a "theorist for cyborgs" (ibid.), Butler creates characters who break all boundaries and "make very problematic the statuses of man or woman, human, artifact, member of a race, individual entity and body" (178). Butler's sf parallels Haraway's description of the move in feminism from essentialist Earth Goddess to cyborg monster, moving from a focus on essential identity to a created one. Some 1970s feminist sf utopias engage with advanced technologies; Joanna Russ, another cyborg theorist identified by Haraway, creates in *The Female Man* (1975) the character Jael, who might be the very first feminist cyborg, and Marge Piercy imagines a utopia in *Women on the Edge of Time* (1976) dependent on artificial reproductive technologies that free women from childbirth and enable men to breastfeed babies. However, Piercy and Russ focus on technologies, such as the reproductive and the labor-saving ones, that directly add to the utopic or dystopic quality of their imagined communities. While Russ's violent man-hating cyborg Jael may be a hero of sorts, she clearly lives in a dystopia, and the technologies she draws on are also dystopian. Both novels include utopian communities that make use of utopian technology and dystopian communities that make use of advanced weapons and other dystopian technology, but neither significantly question the "essential" qualities of the technology itself.

Others, most notably Sally Miller Gearhart's *The Wanderground* (1979), repudiate advanced technology altogether, which is characterized as the realm of men, and celebrate women's connection to nature. Such texts emphasize the positive power of women, mothering, and the importance of the natural world and, at the time, provided an antidote to the denigration of traditional women's work and the contemporary rampages of advanced technologies—including industrial pollution and chemical weapons—on both land and people. However, it is important to remember that this supposed connection between women and nature has been used historically to justify tying women to the home and keeping them out of the "real" business of the world. In the technology driven world of the 1980s and beyond, such a focus—as Haraway reminds her contemporaries—is somewhat beside the point.

The costs of the "woman equals nature" equation have been even higher for African-American women. Black women's supposed closeness to nature, during slavery and afterwards, justified rape and forced childbearing; after all, breeding is the *natural* function of female animals. Thus while Butler is intensely concerned with how biology has been used to define people, she—like Haraway—is more interested in how it has and can be used to change people and their relations to others. In contrast to Piercy and Russ, Butler also engages with technologies that appear, in many cases, to threaten the happiness and the peacefulness of the lives of her characters but that cannot be ignored or simply replaced by more utopian technologies. Butler is interested in looking at how her characters might deal with these technologies and their effects instead of showing how certain technologies are central to a utopian community. Thus, while Butler's fiction, like that of her contemporary feminist sf writers, focuses on created communities, it differs in that it is not either utopian or dystopian.[10]

Haraway's characterization of cyborg monsters and Butler's stories about them, then, are crucial to the development of hybrid feminist identities and concerns with technology that I see as the most exciting and relevant aspects of current feminist sf. Haraway points out some of the specific characters she sees as embodying cyborg practice, including Butler's "African sorceress pitting her powers of transformation against the genetic manipulations of her rival (*Wild Seed*),…time warps that bring a modern US black woman into slavery where her actions in relation her white master-ancestor determine the possibility of her own birth (*Kindred*)," as well as Lilith (*Dawn*) who "mediates the transformation of humanity through genetic exchange with extraterrestrial lovers/rescu-

ers/destroyers/genetic engineers" (179). When analyzing Butler in relation to feminist cyborg identity, most critics—including myself, Sherryl
Vint, Patricia Melzer, and Haraway—focus on Lilith, the alien, genetic-
engineering Oankali, and their hybrid offspring from Butler's Xenogenesis trilogy and how they upset our notions of what it means to be human
and whole—as well as any notions of "normal" sexuality or gender.[11]

However, while many of us are happy to take up Haraway's terms
and descriptions in describing Butler's work, we are also eager—in an effort to be original and appropriately critical—to set ourselves apart from
her original theory. Looking back at Haraway's "Cyborg Manifesto," we
often take the easy route of criticizing it for being too general, over-
celebratory, not particularly effective for political practice, or simply limited in its applications.[12] For example, Melzer claims that Butler's fiction
not only reflects certain feminist theories such as Haraway's, but also
"points to the theories' limitations, especially in their generalizations and
their attempts to erase contradictions" (2006, 32). In a piece published
in 1998, I argue that while Haraway seems to offer us a simple choice to
either embrace cyborg positions or "become essentialist goddesses who
will eventually undergo dispersion" (Holden 1998, 52), Butler's depiction
of Lilith demonstrates that such survival has much higher costs than
Haraway implies. However, instead of focusing on what Haraway missed
or failed to take into account—after all, Haraway herself does this in later
discussions of the "Cyborg Manifesto"[13]—I want to use her cyborg myth
as what she initially intended it to be: a jumping off point for re-imaging
our relationships to science, advanced technologies, and fluid feminist
identity positions.

I would like to first extend Haraway's cyborg theory with Judith
Butler's notion of sedimented construction. Addressing the "[p]ainful
fragmentation among feminists" (1991, 155) in the manifesto, Haraway calls on feminists to move beyond "endless splits and searches for a
new essential unity" (ibid.) and embrace coalition based on "affinity, not
identity" (ibid.). Referring to Chela Sandoval's writings on oppositional
consciousness, Haraway argues that the political identity of "women of
color" provides a model for this type of cyborg political affinity.[14] Sum-
marizing Sandoval, Haraway writes:

> The category "women" negated all non-white women; "black"
> negated all non-black people, as well as all black women. But
> there was also no "she," no singularity, but a sea of differ-

ences among US women who have affirmed their historical identity of women of colour. This identity marks out a self-consciously constructed space that cannot affirm the capacity to act on the basis of natural identification, but only on the basis of conscious coalition, of affinity, of political kinship. (1995, 156)

Mary Ann Doane takes issue with "The opposition between identity and affinity (the latter espoused by Haraway)...: one is condemned by nature to an identity but one chooses an affinity.... But I would argue that there are identities—crucially important identities—which are neither natural nor chosen but constructed, mapped" (1989, 221). Doane's criticism of Haraway's implied binary—identity tied to a false "nature" versus affinity tied to a conscious political choice—points out aspects of such coalition-building and identity Haraway doesn't explicitly engage with in the manifesto that are crucial to a reading of Butler's fiction. We might ask, like Joan Scott does in her piece on Haraway's cyborg, "How have 'women of color' been able to claim affinity without evoking a 'natural' identity?" (1989, 217).

Judith Butler's corrective to some of her own theories helps to answer that question and complicates our understanding of "natural" identity. In her second book, *Bodies That Matter*, Judith Butler explores the place of material bodies in gender construction. This exploration helps illuminate the non-constructed parts of cyborg bodies and furthers the usefulness of the cyborg metaphor in reading Octavia Butler's work. Like Haraway, Judith Butler claims that there can be no "nature" without history; nature is not a blank surface written on by the social or cultural (1993, 5). Judith Butler goes further by clearly indicating that there can be no construction without history. The process of construction is not simply the act of applying cultural interpretations on top of a physical body or reality; for example, "gender" is not simply the cultural and social interpretations of a biological sex. Nor is it the taking on or off of an identity at will; as Judith Butler explains, it does not mean that "one woke in the morning, perused the closet or some more open space for the gender of choice, donned that gender for the day, and then restored the garment to its place at night" (x). Instead, Judith Butler proposes "a return to the notion of matter, not as site or surface, but as *a process of materialization that stabilizes over time to produce the effect of boundary, fixity and surface we call matter"* (9). Construction itself, then, takes on a more organic character. It becomes a process that takes place over time.

Furthermore, Judith Butler asserts, "The forming, crafting, bearing, circulation, signification of that sexed body…will be a set of actions mobilized by the law, the citational accumulation and dissimulation of the law that produces material effects, the lived necessity of those effects as well as the lived contestation of that necessity" (12). In other words, bodies accumulate sedimented meaning over time, and this bodily history produces recognizable sexed, gendered, and racialized bodies. What the bodies live through produces the material reality of those bodies at the same time that those experiences result from the specific material markers of those bodies. Such effects cannot be easily put off, but they can be questioned in a way that might lead to a redefinition of that "lived necessity" as constructed and ultimately result in a rebellion against any accepted "essential" characteristics.

Octavia Butler's protagonists eventually develop into, I argue, constructed cyborgs aware of both their hybridity and the accumulated bodily effects that Judith Butler describes. Transformed by biological or medical technology into what we might define as more or less than human, these women navigate their survival in societies riddled with complex hierarchies of power, places where survival is difficult at best. Throughout her fiction, Butler plays with varying hybrid identities, bioengineering, and genetic technologies to figure out how her protagonists can survive and have agency in the futures she imagines while remaining true to themselves as African-American women. As Butler investigates potential feminist cyborg identities, her characters become increasingly grounded by their connections to actual bodies and histories as well as to the pain tied to these bodies and histories—they become more aware of the accumulated material effects of their bodies.[15] These characters, in the words of Judith Butler, "cite" the law that has defined them as black, female, and abnormal "in order to reiterate and co-opt its power" (15). Such reiteration relies on knowledge of the past—a history written on their racialized, gendered bodies—that sets them apart from the dominant culture. Combining this reiteration with the advanced technologies makes them cyborg and in this way, these women reconstruct themselves as successful survivors. In this manner, Butler's stories lead the way within feminist sf to a complex but still empowering hybrid or cyborg feminism, a move necessary for feminists such as myself, who came of age during the so-called post-feminist (and postmodern) '80s and '90s.

The Patternists

Butler's first group of novels, begun in 1976 with her first novel *Patternmaster*, focuses on a group of genetically engineered humans, known as the Patternists, who have psionic (mental) abilities such as telepathy, psychic healing, and psycho-kinetics. *Patternmaster*, which is set in the distant future, shares some characteristics with the contemporary 1970s feminist sf utopias; as in those worlds, the Patternist society appears to have moved beyond racism.[16] Furthermore, because mental strength determines a person's position in the Patternist hierarchy, both race and gender initially seem beside the point. The Patternmaster controls the Pattern, the psychic web that links the Patternists together, and ranks at the top of the hierarchy. Men or sometimes women with strong mental powers become Housemasters, rulers over their own houses of journeymen, apprentices, outsiders, wives, and husbands. Journeymen and apprentices work for their respective Housemasters but are free to make their own decisions and often become Housemasters. Outsiders (usually weak male Patternists), wives, and presumably husbands (though we don't see any) are owned by their Housemasters; they cannot travel or have children without the permission of their masters and can be sold or traded without explanation. Even lower in this society are "mutes," men and women without any mental abilities at all. Most domestic work and physical labor falls to the mutes, who, controlled mentally by their masters, are rarely even allowed to think for themselves.

Patternmaster centers on Teray, a strong young Patternist who is one of the sons of the current Patternmaster, and his struggle with his brother Coransee, an extremely powerful Housemaster who hopes to take over the Pattern. In Coransee's house, where Teray has been forced to become an outsider, he meets the healer Amber, a rare Independent "who possessed some valued skill that made [her] welcome at the various sectors.... And...enough strength to make holding on to [her] not worth Housemasters' trouble" (67). Amber agrees to become Teray's ally—but not his wife—in Teray's fight against Coransee.

Despite Butler's deliberate choice to de-emphasize race and gender as potential sources of discrimination, she highlights throughout the text the most important aspect of racism (and sexism) in any society—that of power. In American culture, most often only people of color are seen as possessing race and only women as possessing gender, while white Euro-American men are presented as the standard. In *Patternmaster*, it is those with the clearest access to power—such as male or female House-masters—who appear "race-less." They are described in terms of body shape, muscular strength, beauty, or age but never in terms of skin color, hair color or texture, or facial features that might indicate their race or ethnicity. I first noticed this curious omission after reading an article by Ruth Salvaggio in which she states that "[b]ecause Teray is white and Amber black, their relationship continually reminds us of racial distinctions" (1984, 79). Salvaggio's comment surprised me because in my first two readings of *Patternmaster*, I had assumed that Teray was black. This may have something to do with the picture on the cover of my 1995 edition of *Patternmaster*, which depicts a bald black man, or the fact that most of Butler's protagonists are black or of mixed race.[17] When I went back through the book page by page, I discovered that there were no clues about Teray's race. My assumptions regarding his race, as perhaps Butler had intended, had to do with factors outside the story.

Racialized descriptions, however, are not absent from the novel, but are reserved to describe those without power—mutes or weak Pattern-ists, or those like Amber who seem to exist outside of the usual power hierarchies. For example, there is the "blonde mute woman" who serves Coransee's breakfast (41) and one of his outsiders who is "a tall, bony man with straw-colored hair and mental strength so slight that he could easily have been a teacher at the school" (49-50). This novel, thus, makes explicit the fact that race does not refer to one's physical body but marks one's place within the hierarchy. Those marked by race are the owned, while those with no discernible race wield the power and are the "true" citizens of the society.

Amber, described as "a golden-brown woman with hair that was a round cap of small, tight black curls" (64), is the African-American wom-an who exists in between; she is neither the race-transcendent House-master nor the raced slave. Her healing ability, we learn early in the story, "had little to do with mental strength. It was a different sort of power" (61) that didn't usually allow a Patternist to rise in the hierarchy. Perhaps for this reason, she is marked as a woman of color, a woman whom both Teray and Coransee hope to make their wife or property. However, like Haraway's ironic cyborg, Amber indulges in her multiplicity—her race, her gender, her unrecognized power—and is not concerned with maintaining an identity that answers to any single definition. Taking *"pleasure in confusion of boundaries"* (Haraway 1991, 150), Amber takes male and female lovers, heals and kills, and loves Teray and refuses to become his wife. Amber's cyborgness is less explicit than that of Butler's later protagonists, but she is what I see as an early experiment with the effects of biotechnology on bodies and identity. Amber is a product of generations of genetic manipulation and selective breeding, and her power a happy, though somewhat anomalous, byproduct of that practice.[18] That proto-cyborg power is what allows her to make partial connections to others and to exert some control over her life. For example, Amber has multiple ties: to Housemasters like Coransee who have been her lovers and teachers, to the mutes whom she heals and tries to protect from cruel masters, and to those whom she loves like Teray. Still, no one group controls her loyalty or her identity. As she tells Teray, "'I could have given my life for you back there if we had had to fight. But I could never give my life *to* you'" (134). She uses her power not to dominate but to survive without effacing herself completely.

Amber's position allows her a certain type of freedom, but her success and power is not without a price. To ensure her survival, she must move from House to House without making lasting connections with others. Toward the end of the story, like her slave ancestors before her, she must submit to sex with the "master," Coransee. In Butler's future world, genetic engineering and alien viruses have changed the definitions of humanity and, thus, race and gender do not have the same meaning as they did in 1970s America. However, Butler makes it clear that the issues of power that infused the racial and sexual inequities of the 1970s, making black women invisible participants, still play significant roles. Unlike her ancestors, Amber can use her power over the biological processes of her body to avoid pregnancy with the "master's" child, but her raced and gendered body is still subject to rape. Amber survives and may become a Housemaster herself someday, but she must cut herself off from her body's suffering, as well as her past and present loves, to maintain her position and power.

In *Mind of My Mind* (1977), Butler's second novel and a prequel to *Patternmaster*, Butler takes us backward in the timeline of the Patternists as she moves forward in her experiments with the intersections of power, race, and hybrid identities. The characters are not already part of any race-transcendent society, but we witness how such a society comes to be and what is lost in its creation. In particular, Butler explores how Mary—a poor black woman from contemporary 1970s Los Angeles—changes herself, her world, and her perspective when she is placed in a position of power. While Mary is eventually successful and takes on a leadership role usually reserved for white men, Butler reminds her readers how African-American women who join Mary's new Patternist society, in the words of Nellie McKay, "tak[e] sides against themselves" (qtd. above). Thus even though Mary may choose to forget her history and its pain to make her new race-transcendent society a success, Butler does not allow her readers the same indulgence.

Mind of My Mind tells the story of the genesis of the Patternist society. Doro, originally born a Nubian, has lived for four thousand years by literally taking over other people's bodies, moving from one to another as necessary. For most of his life, he has been breeding people in an attempt to create a race of telepaths. He hopes that his daughter Mary, a young, poor, African-American woman of mixed race, will become a special telepath who can link with other telepaths. During her transition from latent to active telepath, Mary creates the first Pattern by mentally latching onto minds of six active telepaths, including the mind of her new white husband whom Doro has forced her to marry. These telepaths are drawn to Mary, both physically and mentally, and she can draw power from them. After two years, during which Mary adds 1,500 people to her Patternist community and network, Doro thinks that she has too much power and orders her to stop acquiring telepaths. However, Mary cannot stop without destroying herself and thus all the Patternists. Drawing on the strength of her people, Mary fights and kills Doro. Many Patternists die in the fight, but Mary is free to continue building and protecting her Patternist society.

Initially, Mary's choices in life, and in any identity she adopts, are severely limited by the racism and sexism of 1970s America. Like her slave ancestors before her, Mary is expected to be a whore, a breeder, and a dutiful slave for her owner, Doro. For example, when Mary defends herself against one of her mother's johns who attempts to rape her, Doro chastises her. Demonstrating how horrible jail would be for a telepath like Mary, he asks her: "Wouldn't you rather even be raped than wind up in a place like this even for a short time?" (29). Rape, her father/owner Doro indicates, is simply a survivable side effect of her position. Doro also expects her to marry one of his white sons and breed with him. Mary thinks, "Somehow, I'd never thought of myself as just another of Doro's breeders—just another Goddamn brood mare" (33). Mary struggles against Doro's orders, accepting them only unwillingly, but cannot bring herself to step outside of the bounds set up for her, by both Doro and herself. For example, she aligns herself with the black cook at her husband's house simply because the woman is black like her.

Mary's connection to her race, as well as the limitations such a connection implies, fades as she becomes "one of the owners" (102). The society she creates out of her Pattern effectively erases both the differences between her and the white men typically in power as well as the connections that existed previously between Mary and the black cook. In this book, we become much more aware of how Mary has been carefully constructed by Doro—both by his breeding program and social conditioning. Mary, however, breaks from Doro's careful programming and becomes one version of the boundary-breaking, post-gender, and post-race cyborg that Haraway celebrates.

Mary's cyborg identity does not acknowledge its history or Judith Butler's sedimented lived reality, but such an identity has many benefits for Mary: Mary's telepaths form a supportive community based on their *affinity* despite their differences of race, gender, and wealth; their telepathic powers become more efficient; and the Pattern serves to make latent telepaths active ones, freeing the latents from their previous lives as violently abusive alcoholics unable to hold a job or care for their children. The Patternist community thus has many utopian aspects, but its success seems tied to a questionable forgetting of the past. As in 1970s feminist utopias, the black woman begins to disappear.

Butler, unlike some of her contemporary feminist sf writers, does not let this erasure happen without comment. She celebrates Mary's power but simultaneously questions the price Mary and her community pay for that power. In creating their community, the Patternists mentally control numerous non-telepathic "mutes." Mutes take care of Patternist children, help run the households, and are programmed to be content. Emma, Mary's over six-hundred-year-old ancestor who has lived in the United States since slave times, appropriately acts as the voice of history regarding these countless "conscripted servants" (160). When Doro tries to explain what he calls the "convenient term" (161) "mute," Emma protests against any such terms: "I know what it means, Doro. I knew the first time I heard Mary use it. It means nigger!" (161).

Mary's selective amnesia regarding the ways in which her own body and the bodies of African-American men and women before her have been marked by a social system not unlike that of the Patternists troubles others in her community. For example, a young telepath named Page, who has been rescued from her abusive parents, realizes that her foster parents—non-telepathic "mutes" controlled by the Patternists—are, in effect, slaves. Disgusted, Page exclaims, "I know about being a slave! My parents taught me. My father used to strip me naked, tie me to the bed, and beat me, and then—… I don't want to be a part of anything that makes people slaves" (183-84). By bringing Page into the Patternist community, Mary frees her from the position forced on her by her father—that of the black female slave forced to submit to rape. At the same time, Mary has made Page one of the slave-holders, a position she rebels against because, despite her new mental powers, Page cannot easily forget what the experience of her young, powerless, black female body has taught her. The objections of both the long-lived Emma and the youthful Page to Mary's new slave society are borne out of the lessons enacted on their African-American female bodies, lessons that have taught them the dangers of such hierarchical societies, regardless of who takes on the position of power.[19]

The Patternist society in Mind of My Mind does, like other late 1970s feminist sf, shakes up the hierarchy of the present world; at the same time, Butler highlights, unlike texts such as Piercy's Women on the Edge of Time and Gearhart's Wanderground, the problems with the kind of alliances Mary creates to achieve success. Mary's acquisition of power and position as a boundary-breaking cyborg provide an alternative ending to the story of the poor black woman. Mary does more than simply survive; she triumphs. However, through Emma and Page, Butler points out what Mary's success might mean for those who now end up at the bottom of the hierarchy and reminds us about the current world where black women still struggle to survive. Such reminders highlight the dangers of not acknowledging the "lived necessity" (Judith Butler 1993, 12) of any physical body and casting off history, dangers that include the repetition of the history it denies—the replication of slavery and gender discrimination (as seen in Patternmaster).

In *Wild Seed* (1980), Butler goes even further back in the history of the Patternist world and reinvents Emma, Mary's grandmother several times removed, as a strong African-American woman who survives and acquires power in the world without taking sides against herself. In this story, Emma—who goes by her Igbo name Anyanwu—is a hybrid character who continually constructs and reconstructs herself in relationship to a very specific African-American history. Such a history, like the character herself, is of necessity cobbled together from a variety of African myths and languages and combined with other histories and technologies brought to the "New World," making it a history particularly relevant to Anyanwu's cyborg position.[20]

Wild Seed narrates the relationship between Doro and Anyanwu. Doro finds Anyanwu in her Onitsha village in 1690 when she is almost three-hundred years old. After a terrible sickness at the age of twenty, Anyanwu gained complete control over the biological processes of her body, which made her an effective healer and enabled her take on alternate shapes, both animal and human. Doro convinces her to come with him to America as his wife, but once they arrive, he marries her off to one of his white sons. From this time onward, Anyanwu and Doro become adversaries; he uses her children to enforce her loyalty, and she continues to resist him. After her husband's death, Anyanwu escapes Doro by taking on various animal forms. In the guise of a white man, she eventually becomes the owner of a Louisiana plantation where Doro finds her in 1840. Anyanwu, tired of fighting with Doro for the lives and rights of her children and herself, decides to die. Doro finally realizes the worth of his only long-lived companion and makes a reconciliation with her that convinces her to go on living.

An initial glance at Anyanwu's story may align her with the "archetypal" mother figures, such as those found in Gearhart's *Wanderground* where women are considered to be naturally less violent, more nurturing, more connected to nature, less competitive, and more communal than men. Critics writing in the 1980s often stressed what they saw as the biologically-determined aspects of gender in *Wild Seed*. For example, Sandra Y. Govan states that Doro's "is the more terrible power; he kills instantaneously whenever he takes a host body. But [Anyanwu's] is the nurturing healing power of the archetypal earth mother" (1984, 83). Similarly, Ruth Salvaggio states that "Doro's paternal concerns revolve around his mechanical breeding experiments: He does not create children, but

Frankenstein monsters. Anyanwu's maternity, however, is the main source of her being, the principal reason for her existence" (1984, 81). Some later critics, like Hoda Zaki, highlight the problems inherent in the gender essentialism that they see in the work of Butler and her contemporaries: "Butler, in describing her heroines as nurturing, freedom-loving women who employ violence only for the sake of survival, shares with other feminist sf writers the same truncated assumptions about women's and men's natures even though she does not place gender concerns conspicuously at the center of her novels" (1990, 246).

Butler often seems overly insistent about the innate gender of her characters, but I agree with Michele Erica Green that "Butler's 'essentialism' is tricky" (1994, 167). Green claims this trickiness comes out of Butler's focus "on the exceptions to the rule she posits as human norms rather than on those who exemplify it" (167).[21] Patricia Melzer further complicates Green's supposition by showing how Butler negotiates constructionist and essentialist notions of gender identity through Anyanwu. By maintaining "a stable *gender* identity while constantly changing *bodies*," Melzer claims that Anyanwu (and Doro) destabilize both "a constructivist claim that the discursive body determines one's identity and as essentialist insistence on the physical experience of a naturally gendered body as fundamental to gender identity" (2006, 230). At the same time, Melzer argues that "Butler's insistence on Anyanwu's female identity and Doro's male identity contradicts their symbolic function as gender-transgressive" (234).

However, we must not overlook the role of choice in Anyanwu's insistence on the stability of her gender identity as well as what that gender identity means to her, and presumably to Butler. For example, Anyanwu's desire to mother goes beyond any simple, biologically-determined need to nurture but instead reflects her choice to physically and emotionally mother. She is aware that this choice does not reflect any biological inevitability, or the power of any "femaleness," but rather reflects her ability—given the control she has over the functioning of her body—to *choose* motherhood. She co-opts the nurturing mother role as one of power and influence, but does not believe being a "true" or good woman means being able to mother effectively. When Doro brings one of his women, Susan, to Anyanwu's plantation, he is disappointed that Anyanwu's people have not been able to make Susan more "useful" (264) to him—that is, a better mother to the three children he has forced her to bear.[22] Anyanwu replies that as a strong field hand Susan is "useful" (ibid.) and despite her inability to care for her children is a "good woman" (ibid.).

Anyanwu's ability to change shapes, to become outwardly a woman, man, black, white, or animal, literalizes the multiplicity that exists within all people, particularly those whose backgrounds encompass multiple narratives of identity. Within the character of Anyanwu, Butler celebrates that multiplicity without letting one narrative take over all others. The way in which Anyanwu must become the "other" on a cellular level in order to transform herself means, as Melzer argues, that "Anyanwu's seemingly essential identity *incorporates* the 'other'" (2006, 232). Furthermore, despite her sense of herself as a black woman, she never simply reverts to any original self but must maintain a conscious connection to her varied narratives of identity in order not to lose herself in the construction—as one might argue Mary has by the end of *Mind of My Mind*. For example, when Anyanwu transforms herself into a white man in Louisiana in 1840, she learns how easy it is to "become" what other people see and let that privileged position blind her. She explains: "Slaves were passing in front of me all chained, and I was thinking, 'I have to take more sunken gold from the sea, then see the banker about buying the land that adjoins mine….' I was not seeing the slaves in front of me. I would not have thought I could be oblivious to such a thing" (211). Anyanwu's experience does not excuse the actions of white slave owners, but it does point out how the specifics of a given body and the way it is perceived significantly affect the world it experiences. Butler shows how easy it might be to accept being "one of the owners" as Mary does in *Mind of My Mind*. Anyanwu learns that she must incorporate what Judith Butler called the "lived necessities" and histories of her past bodies in any new identity or community she constructs to truly change anything around her.

Key to maintaining this necessary connection to her past is Anyanwu's construction of a history relevant to her cyborg identity, one that allows her to retain certain aspects of her past without idealizing any one version of human culture. As such, Anyanwu's commitment to her Onitsha Igbo culture is only partial; she holds onto it for some reasons but does not completely embrace it for others. For example, Igbo culture follows a strict, patriarchal structure that Anyanwu does not endorse. Even before she left her native Igbo village, she "found it difficult to be a good wife in her most recent years because of the way a woman must bow her head and be subject to her husband" (9). Still, in spite of the fact that

Igbo culture does not represent any sort of paradise to which Anyanwu or her African-American descendants should retreat, she recognizes the importance of bringing the positive aspects of this African culture into her life as an African-American. Upon entering the New World, Anyanwu thinks: "It would be good for the children of their marriage to know her world as well as Doro's—to be aware of a place where blackness was not a mark of slavery" (114).

In America, Anyanwu continues to construct this hybrid history by bringing disparate traditions together, challenging the authority of one over the other. For example, the "Madonna and Child" portrait of Anyanwu and her child that she displays in her American home forces her Euro-American visitors to confront the narrowness of what they might see as their own sacred traditions: "The portrait was a black madonna and child right down to Anyanwu's too-clear, innocent-seeming eyes.... Some were appreciative, looking at the still handsome Anyanwu.... Others were deeply offended, believing that someone actually had tried to portray the Virgin and Child as 'black savages'" (142). Anyanwu realizes that there is no perfect past—no mythical paradise—to build a successful identity on and thus continually combines a variety of cultures to form new modes of identity and a better future for herself and her children.[23]

Anyanwu refuses to be contained by the gendered, raced, cultural, and social boundaries society puts upon her bodies; she breaks free, and even though at times the "lived necessities" and accumulated effects of race and gender threaten both her survival and will to survive, she ultimately decides to live, to embrace but not unify all parts of herself. The black woman in *Wild Seed* is not invisible, nor is her narrative subsumed by that of white women or black men. Her difference is thus not elided nor used to separate her from those not like her.

Butler's experimentation with feminist representations of powerful African-American women in these three novels shows a certain evolution of hybrid and cyborg characters. In *Patternmaster*, she explores what the apparent absence of race might mean and shows how race, uncoupled from skin color, continues to describe the power relations of society. The Patternist society grants the hybrid Amber a place, but does not recognize the significance of any difference she might represent or the multiplicity that underlies that difference. In *Mind of My Mind*, Butler demonstrates that as Mary gains power, she loses her ties to her past and thus cannot carry the lessons of her racialized and gendered history, of being different, into what I see as her new cyborg identity and society. Finally, in *Wild Seed*, Butler creates a more complicated cyborg, who embodies Haraway's cyborg "not afraid of [her] joint kinship with animals and machines, not afraid of permanently partial identities" (1991, 154), and well aware of the sedimented construction of those identities that Judith Butler describes. Anyanwu has learned to accept and simultaneously contest her pasts in creating a new identity that draws on her history and allows her to survive the ultimate diaspora.

As Butler worked through her various renditions of feminist characters, she significantly affected the course of feminist sf. More than simply focusing on African-American female protagonists, Butler raised new questions about women's bodies, relationships, and responsibilities but rarely left us with definitive answers or visions of feminist triumph found in other feminist sf of the time. Her development of hybrid characters who were capable of representing multiple narratives of identity and making connections marked a move within the field away from the utopian trend of 1970s feminist sf. Butler readjusted readers' notions of what was a suitable topic or "hero" in science fiction at the same time that she—black, female, and powerless in her own view—challenged the popular conception about *who* could be a science fiction writer.

Perhaps it was fate that I read *Wild Seed* first of all of Butler's novels. It was certainly a lucky choice for someone searching for a feminist identity that could encompass, without suppressing or constraining, my varied identities as well as my newly acquired appreciation of differences among women and feminists. For me and others of my generation, the successful fights of 1970s "Women's Lib" against obvious discrimination and prejudice were like tales of life on the frontier—exciting and necessary in terms of the place we were starting from as 1990s feminists—but ones that seemed distant and not directly applicable to the current world and our positions as young women in the postmodern age of advanced technologies and multiple sexualities.[24] In addition, the popular notion that feminism was no longer necessary in the 1980s and 1990s made defining oneself as a feminist a somewhat paralyzing task. As I struggled with this self-definition and with finding outlets for feminist action, Butler's character Anyanwu provided me with a feminist model that could incorporate disparate life stories, participate in society, encourage deep connections to others, and still remain true to herself. Such a position, as Anyanwu's life and perhaps the eventual outcome of her alliances demonstrate, is not without pain and conflict, as well as self-doubt, but powerful possibilities exist within her cyborg, mutable self.

In spite of the fact that we "know" what happens to Anyanwu's descendants in *Patternmaster* and *Mind of My Mind*, I choose to believe that the Anyanwu of *Wild Seed* might have led her people to an alternative future. Sometimes, I wonder what would have happened to the Patternist world if Butler had "discovered" the *Wild Seed* version of Anyanwu first—but then again I believe that it was the explorations of difference, power, and multiplicity in the first two books that allowed Butler to create such a moving character in the first place. Octavia E. Butler may have begun writing about power because she herself had so little, but through her writing and life, she ended up exerting great power in multiple worlds, and certainly in mine.

Works Cited

Attebery, Brian. 2002. *Decoding Gender in Science Fiction*. New York: Routledge.

Butler, Judith. 1993. *Bodies That Matter: On the Discursive Limits of "Sex."* New York: Routledge.

Butler, Octavia. 1978. *Mind of My Mind*. New York: Avon Books.

———. *Patternmaster*. 1976, 1995. New York: Warner Books.

———. *Wild Seed*. 1980. New York: Warner.

Charnas, Suzy McKee. 1978. *Motherlines*. New York: Berkley.

Crosby, Christina. 1989. "Commentary: Allies and Enemies." In *Coming to Terms: Feminism, Theory, Politics,* edited by Elizabeth Weed, 207-8. New York: Routledge.

Doane, Mary Ann. 1989. "Commentary: Cyborgs, Origins, and Subjectivity." In *Coming to Terms: Feminism, Theory, Politics,* edited by Elizabeth Weed, 209-14. New York: Routledge.

Federmayer, Eva. 2000. "Octavia Butler's Maternal Cyborgs: The Black Female World of the Xenogenesis Trilogy." *Hungarian Journal of English and American Studies* 6.1: 103-118.

Gane, Nicholas. 2006. "When We Have Never Been Human, What Is to Be Done? Interview with Donna Haraway." *Theory, Culture & Society* 23.7-8: 135-158.

Gearhart, Sally Miller. 1979. *The Wanderground: Stories of the Hill Women.* Boston, MA: Alyson Publications, Inc.

Giddings, Paula. 1984. *When and Where I Enter: The Impact of Black Woman on Race and Sex in America.* New York: Bantam.

Govan, Sandra Y. 1984. "Connections, Links, and Extended Networks: Patterns in Octavia Butler's Science Fiction." *Black American Literature Forum* 18: 82-87.

Green, Michelle Erica. 1994. "'There Goes the Neighborhood': Octavia Butler's Demand for Diversity in Utopias." In *Utopian and Science Fiction by Women: Worlds of Difference,* edited by Jane L. Donawerth and Carol A. Kolmerten, 166-189. Syracuse, NY: Syracuse University Press.

Haraway, Donna. 1991. *Simians, Cyborgs, and Women: The Reinvention of Nature.* New York: Routledge.

Holden, Rebecca J. 1998. "The High Costs of Cyborg Survival: Octavia Butler's Xenogenesis Trilogy." *Foundation: the International Review of Science Fiction* 72 (Spring): 49–56.

Hull, Gloria T., ed. 1981. *All the Women Are White, All the Blacks Are Men, But Some of Us Are Brave.* Old Westbury, NY: The Feminist Press.

Kenan, Randall. 1991. "An Interview with Octavia Butler." *Callaloo* 14.2: 495-504.

Larbalestier, Justine. 2002. *Battle of the Sexes in Science Fiction.* Middletown, CT: Wesleyan University Press.

Lefanu, Sarah. 1989. *Feminism and Science Fiction.* Bloomington, IN: Indiana University Press.

Littleton, Therese. "Octavia E. Butler Plants and Earthseed." *Amazon. com.* http://www.amazon.com/exec/obidos/tg/feature/-/11664/.

McKay, Nellie. 1992. "Remembering Anita Hill and Clarence Thomas: What Really Happened When One Black Woman Spoke Out." In

Race-ing Justice, En-gendering Power: Essays on Anita Hill, Clarence Thomas, and the Construction of Social Reality, edited by Toni Morrison, 269-89. New York: Pantheon Books.

Melzer, Patricia. 2006. *Alien Constructions: Science Fiction and Feminist Thought.* Austin, TX: University of Texas Press.

Merrick, Helen. 2009. *The Secret Feminist Cabal: A Cultural History of Science Fiction Feminisms.* Seattle, WA: Aqueduct Press.

Morrison, Toni, ed. 1992. *Race-ing Justice, En-gendering Power: Essays on Anita Hill, Clarence Thomas, and the Construction of Social Reality.* New York: Pantheon Books.

Piercy, Marge. 1976. *Woman on the Edge of Time.* New York: Knopf.

Russ, Joanna. *The Female Man.* 1975. In *Radical Utopias.* 1990. New York: Quality Paperback Book Club.

Salvaggio, Ruth. 1984. "Octavia Butler and the Black Science-Fiction Heroine." *Black American Literature Forum* 18: 78-81.

Sandoval, Chela. 1995. "New Sciences: Cyborg Feminism and the Methodology of the Oppressed." In *The Cyborg Handbook,* edited by Chris Hables Gray, 407-21. New York: Routledge.

Scott, Joan. 1989. "Commentary: Cyborgian Socialists." In *Coming to Terms: Feminism, Theory, Politics,* edited by Elizabeth Weed, 215-16. New York: Routledge.

Siegel, Deborah. 2007. *Sisterhood Interrupted: From Radical Women to Grrls Gone Wild.* New York: Palgrave Macmillian.

Vint, Sherryl. 2007. *Bodies of Tomorrow: Technology, Subjectivity, Science Fiction.* Toronto, ON: University of Toronto Press.

Weed, Elizabeth, ed. 1989. *Coming to Terms: Feminism, Theory, Politics.* New York: Routledge.

Wolmark, Jenny. 1994. *Aliens and Others: Science Fiction, Feminism, and Postmodernism.* Iowa City, IA: University of Iowa Press.

Zaki, Hoda M. 1990. "Utopia, Dystopia, and Ideology in the Science Fiction of Octavia Butler." *Science-Fiction Studies* 17: 239-51.

Endnotes

1 I am consciously avoiding the term "diabetic." Somehow, being called a "diabetic" instead of a person with diabetes makes me feel like I am the disease.

2 I had to talk my advisor, Dr. Susan Stanford Friedman, into taking on a feminist sf dissertation. Once onboard, Professor Friedman became, and still is, a staunch supporter of my work. Other feminist scholars refused to be on my doctoral committee because they didn't see the connection between their work and mine.

3 As an adjunct lecturer, I remain on the outskirts of academia. However, the world of feminist sf continues to provide a welcoming venue for my interests and work.

4 The world's largest feminist science fiction convention, WisCon, has been held each year in Madison, WI, since 1977.

5 Butler published another book, *Survivor* (1978) loosely set in the Patternist series sometime after the events of *Clay's Ark* (1984) and *Patternmaster*. This novel, later dismissed by Butler as "my Star Trek novel"(Littleton), is set off-world and centers on a group of humans who leave Earth to escape the clayark plague, and has little to do with either the clayark or Patternist societies. See Melzer for an interesting reading of *Survivor* in tandem with the first book of Butler's *Dawn* in terms of cyborg hybridity as resistance to colonizing powers.

6 Science fiction scholars like Brian Attebery have noted the "wave of powerfully feminist sf in the late 1960s and 1970s" (2002, 6), calling the 1970s "the decade when women writers of sf ceased to seem exceptional" (107). Sarah LeFanu tells us that "while between 1953 (the year of its inception) and 1967 there were no women winners of the Hugo Award, between 1968 and 1984 there were eleven" (1989, 7). See Chapter 5 of Justine Larbalestier's *Battle of the Sexes in Science Fiction* (2002) and Helen Merrick's *The Secret Feminist Cabal: A Cultural History of Science Fiction Feminisms* (2009) for alternative arguments regarding the "explosion" of women into the field of science fiction during this period.

7 See *When and Where I Enter: The Impact of Black Woman on Race and Sex in America* (1984) by Paula Giddings for a discussion of the way such antagonism was encouraged.

8 The title of the ground-breaking collection of essays, *All the Women Are White, All the Blacks Are Men, But Some of Us Are Brave: Black Women's*

Studies (1981) edited by Gloria T. Hull highlights the traditionally ignored position of black women and black feminists as well as the difficulty for black women to maintain ties to both feminism and the civil rights movement.

9   See *Race-ing Justice, En-gendering Power* (1992), a collection of essays on Hill and Thomas edited by Toni Morrison, for a discussion on this topic.

10 Some critics insist on defining Butler's fiction as part of the 1970s feminist utopian tradition. For example, Hoda Zaki ties Butler's fiction to "the post-1970 feminist and utopian SF trend" (1990, 239) because Butler "allows (unique) individuals occasionally to escape the grip of instinct and genetic structure on human behavior" (243) and because the alien societies in Butler's fiction "not only stand in the sort of political comparison to existing human social arrangements which is typical of utopias, but are also ideal in themselves" (243). However, if all narratives in which individual characters "occasionally escape" their biological destiny are defined as utopias, the term would cease to be meaningful. In addition, the alien communities in Butler's fiction—only one of which could be defined as utopian—do not continue in the traditional isolated utopian mode. Michelle Erica Green sees Butler's texts as critiques of the bulk of 1970s feminist sf because they do not focus solely on gender discrimination but address multiple problems in society. However, Greene still defines Butler's fiction as part of that utopian tradition (168).

11 See Federmayer, Holden, Melzer, Vint, and Wolmark. Haraway analyzes *Clay's Ark* briefly and *Dawn* in more detail in "The Biopolitics of Postmodern Bodies: Constitutions of Self in Immune System Discourse." She loosely connects Butler's characters to the cyborgs she describes in her manifesto and claims that "Butler has been consumed with an interrogation into the boundaries of what counts as human and into the limits of the concept and practices of claiming 'property in the self' as the ground of 'human' individuality and selfhood" (226). She further notes that in *Dawn*, Butler is "[p]reoccupied with marked bodies" and writes of "the woman of colour whose confrontations with the terms of selfhood, survival, and reproduction in the face of repeated ultimate catastrophe presage an ironic salvation history" (227)—but one that ends in an unresolved dilemma (229). A few scholars have investigated the dissolution of boundaries—primarily of gender, sexuality, and race—that Butler presents in the Patternist series, focusing mainly on the shapeshifting Anyanwu from *Wild Seed*. For example, Melzer notes that Anyanwu "is Butler's most explicit translation of the technological metaphor of the synthesized human into a consciousness" (98) and that "her transgression of boundaries is complete" (98).

12 Christina Crosby asks "whether [the manifesto's] inclusivity is as powerful politically as it is intellectually pleasurable" (1989, 207) and notes that it "tends to juxtapose theoretical positions rather than make the connections Haraway recognizes are so necessary" (207).

13 See the 2006 interview of Haraway by Nicholas Gane.

14 In her piece "New Sciences: Cyborg Feminism and the Methodology of the Oppressed," Sandoval argues that the "cyborg consciousness" Haraway sets up in her manifesto "can be understood as the technological embodiment of a particular and specific form of oppositional consciousness that I have elsewhere described as 'U.S. third world feminism'" (1995, 408). Sandoval agrees that the practices of women of color are cyborg but points out that Haraway's work, as picked up by other feminist critics, has "inadvertently contributed to [the] tendency to elide the specific theoretical contributions of U.S. third world feminist criticism by turning many of its approaches, methods, forms and skills into examples of cyborg feminism" (414).

15 Melzer's readings of Butler's work in relation to Haraway's cyborg theory and other feminist theories of fluid identities such as Rosa Braidotti's "nomadic subjects" and Gloria Anzaldúa's borderland *mestizas* highlight the fiction's useful contradictions. However, Melzer primarily reads Butler's cyborgs as parallel to one another except in the case of her queer reading of *Wild Seed* in relation to *Imago*, in which she sees *Wild Seed* as less transgressive than *Imago* because of Butler's insistence on Anyanwu's female identity and Doro's male identity and the resulting heterosexuality of their relationship (234).

16 See Green's discussion of race and 1970s feminist sf in "'There Goes the Neighborhood': Octavia Butler's Demand for Diversity in Utopias."

17 The cover of the first edition of *Patternmaster* displayed a sketch of a bald man of indeterminate race.

18 Butler does not focus on this genetic manipulation in *Patternmaster*, but the later books in the series highlight how the Patternists and clayarks are products of manipulated biology.

19 Interestingly, Melzer claims that Butler's women "in positions of influence," like Mary, "refuse to misuse power on any level" (98). She argues that "The rejection of the use of power for personal goals is defined by Butler as an explicitly female trait, born out of a marginalized social location" (98). I see Butler as continually playing with the use of power—and Mary's intentional "forgetting" constitutes a misuse of power or at least a blind spot.

20 Butler creates a history drawn from the various myths and African cultures she has come across: "I used in particular, the myth of Atagbusi, who was an Onistsha Ibo woman. She was a shape-shifter who benefited her people while she was alive and when she died a market-gate was named after her, a gate at the Onitsha market. It was believed that whoever used this market-gate was under her protection…" (Kenan 1991, 499). Butler also mixes her personal fantasies with pieces of African culture: "Doro comes from an adolescent fantasy of mine to live forever and breed people…. I decided that he was going to be Nubian, because I wanted him to be somehow associated with ancient Egypt. And by then his name was already Doro, and it would have been very difficult to change it. So I went to the library and got this poor, dog-eared, ragged Nubian-English dictionary. I looked up the word Doro, the word existed and it meant: *the direction from which the sun comes; the east*" (499). Butler adds another partial memory of an Ibo tale to fill in gaps in this created history: "I found a myth having to do with the sun and the moon. Anyway the problem with that is: I lost it. I didn't write it down and I never found it again and all I had was one of the names: Anyanwu, meaning the sun. That worked out perfectly with Doro, the East" (500).

21 While this notion regarding Butler's focus on the exception to the rule may be true in some way for Mary, it is not for Anyanwu, who in some ways overflows the so-called biological norm and explodes it. Green's piece provides interesting readings of much of Butler's fiction, but does not analyze *Patternmaster*, *Mind of My Mind*, or *Wild Seed*.

22 All quotations from *Wild Seed* come from the 1988 Warner edition.

23 This combination of African (or other non-white culture) with European culture has been practiced throughout history by those colonized or enslaved by European cultures. The religious practices of African slaves in America and Haiti provide useful examples of how oppressed peoples make the cultures forced on them their own.

24 See Deborah Siegel's *Sisterhood Interrupted: From Radical Women to Grrls Gone Wild* (2007) for a discussion about the parallels between second wave and third wave feminists.

Mary's Children *(syfy poem for Octavia)*

doris davenport

1   Anatak

Emma suicided herself the night Mary absorbed Doro. When
she heard about Doro, she decided
to die. We were weary & bored with her sameness, tired of
hearing stories stones and Doro Doro Doro's *abominations* &
how it was. Mary was our savior, they said. They say. But
some of us tire of emaciated Mary the Patternmaster.

2   Adnaloy

i don't need words, born
an active telepath.
Emma was a "writer." A writer.
She used *words*, wrote on
pa perr. I don't need words
like her but

no one wants
her n-n-n notebooks. So, I, curious,
took them. And read her, and
the notebooks. This is my
first writ ting. I can w-w-write. Mary
is my grandmother.
I can heal, too, and kill.

3   Ignusa

Mutes don't. They don't
have to think merely feel
and do what / as they
are twisted to do.
The Pattern knows, I wish
I were a mute. Want to be
mute.

4   Siroda

We are connected.
We belong to
the First Family.
We have an identity; we
don't know who we are.
Teleporting minds &
bodies at will, entangled
in each other forever we
are one. We don't know
what one…

5   Onetta* (the One)

(*pronounced like Juanita)

Eons centuries decades
millennia measurements
of "time," meaningless.
Pointless. Long before
the Doro there was
one. i am that one. i am
the One.

An earlier version of this poem was published in
a hunger for moonlight, poems, 2006.

Notes on "Mary's Children"

In the early '80s i "met" Octavia Butler, in Los Angeles, via *Patternmaster*, thanks to a good friend, Asungi, and became an Absolute Butler Fan. We met Octavia on April 4, 1981, at a book signing for *Wild Seed*, and thereafter, i sent Octavia snail mail "love notes" on holidays and other occasions. Sometimes she answered. When teaching, i include Butler in one course per semester, somehow, and i read *Mind of My Mind* almost once a year. This, and more, is what Butler's life and work mean to me. i meant to send this poem to Octavia, just to amuse her [she had a great smile], but then, it was too late. i am honored to have this poem, compressed possible sequels to *Mind of My Mind*, included here.

Excerpt 2 from "A Conversation with Octavia E. Butler"

Nisi Shawl

(Interview Conducted at the "Black to the Future Conference: A Black Science Fiction Festival," Seattle, June 12, 2004)

Nisi: Let's talk about research a little bit. Do you research what you write?

Octavia: Yes. I…when I knew I was writing a vampire novel I read a lot of vampire novels and no names here because of what I'm going to say. But I read somebody's vampire novels who doesn't do any research at all. I don't mean researching vampires. I mean researching places. For instance, if you're going to set a novel in Paris, France, you probably should know something about Paris, France, and it should show up in the book some place. And there should probably be one or two French people in the book. [AUD: laughter] It's sort of like those old stories they used to read or I used to read about Africa where the only Africans were kind of shadows who couldn't really… I mean, even their names didn't come into the picture. And I live in terror of writing a book like that. So yes, I do research.

When I was doing the Xenogenesis books, I got a good contract for the first time in my life—good for me. And, I don't think Walter [Mosley] would like it, but I got a decent contract. And I went off to Peru because all of a sudden I could, and the books took place in the Peruvian Amazon. I read books that said one thing, books that said another, and I figured the best way to learn something about the place was to go. And that was probably the best trip I've ever had in my life, in spite of being bitten by every bug in the world. It's one place where you can go and be lunch. You don't really have to worry about the great big animals. They're dead. It's those little ones that are going to get you.

Nisi: So you research the place where the novel is set?

Octavia: Not just the place. When I did *Kindred*, for instance, I went up to Maryland because I had never lived in the South. My character was going to be going back in time to her ancestors, white and slave, in Maryland. So I wanted to know something about Maryland, and the first thing I found out was where my story takes place is on the Eastern Shore. And I set that up because I wanted my character not to be in a city. I wanted her to be out in the country. And I wanted her to have some notion, realistic notion, that she could escape. So I set the book there, and I had to go to Maryland. I didn't have any money.

Ummm…this goes back to a story that someone has reminded me of earlier today about *Survivor*. *Survivor* was the book that I used to get myself to Maryland, which is why *Survivor* is not a very good book. And I tell people not to buy it, which for some reason makes them go out and buy it. But, what can I say? It's really something that I sold too soon and got the money to get a Greyhound bus ticket to Maryland. Three and a half days on the bus. I don't recommend that anyone do this. Got to Maryland and did something—got to Baltimore actually—and did something that I had done before that, in New York. I went to the Travelers Aid people and said, "Can you recommend to me a hotel that is inexpensive?" No one asks about a cheap hotel, "inexpensive" but not actually dangerous. And they sent me to one. It was a terrible place, and when I went in, I was a little afraid to go in. There were a lot of guys standing around out front. I guess the only thing that I was glad about was there were no women pacing up and down out front. [AUD: laughter] So it was an only intermediately bad hotel.

And I went in and whispered to the woman at the desk, "Do women stay here?" And she said, "I live here." So I thought, well, okay, it can't be too bad, but I went upstairs to my room, and once I got to my room, the hotel acquired a nickname and stayed that way in my memory for ever after. I don't even remember what the actual name was, but for me it was The Hotel Sleazy because when I got into the room I noticed that there were cigarette butts on the furniture, lying there the way people put them there so they burn down and scar the furniture. And the cigarette butts were dusty. [AUD: laughter]. Definitely The Hotel Sleazy.

I was feeling sorry for myself, but I discovered that I was right around the corner from the Eli Pratt Free Library, where I practically lived when I wasn't on the Eastern Shore. I was right across the street from the Maryland Historical Society, where I developed an extra love for free libraries, because every time I used the Historical Society's, I had to pay. Not very much, but when you're eating one meal a day, you know, it starts to tell. Don't feel sorry for me. I could live on this fat for ages.

I did a lot of walking around on the Eastern Shore, I did a lot of hanging out at the library and learning whenever I could, both libraries actually. And at the Historical Society, I was able to go into period rooms and describe them. I had no camera, but I could describe them in one of my notebooks. So in a sense, having no camera was almost a good thing because you remember it better. The way my memory works, I remember it better when I have to look at it and write what I'm seeing. So I did that.

And I think I probably did more research on *Kindred* than anything else I've written, just because doing the book scared me to death. I didn't know how to do it. And the research didn't so much help me know how to do it as give me the clay to mold.

"Gambling Against History": Queer Kinship and Cruel Optimism in Octavia Butler's *Kindred*

Susan Knabe and Wendy Gay Pearson

> "Cruel optimism" names a relation of attachment to compromised positions of possibility. What is cruel about these attachments, and not merely inconvenient or tragic, is that the subjects who have *x* in their lives might not well endure the loss of their object or scene of desire, even though its presence threatens their well-being, because whatever the *content* of the attachment, the continuity of the form of it provides something of the continuity of the subject's sense of what it means to keep on living and to look forward to being in the world.
>
> —Lauren Berlant, "Cruel Optimism"

> "Queer belonging"…names the longing to "be *long*," to endure in corporeal form over time, beyond procreation. Though I offer a false etymology here, "belonging" contains the verb "to long," from the Middle Dutch *langen*, to be or seem long; "to 'think long,' desire; to extend, hold out, offer." To want to belong, let us say, is to long to be bigger not only spatially, but also temporally, to "hold out" a hand across time and touch the dead or those not born yet, to offer oneself beyond one's own time.
>
> —Elizabeth Freeman, "Queer Belongings: Kinship Theory and Queer Theory"

What, you might ask, is queer about *Kindred* (1979)? What can queer theory bring to the study of Butler's writing that has not already been covered in detailed considerations of the relationship between desire, subjectivity, race, and history in her novels and short stories? Indeed, the title of this anthology—*Strange Matings*—suggests some of the connections one can begin to make through a queer reading of what is, perhaps, one of the most resolutely heterosexual of Butler's *oeuvre*. "Matings" reminds readers of the extent to which reproduction and motherhood (and, in other senses, fatherhood and/or its failures) permeate not only *Kindred* but also many of Butler's other writings, while "Strange" inevitably brings to mind queer, albeit perhaps mainly in its denotative sense of "odd" or "peculiar." But, as we have so often argued, it is impossible to separate the "oddness" of queer from the queerness of odd. Thus "strange matings" invites consideration of non-heteronormative experiences and imaginings and of alternative forms of sexuality, reproduction, and kinship itself.

We will propose here several ways in which queer theory might illuminate the possibilities for a queer reading of *Kindred*, with potential application to all of Butler's work, and also the ways in which that queer reading might, in turn, highlight new aspects of Butler's intervention into discourses of race, desire, intersubjectivity, and the particular history of race-based slavery in the US. While the structuring concept of this reading involves Lauren Berlant's "Cruel Optimism" (2006), we will also draw on the concept of queer reading as an approach to science fiction, as well as three other major strands of thought within contemporary queer theory: queer phenomenology, predominantly as expressed by Sarah Ahmed, and ideas about queer time; the notion of queer kinship and queer belonging, as developed by Judith Butler, Elizabeth Freeman, and others; and finally the over-arching identification and deconstruction of (hetero)normativity that is so central to the development of queer theory.

In brief, the narrative involves Dana, a young African-American would-be writer who, without any warning, is transported on her 26th birthday from 1976 to the 1810s, where she saves the life of a young white boy, Rufus. She is briefly returned to her own time, but minutes later finds herself once more in the nineteenth century, where she again saves Rufus—mysteriously several years older—this time from the fire he is setting in his own house. Eventually she works out that she will travel to the past whenever Rufus's life is threatened and can return to her present only when she believes her own life is in danger. But while she remains in the nineteenth century as a black woman in the slave-holding south, Dana experiences both first-hand and by observation the miseries of slavery as an institution. On her next trip, her white husband, Kevin, throws his arms around her and is transported to the past along with Dana, who by this time has worked out that Rufus is the ancestor named in her family Bible as the father of Hagar, from whom Dana is descended. Dana and her family were unaware that one of their ancestors was a white man, but this discovery becomes more sinister as Dana meets Alice, the woman who will bear Hagar. As Rufus grows up and enters into manhood as a plantation owner, he forces the free born Alice into a sexual relationship, one which Dana feels that she must facilitate, or at least cannot oppose; she understands that her existence in the present is entirely dependent on Hagar's birth. Dana thus sees herself as unable to escape from Rufus because of the importance of ensuring the existence of the child who will become Dana's own great-great-grandmother.[1] Both Dana and Kevin discover that their knowledge of American history—and, in Dana's case, of African American history—is inadequate to assist them in surviving life in the past, but both also discover that additional historical research does not help.[2] The embodied experience of being in the past overwhelms the hands-off nature of historical knowledge, a fact rather brutally summed up in Dana's oft-cited description of watching, hearing, and smelling a whipping, during which she realizes that, "I was probably less prepared for the reality than the child crying not far from me" (*Kindred* 26). Dana cannot, however, keep herself from attempting to ameliorate the realities of slave life by trying to educate Rufus about the humanity of the black people on his father's estate and by showing him, in part through her relationship with Kevin, that things in 1976 will be different: interracial marriage will be legal, although its legality will be relatively recent,[3] and men and women will be, in theory, equal within that institution. The novel ends (after Hagar's birth and Alice's suicide) with Rufus's attempt to rape Dana, who knifes him and returns to her own present, but loses her left arm, which is caught in Rufus's death grip. *Kindred* thus returns to the beginning, with Dana in the hospital and Kevin suspected of maiming her, and continues only long enough to take the couple to 1976 Maryland, where a search reveals very few historical traces of either the incidents or people whom Dana and Kevin encountered in the past—a fact that is itself revealing of the nation's unwillingness to come to terms with this part of its past or to recognize minoritized peoples as having (a place in) history.

Queer Reading and *Kindred*

Queer theory predominantly deconstructs the naturalization and normalization of ontological sexual categories (straight, lesbian/gay, bisexual) that are taken as the inevitable corollaries of a binary notion of gender (male, female, at the expense of both trans and intersex). Queer theory's application to science fiction has not primarily addressed those works that can be identified as lesbian and/or gay; however, there is a parallel mode of scholarship, beginning pre-eminently with Eric Garber and Lyn Paleo's *Uranian Worlds*, that historicizes and analyzes LGBT science fiction. Inevitably, there is considerable cross-over between these strands of sf criticism, because both reference human sexuality (although in queer theory, this is more pertinently addressed in terms of desires, pleasures, and intimacies). Nothing about queer theory prevents its application to LGBT works, although queer readings may well find some of those works homonormative.[4] Nevertheless, the "queering" inherent in queer theoretical approaches provides a powerful tool for the critique of normalizing moves of all kinds, even those not directly involving human sexual relations. Queer theory thus provides useful strategies for analyzing and making visible the (hetero)normalization of racialized sexualities (which describes both the prohibition and the fetishization of interracial sex). The racialized sexual epistemology of the slave-owning Antebellum south is ripe for queer theoretical intervention, particularly, in the context of science fiction, when it is taken up by a writer like Octavia Butler with a demonstrated interest in questions of difference. There are many potential approaches to understanding Butler's apostrophizing of difference, including feminist sf studies, African American studies, literary studies (e.g., the genre of the neo-slave narrative), American history, critical race theory, and so on. We ask in this essay what a theoretically-informed contemporary queer reading can bring to this mix.

While queer readings of Butler's work are not common, they do exist. The most common subject of queer reading is probably "Blood Child"—not surprising given the obvious queerness of a tale about an alien female impregnating a human teenage boy. In terms of *Kindred*, Guy Mark Foster's "'Do I Look Like Someone You Can Come Home to from Where You May Be Going?': Re-Mapping Interracial Anxiety in Octavia Butler's *Kindred*" (2007) stands out. Foster "argues that *Kindred* manages to conceal the subversive nature of what initially appears to be a genuinely loving, healthy interracial relationship between a black female writer and her white husband by shrewdly masking the cultural and political implications of that relationship behind a rather sophisticated narrative ruse," i.e., time travel to an era when such a relationship is impossible (143). The "'sanctioned social plot' of racial oppression" partially obscures *Kindred's* destabilization of "key assumptions regarding the supposed causal relations between race, politics, and sexuality that has been a stubborn, if historically variable, feature of African American cultural discourse" (144).

Kindred thus engages in a *queering* of both African American and white American takes on interracial relationships, a queering that is founded on the apparently confounding fact that Dana's marriage with Kevin survives their various trips to the past.[5] Foster notes that:

> If contemporary critical paradigms for exploring interracial sex are recalibrated to acknowledge the mutual interdependence of discourses of race and desire rather than the more usual practice of viewing them as separate and unrelated, then scholars would recognize *Kindred's* protagonist as queer. (146)

This dual queering—of the novel and of its protagonist—reflects the simultaneous working of discourses of race and desire, on the one hand, and of race and gender identity on the other. The concept of race and the idea of sexuality are both products of Enlightenment era thought, colonial practices, and biopolitics. Race as a concept supposedly rooted in biology is self-policed (individuals are forced to self-identify and to self-surveil for racially appropriate behaviors and ideation) in ways that, while not identical, are related to the self-surveillance that biopolitics produces as the naturalized effect of sexual biology. Siobhan Somerville argues, however, that:

> By the early twentieth century, medical models of sexuality had begun to shift in emphasis, moving away from a focus on the body and toward psychological theories of desire. It seems significant that this shift took place within a period that also saw a transformation of scientific notions about race....
>
> In what ways were these shifts away from biologized notions of sexuality and race related in scientific literature? One area

in which they overlapped and perhaps shaped one another was through models of interracial and homosexual desire. Specifically, two cultural taboos—miscegenation and homosexuality—became linked in sexological and psychological discourse through the model of "abnormal" sexual object choice. (1997, 45)

Connections between aberrant sexuality and race as a site of perverse desire have been culturally expressed through racialized discourses of sex and sexualized discourses of race: obvious examples include the fetishization of the body, and particularly the genitalia, of African women (summed up most notoriously in the case of Saartjie Baartman[6]); white myths—and fears—of black male virility, expressed particularly in terms of penis size; and white (male) expectations of the sexual availability (also often the sexual voraciousness) of women of color. In relation to this latter myth, Jeffrey Pokorak (2006) argues that current racially-based disparities in the prosecution of rape stem from both historical legal distinctions between white and black people and the "powerful myth of slave sexuality: Black men were lascivious and must be kept from unrestrained sexual intercourse and assault, while Black women were portrayed as lascivious and therefore incapable of being raped" (9). He notes that, "Raping a Black woman was not a crime for the majority of this Nation's history" (8). Thus neither legal nor cultural discourse admitted the right of a black woman to the control of her own body and sexuality. This is a fact that Dana confronts throughout her time in the past, both in relation to her own ability to avoid rape and in relation to the treatment of black women around her.[7]

While many critics focus on "the historical narrative of interracial rape," Foster refers to the concurrent and co-dependent development of racial and sexual discourses within dominant culture to argue that such analyses "do so at the expense of marginalizing the narrative of consensual interracial desire, represented by Dana and Kevin's marriage" (2007, 148). Added to the dominant culture's racist stereotyping and fetishization of black sexuality, however, is African Americans' knowledge of the historical record of racism and of slavery itself, particularly the knowledge of the rape of black women by white men. Since many Americans assume that "blackness and whiteness are historically stable," they also take for granted that "interracial sexual liaisons of the past and those of the present, despite being implicated within radically

contrasting historical and socioeconomic conditions are conceptually in-
distinguishable from one another" (ibid.). These discourses of stability
foster two false assumptions: that whites are inevitably racist because
their ancestors presumably were; and that contemporary interracial relations mark the African-American partners as "self-haters and racial
traitors" and the white partners as "at best, politically radical, and, at the
worst, sexual fetishists" (ibid.). In presenting Dana and Kevin's marriage
as loving, enduring, and devoid of race-based sexual fetishism, Butler
effectively normalizes interracial relations, which had been discursively
rendered as queer by a racist, sexist, homophobic culture. Or, to put it
the other way around, she queers interracial relations by reclaiming them
from a series of conventional, but historically inaccurate, assumptions
about race and sexuality. Butler explicitly refutes the dominant perspective that "[Black/white] relationship(s) cannot be built on anything other
than sex" (Rosenblatt; cited in Foster, 150). It remains for us to point out
the similarity between this and the contemporary homophobic discourse
that insists that lesbian and gay relationships cannot be built on anything
but sex.

The second queering in *Kindred* can be symbolized through Dana's
clothing. The first time Dana is transported to the past, she is wearing
pants, as she is when Rufus catches a brief glimpse of her in 1976: "You
were wearing pants like a man—the way you are now. I thought you were
a man" (*Kindred* 22). Other characters criticize Dana's clothing or pity
her for having a master so poor or so cheap that he will only give her
men's clothing to wear (73). Dana's clothing is later accepted as Kevin's
eccentricity, but remains linked to her strangeness because she also uses
a New York origin as the alibi for the educated ("white") way she speaks.
Dana's accent brings her race into question while, as Foster also points
out, her clothing destabilizes the recognizability of her gender expression.

> The sheer frequency with which such comments about Dana's
> sartorial style appear in the text suggests that not only is the
> protagonist's gender in question, but since in western cultures
> who one sleeps with is so bound up with what Judith But-
> ler would call gender performativity, so is Dana's sexual ori-
> entation in question as well. And since the novel understands
> human sexuality in terms of an intraracial-interracial binary
> framework, rather than the usual heterosexual-homosexual

framework…, it would seem that Dana's gender instability is linked, not to lesbianism, but to her close relations with white men, in this case with Kevin and Rufus. (2007, 156-7)

We argue that while her "masculine identification" (ibid.) may not make Dana a lesbian—indeed, she shows no sign of same-sex desire—it does make her queer. More importantly, it makes her queer in ways that profoundly link the improper performance of gender with a failed performance of race. Dana herself comments mid-novel that she is only "playing at" being a slave (*Kindred*, 91), although that changes during the time she and Kevin spend on Weylin's plantation, particularly when she sees black children playing at slave auctions. Even when she realizes "how easily people could be trained to accept slavery" (101) or when she herself is brutally whipped for teaching slaves to read, Dana's embodied experience of race never quite matches that of black people born into nineteenth-century slavery (or even nineteenth-century freedom). "Dana's textual transgenderedness—one linked to an overtly *racialized* sex/gender system rather than one in which race is suppressed—" allows her to extend a kind of "black masculinist protectionism" to the other black women on the estate, particularly Alice (Foster 2007, 157). However, Foster points out that "Dana's efforts are hardly altruistic; rather, they are marked throughout by self-interest and anxiety about her own identity concerns as a contemporary black woman who is married to a white man, concerns that she has been unable to confront except by traveling back in time" (ibid.). This reading of Dana's "textual transgenderedness," more than her actual race/sex/gender queerness, links to Foster's thesis that the narrative trajectory of the novel is one of interracial romance and that when the couple travel to the past, at great personal cost (Dana loses an arm, Kevin loses four years while stuck in the past), their experience of history involves coming to a "shared" insight into "how their relationship as an interracial couple is deeply entwined with the past" (145).

Foster's argument about this interracial romance is compelling and provides a useful jumping-off point for thinking about the functions of orientation and disorientation in the novel. Both are devices that queer the present by illustrating its estrangement from the past, while also showing how the limits of historical knowledge orient the present in specific, and often harmful, directions.

Queer Phenomenology and the Queerness of Time (Travel)

If time travel is a form of history, a way of entering into the past, that should not obscure the fact that history is also a form of time travel, enabling the fictions that make life livable (or, as Judith Butler points out, unlivable [*Undoing* 2004, 2-4]) in the present. Time travel facilitates *Kindred*'s explorations of the past and of the way in which the past shapes the present, both exposing the limits of historical knowledge and the queerness of time travel itself. Not only should the day-to-day experience of the past be inaccessible to Dana in the present, the queer temporality of her translocation through history showcases the failure of normative readings of time as linear. Dana's past does not guarantee her present, which, in turn, does not guarantee her future. Furthermore, time is not history, but exists in a dialectical relationship with it (Freeman, *Time*, 2007, 9). The queerness of time travel thus inheres in its inability to guarantee the actuality (factuality?) either of the past (or future) that is its destination or the present of its supposed return. Part of the queerness of Dana's time-traveling is that she cannot know the "truth" of this past, but must assume it in order to arrive at a bearable (or at least livable) response. Thus the queerness of time travel catches Dana in a kind of temporal double bind, in which it both seems to fill in the blanks of historical knowledge and to remind the reader that this reparative strategy is literally fictional (to us) and thus possibly also to Dana. The past, queered by Dana's travel to it, is both real and not real, a truth exposed and a story imagined.

But time travel is also a corporeal experience: it involves the body moving through time, or between times. This is notable in the ways in which Butler describes Dana's experience of dislocation across time. The first time she returns to 1976 after saving Rufus from drowning, she says, "I felt sick and dizzy. My vision blurred so badly I could not distinguish the gun or the face of the man behind it" (*Kindred*, 14). After experiencing minutes in the past that turn out to be only seconds in 1976, Dana's physical condition is changed: not only does she experience dizziness and disorientation, she also returns "wet and muddy" (ibid.). Kevin perceives her travel only as unexplained movement across the room. The variance of their perceptions introduces the reader both to Butler's insistence on the corporeality of time travel and also to the disjuncture between time experienced in the past and time lapsed in 1976.

When Dana's twentieth-century body is dropped into the nineteenth century, she experiences the type of disorientation that Sarah Ahmed describes in *Queer Phenomenology*. Ahmed argues that:

> Moments of disorientation are vital. They are bodily experiences that throw the world up, or throw the body from its ground. Disorientation as a bodily feeling can be unsettling, and it can shatter one's sense of confidence in the ground or one's belief that the ground on which we reside can support the actions that make a life feel livable. (2006, 157)

Ahmed's discussion of disorientation meshes remarkably with Dana's experience. Disoriented by her translation into the past (which is also a geographical dislocation, from California to Maryland), Dana is not only deeply unsettled, but all her assumptions about what makes life livable become ungrounded. This becomes most clear when she realizes how poorly her reasonably well-educated and materially-secure life in 1976 has prepared her to confront the evils of life as a black person on a slave plantation.

Her disorientation is reinforced when she realizes that the child she has saved, Rufus, is the father of her ancestor, Hagar. To come so late to the realization that her family is not wholly African American is also deeply disorientating. It changes her understanding of the ground in the most literal sense. It forces her away from what she understands as home—a process that has already begun with her aunt's and uncle's reactions to her marriage to Kevin—and what she knows of as the truths of her personal, familial, and national histories. This is an experience Dana shares with many African Americans, who have had to confront a similar disorienting moment embodied in concepts of kinship that disallow the recognition of genealogies that include "the history and memory of nonconsensual miscegenation, specifically, the pervasive rape of Black women by white slave masters" (Van Thompson 2006, 111). Dana's disorientation from a previously comforting sense of the United States as home and a belief in her identity as an African American woman is exacerbated by her growing realization that the birth of her ancestor, Hagar, is dependent on the rape of her great-great-grandmother by her great-great-grandfather. This amounts to both a form of queer kinship (one created by its distance from the norms of what bell hooks refers to as "imperialist white-supremacist capitalist patriarchy" [2004, 17]) and a queering of kinship in that it requires Dana to do kinship differently.

Dana's experience of the past becomes one of continual disorientation: she is ungrounded by the realization of how easily people are enslaved and by her encounters with the casual but brutal violence meted out toward black people. At the same time, her disorientation from the past is partially deliberate, a desire not to become part of a system she despises and a continued orientation toward an ideal of 1976 as a place where she can be free, and free to choose an interracial marriage with Kevin. As part of her chosen disorientation, she understands both herself and Kevin to be, as David Lacroix notes, "oscillating between two possible positions: performing roles, and observing from a detached point of view" (2007, 114). Both positions keep her oriented toward her present in 1976 and away from interpellation into a past where she has to confront the loss of everything she holds valuable in the world and of the taken-for-grantedness of that world.

Orientation is necessary for a sense of the familiarity of the world. As Ahmed points out, "The question of orientation becomes, then, a question not only about how we 'find our way' but how we come to 'feel at home'" (2006, 7). One of Dana's most disorienting moments occurs on her fourth trip to the past, when, after saving Rufus, she has to walk through the darkening woods to the Weylin house to get help and uses bits of paper to mark her trail, so that she can find her way back. She is able to orient herself to find the way, in the most literal sense, but is utterly disoriented when, on sighting the Weylin house, she catches herself "saying wearily, 'Home at last'" (*Kindred*, 127). Repeated trips to the nineteenth century make the Weylin plantation, despite being the setting for pain, despair, and racial ugliness, increasingly familiar, so that Dana is caught between orientations: the nineteenth century that she does not want to be home and the 1976 apartment to which she returns. "My bed. Home. Kevin?" she thinks, when she awakes after her fourth trip. "Kevin?" because she fears that once again she has been returned to 1976 without him.

He too has undergone profound disorientation, being left in a past for which he is as little prepared as Dana. In his case, four years in the nineteenth century have not altered him in the ways Dana fears; instead of being corrupted by the past, he has found his way into the Underground Railroad and survived by helping slaves to escape. His orientation, like

Dana's, remains to the ideals of 1976 even while he discovers corpore-
ally the facts behind the whitewashed histories fed to twentieth-century
school children. As Ahmed says, "In a way, we learn what home means, or
how we occupy space at home and as home, when we leave home" (9). No
one leaves home more profoundly than Dana and Kevin, although Rufus,
by virtue of learning about Dana's time travel and about a future that
seems, superficially, profoundly different from his present, is also disoriented from a simple ability to feel at home in the early nineteenth century.

Such queering orientation disrupts or reorders relationships we name
"home" or "belonging." By not following accepted paths, queer orientations put other objects in reach that might seem far away. Thus Dana
disorients the social relations that Rufus knows—an effect of her textual
queerness. The most superficial of these orientations and disorientations
involves the physical artifacts that Dana brings with her into the past:
coins, her clothing, pens, paper, aspirin, and so on—all of these embody
a type of queerness due to their distance from the 1830s. Dana becomes
a queer force that moves through Rufus's life, at once disorienting him
from his present and opening up possibilities that, as we will explain
later, embed him in relations of cruel optimism.

Time travel thus spirals through all aspects of the characters' lives,
disorienting personal identification and the sense of being able to be at
home or to have a livable life, re-orienting received notions of kinship,
and orienting the reader toward a profound social critique of the ways in
which partial histories, history as metanarrative, affect the shape and possibilities of the present. Time travel allows for multiple levels of queering—queering Dana, queering kinship, queering history, and queering
ideas about belonging. Butler seems in this novel to "long to be bigger
not only spatially, but also temporally, to 'hold out' a hand across time
and touch the dead or those not born yet, to offer oneself beyond one's
own time" (Freeman 2010, 299). In *Kindred*, crucially, Dana reaches out
to touch her ancestor Hagar—who is both the dead and the not yet born.

Queer(ing) Kinship

In respect to kinship, two strands in the history of critical responses
to *Kindred* particularly stand out. The first is the inclination to focus on
Dana's relationship to both Rufus and Alice, particularly in terms of the
inability of Alice, though born free, to resist rape at Rufus's hands. Dana,
by contrast, is characterized primarily by her ability to refuse Rufus's ad-

vances and to make that refusal stick even when she has to kill him to do so. The second is more of a disinclination to attend to Dana's marriage to Kevin as either a sexual relationship or as a relationship between equals. In particular, some criticism emphasizes a doppelganger effect in the novel between people who look similar—Dana and Alice, who are viewed by those around them as so similar that they might be sisters or even, as Dana puts it, two halves of a whole; and Kevin and Rufus, who are both white and have green eyes. The first parallel is very strongly suggested in the novel and repeated several times by Dana herself and serves, in part, to reinforce her guilt at having to facilitate a "sister's" rape in order to ensure her own future existence.

We want to begin with the question of rape. There is absolutely no doubt that the novel exposes—and is intended to expose—the extent to which black women were raped by white men as part of the institution of slavery. The fact that Tom Weylin's wife, Margaret, hates the women her husband has raped and is pettily cruel to Weylin's half-breed children emphasizes how much slavery is institutionalized. When Margaret catches Dana leaving Kevin's room and leaps to (semi-correct) conclusions about their relationship, her cry that this is a "Christian household" merely reinforces her inability to influence her husband's behavior. Margaret attacks the black women who are victimized by the white men with whom she lives because she is powerless in the face of white male superiority, enshrined in law as much in terms of gender as of race. In 1813, of course, Margaret Weylin can no more vote than can Alice or Nigel or Carrie or any of the other black people in the novel, slave or free. Her legal status as the property of a man is emphasized in Butler's relentless depiction of her childishness: deprived of usefulness in a system that operates primarily between the power of the white slave owner and the powerlessness of the black slaves, Margaret exists in the limbo between being toy and burden. The vacuity and tenuousness of her position provides Margaret with no moral high ground; her choice to behave badly to her husband's other victims (and thus her relatives by marriage) makes her a largely unsympathetic character. Nonetheless, Butler refuses a simplistic moral binary: none of the white characters are wholly bad, while none of the black characters are wholly good. Yet this embrace of moral complexity in her characterizations and in her assessment of life for black and white people together in both present and past does not mean that Butler at any point neglects to face fully the ethical failure at the heart of the novel: the refusal of white fathers to acknowledge their mixed-race children. This historical refusal of recognition, the unwillingness to acknowledge genetic relationships—or, more simply, to name one's family as family—resonates from the past into the present. White families continue to insist on a historically unviable racial purity (for example, the annual Jefferson family reunion on his Monticello estate where European-American and African-American descendants have fought for decades over the failure of the former to recognize the latter), but Butler notes in an interview that, for many black families, being confronted with a previously unknown white relative is also a shock.

This insistence on not only forced sex but also forcible exchange of genetic material (which is what factually happens in the births of interracial slave children and which links this novel thematically in many ways to the Xenogenesis trilogy) serves to confront the reader with the centrality of rape and forced breeding to American history. *Kindred* several times reiterates scenarios in which Tom Weylin sells either his own children or children he has allowed to be bred and born on his estate. What seems central here is that the novel's focus is not just on the possibility that Alice will be raped by a white man, or that Dana will, but that both will be or might be raped by Rufus. While rape itself is grotesque enough, the reader is also confronted by the fact that Rufus is attempting to rape his own great-great-grand-daughter. If Rufus had succeeded in raping Dana, it would have been not only rape, but incest. The novel's very title—*Kindred*—signals the concept's centrality and raises the question of what constitutes kindred and who is kin to whom. Rufus does not know that Dana is his kin, which makes his desire for her slightly less grotesque than it seems to Dana and to the reader. Dana has to come to terms with the fact of her ancestor's whiteness—which, in turn, changes the valence of her interracial relationship with Kevin, as she is no longer the first in her family to have a white partner (even if she is the first to do so willingly).

Heteronormative narratives position family as a simple and often linear concept, one easily expressed through the graphic model of the family tree. But the history of race-based slavery mitigates the simplicity of such a model, just as it vitiates the claims of racists to embrace "family values." People who truly value family neither sell their kin nor allow kinship to be determined by skin color. What we see in *Kindred's* exploration of Dana's family tree, then, is both a queering of kinship and a correction of race-based heteronormative kinship models.

Dana's very relationship with Kevin can be described as queer, even though it involves two people of "opposite" sex. Foster explores the queering of this relationship at some length through close readings of the reactions of contemporary characters to their marriage. He notes that, "In each case, one or two characters send home the message that mutually consenting heterosexual relationships between blacks and whites are deviant and, hence, should…be *dis*couraged" (2007, 148). Buz, a co-worker in the auto-parts warehouse where Dana and Kevin are temps, suggests that Dana and Kevin write some "poor-nography together" (*Kindred* 54), a suggestion he repeats with more overtly racist overtones when he mutters, "Chocolate and vanilla porn!" (56). Buz's "assessment of Dana and Kevin's relationship is remarkably close to what social scientists and other scholars frequently report as the dominant social view on interracial couples" (Foster 2007, 149). Both Dana and Kevin have less obscene, but similarly negative responses from their relatives: Kevin's sister, married to a man he describes as a potential Nazi, refuses to have Dana in her house; Dana's aunt, by contrast, accepts the relationship precisely because Kevin's genes will probably produce lighter-skinned babies, while her uncle is deeply disappointed because, Dana tells Kevin, "he wants me to marry someone like him, someone who looks like him" (*Kindred* 111). Indeed, the dominant expectation that the novel critiques is that most people are willing to recognize as kin only those who look like them. In the Antebellum South, this discriminatory luxury was more available to slave owners than to the enslaved; the latter were more likely to have biological or affinal kinship disregarded or legally denied.

This is a situation familiar, albeit in very different ways, to current LGBT Americans, regardless of race, as the patchwork and contentious nature of legislation around same-sex relations, from the legalization of same-sex marriage to the state use of Defense of Marriage Acts, means that most people's kinship relations are either not recognized or recognized only in particular locations. In 1967, an interracial couple could legally marry in DC, yet be arrested for breaching the Racial Integrity Act in Virginia; today, a same-sex couple can get married in New York, yet have that marriage invalidated in Florida. In fact, the rollercoaster ride that has been same-sex marriage law in California means that some couples have legally married, had their marriages annulled by the state, but will likely soon be able to marry again, given the current state of court rulings on the issue. Black Americans have been affected not only by anti-miscegenation laws, but also by the historical denial of their own marriages and kin relations. Some slave owners allowed slaves to "jump the broom"—and some slaves did so without their owners' knowledge—yet the requirement that a civil contact be entered into only by free people meant that no slave marriage had legal force. Slave owners could break apart and sell off members of a slave's family at will: Dana encounters the sale of children and other family members several times in the novel, and the threat of this by Rufus, in his inept attempt to make Alice love him, precipitates her suicide.

We can think about queering kinship here in two ways. In the normative sense, black people's familial relations were rendered queer by slavery—estranged, defamiliarized, disorientated. From the perspective of queer theory, however, as Elizabeth Freeman argues, "Kinship matters... in a way that Judith Butler reminds us that 'bodies matter'; (1) a culture's repetition of particular practices actually *produces* what seem to be the material facts that supposedly *ground* those possibilities in the first place, and (2) when those repetitions are governed by a norm, other possibilities are literally unthinkable and impossible" (2010, 297). Freeman notes that definitions of kinship, specifically procreative definitions, are regulated by "heterosexual gender norms" (ibid.), but it would be more accurate to say, in reference to the "white-supremacist capitalist patriarchy" (hooks), that those heterosexual gender norms are always definitively white, as are the babies that are the normative end goal. Thus the queer call to rethink kinship moves away from ideas about *being* and *having* kin, which the procreative requirement makes unintelligible within queer relations, and reorients itself toward the idea that kinship is something we *do*. Doing kinship thus becomes a way of belonging, as it is also for Dana: while she may not be understood as kin to Kevin while she is in the past (and they are frequently misrecognized as not being fully kin to each other even in 1976), she *does* kinship, as does he. Dana also does a form of kinship with other slaves on the Weylin property, even those to whom she does not have the biological, if inverted, relationship she has with Alice: this is notably true of her relations with Carrie and Nigel, the slave couple whose children Rufus briefly allows Dana to educate. Within anthropological kinship theory, it is recognized that "kinship is a social and not a biological fact, a matter of culture rather than nature" (Freeman 2010, 299).

This becomes self-evident in *Kindred*, given Tom Weylin's willingness to enslave and then to sell the children he has fathered—and also Rufus's pretense at doing this when he is trying to manipulate Alice. The practice of kinship requires recognition. As Freeman says, however, "recognition is based upon identity: it asks the needy to abstract their needs into a name that grants them legal personhood and the privileges attending it" (ibid.). The corporeality of the black slave defies recognition because it cannot access recognition's requirements. Slaves, like LGBT people, are thus forced into one of two strategies: the assimilative one of requesting recognition by becoming as much like those denying that recognition as possible, and the much queerer one of finding alternative paths to forging kinship and belonging. In queer terms, this is often the "chosen family," but the term appears also to have a significant valence for Dana's methods of forging kinship, both in the nineteenth and the twentieth centuries. Dana's version of the chosen family marks Kevin as her kin in a way that the legalities of marriage, a mere nine years after interracial marriage was legalized, cannot. At the same time, it negotiates some of the problematics of kinship to those whom one would not choose: certainly Tom Weylin and his wife, most likely Rufus, and possibly even Alice. It allows Dana to negotiate both black and white treatments of her race, and in both nineteenth and twentieth centuries. Foster argues that, "It is Dana's blackness that has created the conditions for both black and white characters in the novel to demean and infantilize her on the basis of her decision to become romantically involved with a white male" (2007, 147). Models of queer kinship that re-orient questions of recognition not only allow the reader to recognize the validity of Dana and Kevin's contemporary relationship, in the face of both black and white disapproval, but also provide alternative possibilities for thinking about the ways in which slaves and their descendants attempt to mitigate, first, the refusal of their chosen kin relations and, second, the horror of those enforced by the brutality of white ownership.

Following Gayle Rubin, Freeman argues in "Queer Belonging: Queer Theory, Kinship Theory" (2007) that the inseparability of "kinship" and "gender" produces kinship as "a mode not just for the exchange *of* women but for their enculturation *as* women" (301). For black women in the Antebellum South, their enculturation as a specific type of woman comes not through their recognition as kin, but through the refusal to recognize their existence within kinship systems. Black people during the slave era were left to reorient themselves to a place outside recognizable kinship systems, their own and that of their white masters. As Hortense Spiller has noted, being removed from recognizability within kinship structures made enslaved black people "unintelligible as gendered (and thus human) beings" (qtd. in Freeman 2007, 302). Freeman notes that "critical race theory [cannot] necessarily afford to abandon kinship theory in the way that a white-centered queer theory might want to" (303). Removing African Americans from kinship structures, the institution of race-based slavery allowed white-supremacist heteropatriarchs[8] "to produce bodies that, by virtue of seeming without kin, were marketable, and that by virtue of being marketable, seemed bereft of kin" (ibid.). Ironically, white slave owners rationalized their ownership of black people through recourse to "another familial discourse, paternalistically claiming that their slaves were children who could not survive without them" (ibid.). However, Freeman does not tackle the equally problematic misrecognition that was required for slave owners to justify the refusal of kinship to their own biological children, one that equally left them "marketable."

Freeman turns to Toni Morrison to think about how "bodies have been central to conceptualizing the renewal of African American individuals and collectivities beyond the dominant kinship grid" (ibid.). This involves a historical re-membering, which suggests "the knitting together of individual bodies that have been ideologically and physically objectified, fragmented, or shattered…. Again, it suggests an embodied but not procreative model of kinship that has powerful resonances for theorizing in a queer mode" (ibid.). While the value of an embodied non-procreative model seems evident—it suggests that ways of *doing* kinship are what matter—the idea of a historical *re*-membering seems more difficult to relate to *Kindred*, where Dana is clearly *dis*-membered by her encounter with the past. Much critical work has attempted to think through the relationship between Dana's encounter with history and the loss of her arm, yet none of the arguments about it are wholly compelling. The most powerful way of understanding Dana's amputation might be to consider it as a corporeal metaphor for the ways in which black kinship has been dis-membered by the past and black people, through their unrecognizability as kin, deprived of recognition as fully human. Dana must live with the bodily reminder that her people have historically been rendered unintelligible as *people* and that black corporeality, bound up in disavowed kinship relations, has been the mechanism of that rendering.

To deal with this requires a re-orientation toward other understandings of kinship, which in fact brings us back to Morrison's "sense of a resolutely embodied community renewing itself through bodily strategies" (Freeman 304), but at a point where it highlights the potentials of merging with the model of the chosen family. The merged model suggests more dispersed ways of doing kinship, ones that do not depend on a notion of reproductive futurity but also do not entirely turn away from the biological.

For Dana and Kevin, their ability to do kinship under adverse circumstances re-imagines new and dispersed kinship networks that can take in both Dana's biological kinship with Rufus-the-ancestor and her contingent acceptance of Rufus-the-boy as chosen kin. Dana sees herself not as Rufus's great-great-grandchild, however often she reminds herself of the necessity of keeping Rufus alive to father Hagar, but rather as Rufus's mentor, almost as his older sister—someone he can turn to for protection from his father, defense against his clinging mother, and education in how a slave owner-to-be can grow up to be a human being. This latter is Dana's gamble with history. It is a gamble that reminds the reader that slavery, while keeping white people legal persons and intelligible as such, actually renders them less than human from a contemporary perspective. Indeed, the doppelganger relationship that some critics have focused upon between Rufus and Kevin, mediated as it is through these "queer" or reimagined notions of kinship, is not, as it has sometimes been read, a condemnation of Kevin as necessarily "like" Rufus because of his race, but rather an offering up of Kevin as a new form of kin, a better model of white masculinity than Rufus's macho, racist slave-owning father can provide. Dana wants Rufus to be like Kevin, to become as close as possible to a late twentieth-century boy and to grow into a non-racist, indeed anti-racist, man appalled by the notion of slavery—as Kevin is. For if Kevin is ignorant of racial realities, a special privilege accorded to white people within American race politics, and if Dana fears his contamination by the past, it becomes instead his proving ground. Through his years with the Underground Railroad, Kevin grows into the anti-racist white man that Dana would like Rufus to be. Indeed, for a brief period in the novel, Rufus seems closer to Dana and Kevin than to his own parents. Kevin recognizes Dana's attempts to change Rufus, to educate him into being to all intents and purposes a twentieth-century boy, adolescent, and young man living in the nineteenth century, and tells her that she is "gambling against history" (*Kindred* 83), a gamble she partially loses when Rufus resorts to rape.

Rufus's rape of Alice is not simply a personal failing of individual moral values and empathy (although it is also this); it is a failure brought about by the very conditions and ideologies of the white slave-owning classes in the Antebellum South. It is a failure brought about by slavery as a system. While Rufus is not a victim of slavery in the same sense that the enslaved are, the system costs him a great deal: in the end, it costs him his life and (possibly) his humanity, at least as that is gauged by (the reader's) contemporary standards. It—and Rufus—also cost Alice her life, in the most direct sense; his games with her, in his attempt to win her love, cause her to despair over his (fictional) selling of their children. Dana's gamble with history cannot defeat the institution of white-supremacist capitalist heteropatriarchy, and Rufus can no more escape this than his slaves can. Even escaped slaves are marked by their history, and the man who could grow up unmarked as the son and heir of a slave-owner would be very rare (and perhaps very queer) indeed.[9]

Cruel Optimism

Complicating the potentials of acknowledged and unacknowledged kinship and incestuous rape in the novel is the fact that Dana spends barely a year in the past, while Rufus grows from child to young man. For Dana, because of the compressed time frame through which she experiences the past, Rufus remains to some degree the small boy that she first rescues from drowning. Furthermore, this is a small boy whom, as noted above, Dana attempts to educate not only to make her own life in the past easier, but also to ameliorate the lives of the slaves whom he will one day own. In fact, it is possible that Rufus's complex relationship with Alice is a result of Dana's teaching and of the example she and Kevin set of the possibility of a loving interracial marriage. Because Dana explains to Rufus where she comes from and teaches him that, in the future, interracial marriage will be legal, she opens up for him a host of possibilities in relation to his desire for Alice that his father never contemplates. Tom's relationship to black women is much simpler: because he owns them, he sees them as his to use as he pleases. By contrast, it is quite clear that if interracial marriage were an option, Rufus would have married Alice. Whether or not he would have allowed her to turn down his proposal is another question. What Rufus cannot negotiate in the nineteenth century, even with his (little) knowledge of twentieth-century possibilities, is a way to mesh desire, romance, and mutuality within the strictures of institutional slavery, racism, and male supremacy. And that undoubtedly reflects on the present, in which recognizing women's agency in terms of sexual desire and sexual consent remains one of our most conflicted issues today.

In this sense, both Dana's knowledge of her present and Rufus's awareness of the future place these two characters in a specific condition of cruel optimism. Dana's attachments are to her own life, her writing, and her husband Kevin, but they are also to contemporary (1976) ideologies of freedom, race, race relations, sexual relationships, and notions of kindred. Rufus's attachments are to Dana, as a mentor and friend, but also as someone he has been taught to believe is racially inferior, and to Alice, whom he both loves and desires. Because of Dana and because of his lack of real education, his attachment to the ideologies of his own time are strained and complicated, so that he is frequently in the position of believing two opposing things at once (interracial marriage is illegal and impossible and also legal and possible). Because Dana presents him with the possibility that his desire for Alice might, in the future, allow him to wed her, while his father presents him with the example of the white slave owner who takes for granted his sexual ownership of both his black slaves and his white wife (statuses of ownership at once similar, through sex and gender, and dissimilar, through race), Rufus in many ways exemplifies the condition that Berlant names as cruel optimism. He is subject to "compromised positions of possibility" precisely because he has been offered the nearly impossible: a vision of a relationship with Alice that he is constitutionally unsuited to obtain, both because of his own racialized position and upbringing and because of Alice's. Alice, unaware of the future Dana has shown Rufus, can imagine no relationship with him that is not forced and unwanted, a situation exacerbated by the fact that she has her own desired relationship with a black man, a relationship that Rufus severs in his (to us) unprincipled, and certainly compromised, pursuit of her. Dana both deliberately, yet also inadvertently, exerts an influence on Rufus that places him in a duplicitous and compromised position: on the one hand, he knows that he can have what his father had (simple, forced access to the bodies of black women); on the other hand, Dana has taught him the possibility of wanting more, yet that "more" is not obtainable in his lifetime. Dana is also attempting to educate Rufus in a more literal fashion, as even on her third trip, with Kevin, the boy can barely read and knows almost nothing of the world outside the plantation. Furthermore, unlike the slaves and their children whom Dana risks her life to teach to read, Rufus does not understand education as either a privilege or a tool for survival. To address this in metaphorical terms, it is as if Rufus's status on the top of the dungheap, lording it over those at the bottom, obscures any possibility of him seeing that there's anything beyond the dungheap. Yet that vision is precisely what Dana must open up for him if her gamble is to have any chance of succeeding. Dana is thus literally gambling against history because, although she will not take the chance of walking away when Rufus calls her and letting him die, she gambles continuously in small ways meant to make life more livable for herself and for the black people around her. Educating Rufus is Dana's "insurance."

Berlant argues, at the start of "Cruel Optimism," that "all attachments are optimistic. That does not mean that they all *feel* optimistic.... But the surrender to the return to the scene where the object hovers in its potentialities is the operation of optimism as an affective form" (2006, 20). In other words, "we" have a particular emotional investment in allowing ourselves to return, at least imaginatively, to the site of our attachment to the object, whatever that may be. Both Dana and Rufus are continually engaged in this surrender: Dana's time travel literalizes "the return to the scene where the object hovers" in a truly science fictional fashion, i.e., in the sense that Samuel R. Delany has long argued that science fiction is a mode that literalizes metaphors. Dana's desire to remain in the present and not return to the past does not obscure her attachment to "the object" that "hovers"—although it does raise the question of what constitutes the object.

In one way, we may read Rufus himself as the object of Dana's attachment. Indeed, he is literally so, since Dana ends up at Rufus's side in moments of imminent crisis and is thus able—optimistically—to preserve her own family line and future. From another perspective, we might see Dana's kindred, as she understands them (that is, the black family that in only four generations has lost its awareness of the white great-great-grandfather) as the objects of her attachment. Other readings of Dana's attachments, her investments in "cruel optimism," are also possible. Berlant quotes Barbara Johnson's reading of Zora Neale Hurston through apostrophic address (talking to a "you" who cannot talk back) that allows for the optimism of recognizing that "objects of desire…make you possible," but also that they do so in part by "not being there" (2006, 22). Apostrophic address imagines the object "you" desire because its absence makes your own existence, as a desiring subject, possible. At the same time, it catches "you" within the bind of cruel optimism precisely because your attachment to the object cannot bring it into being. In *Kindred* the ultimate object of apostrophic address is Hagar, in whom all optimism (cruelly) rests: Hagar's "promising qualities" are the assurance of Dana's existence in 1976, Hagar's distant future, yet throughout the novel she has the distinct quality of "not being there" (ibid.). Again Berlant's reading of optimistic attachment is literalized in *Kindred* both through the mechanism of time travel and because Hagar is so minimally present in the novel and never exists as a character in her own right. Reading *Kindred* this way is itself a queer reading, a reading against the grain of apostrophic address, since the novel is written in the third person. Like Hagar, "you" does not directly exist in the novel, yet remains suspended: the "yous" that Butler addresses (readers, black, white, both, and neither), the "yous" that Dana addresses, which include Rufus, Alice, Hagar, and the unseen family that bridges the gap between them and Dana, and her husband, Kevin. The "you" that the novel cannot address, the "you" who remains closeted in the obscurity with which the novel cloaks the author's (and readers') future is Dana's own unconceived and unborn child. Indeed, the novel refuses to imagine a reproductive future, something that is a distinct departure for a writer whose oeuvre is so heavily focused on reproduction. Dana and Kevin never talk about their own desire for children; nor does the novel even mention the fundamental concern for birth control. Whereas Lee Edelman (2004) reads the queer lack of reproductive futurity as a larger refusal of American culture's investment in "the Child" (for Edelman, unlike Berlant, the Child is symptomatically white and male), what Butler sets up here mimics the very structure of the novel (or perhaps vice versa), as Dana remains caught in a loop between past and present that, in fact, never admits concepts of futurity: what Hagar's birth ensures is not Dana's future, with all of its diverse potentials for children and grandchildren, but Dana's present. The mixed-race children that Dana might have with Kevin (children who will be legally black, but racially somewhat more white than black—unless Kevin, too, has unacknowledged biracial ancestors) cannot be represented in *Kindred*. Thus a significant part of *Kindred*'s cruel optimism lies in Dana's attachment to a future that cannot exist. Such a future would be the 1976 she imagines for Rufus, the one in which people can marry freely across the racial divide, and in which men and women, not only black people and white, are equals.

To jump forward almost forty years from *Kindred*'s publication, this is the cruel optimism of Barack Obama's election as the first black (biracial) President of the USA. In a truly cogent piece called "Fear of a Black President" (2012), Ta-Nehisi Coates points out that "Barack Obama governs a nation enlightened enough to send an African American to the White House, but not enlightened enough to accept a black man as its president." In this distinction between the electable African American and the unacceptable black President, Coates captures the "cruel optimism" both of Obama's election and of the future *Kindred* would like to, but cannot, imagine. Like Butler and like many of her readers, a significant number of those who voted for Obama in 2008 did so because of their affective attachment to an "object," in this case the vision of a near future (almost a present) in which Americans abandon racism and embrace a post-racial world where it suddenly becomes possible to "imagine a black president who love[s] being black" (2012). Yet even as he recognizes Obama's skill in signaling his affinity with African American culture and thus validating a form of cultural capital previously only accessible to white Americans, Coates concludes that, "After Obama won, the longed-for post-racial moment did not arrive; on the contrary, racism intensified."

Kindred signals the possibility for an optimistic attachment to not one, but two futures, which the cultural imaginary of the US sees as fundamentally incommensurable: the first is a future in which African American pride is both embodied and expressed in culture; the second is the vision of a post-racial future in which race can exist but will cease to matter. This is not a validation of the idea of a "color-blind" nation, but rather—as queer people too have imagined—the institution of a world in which difference can be celebrated while disallowing what Coates refers to as "broad sympathy toward some and broader skepticism toward others" (ibid.). The question becomes, then, whether Dana is attached to either (or both) of these imaginable, but seemingly unrealizable, futures.

Gambling Against History

We have argued above that Dana's gamble against history can achieve, at best, a partial victory. Nevertheless, it is a necessary gamble. It does not simply have the effect of mitigating for Dana and for the slaves on the Weylin plantation some of the worst effects of Antebellum slavery, or of teaching Rufus that another world is possible, if not achievable in his own time. In fact, the whole novel is a gamble against history. It gambles that the history of slavery and its effects on black, white, and biracial people may be properly acknowledged and that doing so may produce for African Americans and for Americans more generally a more generous, comprehensive idea of the United States than is encompassed by the official bicentennial celebrations. To do so would mean to do kinship more actively, to acknowledge kindred more truthfully where they exist, and to imagine relationships between people more expansively and, yes, more queerly. While the US remains a place where gender and relationship are demarcated by race, where rape of black women is treated as far less serious—and indeed less possible—than rape of white women, where an African American can be elected, but a black President is unacceptable, it will remain, like Dana herself, dismembered by history. A gamble is, after all, needed, if we are to be able to orient ourselves and to learn to create a home that allows for a livable life in the world.

Works Cited

Ahmed, Sara. 2006. *Queer Phenomenology: Orientations, Objects, Others.* Durham, NC: Duke University Press.

Bast, Florian. 2012. "'No.': The Narrative Theorizing of Embodied Agency in Octavia Butler's *Kindred.*" *Extrapolation* 53.2(Summer): 151-182.

Berlant, Lauren. 2006. "Cruel Optimism." *differences: A Journal of Feminist Cultural Studies* 17.3: 20-36.

Butler, Judith. 2002. "Is Kinship Always Already Heterosexual?" *differences: A Journal of Feminist Cultural Studies* 13.1: 14-44. Print.

——. 2004. *Undoing Gender.* New York: Routledge.

Butler, Octavia. 1986. [1979]. *Kindred.* Boston, MA: Beacon Press.

Coates, Ta-Nehisi. 2012. "Fear of a Black President." *The Atlantic Monthly*, September.

Edelman, Lee. 2004. *No Future: Queer Theory and the Death Drive.* Durham, NC: Duke University Press.

Foster, Guy Mark. 2007. "'Do I Look like Someone You Can Come Home to from Where You May Be Going?': Re- Mapping Interracial Anxiety in Octavia Butler's *Kindred*." *African American Review* 41.1(Spring): 143-164.

Freeman, Elizabeth. 2007. "Queer Belongings: Kinship Theory and Queer Theory." In *A Companion to Lesbian, Gay, Bisexual, Transgender, and Queer Studies*, edited by George E. Haggerty and Molly McGarry, 295-314. Oxford: Blackwell.

———. 2010. *Time Binds: Queer Temporalities, Queer Histories.* Durham, NC: Duke University Press.

Hampton, Gregory. "Kindred: History, Revision, and (Re)memory of Bodies." *Obsidian* 6.2-7.1 (Fall 2005/2006): 105-117. Web. ProQuest.

hooks, bell. 2004. *The Will to Change: Men, Masculinity, and Love.* New York: Atria Books.

LaCroix, David. 2007. "To Touch Solid Evidence: The Implicity of Past and Present in Octavia E. Butler's Kindred." *The Journal of the Midwest Modern Language Association* 40.1(Spring): 109-119.

Pokorak, Jeffrey J. 2006. "Rape as a Badge of Slavery: The Legal History of, And Remedies for, Prosecutorial Race-of-Victim Charging Disparities." *Nevada Law Journal* 7.1(Fall): 1-49.

Somerville, Siobhan B. 2000. *Queering the Color Line: Race and the Invention of Homosexuality in American Culture.* London and Durham, NC: Duke University Press.

Van Thompson, Carlyle. 2006. "Moving Past the Present: Racialized Sexual Violence and Miscegenous Consumption in Octavia Butler's Kindred." In *Eating the Black Body: Miscegenation as Sexual Consumption in African American Literature and Culture*, edited by Carlyle Van Thompson, 107-144. New York: Peter Lang.

Endnotes

1 Different scholars variously refer to Rufus as Dana's grandfather (which he could not be, given the time frame), her great-grandfather, and her great-great-grandfather, as well as by less precise terms. This lack of clarity about Rufus's exact place on Dana's family tree comes from the novel itself, where Dana extrapolates that "maybe [Rufus] was my several times great-grandfather, but still vaguely alive in the memory of my family" because his name is in Hagar's family Bible. She then goes on to refer to "Grandmother Hagar," although it is also clear that Hagar, born in 1831, could not have literally been the grandmother of a woman born in 1950 (June 9, 1976, is Dana's twenty-sixth birthday). With access to the family Bible, Dana could work out her exact relationship to Rufus and Hagar and the fact that she does not do so may indicate her discomfort with the idea of a white ancestor.

2 We do not mean to suggest here that Kevin should not know African American history, but rather that mainstream culture understands Dana as "naturally" having more of an investment in knowing about 'her' past. *Kindred* exposes the problematic nature of this assumption.

3 Interracial marriage was legalized across the United States in 1967 in the Supreme Court decision in the case of Loving v. Virginia. Prior to 1967, the legality of interracial marriage varied from state to state, with Ohio being the first state to legalize interracial marriage in 1887, while still other states voted to criminalize it as late as 1940. However, Alabama only voted in 2000 to overturn its unconstitutional anti-interracial marriage law, with 40% of voters opposed to removing the ban.

4 "Homonormative" refers to the idea that lesbian and gay people are "just like" heterosexuals except for the sex of the people with whom they have sex. A homonormative result has been the goal of much LGBT rights organizing, which is focused on assimilation into the mainstream heterosexual world, not on the celebration of difference.

5 Some critics have read *Kindred* as a criticism of Dana and Kevin's relationship and of the possibility of healthy interracial relationships in general; some criticism never mentions Dana's marriage or Kevin's existence.

6 See Rachel Holmes, *The Hottentot Venus: The Life and Death of Saartjie Baartman: Born 1789—Buried 2002* (London: Bloomsbury, 2008) and *African Queen: The Real Life of the Hottentot Venus* (London: Bloomsbury, 2007).

7 Indeed, much of the critical work on *Kindred* has focused precisely on the apparent conundrum of Dana's absolute refusal of rape for herself, while

also enabling (or at least not preventing) Rufus's rape of Alice in order to ensure Hagar's birth. See most recently Florian Bast's argument in "No."

8   This is a common variation on bell hooks' original phrase.

9   With thanks to Rebecca Holden for pointing this out.

Sunday Morning

JT Stewart

for Octavia Butler

Sun's up
they say it's Sunday
come to us again

Bacon and egg smells
float over from Master's House
somebody's smoking cigars
maybe two some bodies

Cigars they come here
by big riverboats
breakfast china dishes
they come too
and ice for fancy get-togethers

Cost lots and lots of money

Last Sunday
they traded Jubilee
my grownup cousin
and Vashti my little sister
to pay for all the cigars
all the breakfast dishes
but not for all the ice

They said too much
had melted on the way

"Sunday Morning" Notes

What's the origin of my poem "Sunday Morning?" Why do I dedicate it to the writer of the novel *Kindred*? I believe Octavia Butler has the power of summoning.

Like Octavia Butler, I am a woman of African descent. Yet I can only speak of my kin in terms of two generations. My family tree as I know it begins and ends there: so much in the present, or near present—so little in the past. However, on occasion, something pulls me back—summons me into someone's past. A congregation singing a long-meter hymn in a Black urban church; Fats Domino decked out in a three-piece white suit, playing on a small upright piano in pre-Katrina New Orleans; somebody wearing small, white shoes with buttons refusing to walk along a wide, cobblestone street made by slaves in Trinidad Province, Cuba. And now, *Kindred*.

At the end of that novel, Dana—who has now voluntarily returned to the South—reflects on her catastrophic yearlong travel between the nineteenth and twentieth centuries: "Why did I ever want to come here. You'd think I would have had enough of the past."

Indeed. Why would any American—especially an African American woman like Dana (or like me) want to go back to the slaveholding South of pre-Civil War days…unless this woman has been summoned? Summoned to make a change—perhaps to correct her own personal consciousness and to challenge the collective American fantasy of iconic Scarlett O'Hara and her idyllic plantation, Tara.

Through *Kindred* Octavia Butler has summoned my countless students—summoned them and me—to both bypass and go beyond certain traditional labels: Ante-Bellum South, Post-Modern Sensitivities, Deconstruction of the Master Narrative. No. Absolutely not. We/I Be Here. This new-ness of *Kindred* remains. Lingers.

In the spring of 2007, as I sat outdoors on the deck of my Seattle apartment, looking at the cityscape and Portage Bay—a southern marker of the University of Washington's campus—three aromas drifted in from somewhere, summoning me into that place where Dana and Rufus clash—and both Jubliee and Vashti could well be kin. Mine. Thank you, Octavia. I dedicate this poem, "Sunday Morning," to you.

"Sun Woman" or "Wild Seed"? How a Young Feminist Writer Found Alternatives to White Bourgeois Narrative Models in the Early Novels of Octavia Butler

L. Timmel Duchamp

Novelists of Octavia E. Butler's stature make a posthumous impact on the world in two ways. Most obviously and visibly, their work continues to affect readers and critics who, moved by its power or struck by its brilliance, speak and write about it, ensuring that the world's engagement with the work continues long after the writer has left the world. Less visibly, other writers, influenced by the work, use and develop the narrative models it produced. Although writers and critics often talk about Writers X, Y, and Z having "influenced" writer W, more often than not they use the word "influenced" loosely rather than specifically to refer to apparently intangible elements of style. Such talk of "influence" does not fully acknowledge this important, indirect legacy that inheres in the work of bold and powerful writers and tends to pass unnoticed except by the conscious writers who make use of the narrative models such influential authors produced. In an effort to acknowledge and address this less visible contribution of Butler, I explore here in highly specific terms the influence of her early novels, particularly *Wild Seed*, on my own fiction.

I.

In *About Writing*, Samuel R. Delany (2005), one of Butler's instructors at the Clarion Writers Workshop in 1970, speaks of literary talent in rather unusual terms. The first side of talent, he says, "is the absorption of a series of complex models—models for the sentence, models for narrative scenes, and models for various larger literary structures" (118). He declares that the training of such talent requires "the repetition of the experience of reading" but *not* "the repetition of the experience of writing." And he names the second side of talent as "the ability to submit *to* [*sic*] those models" (119). For this to happen, the writer "must encounter that model…*through* [*sic*] the body," must experience it "as a force in the body, a pull on the back of the tongue" (120).

The first time I encountered Delany's notion of "submission to the models," I felt a sense of profound recognition. Excitement at having been given the key to understanding my own experience as a writer as well as the difficulty of forging new narratives swiftly followed. I had long since understood that only by imagining new narratives and creating diverse characters can writers hope to represent more than the standard male-dominated white bourgeois view of the world in their fiction, and I had struggled from the beginning to do so. But Delany's insight explained in practical terms the resistance the writer faces when attempting to create new narratives. If internalized submission to the existing models is an essential requirement of writing fiction, then conscious efforts to create new models are likely to fail, having a tendency to be awkward and obvious, and lacking the flexibility and capaciousness of the existing models. New narrative forms, that is to say, can't simply be created out of whole cloth. They must evolve through tweaking and hybridization and subversion.

Lacking the range of models available to writers perfectly happy with the white bourgeois realist narrative, writers like myself who wish to represent perspectives that deviate from the dominant values of Western societies face the problem of how to create such narratives without making them wooden and didactic, much less shrill and polemical. This is a problem that dogs writers of color as well as white writers dissatisfied with the standard narratives. When I heard Tananarive Due talk at the "Black to the Future Conference" (Seattle, 2004) about how she initially wrote fiction with only white protagonists, her reflections resonated with Delany's insistence that talented writers are those who have internalized their submission to the models. Due said she hadn't even *noticed* that her protagonists were white until someone pointed it out to her and asked her why that was. The models she absorbed featured and accommodated white protagonists. Having submitted to them and encountered them "as a force in the body, a pull on the back of the tongue," Due unconsciously reproduced them rather than her own experience as a black woman living in a white racist world.

When I first began writing fiction—after having written a roman à clef murder mystery that set me on that path—I worried constantly about how not to write shrill and polemical fiction and yet still incorporate a critical political attitude into my work even as I aimed to create women characters who acted powerfully in making the worlds they live in. I chose the fiction I read at that time almost exclusively for its feminist appeal. I read science fiction as well as literary fiction but felt that science fiction was too difficult for me to attempt to write. The novel I worked on in the early eighties was a literary narrative with the working title of "In Silence, the Maze." Of the contemporary feminist literary fiction I read, Marge Piercy's most interested me, probably because her protagonists either possessed or acquired political consciousness and engaged in political struggle as activists as well as in their personal relations. But I found Piercy's fiction annoyingly didactic and polemical, and that made me acutely sensitive to the same problem in my own fiction. Significantly, Piercy's *Woman on the Edge of Time* (1976), a science fiction novel, struck me as an exception. Though just as political and didactic, it felt alive and open and rich with subtext, as her literary novels did not. At the time I did not consciously make comparisons between the feminist science fiction and the feminist literary fiction I was reading; if I had, I would have realized that science fiction allowed a less direct approach to the aspects of social and personal life I was determined to write about and was better able to accommodate the questions I wished to raise. That my literary novel-in-progress soon came to include magic realist elements, which I used to offer subtle social and political revelations, suggests that I intuitively understood the limitations of bourgeois "realist" narrative, even if I knew little then about the politics of narrative.

As I worked on composing "In Silence, the Maze," my dialogue and narrative became less didactic and more lyrical and complex. Still, though the manuscript grew to more than 900 single-spaced pages, it never acquired the recognizable shape or structure of a novel. The story could, I realized after three years of work, simply go on and on for thousands of pages, showing the characters having fascinating experiences, changing, developing new relationships, practicing their art (for the characters included a dancer, a writer, a composer, and a pianist), in a lyrical, increasingly complex narrative without end. Fascinating but shapeless, it resembled life (albeit richly examined and glittering with insight) more than it did art.

I had not, as Delany would say, submitted myself to the existing models for narrative form. This was conscious on my part, for I wanted to create a new model and in my naiveté imagined that I could. But I had failed to tell a structurally unified and coherent story. I knew that I could do this, for my mystery novel had taken on the classic narrative arc of the genre without my even being conscious of it. Submitting to the standard narrative models, though, would, I felt, contradict everything I hoped to do in my novel-in-progress.

2.

Everything changed for me as a writer in October 1984.
As Delany (2005) notes:

> the sign that the writer has internalized a model deeply enough to use it in writing is when he or she has encountered it enough times so that he or she no longer remembers it in terms of a specific example or a particular text, but experiences it, rather, as a force in the body, a pull on the back of the tongue, an urge in the fingers to shape language in one particular way and avoid another. (118)

When in 2005 while reading *About Writing*, how could I not have recognized Delany's description of the writer's internalization of a model so thoroughly that her body is moved by it without conscious volition? I had long marveled that my first science fiction novel appeared from nowhere and seemed simply to write itself, for one evening after dinner in early October 1984, I sat down at my desk, opened a new WordStar file, and wrote the first two chapters of *Alanya to Alanya* in a single sitting. Without my even thinking about it, science fiction flowed out of my fingers onto the green phosphorescent screen. My literary novel-in-progress vanished from my mental landscape. Writing *Alanya to Alanya* seemed like magic to me, for it was as though the novel wrote itself without my conscious intention. For seven weeks of intense writing that prevented me from sparing the time to prepare meals and often even to sleep, I typed as fast as I could, on edge and aflame to discover what was going to happen to my characters next. But it wasn't magic, of course: my fingers and unconscious were in charge.

Perhaps two-thirds through the novel, I began to see the traces of the feminist sf I'd been reading for the last ten years, present, like ghosts in the text. My protagonist, I decided, was a cross between Irene in Joanna Russ's *The Two of Them* (1978) and Lyle Taney in Kate Wilhelm's "The

North Beach" (1981). I saw that Sweetwater, my fictional anarchist collective, resembled Marge Piercy's twenty-second-century Mattapoisett. I knew that my construction of different systems of gender and sexuality for each of the three classes in my world's rigid class structure as well as my approach to writing narrative scenes I'd picked up from reading Delany. I also realized that one of my alien characters, Leleynl l Absq san Phrglu, who was very, very old and powerful, brown-skinned, and a healer, used techniques similar to those used by Butler's very, very old and powerful, brown-skinned healer, Anyanwu.

Though I recognized these discrete elements, I had no consciousness of submitting to models. It did not occur to me that I had done so until I read Delany's essay, at which point I began mulling over my memories and re-examining *Alanya to Alanya*. Following the novel's publication in 2005, I was struck by how frequently reviewers commented that though overtly political, the novel had surprisingly escaped being shrill and polemical, which reminded me of my early worry about how to write politically critical fiction. Since I never actually worried about this problem while writing the Marq'ssan Cycle, however, I concluded that I must have internalized a model or models for how to write overtly political fiction without being shrill.

I found that model when I reread Butler's *Wild Seed* (1999). *Wild Seed*, which is set in the late seventeenth and eighteenth centuries, narrates the struggle between the four-thousand-year-old vampiric Doro and Anyanwu, a three-hundred-year-old shape-shifter and healer he finds in Africa and whom he is determined to breed. Doro considers Anyanwu "wild seed" that can be used to enhance the "stock" that provide him with especially enjoyable kills. Anyanwu's struggle is both moral and personal; because Doro can kill her, her desire to survive curtails the scope of her opposition. As John Clute (1995) notes, the novel "potently evoke[s] reflections on everything from family romance and sex and feminism to slavery" (180).

I believe that *Wild Seed* works as a model for how to write overtly political fiction for three reasons. First and most obviously, because the story is science fiction, the social and political oppression depicted, though resonant with historical reality, is cognitively estranged, enabling the reader to hold the novel's intense images of oppression at enough of a distance to allow full emotional engagement with the story. Second, although the conflict between Doro and Anyanwu is continual and frequently overt, from the first chapter, Butler translates it into the conflict between two world views and philosophies that not only mirrors but also structures the differences between the two characters. Butler thus lifts the conflict beyond a simple battle of good vs. evil, or vampire vs. victim, to engage the reader's intellectual interest in its ramifications. Third, since Anyanwu, like many of Butler's protagonists, cannot defeat her opponent, she is forced to choose between negotiating the conditions of her oppressive circumstances or suicide—and chooses, for important and interesting reasons, to negotiate with her oppressor. Since the second and third aspects of the model are specific to *Wild Seed*, an elaboration of them is in order.

3.

We know from the first pages of *Wild Seed* that neither Doro nor Anyanwu are ordinary. But although Anyanwu differs from other humans, she is fully human in a sense that Doro is not. Doro cues Anyanwu to the difference between them when he tells her "This body needs rest if it is to continue to serve me" (8).[1] Immediately she senses the significance of his "strange way" of speaking. When he explains that he "wears" the body of those he kills "like a cloth," Anyanwu identifies him as a spirit, which angers him. In fact, Doro's relation to material existence is that of a parasite. His life, which is compulsively peripatetic, depends on physically viable hosts that don't sustain him for long. Since he is stronger and more powerful than any human alive, he feels contempt for the physical. He prefers to believe that he controls the physical without himself partaking of it, even if he is dependent on it. His sole occupation for all his thousands of years of existence is that of breeding "seed"—humans showing traces of paranormal talent—because the experience of living in their bodies gives him pleasure (even though any special powers such a person might have are lost when Doro takes over their body). Not surprisingly, he sees humans as creatures to be bred over generations to develop the characteristics he enjoys consuming. When Doro finds Anyanwu, he categorizes her as "wild seed," gifted with the most perfect talent he has ever encountered, and determines to tame and breed her in order to enrich "his people" (as he refers to those he has taken for breeding stock).

Anyanwu, by contrast, is grounded in the body. While Doro is a spirit that wears flesh, Anyanwu's flesh can change itself. What she values most are her relations with others and the well-being of her loved ones: "It was her way to settle and make a tribe around her and stay within that tribe for as long as she could" (197). When he first meets her, Doro adopts her language, telling her that she "belongs with" him (22), but later tells others that she belongs *to* him. Butler makes the differences in these perspectives explicit:

> Doro looked at people, healthy or ill, and wondered what kind of young they could produce. Anyanwu looked at the sick—especially those with problems she hadn't seen before—and wondered whether she could defeat their disease. (160)

The issue of generation is an index of their conflict. Both Doro and Anyanwu value generation, but generation means something entirely different to each of them. Within himself, Doro conflates the roles of father, master, and owner; he considers "his people" to be his children, slaves, and property. He insists that he has given "his children" their lives and thus has a right to take them when he wishes (202). Anyanwu scoffs at him when he casually refers to having created a man: "Did you create him, then? From what? Mounds of clay?" (123). Although Doro can only use others' bodies, he sees himself as physically reproducing by way of breeding his stock, reinforcing his conflation of the roles of father, master, and owner. As he tells Anyanwu, "I have lived for thirty-seven hundred years and fathered thousands of children. I have become a woman and borne children" (58). Throughout the novel, the narrative opposes Anyanwu's notions of parenting to Doro's constant claim to be father, owner, and master of those he claims to have created, as much by showing her actions and the power of her love as through her verbal opposition to Doro. He believes that childbearing makes women weak and vulnerable to domination (27); Anyanwu sees it as the source of great power and pleasure. Doro may use Anyanwu's love for her children and grandchildren to control her, but her reason for leaving her home and going with him is his promise to give her children she won't have to bury (22).

If Butler had treated these differences as simply the context within which the conflict between Doro and Anyanwu unfolds, though the story would have been just as dramatic psychologically, it would also have been flatter: for the conflict would, then, simply have been the contest between two powerful beings, in which the ruthless, murderous male seeks to tame and enslave the humane and caring female. On the fourth page of the novel, however, Butler signals the reader that the novel's conflict is not merely between individuals, but is between two opposed views of the world. Doro and Anyanwu, as they meet, tell one another their names. "Among my people," Doro tells her, his name "means the east—the direction from which the sun comes" (6). This frightens her. She says, "Do you know who I am? Did you come here knowing?" (7). Her name, she tells him, is the word in her language for Sun. The reader soon discovers that Butler is offering us a striking irony with this apparent coincidence, an irony that repeatedly surfaces throughout the novel. Although Doro reacts impatiently to Anyanwu's fright when he thinks she sees metaphysical significance in this coincidental relation between their names (as he always reacts when he suspects her of superstition), this coincidence symbolically supports his view of their relationship. As he sees it, she is a descendant of people he bred, a line of his seed that strayed and became wild.

Even as a fairly inexperienced reader back in 1980 when I first read *Wild Seed*, I had no trouble picking up the cue from the apparent coincident relation between their names to be on the lookout for a metaphorical subtext. Although the narrative never directly mentions the appropriateness of Anyanwu's name, it offers ample evidence for the reader to infer it. The Sun gives life and warmth and nourishment to all living things; it is the body the earth revolves around. Anyanwu gives life to the tribes she collects around herself, nourishes and heals them and provides the gravity around which they center themselves. She is constant and faithful. Her love is a given in others' lives. As a result, narrative exposition that I would ordinarily have read as mere context for the interpersonal conflict driving the book resonated powerfully with elements of feminist theory current in the late 1970s US. In particular, Doro's and Anyanwu's opposing views of the world evoked for me the differences between the sexes that Simone de Beauvoir focused on in *The Second Sex*, noting that for Europeans, woman is body, man is culture. This dualism renders men and women different categories of beings, such that women are perceived as immanent and material, men as transcendent and acting on the material; women as existing for others, men as existing for themselves; women as giving and serving life, men as disposing of and acting upon it; women's social identities defined by their relationships with others, men's social identities defined by their accomplishments, exercise of agency, and effective instrumentalization of the people and world around them.

During the 1980s, theory arising from what in the US is frequently referred to as the "third wave" of feminism complicated my understanding of gender dualism. Much of third-wave theorizing developed from theory that originated in the second wave. Perhaps the late second-wave work most influential in bringing about the third wave was the Combahee River Collective's *Black Feminist Statement*, first published in 1977 and reprinted more than twenty times since, which drew attention to the necessity of understanding the ways in which race, class, sex, gender, and other oppressions are "interlocking." Although I had encountered the seemingly intractable problem of dual oppressions (class and gender and gender and race) in socialist-feminist theory in the 1970s, my first exposure to the notion of *interlocking* oppressions came in 1981, when I read Moraga and Anzaldúa's anthology *This Bridge Called My Back*, which reprinted the Combahee River Collective's *Statement*. Many white feminists assumed that shared gender oppression made all women equals, without noticing that race and class privilege positioned individual women differently. Faced with the anger of feminists of color, many white feminists worried that such differences among women threatened feminist unity. I immediately sensed that the key to breaking through the supposed intractability of dual oppressions lay in the theory of interlocking oppressions, but it took me several years to fully grasp.

My recent reading of *Wild Seed* resonates with the early twenty-first century theorization of politics by Linda M.G. Zerilli, inspired by Hannah Arendt's political philosophy. An important consequence for feminists of recognizing the problem of interlocking oppressions is that third-wave feminisms discarded, once and for all, the white bourgeois notion of the individual as a sovereign being and rejected it as a goal of personal liberation. Gender oppression, feminists like myself realized, is too complicated to be seen as a simple matter of men exercising power over women, and new ways of conceptualizing not only the complexity of political and social oppression but also personal agency and political freedom are needed. Zerilli's theorization of politics offers me an alternative way of reading Doro and Anyanwu that takes such complexities into account. In this reading, rather than equating man with culture and woman with body, the narrative instead challenges the notion that freedom and personal agency are constituted by individual sovereignty. As Zerilli suggests:

> Equating freedom with sovereignty, the Western tradition
> since Plato, argues Arendt, has held plurality to be a "weak-
> ness," at best an indication of our unfortunate dependence
> on others, which we should strive to overcome. (2005, 16)

And so in more recent rereadings I've been struck by the way in which
Doro constantly asserts his sovereignty as an individual and is certain
that childbearing weakens women because it does not allow them to
enjoy total individual sovereignty. Anyanwu, in contrast, sees her world
as a plurality of relations and interdependence. Her position as a black
woman in antebellum America, for instance, is complicated by her power
to shapeshift, a gift which allows her to pass as a white male when she
wishes. In a sense, her shapeshifting emblematizes the fluidity of her
identity, though it's important to note that she never regards the transformation of her identity as a means of overcoming oppression: for her,
neither blackness nor femaleness is inherently inferior and thus passing,
while sometimes expedient, offers no solution. If maternity and plurality
make her "weak" as Doro believes, it's a weakness she is not only happy
to live with but that she pities him the lack of.

Doro's and Anyanwu's opposing views of the world resonate with
each of these theories in turn and would likely resonate with other theories. Butler is not preaching a single political theory or proposing a new or
existing system of philosophy, but providing readers with elements they
can use to elaborate a subtext resonating with philosophies that challenge
the dominant European view of the individual as sovereign. In this way,
many of the elements of *Wild Seed* form a subtext that evokes the power
and significance of a set of ideas it does not actually spell out. Thus Doro
is not merely a monster; rather, he embodies the characteristics of what
traditional European philosophers have defined as "man"—albeit taken
to the extreme. And Anyanwu is not merely Doro's opponent, lover, and
victim; though she is non-European, she embodies the characteristics
of what traditional European philosophers have defined as "woman"—
albeit one more powerful than any they have ever imagined.

All of Butler's fiction works for me in this way, in each case providing a resonant subtext, though the subtext and the ideas it resonates with
change from novel to novel. It is her creation of such resonant subtexts,
I believe, that allows her to depict such harsh, powerful conflicts without

seeming to preach. Her subtexts' subtle evocations of grand philosophical narratives make her stories about more than villains vs. their opponents and the particular evils of racism, sexism, and ethnic subjugation. She shows conflict as it plays out in the details of the characters' lives as signs that can be read for a larger battle of ideas. As a result, her narratives provide readers with a rich context in which to understand the political issues in play throughout the work, and the choices the characters make, the positions they take, and the values they articulate. In Butler's novels, not only is the personal the political, but the political is the cultural as well.

4.

Besides offering me a model for writing non-polemically about social and political conflict, Butler's early novels also expanded my idea of authentic feminist narrative. For most of 1970s feminist sf, the usual narrative model depicted an oppressed woman accomplishing her liberation, either by defeating or outwitting her oppressors or escaping them. (The latter could include a heroic suicide.) For many feminists in the 1970s, it seemed a given that a depiction of struggle in feminist sf must result in victory. *Mind of My Mind,* which I read before *Wild Seed,* fit the model perfectly: the outcome of Mary's conflict with Doro ends in his destruction and the triumph of community. In its precursor, *Wild Seed,* published three years later, Anyanwu's accomplishment is not the destruction of Doro, but a forced negotiation that allows her to live with her oppressor as a person of special privilege. Anyanwu thus settles for a slightly altered status quo that I knew from reading *Mind of My Mind* would both remain oppressive and entail Anyanwu's collaboration. Butler's next novel, *Kindred,* did not follow the model of feminist liberation, either. Its narrative demands that Dana, the twentieth-century black protagonist, repeatedly rescue her white slave-owning ancestor Rufus and see to it that one of his slaves bears the child who becomes Dana's ancestor. In this case, her own existence in the world is contingent on her active collaboration with the horrors of slavery. The usual feminist model simply could not have worked in that novel: had Dana heroically liberated Rufus's slaves and declined even once to save his life, her own life would have winked out of existence. *Kindred* made me realize that the standard feminist liberation model was at bottom a white bourgeois narrative, premised on the notion of sovereign individualism.

Most women's lives can't be seen in such terms. Must all protagonists, even of feminist sf, conform to the terms of the white bourgeois narrative? Most of Butler's protagonists don't. For Butler, the feminist story isn't an all-or-nothing struggle; it isn't simply about overthrowing patriarchy. It's about understanding how oppression works in all its complexity and finding ways to negotiate with what can't in the particular situation be changed. Plurality, as Zerilli writes (again following Arendt), means that the consequences of actions are boundless and unpredictable—as *Kindred* so clearly shows.

In 1984 when the Marq'ssan Cycle, *Wild Seed* and *Kindred* were the only models available to me of feminist protagonists acutely aware of the "boundlessness and unpredictability" of actions in their struggle against oppression. I believe that Butler's creation of such protagonists came about as a direct result of her choosing to write about women of color and finding the standard bourgeois narrative inadequate. Anyanwu's non-Western perspective with its non-bourgeois conception of family and maternity dictated the creation of a strong character for whom the illusion of individual sovereignty was irrelevant and dysfunctional. Although Dana does not share Anyanwu's perspective on the family, the illusion of individual sovereignty is rendered irrelevant and dysfunctional for her when she discovers that the exercise of absolute sovereignty (refusing to help her white slave-holder ancestor Rufus) would end her life.

Feminist sf ceased to follow the narrative model of liberation or escape from patriarchy in the 1980s as US feminists shifted their efforts from achieving liberation to surviving within the existing system—or as a character from James Tiptree Jr.'s "The Women Men Don't See," who joins a group of aliens to escape patriarchy, put it, "living within the chinks of the world machine." Some writers dismissed the model of liberation or escape from patriarchy because they ceased to believe that liberation was possible or even desirable. Other writers, like me, intuitively understood that another model was needed to create a narrative that embraces plurality and refuses the impossible fantasy of individual sovereignty. The current generation of feminist sf writers owes Octavia E. Butler a tremendous debt.

Works Cited

Beauvoir, Simone de. 1971. *The Second Sex*, tr. H.M. Parshley. New York: Knopf.

Butler, Octavia E. 1981. *Kindred*. New York: Pocket Books.

_____. 1999. *Wild Seed*. New York: Warner Aspect.

Clute, John. 1995. "Butler, Octavia E(stelle)." In *The Encyclopedia of Science Fiction*, edited by John Clute and Peter Nicholls. New York: St. Martin's.

Delany, Samuel R. 2005. *About Writing: Seven Essays, Four Letters, and Five Interviews*. Middletown, CN: Wesleyan University Press.

Moraga, Cherríe and Gloria Anzaldúa, eds. 1981. *This Bridge Called My Back: Writings by Radical Women of Color*. Watertown, MA: Persephone.

Norman, Brian, "'We' in Redux: The Combahee River Collective's Black Feminist Statement," *differences* 18,2 (2007): 103-132

Zerilli, Linda M. G. 2005. *Feminism and the Abyss of Freedom*. Chicago, IL University of Chicago Press.

Endnote

1   The quotations from *Wild Seed* come from the 1999 Warner edition.

While researching her last novel, *Fledgling*, Octavia experienced her
first face-to-face encounter with a horse.
❧ *Photo by Leslie Howle*

The Spirit in the Seed

Luisah Teish

At first, I didn't see it, the Spirit in the Seed, even though it was right there. I did not see it.

I can't remember what day it was. It was in the '80s; that at least I know. I think the sun was shining, so it could have been spring. But then again, I do recall snuggling under my bedcovers with a book fused in place between my fingers. The book was titled *Wild Seed,* and a black woman named Octavia E. Butler had written it.

As far back as the '60s, I'd been in love with edgy TV programs that straddled the genres of mystery and science fiction. I favored *One Step Beyond* and *Kolchak: The Night Stalker* and *Star Trek.* I absolutely loved Rod Serling's introductions to *Night Gallery* and *The Twilight Zone.* I had read H.P. Lovecraft, Ray Bradbury, and Isaac Asimov. Their works took me into other worlds, "outer space," the mind of madness, and the realm of the absurd. I remember reading Asimov's *Foundation Trilogy* and being sorely disappointed that far into the future and even in deep space, his important characters were still fair-skinned, and women in leadership roles almost nonexistent.

I imagined that I would write something unique someday. My characters would have purple skins and orange hair. They would be gynandrous, able to impregnate themselves as well as others. And they would possess unheard of powers. I dreamed about what I would write, but I wasn't sure that such things could be written.

But now an amazingly magical book had appeared in my library. I was thrilled to be reading the work of a woman whose main character was a woman — and both author and main character were black.

Unlike the writing of Asimov, Bradbury, and Lovecraft, which I'd read and processed with my head (pondering possibility and modes of expression), this story touched my heart and took me on a voyage of historical and personal remembrance. Remembrance? From my personal life I remembered Goree Island, off the coast of Senegal, walking through the last door that took slaves onto ships bound for who-knows-where. I was awestruck by this newly-discovered author's ability to make me *feel* her main character Anyanwu, as Octavia chronicled our history from the Motherland through the Middle Passage and on to the plantation. Yes, this woman's writing was remembrance!

For me it was remembrance of reality wrapped in a dream: the dream of the fantastic, fueled by the power of imagination.

I've tried to account for my feelings, my perceptions that something important was transpiring between the book and me. It has taken several readings over a period of twenty years to begin to understand my attraction to this work.

The first time, circa 1989, I read it from cover to cover. I read day and night and finished it in a week. After that first reading I tried to figure out why I was so engrossed in this story. What could the connection have been?

It could have been my late '60s and early '70s civil rights and Black Power experiences that conditioned me to identify with Octavia's characters. They were "wild seed" bred and born to wreak havoc on the Establishment. I'd grown up in the segregated South. I'd stood up to racism, survived poverty, and learned to empower other people. Octavia's characters were fictional expressions of factual people and events. They were revolutionary, and I counted myself among the many "everyday people" who maintained their power and dignity in the face of colonial oppression.

It could have been my late '70s to early '80s struggles as a feminist woman of color who was fortunate enough to find Zora Neale Hurston, Toni Morrison, and Maya Angelou. Those authors helped me to understand imaginative renderings of our lives as black women.

Starting in the late '60s, I'd fought alongside other African American students for Black Studies in college curriculums and had insisted that literature classes include the works of black writers. Yeah, we won, but all the writers were men: Richard Wright, Ralph Ellison, and James Baldwin. The women in these men's novels were often wax-paper thin and secondary, if not powerless or insignificant. I wasn't willing to become an "honorary man" in order to identify with their main characters, and I gloried in the stories those three women gave us.

When I read *Wild Seed* I identified with Anyanwu as a powerful woman fighting to liberate herself from patriarchy. I stood behind her energetically whenever she stood up to Doro. In Octavia, I'd found a writer whose works fed my imagination, so I consumed them like soup on a rainy day. I read *Kindred*, *Imago*, and *Dawn*. These stories dealt with important cultural issues. I saw *Kindred* as a form of ancestor reverence, while *Imago* and *Dawn* addressed issues of transgenerational slave syndrome and racial trauma.

I began to realize that "inner space" was truly Octavia's terrain and that she was taking Us (her African American readers) through a confrontation with fear, the most important part of a rite of passage. For example, in the past black women had been used as breeding chattel on the plantation. In *Imago*, she posed the possibility of that happening again in the future. My response was to redouble my efforts in defending our reproductive rights. Octavia's works pointed out recurring historical patterns and warned against them.

This woman's writings were transformative, and they became deeply impressed upon my consciousness. In Anyanwu, Octavia had created a shape-shifting character that embodied the abilities of ancient African mythological beings. And she had allowed that character to affect the world in ways that "history" (his-story) would deny anyone ever could have done.

Her example affected and empowered not only my political practice, but also my own writing, books and essays I create to popularize the concepts and philosophies of living African religious traditions. In 1984, I wrote *Jambalaya: The Natural Woman's book of Personal Charms and Practical Rituals*, in which I created a "generic African woman" (71) to give the reader a more realistic view of African women's lives. Anthropologists and cultural fundamentalists raised their eyebrows as I lifted the veil from these women's faces. But Octavia's own imaginative reconstruction of the past was there for me, a positive assurance that I could write what needed writing.

Around 1993, I read *Wild Seed* again, more slowly, underlining certain passages and making notes in the margins. This time I dared to ask, "What if?" of spiritual material and to postulate, "If/then" in writing about aspects of our past that fell into the categories of ancestral wisdom or forgotten knowledge. For example, I asked the question, "What if our ancestors, like Anyanwu, knew as much (if not more) about the universe as modern science does? What if their scientific devices were lying deep in the earth or under the sea? Better yet, what if they had a way to perceive that knowledge without a telescope, via shamanism? If so, where would this knowledge be stored?" I examined both spiritual and scientific material and found an answer. In 1994, I published that answer in *Carnival of the Spirit*, theorizing that seasonal rituals embody the ancestral understanding of the construction of the cosmos. The creation story in the first chapter of this book is a composite tale that reconciles the deities of West African mythology with the Big Bang theory of quantum physics (11-13). In addition to showing how science and spirituality connect, *Carnival* shows common elements between African and non-African traditional cosmologies, just as Octavia referred to and connected cultural elements from all over the globe.

Octavia also showed me how to successfully combine spiritual and scientific concerns and viewpoints by writing stories in which extrapolations of scientific change have implications on *all* levels—for example, the psychological impact of alien reproductive techniques on Lilith and her offspring in Imago. And the way her characters take on spiritual qualities because of scientifically plausible attributes was enlightening, too. That helped me visualize how scientific knowledge can resonate with traditional wisdom. Which, in turn, helped me find a place for our African religious heritage and for myself as a teacher among proponents of the Spiritual Science movement, including the Institute of Noetic Sciences and the School of Conscious Evolution.[1]

In 1999, I picked up *Wild Seed* again, and this time I clearly saw the Spirit in the Seed.

Perhaps it was because I now had seventeen years of experience as a priestess, healer, and diviner that allowed me to recognize the encoded wisdom in the book. I could now see more clearly the spiritual elements in Octavia's work. I've come to see her acting as a spiritual director who uses the science fiction genre to introduce Us to ideas of the sacred that we may have lost.

Wild Seed's main character is named for the Ibo Sun Goddess, Anyanwu. She also has characteristics of Sekhmet, the bloodthirsty Lion Goddess of the Egyptians, and of the Daughters of the Gelefun: Yemaya, Oya, and Oshun. These three Yoruba Goddesses appear altered but intact throughout the African diaspora.

Because of her determination to keep track of all her descendants, Anyanwu is similar to Yemaya, the Great Mother Goddess who governs the family and social order and accompanied Us through the Middle Passage. Then again, Anyanwu is like Oya, the Goddess of the Winds of Change, in Her ability to shift shapes, dress in camouflage, and go to battle. And Anyanwu uses the wiles of Oshun, the Goddess of Love and Beauty, when she enchants Isaac and seduces Doro in order to survive.

In *Wild Seed*, Octavia makes us comfortable with the powers of the Yoruba goddesses as well as the controversial powers of Iyaami (in Yoruba, "our mothers"), the bird women who fly at night and consume flesh in order to bring about justice in oppressive situations. Butler's Anyanwu can become a flesh-eating beast to defend herself, but is repulsed by the drinking of cow's milk. Through Anyanwu's emotions and actions, we come to understand the power of taboos, oaths, and curses.

Although Octavia never claimed to be such, I see her as a Theascribe, a Priestess of the Pen. I am convinced that the ancestors called upon Octavia to record their powers, to preserve their memory, and to teach us their secrets.

And then I imagined that I would finally write that unique piece. You know, the one where the people have purple skin and orange hair. The one I dream about. So I applied to the Clarion West Writers Workshop in hopes of taking a class with Octavia Butler. The demands of the time got in my way, though, and I couldn't go. I consoled myself by swearing that I would attend and learn more from our Theascribe another year. But Time has taken Octavia away from us! I place her name on the ancestor shrine and pray that one day she will speak to me.

In the meantime, I assign *Wild Seed* to my students in Women's Studies classes and diversity training sessions. As a prelude to these assignments, I talk about the beauty of Octavia's style. I praise the clarity and brevity of her prose but say nothing about the characters. Then I give the students a month to read the book and ask them not to discuss the material outside of class.

Once the in-class discussion starts, my students see the Spirit in the Seed, the spiritual legacy of Octavia's work. I find that like me they are amazed by Octavia's multidimensional characters and by these characters' depth of emotions. They wonder what Doro might really be. They are inspired by Octavia's ability to enliven history with portrayals of desperation and triumph. And they are grateful for her lessons in the use of female power, lessons that they can absorb, embody, and share with other women. They come to realize that the stories of their lives both reflect and contribute to Goddess lore. They are encouraged to take risks, to shape-shift, to try new things.

Even today, as I read *Wild Seed* for the fifth (or is it sixth?) time, I get wild ideas! I see remembrance of reality wrapped in a dream. I imagine sitting with an illustrator, a costume and set designer, and a choreographer. Together we recreate the novel's African villages, the dolphin's dance around the slave ship, and the many bodies of Anyanwu, Doro, and their wild seed. I see a feature-length film in animation that is absolutely captivating. In my vision, we incorporate all the dance styles of the African diaspora set to world-beat fusion music. This film rivals anime in its popularity with our young people, and over-dollars Disney at the box office. Instead of a black Barbie for Christmas, how about an Anyanwu doll that can transform herself as needed? What if Octavia's works inspire our boys to create video games? I'd like to see Junebug defeat Doro in a game called "Bodysnatch." I'd like to see our girls draw, paint, write, tell the stories, and create the environments Octavia's words inspire in them. We need to scatter these wild seeds so that they can inspirit everybody, everywhere they fall.

If anybody else has seen the Spirit in the Seed and is dreaming these wild dreams, please plant them now. Let them take root so we can all enjoy their blossoming, and, one day, their fruit.

Works Cited

Teish, Luisah. 1994. *Carnival of the Spirit: Seasonal Celebrations and Rites of Passage*. New York: Harper Collins.

———. 1985. *Jambalaya: The Natural Woman's Book of Personal Charms and Practical Rituals*. San Francisco, CA: Harper Collins.

Endnote

1   The recent book/DVD set *Living Deeply: The Art & Science of Transformation in Everyday Life* cites my work in this area.

During Howard University's Black Science Fiction Conference held in March 2003, Octavia smiles in the embrace of Steven Barnes, Nalo Hopkinson, and Tananarive Due, whom she often referred to as her science fiction family. With Samuel R. Delany, the four formed a core group frequently called upon to represent African American voices in the fantastic genres at conferences and conventions.

❖ *Photo by David Findlay*

Part Two

Tendencies Towards Hierarchicalism

and the Breakdown of Society:

Butler in the 1980s

Near and Dear

Steven Barnes

For a period of three years in the late '80s, I lived within walking distance of Octavia E. Butler. My mother had passed away, and I had moved back into her house on West View Street in Los Angeles, the home I'd grown up in. Octavia lived on West Boulevard, about eight blocks away, in a side-by-side duplex with barred doors and windows. I remember the first time I saw her house. I was dropping her off from a signing we'd both attended, and she invited me in.

Such an honor. More than that, it was the beginning of a twenty-year friendship.

At that point, Samuel Delany was no longer active as a science fiction writer. Octavia and I were the only ones doing the work, and in my mind she towered like a giant over the field. There is an issue with artists, in fact with human adulthood and simple existence: everyone craves the mentorship of SOMEONE who has gone further down the road of life than they have. In this regard, Octavia was close to perfect for me. Brilliant, utterly committed to her craft, of singular voice, and possessing an awesome penchant for field research (listening to her speak of her journey up the Amazon was an inspiration), she was absolutely the Real Deal. Her house was crammed bottom-to-top with books: novels, histories, science texts, and poetry, choking the walls from living room to kitchen. Wonderful. The little duplex on West Boulevard was a writer's house. It was at that moment, the moment when I saw her home, that I first began to suspect that Octavia was the purest writer I'd ever met. She simply put more of herself into her craft than anyone else. And for most of us, the answer to one question holds the secret to success in life: how much of yourself are you willing to give?

Octavia gave everything. There are times it seemed she gave until there was nothing left at all.

⇒ ⇐

While I lived on West View, Octavia and I exchanged dinner invitations frequently. She would either walk over to my house, or I would pick her up and we'd go to a restaurant. Whatever the setting, we always talked a blue streak. And it was during one of these conversations that she said the single most interesting thing I ever remember from her. It was a political conversation. Octavia was disappointed with my naiveté in political matters. For instance, at that time I believed in Trickle-Down Economics—Ronald Reagan's pet theory that economic benefits granted to the wealthy would eventually help the poor. She tsked and took me to school rather ruthlessly, puncturing that flimsy balloon of a world view in about ten minutes. Ouch.

Octavia had a philosophy grounded in a kind of down-home feminism, an "outsider" mentality rooted in an awkward girlhood and slight speech impediment that made her uncomfortable in public speaking for all but the last years of her life, and an intellect that devoured texts on biology and behaviorism and history until it all collapsed into a rather remarkable singularity. Deeply humane but at times profoundly pessimistic, Octavia could walk a fine line between depression and evangelism, without ever falling off the resultant tightrope.

That single most remarkable comment arose during a conversation at a soul food restaurant on Pico Boulevard in Los Angeles. I was having red beans, rice, and collard greens. She thought the corn bread was good. At one point after our blood sugar had stabilized, she said that there were two human tendencies she believed to be the most challenging for our species:

(1) The human tendency toward hierarchicalism.
(2) The tendency to place ourselves higher on the hierarchy than others.

She felt that these two things were responsible for sexism, racism, and wars of all kinds. They made the rich contemptuous of the poor, stoked nationalism, and…well, had the potential to destroy us all.

She expanded on her theme with enthusiasm and deep knowledge, lecturing fluidly on the behavior of termites and bonobos, the history of Egypt, and the origins of the modern-day Republican and Democratic parties. Fascinating, and all anchored in an odd, personal, and impressive blend of biological determinism and humanistic spirituality.

That was a night to remember. When readers of *Parable of the Sower* comment that Octavia could have started a religion (after all, L. Ron Hubbard did), I think of that night, and of her ability to reach for the stars while remaining rooted in our genes. Yes, she could have founded a religion. And its followers would have been good, decent, aware human beings.

It's possible she may have wanted a little too much from the shaved apes we call human beings, and I suspect our inability to live up to those expectations sometimes brought her to the edge of despair. Optimism and pessimism can be two sides of a very thin coin indeed.

⋙ ⋘

There was a profound loneliness about Octavia that sometimes made it difficult to be with her. I always wondered if I was interrupting something important when I called. It took a little while for her to open up and flow easily into the conversation, but by the end, no matter how long we had spoken or visited, I felt pain when I had to get off the phone or go home. She always seemed to want to hold onto that human connection just a little longer, too. Just a few more minutes.

I always wondered how she felt after she hung up the phone, but never had the nerve to ask her.

⋙ ⋘

The last time I saw my friend was at her house in Seattle. Tananarive and I had driven up for some event or other, and happily, were able to combine it with a personal visit. Her MacArthur "Genius" grant money had enabled her to purchase a beautiful house near the lake, within walking distance of stores and public transportation (she did not drive). I noted that she was walking more slowly these days, as if she hurt somewhere deep in her hips or back. She lost her wind easily: the three of us had to walk at a snail's pace just to prevent her from wheezing.

Octavia was uncomfortably, unhealthily heavy at that point, and spoke of wanting to change that. She complained about writer's block associated with medications she was taking. At our dinner together conversation centered on writing, and life, and the national scene. Despite her discomfort she lightened up after a while, and my old friend was there again: brilliant, funny, kind, wise.

The last time I spoke to Octavia on the phone, she seemed positive, and happy about the way her latest book, *Fledgling*, had turned out. My impression was that writing that book must have been like pulling wisdom teeth sans Novocain. I wish I could remember the last thing she said to me, but I can't. I can't. And I am so terribly sorry about that.

⇒ ∈

If there is one memory of Octavia I hold closest to my heart, it is our encounter in Atlanta, Georgia, in 1997. She, along with Samuel Delany and Jewelle Gomez, was present at the African American Fantastic Imagination Conference at Clark Atlanta University, the conference where Tananarive and I first met. Octavia watched the sparks fly, and I think she knew before I did that I was falling in love.

Tananarive and I drove to the airport together, holding hands, and spent waiting time holding hands and whispering about our future together. Three days after we met.

After I left her gate, I ran into Octavia on the concourse of my own gate. We talked a bit, and I spoke of Tananarive as if wrapping myself in a warm, friendly blanket. Octavia listened, smiling tolerantly as I betrayed my fear that nothing so wonderful could happen so quickly.

She told me that sometimes we don't know what's happening to us, and it doesn't matter. The world flows on whether we enjoy the ride or not. "Just…see what happens," she said.

Octavia's plane was on the other side of the terminal, and she boarded one of the little airport trams and rode away, waving. Somehow that image…her pleasure at the beginning she had witnessed, has always remained with me. That little smile. The wave. The warmth as she said goodbye.

I miss her incredibly.

We human beings have a terrible tendency toward hierarchicalism, she said. I think this is true. And in that spirit I am forced to say that Octavia E. Butler was the most committed writer, and one of the very finest human beings, I've ever known.

I think she'd forgive me for that.

Disparate Spirits Yet Kindred Souls: Octavia E. Butler, "Speech Sounds," and Me

Sandra Y. Govan

The claim, the intention, and the initial premise of this piece is a special relationship between myself and my subject. I posit that despite obvious differences, Octavia E. Butler and I maintained an unusual connection, that in fact we were, notwithstanding our obvious physical and geographical distances, disparate spirits and yet kindred souls. The focus of this personal essay is two-part. First, I begin by delineating the shared traits and commonalties that linked us and how, as we made discoveries about our respective pasts, our connection strengthened. Then, changing gears to the more analytical, I shift the focus to "Speech Sounds," one of Butler's most powerful short stories, a story whose resonance I find particularly appealing because I identify with its protagonist on such a visceral level.

The relationship I had with Octavia E. Butler was neither complicated nor convoluted. Our friendship existed on both a professional and a personal plane. Since 1984, I have spoken with her, interviewed her, introduced her, reviewed her work, presented conference papers on her work (once when she sat in the audience), and published articles about her. She invited me into her home in both Pasadena and Seattle; I invited her to my home in Charlotte. Each time we met, at a conference or casually, I found her to be the same thoughtful, observant, patient, and generous woman though she did not suffer fools willingly. Witty, yet reserved; considerate of others, yet a down-to-earth, forthright, politically astute woman. She was as well an honest and humorous person, a woman of tremendous integrity whose penetrating prophetic vision permeated everything she wrote from her essays, to her short stories, to her highly regarded novels—from her first novel, *Patternmaster* (1976), to her last, *Fledgling*, published in October 2005—a mere four months before she died.

While we were not bosom buddies, Octavia and I established connections that went deeper than "writer" and "scholar." In addition to sharing the joys and disappointments of having summer birthdays and being raised as Baptists, we discovered that we both had somewhat sheltered childhoods and that because of our positions in society, no one expected either of us to amount to much. Both of us were often uncomfortable with children our own age because our differences, even within our own social group, set us apart. Sometimes we were targeted for abuse because our differences were too distinctive—much of Octavia's discomfort sprang from being thought too tall and deemed too dark, both heavy weights for an African American girl of the Fifties to carry. Also, although her extended family knew her to be a "smart little girl," her unrecognized dyslexia adversely affected her performance at school; thus her grades were not stellar but only satisfactory. Looking back to those years, Butler described her psychological or emotional malady in very strong terms. She had been traumatized and tormented; she felt she had been treated, bluntly, as "shit." Extreme shyness was not "cute, or feminine or appeal-ing." Her shyness made her feel awkward, "ugly and stupid, clumsy and socially hopeless," making her want to fade from sight—an impossibility given that in grade school, her height reached well beyond that of most of her classmates, stretching to six feet (Butler, "Positive Obsession" 128).

My physical differences similarly affected my relationships and ex-periences in school. I had been born with dislocated hips that required four hip operations prior to my learning to walk unaided. At four I finally walked without touching either the walls or the furniture. The hip dys-plasia subsequently led to spinal curvature by age 13. As a result, I walked with a distinct limp. Still do despite corrective surgery for scoliosis, seven successive hip replacements, and an elevation on one shoe. Following my transfer in the fifth grade from a Chicago public school that specialized in serving children with disabilities (and thus was rather sheltered), to a mainstream normal neighborhood public school, like Octavia I encoun-tered all manner of physical and psychological abuse from my peers. Big-ger girls would catch me in the bathroom and lean on the stall doors so I could not get out. Other large girls would snatch up my petticoats fol-lowing gym class and hold them up to announce to all gathered around, "my baby sister can wear this." My fifth grade peers teased me for being too small, too smart (and thus a teacher's pet), too talkative (especially to teachers), and for being "a cripple" (as they used to say before that term became politically incorrect.). Often the target of teasing, cruel joking, and the usual playground bullies, I found it useful to have an encouraging mother who guided my education, a protective big brother at school to defend me, and a doting father wrapped around my baby finger at home.

As social outcasts disdained by our respective peer groups, Octavia and I found our greatest refuge in books. Voracious readers, we haunted our public libraries. We read books of all kinds, and our tastes were surprisingly similar. We read DC and Marvel comic books (I still have my collection, and when Octavia came to Charlotte for a lecture and visited me in 1999, I think she still had her collection too.)[1]; we read romance stories, horse stories, and murder mysteries. Our proclivities as avid young readers and our imaginative inner lives led us each to harbor the dream of becoming writers, despite mixed messages from our families. Butler's aunt, Hazel R. Walker, revealed with some distress that she had been the aunt who told Octavia that "Negroes can't be writers" (Walker). My father did not put it quite so bluntly, but the intent was the same. When, at ten, I announced my intention to become a writer, he quietly took me aside to tell me gently: "Sweetie, let teaching be your vocation and writing be your avocation." In fairness, as adults both Octavia and I recognized that this seemingly harsh adult advice was not meant to squash our dreams but to shield us. Family members understood the difficult rigid career and social barriers facing black children during segregation. Our elders drew their negative perceptions from personal experience; they were African Americans largely confined to limited job opportunities prior to the Civil Rights struggle. They were also largely uninformed about the tradition of African American literature and the many writers who constituted that tradition.

Despite our early childhood traumas and these mixed messages about our ability to succeed as writers, I learned from years of casual conversation that Octavia and I spent much of our childhood surrounded by compassionate adults, adults who taught us important life lessons and made sure that books continued to be a part of our lives. Octavia had her mother, her grandmother (who owned a tearoom in Pasadena), and the older boarders her mother took in to learn from and talk to; she also had several aunts and uncles, whom she looked to provide models of male behavior, living in fairly close proximity. Ironically, though I was fortunate enough to possess *three* grandmothers (the third was my father's stepmother), each lived in a different state, so I rarely saw any of them during my childhood. I did, however, have engaging older women neighbors to talk to, a nearby favorite Aunt who always welcomed me, and two wonderful cousins willing to do battle on my behalf. In fact, rather than play with the girls my age on my block, I usually either babysat for younger kids or I deliberately spent time with the older women on our block and the next one—Mrs. Purnty, Mrs. Purnell, Mrs. Roberts, Mrs. Bell, Ms. Motley—all women who gave me books (Louisa May Alcott's *Little Women*, the expurgated child's version of Twain's *Huck Finn*, a wonderful book called *365 Bedtime Stories*), and/or who talked about various topics: my future; going to college; the need to rise whenever I fell; being careful around boys; being careful about love; and, clarifying questions of race and the then puzzling question of color variations among Negroes—why some neighbors on the block were very light while others were cinnamon brown or pecan-colored or much darker.

Our mothers also kept bringing books into our lives, continuing to feed our dreams and imaginations. My mother brought home WWII mystery and suspense novels from Chicago's Pullman Branch public library where she worked for a time, and we shared Agatha Christie novels. Octavia's mother brought home to her all manner of books and *Mad Magazines* from the houses she cleaned. It was Octavia's mother who encouraged her to follow her dream. As Octavia M. was pressing her daughter's hair, she noticed the child writing something in her ever present notebook. When she asked the twelve-year old what she was doing, Octavia E. told her mother that she was writing a story. Butler reports her mother then said, "Maybe you'll be a writer," leaving her daughter with the realization, "Wow, you can be a writer" (Smith, Shirlee A-14).[2]

Despite the lack of either African American authors or books on our early reading lists (or perhaps because of it), in our separate spaces across the country, we individually devoted serious attention to the goal to become writers, ignoring what we had been told. Octavia has often reported that she began writing at ten.[3] At thirteen, having found Van Vogt, Asimov, and Ellison, Octavia attempted to publish the stories she had written with the help of Mr. Pfaff, her junior high science teacher. Pfaff not only made his science classes engaging, but he typed a manuscript for his young student, thus helping Octavia to submit her first story to an sf magazine (Butler, Telephone interview).

Beyond this point our paths diverged. While I dreamed of acquiring fame for penning the classic American novel, in fairness I never actually *finished* a story to show to anyone. Following high school, I took my father's advice. I went to college, obtained undergraduate and advanced degrees, then surrendered the dream of writing fiction to the goal of becoming a teacher and a scholar—a profession I love though it is unlikely to ever bring me a MacArthur Award or a Pulitzer Prize. Maintaining the toughness necessary to survive, or thrive, in academia proved sufficiently challenging for me. I also became a literary critic focused primarily on African American literary works—which, happily, led to my reading and meeting and forming a friendship with Octavia E. Butler.

Octavia, on the other hand, held fast to her dream. She understood that the four-year college route was not a required road for her. Uncomfortable about going away to school yet strong-willed about her goals, she completed a two-year program at Pasadena City College, took some social science and humanities classes at California State and a few writing courses at UCLA. Principally, however, she gained the skills she needed by attending Writer's Guild of America West, a writer's workshop where, in 1969-70, she met and worked with Harlan Ellison and Sid Stebel. These were the teachers that, as Octavia would later indicate, gave her the best instruction for genre specific writing (Butler, Telephone interview).

While we pursued different professional callings as young women, we both found that teaching and teachers played significant roles in our work. Also we both enjoyed, at times, the teaching and mentoring or advising roles that seemed to accrue to us the more we aged and gained reputations in our respective fields.

As our relationship developed, we exchanged cards, letters, emails, and phone calls. We commiserated with each other over family losses (we both lost our mothers in the nineties); and, too often, we lamented unexpected health challenges, empathizing with each other because our bodies, the initial cause of that lack of expectations the world had for both of us, had begun betraying us again. Octavia changed from a woman who could stride the hills around her Pasadena home (and owned a treadmill) to a woman who, although she hated to accept it, required assistance walking through airports to reach a departure gate on time because she could not catch her breath.[4] She could not, in her last few years, walk to the end of her block without stopping. She was told she had "the beginnings of heart failure" and thus felt tired all the time. Ironically, the various prescribed drugs designed to make her feel better left her frustrated, unable to concentrate, and unable to focus on what had become the chore of the Parable novels—finishing the series. Although she considered herself "essentially a novelist," in order to keep her imaginative life alive

Octavia turned to writing short stories (both "Amnesty" and the "Book of Martha" were first published on-line in 2003) and to revising various drafts she had intended to form the remaining Parable books (Butler, *Bloodchild* 2005 *viii*). She had not yet, as she put it, "found a way in," a serviceable entry point by which to rejoin the Earthseed community as those characters ventured out among the stars fulfilling the established Earthseed destiny. But because she remained a perfectionist, concerned always about carefully crafted prose, shaping, reshaping, and refining it because she never wanted to insult her audience with writing she considered "flat," she never showed these drafts of the final two Parable books (as originally envisioned) to her editor. The medications diminishing her concentration made her doubt her ability to develop the projected novels to a point where she felt her audience would be satisfied. Concern for her audience shaped her unadorned artistic credo— "don't bore people" (Butler, *Bloodchild* 2005 13*)*. For relief, Octavia avidly read vampire novels, "hot" vampire romances (Govan, "Going to see" 10, 27).

My own physical challenges, though causing chronic discomfort, were not debilitating in the same way; I considered them largely structural rather than internal. Born with dislocated hips (later diagnosed as epiphyseal dysplasia), which subsequently led to multiple joint replacements in my hips and shoulders, I coped with these skeletal defects all my life. But 2003 marked a rougher medical year for me as well. I discovered that the osteoarthritis affecting my hip and shoulder joints was also impacting my eyes. I learned that the cartilage in both shoulder joints had completely disintegrated, leaving bone to grind on bone; I found that early corrective surgery for scoliosis (at 13) had not prevented later spinal stenosis. I also discovered that God has a sense of humor. As a middle-aged black woman, I had somehow contracted a condition more typically faced by older white men—chronic lymphatic leukemia or CLL. Octavia laughed with me when I shared this irony. For ten weeks I endured chemotherapy, feeling completely drained and unable to focus on four days of each week. In sum, Octavia and I both faced unexpected physical challenges or system failures. Our assorted ailments not only affected our mobility but they also altered our ability to work on projects dear to us. We each, however, persevered as best we could, comforting each other with cards and laughter and comforting ourselves by turning out what work we could.

In addition to the connections and parallels in our individual lives, both our lives and our work have undoubtedly been shaped by our families' histories, in particular, by the legacy of the strong women who peopled those histories. In 1999, the Charlotte Mecklenburg Public Library invited Octavia to participate in the Novello Literary Festival, an annual [before budget axe fell] Charlotte event. The Library asked me to introduce her. As a result, I heard Octavia speak about her family's Louisiana background for the first time. She illustrated the hardiness and pluck of her maternal grandmother (Estelle Guy), using elements borrowed from personal family history to contextualize Lauren Olamina, the protagonist for the two published Parable novels. To Lauren she gave many of the skills, strengths, and remarkable personal attributes of the grandmother she so admired. In the midst of the Depression, Estelle Guy, who bore nine children, left Louisiana to resettle her family just outside Los Angeles in Pasadena. Enthralled with Octavia's story, I was struck immediately by the similarities of our family heritage. In that same era, my grandmother moved her family from rural Ruston, Louisiana, to Los Angeles, California. Just as Octavia's maternal grandmother owned different properties in California, my maternal grandmother, the iron-willed matriarch Etta P. Wilson who raised six children, also bought, and rented out, several properties in California.

Without access to Octavia E. Butler's literary estate, at this point I cannot assert without qualification that the parallels I've drawn between our lives correspond as precisely as I believe they do. It is, however, as a critical reader that I can attest to the connections or correspondences in her fiction that attracted me and keep my attention. It is at the subjective, subterranean, sub rosa level that I have pondered the several factors that have kept me re-reading her stories. It may be that Butler's tales featuring strong highly capable Black, or multi-racial, women protagonists appeal to me so much because we both emerged from somewhat sheltered childhoods where societal expectations were minimal for us. That her characters also live with or endure some physical or psychological impairment that affects their lives and yet persist and achieve, for me can be read as additional stimulus, as indicators of possibilities existing both within and without the fictive realm. In Butler's novels, *Kindred*'s Dana is one such example; Lilith (whose suggestive name is a burden), from the Xenogenesis series, is another; Lauren Olamina, the empathetic heroine of the Parable books, is a third; and *Fledgling*'s Shori Matthews, whose memories have been brutally stolen from her, is a fourth. Each of these characters is a woman who acts, a woman who is decisive, in command. Each of these characters shows an ability to achieve difficult tasks despite her disability—in fact, in Lauren's case, *because* of her disability. These are all female characters able to wrest control of their lives and empower themselves under extremely trying circumstances. The worlds they inhabit are diseased, decaying, often dysfunctional and violent; and yet, these "disabled" women not only insure their own survival, their perseverance and their determination saves others as well.

Oddly enough, and of great interest to me, each of these protagonists in her own way is also a teacher—a teacher consciously or not abiding by one of the cardinal mantras of the Civil Rights and Black Power struggles from the 1960s—that is to say, "each one, reach one, teach one." These recurrent themes in Butler's novels are also apparent in the short stories of *Bloodchild*—thus Rye of "Speech Sounds" or Lynn of "The Evening and the Morning and the Night" easily melds into this pattern. Although Lynn's tale is gripping, I identify more with Rye (her name, her former profession— "She had been a teacher. A good one" [107]). I like the way Rye protects and defends herself; I like how she copes with and manages around her disability, how she maintains her self-control, her ability to function despite the dysfunctional society surrounding her. I like the way her story ends more than I like any other Butler character in her short fiction collection.

Having placed all of that on the table, I turn now to the highly textured, multi-layered, prescient "Speech Sounds," a story as deep and as rich in its subtle turns, societal critiques, and careful science as any Butler novel. "Speech Sounds" first appeared in *Isaac Asimov's Science Fiction Magazine* in 1983. The story struck an immediate chord with critics and fans; the attention it garnered won Butler her first Hugo Award. When it was reprinted in *Bloodchild* (1995), Butler added a revealing "Afterword." Here she shows the emotional scaffolding she used to build the story. During the 1980s, a friend of hers was hospitalized, dying slowly of multiple myeloma—an incurable cancer. Butler visited her friend weekly, riding the bus through LA to the hospital because she would not risk driving with dyslexia. When she arrived, because her friend had always been interested in her writing, Butler shared with her passages from her novel then in process, the unsettling, ominous, *Clay's Ark* (1984). This fifth novel of the Patternist saga is a tale that illustrates the origins of Clayarks from an alien interstellar microbe driven to reproduce by infecting its (human) hosts and radically altering their bodies. Understandably, coping with a friend's ravaging disease while creating a radical infection for her characters posed a certain level of emotional discomfort for Butler. "Speech Sounds," as she acknowledges, "was conceived in weariness, depression, and sorrow" (Butler, *Bloodchild* 2005, 109).

Although the story stands alone quite well, knowing its origins in her psyche adds to its depth in many ways. Butler's decision to extrapolate from a contemporary event, turning problem to story, is a quintessential science fictional technique. "Speech Sounds" creates an immediate atmosphere of fear and tension. An unknown highly infectious disease has swept the planet creating havoc in a unique manner. The mystery disease trope places Butler's "Speech Sounds" square in the midst of the tradition. For instance, the mysterious affliction with fearful consequences has long been a popular science fiction staple. Think *Andromeda Strain* or several different *Star Trek* episodes; "Miri," for instance, is an original *Star Trek* story where all the adults in an Earthlike city have died of a viral infection. When the children left behind hit puberty, and start becoming adults, they sicken, become irrational, then die.[5] Dr. McCoy, Mr. Spock, and of course, gallant Captain Kirk must find a cure quickly because once in contact with the children, they themselves become infected and must quickly synthesize an antidote or succumb to the disease.

The taut opening scene from "Speech Sounds" reveals compelling contemporary urban reality rather than mythic romantic prose. The story begins: "There was trouble aboard the Washington Boulevard Bus" (89). The brief declaration is both explicit and extrapolative, emerging directly from Butler's regular bus ride through LA's urban corridor. The second sentence, equally brief and intense, introduces Butler's heroine and gives us a quick glimpse of her as wary and perceptive. "Rye had expected trouble sooner or later in her journey." By the third sentence, "She had put off going until loneliness and hopelessness drove her out," we know why this desperate woman is risking her life on a city bus (89). Anyone who has ever ridden on a large urban bus line knows how easily tempers can fray, how quickly fights can start among crowded, tired, irritable passengers. Contributing to the story's complexity is that the nature of the conflict is entirely persuasive; moreover, we learn rapidly that this conflict is both local and universal, at once personal and political.

Arguably, Butler's "Speech Sounds" adopts another classic sf convention—the rhetorical "what if" or speculative question. What if an unknown virus attacked? How would that event affect human behavior? She then proceeds to dramatize that speculation by depicting the answer in a well-told story. Global suspicion about causality, about who or what caused the outbreak, spreads. What nation is responsible for creating then disseminating the illness? More importantly, affected local individual communities and their remaining inhabitants turn in frustration upon each other. Tense, antagonistic, and unable to communicate, people generally attack rather than support; at the slightest provocation they irrationally vent their frustrations, and sometimes their desires, upon the more vulnerable or upon survivors perceived to be less impacted than themselves. Here Butler invokes the base dimensions of human nature—jealousy, envy, lust, territoriality, violence, the tendency to fear and to fight what we do not comprehend.

Butler first uses several dramatic scenes to establish setting and introduce her principal characters. After providing subtle clues about their identity and attributes, she then illustrates for readers some of the psychological complexity underlying the story's conflicts. The story's narrator discloses what is known about the illness in specific terms as she speculates about the origins of the disease and its effects on survivors:

> The illness, if it was an illness, had cut even the living off from one another. As it swept over the country, people hardly had time to lay blame on the Soviets (though they were falling silent along with the rest of the world), on a new a virus, new pollutant, radiation, divine retribution.... The illness was stroke-swift in the way that it cut people down and strokelike in some of its effects. (95-96)

This disclosure does more than showcase Butler's deft economical prose; it reveals several tensions simultaneously. We see a hostile worldwide altered geo-political climate and hear Butler's speculation about possible side-effects of environmental degradation—perhaps an early glance at the effects of climate change or global warming. For some readers "Speech Sounds" may seem an illustration of science run amok. Nor does Butler, steeped in the Baptist church and biblical tale, neglect a nod to religion. For the faith community, or the merely superstitious, the sudden inexplicable appearance of such a horrific disease raises the specter of an Old Testament angry God striking down sinners. From this perspective, God chastises humanity by sending a new plague.

As the passage continues, Butler's narrator cuts to the beating heart of the story. The illness is "highly specific." The hopelessness and depression Butler alludes to in her "Afterword" surfaces in the narrator's description of the aftermath for those stricken. "Language was always lost or severely impaired. It was never regained. Often there was also paralysis, intellectual impairment, death" (96). We further learn from Butler's protagonist, an astute African American woman named Rye, that many of those impaired lost not only their voices but often their self-control, their socialized behavioral norms, and any sense of ordinary personal decency.

Valerie Rye is for me a principal attraction of the story. Like most of Butler's women, Rye is an engaging and fully rounded character, an intriguing individual. Functional in a largely dysfunctional and seemingly dystopian setting, despite terrible painful personal losses—husband, children, parents, and sisters—Rye has managed to hold on to some hope, to refuse to yield to utter despair and hopelessness. When we meet her, she has left her Los Angeles home, headed toward potential refuge in Pasadena, to seek out her brothers in Pasadena that she hopes might also have survived. Having ridden LA buses before, Rye is aware of the risks, prepared for the dangers she might face. Both knowledgeable and intuitive, Rye appears capable, determined, perceptive, compassionate, ready for any event, carefully observant, attentive to her surroundings, wary yet strong. Known by her last name, Rye is a woman who knows when the fighting will begin on the troubled bus and anticipates the reaction of the bus driver. She is both logical and discerning. "When the driver hit the brakes, she was ready," the narrator says (89-90). Rye escapes the fight the moment the bus comes to a complete stop. But when a lone police officer arrives and attempts to quell the violence, though suspicious of his motives, Rye moves to assist him.

Rye's wariness arises because the disease has proven so virulent that there "was no more LAPD, no more *any* large organization, governmental or private. There were neighborhood patrols and armed individuals. That was all" (92). The narrator's explanation resonates because it does more than summarize action or plot. It succinctly describes the present state, addressing the total disintegration of civil authority in the face of the catastrophic social upheaval that Butler envisioned happening here, in the 1980s, in the United States.

The disastrous disease causing havoc in "Speech Sounds" is a tool Butler uses to illustrate how *easily* entire communities can unravel into destructiveness. Possibly drawing upon memories of the Watts race riots of the mid-1960s, the story shows what has happened in the United States. But because Butler was a confessed "news junkie," she could well have extrapolated from contemporaneous headline news more evidence of the human capacity for irrational behavior. People too often fear or to hate those who differ from them. For one reason or another, one group will deny the basic humanity of the other. At the close of the twentieth century and the beginning of the twenty-first, this denial of basic human rights occurred at home and worldwide. Hurricane Katrina in 2005 illustrated the point for the US. Images of poor and abandoned African Americans clinging to rooftops while streets and homes flooded, holding signs that read "We're Americans too," flashed across T.V. screens. From Bosnia, Rwanda, Somalia, and Serbia came televised reports of beatings, beheadings, mass executions, or the designation of one group as "cockroaches" by the other group, the better to "exterminate" them. The communal violence Butler depicts in "Speech Sounds" brings readers into the story on the most gut-wrenching or visceral level. She shows us how people, isolated by loss of speech also lose connections to others and to basic humanity. Such a massive loss of one of our essential five senses graphically illustrates frustration, anger, lashing out at others who are different because *they*, apparently, are not affected by the disease.

"Speech Sounds" highlights several brutal acts of random violence coupled to the erasure of self-control and the diminution of ethical behavior among ordinary American citizenry. And yet, in depicting some characters who still strive to exercise basic human decency, attempting to remain a force for positive moral action, Butler incorporates another of her trademark themes: the significance of a hierarchy. Though he may be the last cop standing, the policeman who helps the passengers escape drives about policing, asserting control over the chaos rocking the bus, as if community policing remains his duty despite the surrounding decay. He has retained both his badge and his gun, symbols of authority. Rather than succumb to predatory practices heightened by the virus, he uses his remaining police presence to maintain order in the community, assisting citizens as a last representative of civic government. The officer, who Rye thinks of as Obsidian, serves as a symbol for a vanished civil order.

While Obsidian clearly represents official hierarchy, in this chaotic world Butler's depiction of power and authority is neither absolute nor phallocentric. Rye also carries a gun and knows how to use it. Rye can maintain control and exert authority when needed. She and Obsidian balance each other; through them Butler shows both mutuality and gender equality. Subtly subverting the Golden Age SF traditional practice of absenting or negating any black presence in the future, relegating African Americans to alien or other, Butler not only shows African Americans surviving but being among the elect who will revive civil society. In either a nod to color-blindness or an inability to recognize major characters as people of color, when Butler first submitted this story to *Asimov's*, Val Lindahan, the story's illustrator, initially drew Obsidian and Rye as white (Williams, Sheila 2007). Lindahan may have assumed all sf characters are white, or simply read hurriedly, overlooking the significance of his name and thus his racial identity. Someone caught the mistake and the illustration was revised before publication.

While the illustrator's error is telling, it points to another Butler signature trait, her love of metaphoric investment in character names. The richness of Obsidian for a policeman's name should be apparent. The very word "obsidian" signifies blackness; further, the word is defined as a hard, dark, glassy volcanic rock with the texture of granite—a toughness suitable for a cop. Butler's distinctive play upon the name occurs when Obsidian hands Rye his name symbol so she will know who he is—a chain with an attached pendant that "was a smooth, glassy, black rock. Obsidian" (97). Speculating silently that "His name might be Rock or Peter or Black," Rye nonetheless determines "to think of him as Obsidian" (97). Actually, the juxtaposition of "Peter" between "Rock" and "Black" is a complex and clever biblical allusion.[6] Pursuing the implications vested in "Peter" has even greater potential ramifications, for in the tale Rye and Obsidian form an attachment. Rye has begun to think of them in serious partnership; perhaps he will come home with her. She is willing to accept his insane drive to try to provide stability to what remains of their world if they can stay together. While Butler's allusion points to the *story* told of Simon Peter in the book of Matthew, I also hear reverberations of an old African American spiritual rendered, appropriately, by the female a cappella group Sweet Honey in the Rock, "I got a home in that rock, ain't that good news."

Rye's personal naming emblem is a pin resembling a stalk of wheat; thus she assumes that anyone who did not know her previously might think her surname was "Wheat." However Butler chose the name "Rye," which as a homonym for "wry" not only *sounds* appropriate for her character but also poetically fits both the meaning of the word (contrary, distorted, twisted) and fits her personality and situation as well. The world Rye now inhabits has become twisted and distorted. These facts drive her to move beyond the boundaries that heretofore confined her. In assisting Obsidian to rescue passengers from the bus, in getting into his car and leaving the scene with him, in finding a way to trust him and in relieving mutual loneliness through (safe) sexual liaison with him, in mastering her own intense jealousy over Obsidian's ability to *read*—a skill the virus has ironically stripped from her and left her disabled in her own eyes—Rye, a former freelance writer and college history professor, lives up to the inheritance encoded in both of her names. "Rye," an annual brown cereal grain, is also a hardy grass used in flour (and thus the creation of [rye] bread—the staff of life), and in the making of whiskey. Her given name, Valerie (a fact we do not discover until the end of the story), derives from the French and suggests valor, courage, bravery, and strength. Rye will need those attributes at the story's close. She will need courage and strength to be not merely a survivor but a mentor and a teacher for a new beginning. It is not dystopian disaster that Butler leaves us with at the close of "Speech Sounds"; rather, she leaves us with the image of the resilient Valerie Rye, a woman who has suffered repeated horrific losses, driving off with two newly orphaned small children, kids apparently uninfected by the disease. Rye will nurture and guide these children, and others like them who will have survived, as they grow. A protector /teacher with new unspoiled pupils, Rye, whose very name is connected to life, represents hope. In a short piece for *Essence* in 2000, Butler maintained, "The one thing that I and my main characters never do when contemplating the future is to give up hope" (165).

That Rye is a black woman; that she has a disability; that she is smart, resilient, capable and strong despite her disability are all appealing factors about "Speech Sounds" for me and other people of color. The most distinctive aspect of the story, however, is its authentic engagement with science. "Speech Sounds" accurately reflects and animates research developments in neurobiology, neuroscience, educational psychology, and neurolinguistics. Butler takes information from these related fields and pulls that information together for readers. Thus through her story can enter the debate about cognitive theory and left-brain, right-brain thinking (with resultant behavioral differences) when much of Broca's area, that segment of the brain responsible for processing language, for shaping speech, and for understanding of the spoken word, has been largely destroyed by the virus. She gives us a world where millions suffer some form of aphasia; she paints characters in perilous situations so she can illustrate artistically the dynamics between different modes of thinking and behaving, showing readers the results of a direct attack upon one brain hemisphere (the left brain) or the other (the right brain). Richard Morris's essay, "Left Brain, Right Brain, Whole Brain?" indicates that the brain's temporal lobe affects sound and speech processing (and aspects of memory), while its frontal lobe controls thinking and conceptualization. Morris examines various theories about left-right brain specialization with respect to language acquisition, learning styles, and the resultant implications for education. He stipulates that "in 97% of right-handed people, language is controlled by the left hemisphere [while] left-handers have a more even distribution of language in both hemispheres."[7]

Morris's discussion, connected to other studies of brain research such as Emotional Intelligence, split-brain research, or brain-mapping, allows knowledgeable readers with similar eclectic interests to examine more closely how Butler wove the science into her tale.[8] She moved from interface with speculation and scientific theory to the whole cloth of near-dystopian drama extrapolated from the speculative "what if" factor. When Rye first sees Obsidian, for example, she watches his hands. Seeing him point with his left hand to the bus, immediately arrests her attention: "Left-handed people tended to be less impaired, more reasonable and comprehending, less driven by frustration, confusion, and anger" (91-92). Rye notices that when the irate bus driver wordlessly threatens Obsidian, he does nothing, refuses to react, and again, attracts Rye's attention. We're told, "The least impaired people tended to do this—stand back unless...physically threatened and let those with less control scream and jump around" (93). The passage points directly to theories regarding split-brain research, to the dominance of one brain hemisphere over the other, and to what scientists think is responsible for controlling speech, thought, or action in a given manner. Though some researchers suggest the differences apparent from the division are more myth than fact, other theorists suggest that individuals indicating a left-brain preference (Obsidian) tend to be more focused, less scatter-brained. They prize accuracy, logic, objective analysis, rationality, precision in word or act. (Think of Mr. Spock, the Vulcan Science Officer aboard the original Starship Enterprise, as a metaphor for the logical human mind.) By contrast, individuals drawing upon the right frontal lobe (the right-brain folks) are apparently less inhibited. They are intuitive, imaginative, holistic, able to pull from creative wells, cable of recognizing symbols and seeing images; they can synthesize, they are risk takers, they can be subjective.[9] Rye is apparently one of the rarest of remaining individuals; she can tap into both sides of her brain, the whole brain. She certainly has right-brain deficits in that she has suffered the loss of her ability to read and to write; she feels intense bitter jealousy because Obsidian has retained those skills. Rye, however, has retained an ability he did not have, the ability few remaining adults kept after the illness, the ability to speak and to comprehend the spoken word. In the final line of the story, she says to the three-year old children she rescues, "I'm Valerie Rye.... It's all right for you to talk to me" (108). We learn here that not only can she speak, but *so can they*. As mysteriously as it came, the virus has evidently dissipated leaving the very young unaffected but with little adult guidance.

The story's last line returns us to the significance of the title. Valerie Rye has not spoken aloud to anyone since the loss of her immediate family. Alert and wary to the last, she has not even spoken to Obsidian although she did reveal that she retained verbal speech. In a manner of speaking (pun intended) when Rye speaks to the children she also relishes the sound of her own speaking voice for the first time since the virus struck.

With "Speech Sounds," Octavia E. Butler created one of the most distinctive sf stories ever to earn a Hugo Award. Both Rye and Obsidian are innovative and compelling characters—each holds our attention. The story's scientific underpinning is fascinating and largely accurate; the use Butler puts it to, her compression of so many distinctive elements into a hauntingly different story of love, hope, and redemption among the ruins, well—her ability to do so is one of the reasons I remain so attracted to her work; why I, along with legions of her fans, will miss my friend and mourn her loss for a long time to come.

A final note. Shortly after I introduced Octavia at that 1999 Novello Literary Festival, she called me to ask whether I "had the time," and if I "would mind," writing an "Afterword" for the Time Warner reissue of *Wild Seed* (1999). She wanted to know if it was "OK" for her to give my name to her editor for that project. Although I wanted to scream, "Yes! Of course it's OK!" I strove to maintain professionalism and merely said, "Sure, be glad to help," or some such. I will always believe that Butler extended that invitation because she had not only read much of my work about her, but also, at Novello, she had actually heard me speak about her in a way she approved. My introduction had been straightforward—informative yet humorous, unburdened by the academic flourishes that general audiences can find so distressing. Our styles meshed; our spirits were in sync, we trusted each other, and we shared a common history. The more I reflect on what she revealed about herself and her family in various venues, the more we spoke over the years, the better I understood why we had connected in the way we had, why I have felt so drawn to her stories. Consciously and subconsciously, I have not only read avidly, and critically, but I have been empathizing with both text and subtext. I have felt a resonance between myself and her characters, identifying not only with these characters as strong black women but as characters who do not let their disabilities limit them, characters who are in some manner also teachers and mentors. All of her protagonists are credible, ethical, people.[10] The lasting impact made by Butler's characters, the vivid fully imagined diverse worlds she creates in her fiction, and the technical finesse of her work is fiction that, as woman, reader, teacher, and scholar speaks to me.

Works Cited

Butler, Octavia. 1995. *Bloodchild and Other Stories*. New York: Four Walls Eight Windows.

Brand, Chad. 2003. *Holman Illustrated Bible Dictionary*. Nashville, TN: Holman Bible Publishers.

Davis, Joel. 1997. *Mapping the Mind: The Secrets of the Human Brain and How It Works*. Secaucus, NJ: Carol Publishing Group.

Falk, Dean. 1992. *Braindance*. New York: Henry Holt and Company.

Holloway, Karla FC. 2006. *BookMarks: Reading in Black and White* New Brunswick. NJ: Rutgers University Press.

Hurston, Zora. 1942. *Dust Tracks on a Road.* Edited by, Robert Hemenway. 2nd ed. Urbana, IL: University of Illinois Press, 1984.

Morris, Richard. "Left Brain, Right Brain, Whole Brain: an examination into theory of brain lateralization, learning styles and the implications for education." (March 2005) *Random Thoughts from a Random Fellow.* http://www.singsurf.org/brain/rightbrain. php.

Endnotes

1   I learned about Butler's early love of comic books when she visited my home and saw my collection; her love of comics was further substantiated in Karla FC Holloway's *BookMarks: Reading in Black and White*, (2006, 182), a book that elegantly blends the scholarly with the personal.

2   In offering such unqualified encouragement to her daughter Butler's mother played the same role as Zora Neale Hurston's mother did when she, more prosaically, told her young daughter to "jump at de sun" (1942, 21).

3   In several interviews where the question rises about her age at the time she began writing, Butler has indicated she started writing at ten years old.

4   In a conversation we had in Chicago, October 2005, where she was inducted into the International Black Writers Hall of Fame, Butler disclosed her injured pride at her lack of stamina. She needed to accept a wheel-chair ride from the passenger assistant who twice offered to wheel her to her gate. On the second offer, Butler took the ride.

5   Adrian Spies, "Miri." Season one, Episode 8, original *Star Trek*, Director, Vincent McEveety; televised on NBC, 27, October, 1966.

6   Peter is symbolically significant if we connect the name to Peter, disciple of Christ. Butler's allusion to the biblical forerunner is too obviously placed in the sentence to ignore, coming as it does between "Rock" and "Black." According to *Holman's Illustrated Bible Dictionary*, Peter, in fact, means rock (Brand 1406). Butler thus directs us to examine biblical lore and affirms in different language, with a different thrust, the concepts of mercy, hope, and love. See the *Authorized King James Bible*, First Epistle of Peter, chapter 1; verses 3 and 22. An examination of Matthew

16, verse 18, makes the biblical correlation firmly. Here Jesus changes Simon's name to Peter and says to him, "upon this rock I will build my church; and the gates of hell shall not prevail against it." While Butler's story does not necessarily allude to building an actual church/the church, it is about withstanding the onslaught of the virus and rebuilding a home, community, a world. That Obsidian is not present at the story's conclusion is not as important as the fact that, however brief their alliance, he has given Rye hope, a foundation to build upon for the future.

7   Morris's essay was prepared as a teaching module, placed on the internet, and invited response. In an email exchange, I suggested Professor Morris read "Speech Sounds" because I thought it fit the information he laid out. Morris wrote in return, "you can see how the virus targeted Broca's area, which plays a large part in language; from what I recall left-handers develop speech in different areas of the brain which may explain why left-handers are less affected" (Morris, Email).

8   Dean Falk argues in *Braindance* that "Patients with Broca's aphasia are fine in the comprehension department. However, they have great difficulty speaking or writing what they wish to say" (1992, 69). Joel Davis discusses aphasia succinctly in *Mapping the Mind: The Secrets of the Human Brain and How it Works*: "Aphasia not only involves damage to a person's ability to communicate verbally," it can "severely disrupt creativity, decision making," and other abilities (1997, 188).

9   This information is of course synthesized from a number of readings pulled from a number of different sources. Dr. Ronald Lunsford, a colleague at UNC Charlotte and a linguistics authority, suggested that this reduction is "too simplistic" and that "recent studies won't support it." I am exceedingly grateful for his careful reading of the essay, but his take on the story derives from the realist not the sf perspective; Butler was speculating, not recapitulating.

10   I am indebted to my friend, Professor Barbara Ann Caruso of Earlham College for the term "ethical character." We had been discussing Butler's work, and she said she liked that all of Butler's women characters were so ethical. I am also deeply indebted to my friend and co-conspirator Professor Helen R. Houston of Tennessee State University. Dr. Houston is always willing to help me sound out and clarify my prose and my ideas.

Excerpt 3 from "A Conversation with Octavia E. Butler

Nisi Shawl

(Interview Conducted at the "Black to the Future Conference:
A Black Science Fiction Festival," Seattle, June 12, 2004

Nisi: Well, *Kindred* is a very obvious example of how African ancestry has influenced your work. Could you talk about that a little bit more and maybe give some other examples of how your African ancestry has contributed to your writing?

Octavia: It's kind of hard to do that because it's not as though I've ever been anything else.

Nisi: There's no contrast.

Octavia: Exactly. When I was a kid in the sixties, in college when everybody was busy with "the Movement," I was told over and over again that I should do something that was more relevant to the Movement. I was shirking my duties because what I was doing had nothing to do with Black people. Well, gee I look Black. I didn't think it was fake. It didn't wash off or anything. So I figured it had something to do with Black people. And you know, I can remember somebody coming into my house and looking at my books and saying "How can you be interested in, how can you waste your time with something so unreal as science fiction?" On the other hand, later I had someone tell me, you know I never bothered about science fiction because we didn't seem to be there. True. But all of the science fiction I've written when I was growing up was…well let me tell you a little bit about how I began writing when I was trying to sell.

I had been reading science fiction for a little while, and when I was thirteen I began to try to sell it. I didn't know what I was doing. It was horrible stuff. If I'd sold any of it I would be deeply ashamed. But on the other hand I wanted so badly to sell it. And what really bothered me was I couldn't find a teacher. It wasn't offered in any of the—just writing, creative writing, or writing for publication—it wasn't offered at my middle school or my junior high. It was barely offered in college. And mostly by English teachers who really didn't have any idea, I mean commercial writing was kind of beneath their radar, for more reasons than one I guess. But anyway I just lost track of the question.

Nisi: Well we were talking about how you got to write science fiction and your writing for publication. What you were writing for publication...

Octavia: Hmm... It's gone...no, I have no idea.... Hey I'm old.

[AUD: laughter]

Nisi: Well what was the first science fiction that you read?

Octavia: Oh gosh, probably something by Heinlein. Because they kept you...where I went to the library, they kept you in the boys and girls room, which they called the Peter Pan room, until you were fourteen. And you know, you might find Heinlein juveniles and those old Winston Juveniles that had the inside cover of all sorts of exciting, wonderful things happening. None of which took place in the book. Kind of disappointing. Those were my first. They did not impress me as different. I didn't realize that science fiction was different from any other kind of storytelling because I was also hooked on horse stories for instance. I was trying to figure out why, and I was talking to someone about "Girl and Her Horse" stories a few days ago. And we worked out that that was the only place—the only stories we were reading where girls were really active—out there doing things as opposed to doing almost nothing, and the boys were out there doing things. I mean I read Nancy Drew, but Nancy Drew always seemed like a middle-aged woman. [AUD: laughter] So I wasn't too thrilled with her you know.

Nisi: Was the action and adventure of both the horse stories and the science fiction what drew you?

Octavia: And the fact that the glands were kicking in, so I wanted to introduce some sex into my writing.

Nisi: Sex was in the horse stories?

Octavia: No. [AUD: laughter]. No, no. Because I had no real contact with horses, I was not traumatized by seeing horses do it. The romances kind of crept in there between the science fiction and the horse stories. When I was ten, I was crazy about horses and wrote about them a lot and talked about them until people would ask me to stop. Because nobody else knew what I was talking about. I mean, nobody I knew liked horses or thought there was anything special about them. And later I was writing romances, and people thought that was very good, that's what I should be interested in—I mean my friends. But the problem was I was terrified my mother would find them, and I wasn't supposed to know about those things, you know. And I didn't really; I had a good imagination. When I was twelve I discovered science fiction and began to read it more as a separate genre, and also when I was twelve I stopped going to the library, and that lasted for two years until I was allowed to go into the adult department. So I wound up going to the supermarket really, and getting things like *Amazing* and *Fantastic* and *Galaxy* and *Worlds of If*— all those marvelous old, corny science fiction magazines that you know if my mother saw the cover I might have to explain. She actually once stopped me from reading a Western novel because it had a racy cover, a woman with a low-cut red dress. In the novel actually I think…well there was one case where a woman actually looked at a man with interest, and the novel treated her as a prostitute. [AUD: laughter]

Nisi: Another thing that you were interested in, as you've told me, as a child, you were a comic book reader?

Octavia: Oh, God, was I ever. I have the first "Spider-Man" in *Amazing Adult Fantasy* and other things like that. And before that I had a lot of really bad DC. You know, where everybody is wearing the same expression, and the women and the men look a lot alike except the women have long hair. Really bad DC. But it was what was out there.

Nisi: It must have had something to it.

Octavia: They were doing wild stuff. Yeah.

Nisi: Adventures….

Octavia: Yes exactly. Some of them were girls, even if they did look a little odd.

Nisi: Do you still have an interest in comics?

ndra K. Gill

n people ask me why I'm so into science fiction, I tell them
s raised on *Star Trek* and Octavia E. Butler. My parents intro-
to sf as a literary and a media experience early on. I remember
Trek reruns on the small black-and-white TV in my parents'
en I was very young; when I was a bit older, my mother's book
pendium of the Xenogenesis books sat on a shelf outside of my
inviting me to what would be my first direct encounter with
ork. I heard Butler's name often before I ever read her. *Pattern-*
r first published novel, was released the year I was born, and my
as one of her readers from the beginning. She was an author
r would recommend to people, myself included. Added to this
nage I had of Butler while I was growing up. The author photos
wed a woman who wore her hair in a short natural, a style my
nd I frequently wore. I later found out that she was tall like
he women in my family, which added to the feeling I had that
have been a relative—one of my aunts, maybe—even though I
her through her writing.

vorite of Butler's books is an unusual choice, I think. When
n people about her work, most bring up her novels, which are
But I have a particular love for her collection *Bloodchild and*
ies. My father gave me a hardback copy when it was first pub-
1995. My copy has the mark of many of the books from my
ars in it—my name and phone number jotted down on the
paper as a protection against loss. Like the stories it contains,
s compact—deceptively so, because it holds so many treasures.
I've taken with me during the times I've had to leave many of
books in storage. I come back to it often, always managing to
hing new in these stories. It's a joy to be able to recognize that
wn as a result of returning to work you know well and seeing

Octavia: Not really, I haven't bought any since I was, oh, a lot younger. But on the other hand I can't let go of them. So there is something there. Every now and then I'll pull something out and read it. The problem with my comic books is I read every one of them. So none of them are pristine or salable for high prices and all that. And what's more, I bought some of them secondhand, so they're in really bad shape, but I've still got them.

Nisi: Your mom didn't throw them away.

Octavia: No, this was after mom. Actually she tore them in half and threw them away.

Nisi: Oh, mom.

Octavia: Well, everybody's mother did that, right? I used to go after her when I was older and say, do you know what that would be worth if you hadn't thrown it out. [AUD: laughter]

Nisi: Have you ever considered writing a comic? Have you ever done it?

Octavia: No, no, no. [AUD: laughter] I'm a really, at this point, especially a really slow writer. And I pretty much have all I can do to get my own work out.

Positive Impact: Growing (Up) with Octavia E. Butler

Candra K. Gill

When people ask me why I'm so into science fiction, I tell them that I was raised on *Star Trek* and Octavia E. Butler. My parents introduced me to sf as a literary and a media experience early on. I remember watching *Trek* reruns on the small black-and-white TV in my parents' room when I was very young; when I was a bit older, my mother's book club compendium of the Xenogenesis books sat on a shelf outside of my bedroom, inviting me to what would be my first direct encounter with Butler's work. I heard Butler's name often before I ever read her. *Patternmaster*, her first published novel, was released the year I was born, and my mother was one of her readers from the beginning. She was an author my mother would recommend to people, myself included. Added to this was the image I had of Butler while I was growing up. The author photos I saw showed a woman who wore her hair in a short natural, a style my mother and I frequently wore. I later found out that she was tall like many of the women in my family, which added to the feeling I had that she could have been a relative—one of my aunts, maybe—even though I only knew her through her writing.

My favorite of Butler's books is an unusual choice, I think. When I talk with people about her work, most bring up her novels, which are brilliant. But I have a particular love for her collection *Bloodchild and Other Stories*. My father gave me a hardback copy when it was first published in 1995. My copy has the mark of many of the books from my college years in it—my name and phone number jotted down on the front endpaper as a protection against loss. Like the stories it contains, the book is compact—deceptively so, because it holds so many treasures. It's a book I've taken with me during the times I've had to leave many of my other books in storage. I come back to it often, always managing to find something new in these stories. It's a joy to be able to recognize that you've grown as a result of returning to work you know well and seeing

it differently than the previous time you'd read it. When Butler died, this was the book I took from my shelf to reread in her memory.

The stories collected in the original edition of *Bloodchild* include, among others, the title story, which won the Hugo and Nebula awards, and "Speech Sounds," which won the Hugo. In addition to the stories, it also features a preface, an afterword for each story, and two autobiographical essays about Butler's life as a writer. This combination of material is why I cherish this book. In the afterword to the essay "Positive Obsession," Butler says in her self-effacing way: "I have no doubt at all that the best and the most interesting part of me is my fiction" (136).[1] But I enjoy the nonfiction parts of the book as much as the stories. I appreciate the glimpses into her writing process, her inspirations, and her life.

It's appropriate that I associate my love of Butler's work so closely with my family. Family, whether biological or found, is a common theme in her work in general and these stories in particular. In fact, the only story where family connections aren't a prominent theme or motivator is "Crossover," and even it focuses on a close relationship. In "Positive Obsession," Butler talks about her mother, whose education was limited, bringing home books that were thrown out by the people whose homes she cleaned, for Octavia to read. I find this story striking because my mother tells similar stories about my grandmother. On a personal level, I appreciate that Butler connected her love of learning for learning's sake with her family, as that is what I experienced growing up in mine.

With the exception of "Near of Kin," which is not a genre story, the stories in *Bloodchild* are emblematic of what I love best about science fiction. They are challenging, thought-provoking, and full of wonder. They show the deep intellectual curiosity of the author. The speculative settings and events allow deft explorations of contemporary issues by letting readers step outside of their lives to see the issues that affect them from a unique point of view. The situations depicted are ethically complex — there are no easy "good guys" or "bad guys." And the writing is beautiful. The structure is meticulous, with exquisite plotting and no wasted words. These are carefully crafted, just plain excellent stories.

⇒ ⇐

"The Evening and the Morning and the Night" is one of my favorite short stories ever. The tale of a woman coming to terms with a terrifying inherited disease, its imagery hits on a visceral level from the start. Every time I read it, I'm amazed that it has never been made into a film. In fact I once briefly (and arrogantly) toyed with the idea of studying to be a filmmaker just so I could be the one to do the adaptation; that's how much I enjoy it. In addition to the strong imagery, the elegance of the story struck me from the first time I read it. It's framed by two visits to wards where people with Duryea-Gode disease (DGD) are sent once the disease reaches the stage where those who have it become a danger to themselves and others; such framing showcases the effects those visits have on Lynn, the narrator and protagonist of the story. After the first visit, she wants to die. After the second she discovers a reason to hope, but not without consequences. The disease itself is a fascinating creation. An unforeseen genetic side-effect of a cancer cure, it results in extreme self-harm, complete detachment from the outside world, and a shortened life. Those with the disease inevitably pass it on to their children. Lynn, whose parents both had the disease, considers herself doubly doomed. Lynn later finds out that her parentage is a key to managing the disease, as women with two parents with DGD have a pheromone that makes other DGD sufferers respond to them. This response allows the mitigation of their self-destructive behavior and the expression of creativity.

Right away, I found Lynn's situation compelling. She goes from despair to hope, but with the burden of unasked-for responsibility. She is gifted with the knowledge that she has a chance to avoid the worst effects of the disease but faces a host of new concerns as a result, from having to reconsider her decision not to have children to the impact the discovery has on her relationship with her boyfriend (who worries that he is only attracted to her because of her ability to control the effects of the disease). The story ends with Lynn leaving the ward after learning about this, so the reader doesn't see what decisions Lynn makes. But we readers think about those decisions. What will Lynn decide? How would we react? What decisions would we make if put in her place?

When I was in college, I was part of a group of students who helped a professor with a program he was a part of in which high school students visited a college campus for a day to engage in various academic activities. We were responsible for choosing a story for this group of students to read that they would then have to give a response to. I suggested using "The Evening and the Morning and the Night" and brought in a copy of the story for the professor and my group to read. The story starts with a high school-aged Lynn and ends with her nearing the end of the college years. With its issues of chronic and inevitable illness, societal response to diseases people fear, the interpersonal dynamics of the characters, and the gender issues explored, I thought it a perfect story for both the visiting students and our group. It turned out to be too long to work for the project, but the professor mentioned that he otherwise would have liked to have used it. I remember this, because this was the first of many times these stories would come up in the context of my academic life. I also remember it because I got to share this favorite of mine with someone who appreciated it.

While I was completing my first master's degree, I taught college composition classes as a graduate assistant. The bylaws of the university where I taught stipulated that only those who held terminal degrees could teach literature classes. We graduate assistants and adjuncts without terminal degrees but with serious literary inclinations would try to skirt this restriction by incorporating as much literature as we could into our composition classes. Of course, exposure to good writing, both as an example of the craft and as a topic to write about, is an important part of writing instruction. But we also wanted to impart our love of reading for its own sake—for the sake of the appreciation of beauty, of seeing the world from someone else's point of view, of being challenged to think.

Anyone who has done the work of choosing a textbook knows how difficult it can be to find one that meets all of the needs of a given class. The best textbook I found during that period was one that featured a balanced selection of readings, both fiction and nonfiction, to go along with its writing instruction. I was especially pleased to find that "Bloodchild" was one of the selections. I was excited for my students because they would get to read this story and write about their reactions to it, and I was pleased to get the chance to share a story I enjoyed. What I didn't anticipate at the time was that not everyone knows how to read science fiction. They get stuck on the strangeness of the situation and can't make their way to what the work is saying or doing. So on the day "Bloodchild" was due, instead of the bright-eyed enthusiasm I had expected, I found a couple dozen frustrated pairs of eyes looking at me. There was a small number of sf readers in my class, and they were able to engage the material. But I spent more time than I'd anticipated going over the story itself with the class before I could get to their reactions to it, as I had to get them to go along with sentient worm-like creatures before I could help them explore the social issues the story presented. It ended up being worth it, though, especially when I read them the afterword Butler had written for the story. That helped them understand the scientific curiosity that led Butler to take the botfly, a creature whose burrowing she found to be frightening, and to control her dread by reimagining its most fearsome characteristic. It also helped them understand why someone would write a story to explore a complex social dynamic created by the symbiotic reproductive relationship of two sentient races who need each other to survive. My students, pushed outside of the familiar, found their footing, and I got to ultimately have one of those moments teachers crave where I watched my students' minds open up along with their conversation. I chose that textbook again the next semester I taught.

Butler's short work came up again in an academic context recently. During a break from a conference I was attending, I met up with some friends at a bar. Put together a group of folks with backgrounds in literature, history, sociology, and media studies, and you're likely to get an interesting conversation out of it. Throw in some alcohol and set the topic to apocalypses, and you'll definitely come up with something memorable. A friend was gathering materials of various media for a class she was preparing to teach whose theme was apocalypses, and someone mentioned "Speech Sounds" as a good story to use. The friend who was teaching the class hadn't read it, so I promised to send it to her. I'm not sure why, but I hadn't thought of the story as apocalyptic before that. Upon rereading it after that conversation, I saw how a total breakdown of communication would be as cataclysmic as any bomb. What struck me as I read this story once again was how well Butler had balanced the larger issue of the impact of this mysterious disease on society with her intimate portrayal of one woman's day-by-day survival. What further struck me was how much I missed teaching. It made me realize how much I looked forward to the day when I would return to the classroom—in part because I planned to bring these stories with me.

⇒ ⇐

The essay "Positive Obsession" was first published in 1989 (as "Birth of a Writer" in Essence). In it, Butler discusses being the only black woman she was aware of who made her living publishing science fiction. Thankfully, this has changed, and I'm glad she lived to see that change. But I'm also glad she published when and what she did.

It was always important to me that Ms. Butler called herself a science fiction writer. There are people who successfully publish what is obviously science fiction but don't want to be connected to the genre, and I'm happy Butler wasn't one of them. In "Positive Obsession" she shares the story of being told by her aunt that black people couldn't make a living off of writing, and her refusal to believe this even though she had no evidence to the contrary. I'm more thankful than I can express that I grew up knowing about her and her work. Because of her, I knew it was possible for us to write in the genre I so enjoy.

I've often encountered the false assertion that black people aren't interested in science fiction. This is usually attached to one of those odd online discussions that end up turning into unintended, consuming arguments. Black people not caring about or liking science fiction is given as a justification or explanation when discussion turns to the issue of racism in sf portrayals of blacks and other people of color. Problematic representations, whether they involve portrayals that could be offensive or an absence of human characters with non-European ancestries, are justified by the presumption that only people of European ancestry will be reading or viewing the material. Or the characters have been written in a "colorblind" manner, so why bring up that race stuff, anyway? Setting aside the thorny issue of writing out of existence the majority of the people on the planet, I have to wonder why people don't want to share the transformative and empowering experiences reading science fiction can bring with as many people as possible.

In "Positive Obsession," Butler answered the question of why sf is important to black people with some rhetorical questions of her own: "What good is science fiction's thinking about the present, the future, and the past? What good is its tendency to warn or to consider alternative ways of thinking and doing? What good is its examination of the possible effects of science and technology, or social organization and political direction?" She goes on to say, "At its best, science fiction stimulates imagination and creativity. It gets reader and writer off the beaten track, off the narrow, narrow footpath of what 'everyone' is saying, doing, thinking—whoever 'everyone' happens to be this year" (135). Sf is inherently about a change of perspective. Why on Earth wouldn't people of color be into that kind of thing?

I want to see Butler's books on the shelves—and books by and about many other people of color—because I want us to be visible, both in terms of being authors and in terms of the characters and cultural experiences portrayed. And while it is thankfully no longer the case, Butler was for a long time one of the few people of color professionally publishing sf in US markets. The perseverance she relates in both of the book's essays and encourages in other would-be writers is an important part of why that isolation is no longer the case, and I want people to continue to read her work because of this. But I also want to see her books on the shelves because of the careful craft of her writing, the depth of her characterizations, and the complexity of the situations she explored. I want people to read her because she was one of the best.

⇒ ⇐

I never got to meet Octavia E. Butler, though I had long wanted to. I felt this most keenly at WisCon 30 in 2006. WisCon is an annual feminist science fiction convention that I've attended almost every year for fifteen years. For WisCon's 30th anniversary, every previous guest of honor was invited to attend. Butler had been one of the guests of honor of WisCon 4. WisCon 30 took place only three months after Butler's death. I don't know whether or not she had planned to attend, but I couldn't help but feel her absence. The community was still reeling, and in many ways, we still are. Octavia E. Butler is much missed.

When I realized I would be writing about these stories, I decided to pick up a paperback copy of *Bloodchild and Other Stories* because I didn't want to mark up my hardcover. At the bookstore I found that a revised edition had been published with two new stories. I'd read one of those stories, "The Book of Martha," when it was first published online. Then I'd gleefully posted a link to it in several of the blogs I frequent and watched as others spread the news with joy (this was sadly paralleled when, stunned, the same people spread the news of her death on the same blogs). But until this time I had been unaware of the other new story, "Amnesty."

I read "Amnesty" for the first time in preparation for writing this piece. It's the story of Noah, a woman who works as a translator between humans and an invading alien race whose ways of communicating are completely outside of human speech. It's a unique take on an alien abduction story, with Noah describing her experience to other potential translators who view the aliens as hostile invaders. As the story unfolds, it's revealed that Noah endured years of abuse before the aliens were able to communicate with humans. When the other potential translators ask her why she went back to work as a translator after what she suffered, she tells them of her abuse at the hands of the military upon being freed from alien captivity. She chooses to work for the aliens to try to help her fellow humans better deal with the aliens, whose overwhelming presence is insurmountable.

Finding "Amnesty" gave me the unexpected pleasure of discovering a new Butler story that, like the other pieces in the *Bloodchild* collection, lingered with me after I had read it. It's a story that feels topical in the face of contemporary events. When Noah expresses the despair she felt at the hands of her human captors because they, unlike her alien captors, knew what they were doing and felt justified in doing it anyway, I can't help but think of the secret prisons and systemic abuses in the name of "security" that have been perpetrated throughout human history. The copyright year for this story is listed as 2003, but it made me think of the 2004 reports on the Abu Ghraib abuses. "Amnesty" is an intriguing science fiction story—the aliens' biology is fascinating—and a relevant, ultimately optimistic commentary on both the worst and best of human nature. Reading "Amnesty" was a bittersweet experience as it exemplified why I'm so taken with Butler's short work while making me miss the stories that might have been.

In the preface to *Bloodchild*, Butler talks of the difficulties she had writing short stories. She describes herself as "essentially a novelist" (x). I believe this is true, but I'm thankful that she wrote these stories in spite of her struggles with them. While I hope people read her novels, I also hope they take the time to read her stories and share them with others. I will continue to revisit them, value them, and grow with them.

Endnote

1   All quotations in this essay come from the Four Walls Eight Windows 1995 edition of *Bloodchild and Other Stories*.

"We Get to Live, and So Do They": Octavia Butler's Contact Zones

Thomas Foster

Critic Fred Pfeil once defined both Octavia Butler's writing and cyberpunk science fiction as postmodernist because he thought both bodies of work self-consciously cited and reworked earlier genre conventions, in the kind of recycling typical of literary postmodernism.[1] This aesthetic reacts against modernism's utopian desire to abandon conventionality entirely in favor of innovation and "making it new" (within the genre, Pfeil associates modernism with the New Wave science fiction of the 1960s and early '70s). Pfeil described this recycling technique as postmodern "SF's return to its subcultural ghetto," a return that was "at one and the same time 'trashier,' 'pulpier,' and far more sophisticated, even more liberatory, than those earlier writings" (1990, 84). I find this analysis useful for explaining some of the difficulties I have encountered in teaching Butler's work, especially the Xenogenesis trilogy (*Dawn* [1987], *Adulthood Rites* [1988], and *Imago* [1989]). My students usually have at best a passing familiarity with the earlier conventions that these novels redeploy, literalize, and displace. Instead of understanding how Butler's repetition of those conventions destabilizes and changes their meaning, students often miss the irony and critical commentary and, in fact, often take less sophisticated treatments of the same themes (usually derived from film or TV) as an interpretive key, as the answer to any question about how to read Butler's fiction.

While this ambiguity is unavoidable in any text that attempts to work critically within earlier representational frameworks, it is especially pronounced with respect to the Xenogenesis trilogy, whose effects depend heavily on its revisionary relation both to previous alien invasion narratives and to African American literary history. I was therefore excited to read Butler's relatively late short story "Amnesty" (originally published in 2003). This story struck me as a deliberate response to the misreadings which the Xenogenesis novels generated. "Amnesty's" theme of necessary coexistence (exemplified by the quotation that provides my title) returns to address the major conceptual difficulty readers have with Butler's earlier work: understanding how she can reject the assumption that the forms of power her aliens wield are coercive or dominating in ways familiar to us from histories of slavery or colonialism, while at the same time she does not celebrate human/alien relations as egalitarian or naively utopian.

Rewriting the Contact Scenario: The Paradoxes of Compulsory Interdependence in the Xenogenesis Trilogy

The first novel of the trilogy, *Dawn*, opens with its main character, Lilith Iyapo, awakening again to confinement, ignorant of her location or the identity of her captors. She shortly learns that she has been either captured or rescued, or both, by an alien race called the Oankali. These aliens are a spacegoing race who, having abandoned their own home planet, travel the cosmos in search of other intelligent species. The Oankali discovered Earth in the immediate aftermath of a nuclear war and collected as many survivors as possible. Lilith's awakenings resulted from the Oankali's uncertainty about how to establish contact with human beings, given the collapse of organized society and institutional authority. After leaving her awake in isolation for some time, they introduce her to a single Oankali named Jdahya who has been physically altered to appear relatively human. Jdahya serves as mediator between Lilith and the Oankali, just as Lilith will later be expected to mediate between the Oankali and other human survivors.

Whether Lilith has been captured or rescued is only the first of the ambiguities the novel systematically exploits. The novel implicitly opens a more general question about the effects of contact between the human survivors and the Oankali when Lilith notes a scar on her belly and asks herself "What had she lost or gained, and why?" (4). The answers depend upon how readers interpret the Oankali's motive for rescuing the remnants of humanity: what the Oankali call the trade, a process of genetic hybridization between the Oankali and other species, which is necessary to the long-term perpetuation of their species. The Oankali are natural genetic engineers, with a third sex, the ooloi, who have special organs for observing and manipulating the genes of other species (20; male and female Oankali do not reproduce through direct sexual contact; instead, their ooloi mixes genetic material from its two partners). Oankali reproduction is therefore symbiotic and involves the progressive alteration of the species's genotype and phenotype—which is to say, for the Oankali reproducing means becoming radically different from their parents (of either species). As a result the Oankali are described as possessing a "long, multispecies… history" (61), and their reproductive process also requires the ongoing loss of previous forms of species identity. This process of becoming other is allegorized as a liberatory loss of origins; the Oankali regard their home-world and, by extension, their original morphology as "the one direction that's closed to us" (34). The loss of homeworld can be read as a loss of cultural origin as well as genetic or physical origin, a reading reinforced by the way in which the Oankali wish to acquire "not only language," but also their trade partners' "culture, biology, history" (59).[2]

The Oankali regard humans as genetically flawed, having evolved to be both hierarchical and intelligent, and they attribute the war to this flaw (36-37). To humans (like all the readers of this novel, of course), the Oankali, and especially the ooloi, appear manipulative and meddlesome. As Jdahya tells Lilith, the Oankali have never been hierarchical, but they are "powerfully acquisitive" (39) and so attracted to difference that they cannot leave any "other" alone. Lilith realizes that Jdahya's early interactions with her, her later adoption into his family, and her bonding with a young ooloi on the verge of puberty have all been carefully designed to recruit and assimilate her. At the same time, Lilith is equally self-critical about how her own xenophobic responses to the Oankali (22) dramatize the differences between the two races and at least partly explain the reasons for the Oankali's manipulations.

The basic conflict in the Xenogenesis novels is between a human logic of identity, of autonomy and integrity (at both the individual and the species levels), of differences between entities; and an Oankali cultural logic of continual change, of attraction to and incorporation of otherness, of differences within a shared framework, which they use the human word "trade" to name. Their insistence that the other species they encounter undergo this same process is what seems, both to Lilith and to readers of the novel like my students, most oppressive about the Oankali, while their own submission to these same processes is what seems most self-critical and liberating about them. In this sense, it is wrong to interpret the Oankali as alien invaders. Their relations to others are always established through exchange, negotiation, and mutual compromise, rather than direct coercion or domination. They demand active partners, not passive acceptance of their own norms.

My students, however, remain resistant to a positive reading of the Oankali in terms of tolerance or mutuality. Their resistance can be explained by the question that still remains: when the difference between human and Oankali ceases to be an external difference and becomes an internal one, between two partners in trade, then hasn't the human race been assimilated to the Oankali reproductive and cultural model? Hasn't humanity lost something that the Oankali haven't lost?[3] Jdahya defines the paradox of Oankali self-definition when he elaborates on the nature of the trade: "We trade the essences of ourselves. Our genetic material for yours" (39). Their essence, the most fixed and unchanging aspect of themselves, is not to have a fixed essence, but to remain always open to change at the most basic levels.[4] The trade is not reproduction in the sense of consistent self-identity, but the production of self as difference. In contrast, the Oankali find that for most other intelligent species, including humans, "Different is threatening" (186). The Oankali culture is organized around this xenophilia, with its concomitant surrender of self or ego.

To engage in the trade and to experience this simultaneous gain and loss is what it means to "be" Oankali. The seemingly common-sense reading of the Oankali as cultural and biological imperialists, forcing their way of life on everyone they meet, is disrupted, however, by how the Oankali's reproductive schema and the culture that has grown up around it also seem to render uncertain what it means to "be" anything. If there is no essential norm to be assimilated to, are humans (or any other trade partner) actually being assimilated, in the sense that immigration or colonial administration and education in our actual human history have assimilated people from other cultures to new, "alien" norms of behavior and identity? The science-fictional framework of the Xenogenesis trilogy has the potential, at least, to defamiliarize not only ontological categories (what it means to "be" something), but also political categories like assimilation.

Within the Xenogenesis novels, this interpretive problem plays itself out in Lilith's relation to the other human characters whom the Oankali recruit her to awaken and educate about their situation and ultimately persuade to bond with ooloi of their own. Lilith and the Oankali withhold the full truth about their situation from the group she chooses to awaken, but the awakened humans become suspicious of Lilith, whose special knowledge and physical modifications single her out as a likely collaborator with their unseen captors. Unable to wait, Lilith's ooloi Nikanj encourages Lilith and a man named Joseph Shing to develop a sexual relationship mediated by the ooloi, who is able to transmit and intensify sexual sensations between the two partners, thereby revealing the extent to which Lilith's bond with Nikanj is an erotic one. The term ooloi, we are told, means "treasured stranger" (104). Later, the other ooloi similarly respond to increasing unrest in the human encampment by revealing themselves and bonding, one by one, with human couples. "The lesson all adult ooloi eventually taught" (160), Lilith reflects, is dependence on others rather than isolated self-reliance (152). But the unevenness of this mutual dependence generates resentment, and that resentment results in a desire to escape the framework of the trade rather than to work within it to redress these inequalities, especially once the human survivors realize that bonding with an ooloi changes their body chemistry to the point that direct contact with their human sexual partners becomes repulsive (195). The presence of an ooloi as a mediating influence on relations to others of one's own species becomes compulsory and unavoidable.

These mutual misunderstandings have the unintended effect of increasing preexisting tendencies to exclude other human beings from the unity of the human community in the name of resistance to the Oankali. Nikanj informs Lilith that the other survivors mistrust her Asian partner, Joseph, because they decide "he's something called a faggot" and because "of the shape of his eyes" (159). However, Curt, the man who becomes the leader of the human resistance movement, had already demonstrated his racism immediately upon being awakened, by his negative reaction to Joseph's slight accent (141). Similarly, the men insist upon a sexist interpretation of their relation to the ooloi and the trade in general, treating their situation of dependence as passivity and therefore feminization (193). The movement to define, as Curt tells Lilith, "a human place" that will be "off limits to you and your animals" (227) often seems to endorse, if not require, a rhetoric of racial and sexual purity.[5] A similar implication emerges at the end of *Dawn*, when Lilith's Oankali partner challenges her to declare whether what the Oankali want from the humans is "unclean" (245). The interpretive problem Butler's novel creates is whether this question is a sincere attempt by Nikanj to understand an alien, human point of view, or whether it is just a rhetorical question designed purely to make Lilith question her race's values without Nikanj having to question its own. Lilith critiques the political logic of distinct and territorialized identities underlying Curt's movement when she describes his group as wanting to "play Americans against the Russians. Again" (176). This critique is driven home by placing Curt's declaration of desire for a "human place" immediately after he has murdered Joseph. The implication seems clear: the unity and autonomy of the "human" have historically been secured by sacrificial processes of exclusion, abjection, and scapegoating. To the extent that slavery depended upon similar processes, it is therefore not only the Oankali's treatment of Lilith that invokes that historical reference, as my students tend to assume, but also the human characters' treatment of one another.

Lilith herself constitutes another sacrificial figure, since she is quite aware that the other survivors will regard her as a "Judas goat" (*Dawn* 65), a collaborator. *Dawn* ends by implicitly citing and rewriting not just science fiction conventions, but figures from colonial history, specifically the figure of La Malinche or La Chingada, Cortes's native translator and mistress during the conquest of Mexico. This transposition of colonial history into a speculative, futuristic framework occurs during a pitched battle between the ooloi and the human separatists. Nikanj is mortally injured, and to save him Lilith has to strip, lie down, and allow him to pierce her body with his sensory tentacles, in order to utilize her human "talent" for cancer to regenerate from his wounds (231). Lilith refuses "to think how she would look to the humans still conscious," knowing they will be convinced she is a "traitor" after observing her apparently sleeping "with the enemy" in the midst of the battle (231).[6]

Lilith understands herself, however, as going along with the Oankali in order to make it possible for the other survivors to "learn and run" (144, 247-248). This kind of sympathy for the separatists forms a recurrent motif in the Xenogenesis trilogy and is ambiguously juxtaposed to another motif, of everyone being "co-opted" in their relation to the Oankali (240) who force the survivors to consider how the Oankali might be "family" even before other humans (196). The extremity of Lilith's willingness to aid Nikanj is also disturbingly juxtaposed to Lilith's plans for escape from Oankali influence, implying that her collaboration with the Oankali is more than just a strategic necessity in an overall plan to achieve independence. In the second two novels of the trilogy, Lilith's "learn and run" is transformed into a project of persuading the Oankali that a truly equitable or symbiotic version of the trade requires them to allow survivors to create their own purely human places—that is, convincing the Oankali that permitting separatist communities to opt out of the trade is required if they are to live up to their own cultural ideal of valuing difference. This shift in Lilith's initial plan is reinforced by the fact that the next books in the trilogy are narrated by hybrid characters: *Adulthood Rites* by the first male human/Oankali hybrid, and *Imago* by the first hybrid born as an ooloi. To them falls the task of revealing to the Oankali the paradox involved in their openness to changing everything about themselves except their openness to change.

The Xenogenesis trilogy therefore revolves around a set of unresolved interpretive questions: is it possible to have separatism or nationalism without demonizing and scapegoating an other, without reducing difference to enmity? Is Lilith right to assert, early in *Dawn*, that "rebirth for us can only happen if you let us alone! Let us begin again on our own" (41)? Is coexistence possible without change? Does change mean complete loss, either of the past or of difference? On the one hand, the novels encourage us to identify with the compromised positions of Lilith and the later hybridized narrators, who are far more sympathetically portrayed than the separatists. On the other hand, these compromised narrators themselves insist on the continuing value of separatism and human specificity or autonomy within the overall context of the trade. The Oankali recognize the need to "moderate" the human survivors' "hierarchical problems" and to mitigate their "natural fear of strangers and of difference," by teaching them "more pleasant things to do" (247, 192). But the Oankali tend to assume that the only trade-off involved in their partnership with the human race is the lessening "of our physical limitations," as in Nikanj's use of Lilith to regenerate lost body parts (247). The trilogy suggests that Oankali xenophilia and acquisitiveness also has to be moderated. But this process of mutual learning is itself uneven, in my view. I read the trilogy overall as implying xenophilia is preferable to xenophobia, even if neither is a utopian solution to all social problems.

"Amnesty:" Coexistence or Capitulation?

Butler's story "Amnesty" reverses the narrative pattern of *Dawn*, since the story begins with its main character already in a situation of negotiated (inter)dependence, then reveals how that situation came to be. There are clear parallels between the main characters of "Amnesty" and *Dawn*. The story begins with a black woman named Noah Cannon working as a translator for an alien race referred to as the Communities. In the opening scene, her employer loans her services to another Community, who wants Noah to conduct an orientation session for a set of prospective new human employees, a task that parallels Lilith's job of preparing a community of human survivors for trade with the Oankali. During the course of her interactions with this diverse group, we learn that Noah was initially abducted by the aliens upon their arrival on earth, before the two races improvised a method of communicating.

The aliens have occupied parts of the earth since they landed here in a one-way transport ship and will require several generations to build new ships and continue their journey, like the Oankali in the Xenogenesis trilogy. For one of Noah's students, this situation means the aliens "came here uninvited, stole our land, and kidnapped our people" (158), an injustice that needs righting. Noah, however, regards the alien presence as an unavoidable fact that necessitates coexistence; the lesson she draws from this history is that "the universe has other children. We knew it, but until they arrived here we could pretend otherwise" (158). There is a basic conflict, or perhaps an uncertain distinction, between resisting invasion and defending against the decentering of human ethnocentrism and assumptions of superiority by reasserting that superiority.

As with the Oankali, the Communities' very morphology constitutes a challenge to human logics of identity and autonomy.[7] The passages I quoted above indicate how these qualities are inextricably bound up with the view that the aliens are invaders who must be violently resisted. As the name implies, each of the Communities is an "intelligent multitude" (162), a colony creature made up of several hundred individuals. Instead of organs, the Communities have "organisms of mobility" or "manipulation" and "specialized entities of sight" (149, 151, 152). While Lilith is initially unable to perceive Jdahya's alienness and therefore concludes he is more humanoid than he actually is, the Communities are so alien that they are almost impossible to "see" clearly. In describing the aliens, Noah says, "When I look at them, I see what you've all seen: outer branches and then darkness. Flashes of light and movement within" (162). The closest visual analogy for the Communities is a twelve-foot-high, moss-covered bush with a canopy of leaves and branches and protruding limbs (149), but this appearance is deceptive: "The Communities were not plants, but it was easiest to think of them in those terms since most of the time, most of them looked so plantlike" (151).

This visual difficulty is reinforced by the fact that the Communities communicate with humans through a gestural language of touch, grounded in a practice of literal incorporation or enfolding, in which a human being is gathered into the body of the Community. This aspect of the story reworks the Oankali trade as a process of learning about other species by incorporating their genetic material into the Oankali's own and vice-versa. In contrast to the Xenogenesis trilogy, "Amnesty" focuses on processes of communication rather than reproduction, and so avoids the accusation of essentialism that has muddied the interpretive waters for critics of the earlier trilogy (Zaki 1990; Michaels 2000, 650). Like the Oankali, the Communities themselves embody a practice of symbiosis and interdependence at the physical level, which colors their relations with the human characters. None of the "individual entities" ("Amnesty" 153) that make up a Community can survive outside on their own; individuality for the Communities is not synonymous with autonomous existence. Nor is autonomy or identity reserved for the group itself, since individuals can move from one Community to another, temporarily or permanently (162). The Communities contain "many selves" (151), and the boundaries between Communities are fundamentally unstable and shifting.

The exchange of individual component organisms is in fact a mode of communication among the Communities, or rather a substitute for human practices of rhetoric or persuasion. One of the difficulties Noah faces in performing her job is that the Communities are able to "change one another just by exchanging a few of their individual entities—as long as both exchanging communities were willing" (153). The Communities often assume that Noah has the same ability to literally change the minds of the humans whose instruction the Communities entrust to her; they expect instant results, rather than a long process of give and take. One of the ways in which contact between humans and the Communities is reciprocal resides in the way in which humans have taught the Communities to understand the process of exchange as more fraught and difficult, as a more figurative process of changing minds (this aspect of "Amnesty" again foregrounds an overlooked dimension of the Xenogenesis trilogy). The play on the words "change" and "exchange" in the quoted passage is especially significant. As in the Oankali trade, exchange is a dynamic process that modifies the two parties involved in it, rather than a flow of tokens between fixed entities.

Like Lilith, Noah's position with the Communities compromises her relation to her fellow human beings. The narrator emphasizes Noah's status as a mediator, someone with a foot in both groups but accepted by neither, by pointing out the contradiction in the group's reactions to Noah: they simultaneously need the information she can give them and distrust her precisely because she possesses that information, since it can only be obtained through a suspect intimacy with the alien "invaders" (156). Lilith similarly reflects that to lead the other survivors she has to be trusted, but every act she performs to prove that she is telling them the truth about the Oankali calls into question her own "loyalties, and even her humanity" (*Dawn* 160).

Noah's class of future alien employees is smaller than Lilith's group of survivors, so that Noah's audience seems to bear a greater burden to represent a range of human types, both racial and gendered, as well as a range of preconceptions about and responses to the presence of the aliens on Earth. This group includes a militant white woman, Thera Collier, who argues for violent resistance, and an angry young black man, James Hunter Adio, who is both hostile toward Noah and distressed by the economic circumstances that require him to "sell out" to the alien Communities (Noah's other students include a Hispanic woman, a white woman interested in alien spirituality, an Asian woman, and a white man). Much of the story concerns Noah's attempts to sort through these interlocutors' misunderstandings about her position, a process that in effect elaborates on Lilith's attitude toward the human separatist movement in *Dawn*. The complex relation between Noah and James Adio, in particular, invites further reflection on the relation between Butler's speculative alien contact scenarios and actual racial histories and political projects, especially nationalist ones. "Amnesty" makes more explicit Butler's double-sided dialogue with both science fiction and African American traditions.

Misreading the Xenogenesis Trilogy

In my classes, there is usually a particular sequence of responses to Butler's Xenogenesis trilogy. *Dawn* is often initially read as an alien invasion narrative in the classic cold war paranoia mode (watch the skies!). Given that *Dawn* focuses on a woman "captured" by aliens and "forced" to "interbreed," students will occasionally note the pulp parallels (Mars needs women!), especially the tradition of magazine covers with scantily clad women ensnared in the tentacled clutches of alien monsters. In a discussion of her story "Bloodchild," Butler has described her goal of doing "something different with the invasion story. So often you read novels about humans colonizing other planets and you see the story taking one of two courses. Either the aliens resist and we have to conquer them violently, or they submit and become good servants.... I don't like either of those alternatives, and I wanted to create a new one" (Potts 1996, 332).[8] While "Bloodchild" represents the consequences of a failed attempt at human colonization, both *Dawn* and "Amnesty" place the human race in the position of having to respond to a technologically-superior alien presence, and both narratives represent attempts to imagine that response in terms of contact and exchange across cultural and biological differences, not just as an "invasion."

The mis- or partial reading of the Xenogenesis trilogy as a simple narrative of human victimization by external forces, with its concomitant assumption that the only right response is a defensive reassertion of human rights and autonomy, is often subsumed by another after I point out how *Dawn* (especially in its opening sections) references the history of slavery; the novel begins with a black woman waking to find herself captive in a ship.[9] In the same more or less indirect manner, Lilith tries to process the Oankali trade as a project of "captive breeding" (58), language that evokes the position of women of African descent under slavery. These historical subtexts become more explicit when Jdahya defines the Oankali as trading "ourselves." The only way Lilith can initially make sense of this statement is to assume that trading "ourselves" is the same as trading "each other" as "slaves" (22). It is important to note the irony involved in the fact that when the word slavery actually appears in the novel it is in reference to the Oankali being traded, rather than trafficking in others.[10] But as the narrator of Butler's story "Amnesty" points out, "People had never been able to be neutral about abductees" (159). As in the Xenogenesis trilogy, these "abductees" are human beings held captive by aliens, but the same point might be made about readers' tendencies to decode such narratives politically, especially when a black author is writing about a black abductee.

Students tend to miss how Lilith's reflex to analogize her experience to a historical model of slavery is problematized by the very juxtaposition of alien invasion, with its focus on human/alien conflicts external to our species, and slavery, with its focus on processes by which "we" other and dehumanize one another. Butler's inclusion of references to both these kinds of invasion has the potential to disrupt any triumphal narrative of human superiority in the face of the alien menace and perhaps even any claims to a generally "human" right to self-determination. After all, the category of the "human" has historically been used to justify slavery through the denial of humanity to whole populations. This reflexive interpretation of the Oankali in terms of human history is also problematized through its association with Lilith's xenophobia (22), which in turn is connected to her resistance to change (74) and her insistence on human specificity, integrity, and autonomy, values which Butler's writing consistently interrogates.[11] The focus of *Dawn's* opening scenes is in fact on Lilith's difficulties in dealing with extreme forms of difference as much as her captivity and loss of control. Initially, those forms of difference are primarily physical and visual, and Lilith's difficulties combine xenophobia with resistance to perceiving the Oankali's physical differences. She tends to assimilate first their appearance and then their behavior and culture to more familiar, human models, even as she oscillates between seeing no significant difference to seeing only the differences. During her first face-to-face meeting with one of the aliens, Lilith is told that "It's wrong to assume that I must be a sex you're familiar with" and "what you probably see as hair isn't hair at all" (11). In this way, the novel also reproduces and displaces questions of racial perception and definition. Butler has carefully designed the opening scenes so that Lilith's education provides an allegory of reading in which the misunderstandings attributed to Lilith's interpretive reflexes should make readers self-conscious about what we might be projecting onto these characters and plot events.

The most devastating critique of Lilith's xenophobia comes during the scene in which she is first released from confinement and offered a tour of the Oankali spaceship (a genetically-modified living creature). When she withdraws from the alienness of the scene, Jdahya asks "Back into your cage, Lilith?" (29). Again, the reading of the novel as a slave or captivity narrative is undercut, since resistance to exposure to difference is represented as another form of captivity—confinement within the familiar, the human. The Oankali's trade in themselves (22) marks one of the key ways in which Butler's novels reimagine—that is, both invoke and displace or resist—histories of slavery and colonialism. The trade requires a willingness to change on the part of both parties. This mutual interdependence tends to be interpreted by the human characters simply as dependence (38) and domination, as a one-way flow of power, and many readers follow suit. But the Oankali understand this process of genetic and cultural hybridization (59) as valuing and maintaining difference as well as opening it to change in a refusal to reify species difference as external.

For the Oankali, the trade is an epistemological process; they know others by becoming them, in the process altering themselves. The challenge this alien epistemological framework poses to modern, European habits of thought—specifically, the distinction between subject and object, knower and known—is ironically dramatized by Lilith's reflections on her former profession of anthropology, when she notes that her captivity among the Oankali might be regarded "as fieldwork—but how the hell do I get out of the field?" (86). The Oankali do not allow Lilith to maintain the classic ethnographic privilege of distance from the "others" being studied.[12] They justify this treatment by denying themselves the same distance. The human interpretation of the trade as domination is not entirely incorrect, however, since the mutuality of the trade and the Oankali's desire to incorporate difference is not in itself enough to ensure equality between the two trade partners, as Lilith repeatedly reminds the Oankali.

Dawn undermines any simple reading of the Oankali as invading aliens or slave traders out to subjugate humanity by demonstrating that the Oankali are capable of learning from their human partners and thereby unlearning their own tendency to think that physical attraction to differences of both biology and culture necessarily translates into comprehension of the intellectual implications of those differences. The Oankali are depicted both as desiring a genuine two-way flow of ideas and influence and as capable of recognizing when that desire blinds them to their failure to achieve it. Nikanj's ooloi parent Kahguyaht states its view of the inequality between the supposed trade partners very clearly: "we know you, Lilith. And, within reason, we want you to know us" (48). Kahguyaht even asserts that "Your children will know us, Lilith. You never will" (111). This attitude is often taken as representative of the Oankali's domineering tendencies with respect to their own rhetoric of mutuality and exchange: they know us in ways that we can't know them, except by becoming them through the mechanism of the trade—that is, we can't know them until we cease to be ourselves and become (more like) them.[13]

However, Kahguyaht's attitude is representative merely of one generation of Oankali, in contrast first to Jdahya and later to Nikanj. Jdahya goes so far as to violate the most basic Oankali social taboos by offering to kill Lilith rather than continue to coax and encourage her to enter into the trade (42). Radical as it is in Oankali terms, this offer still implies that the only alternative Jdahya can imagine to the trade is its pure negation, rather than making it more truly symbiotic. The real work of the trade is then left up to Lilith's partner Nikanj, who notes its difference from Oankali like Kahguyaht. While Kahguyaht and Nikanj agree that "humans—any new trade partner species—can't be treated the way we must treat each other," Kahguyaht believes this difference is absolute, while Nikanj believes "We should be able to find ways through most of our differences" (80). As a result, Kahguyaht feels "coercion" of the human trade partners is justified, while Nikanj asserts that it does not (80). *Dawn* ends with Lilith holding Nikanj to this claim, in the course of an argument over the murder of Joseph. Nikanj insists on sharing Lilith's grief, despite her request that it "leave me what I feel for him, at least," in another example of the basic conflict between the human need for privacy and autonomy and the Oankali drive toward hybridization, interdependence, and boundary-crossing (225). Lilith then turns the tables on Nikanj and asks it to share what it feels with her. Nikanj is only able to reply by reminding her of their biological difference, implying that the traffic between them does not run in both directions. Lilith demands that Nikanj "Approximate!… Trade! You're always talking about trading. Give me something of yourself!" (225). The Xenogenesis novels then emphasize that the trade and the contrast it provides to more familiar human values (perhaps more accurately, the values associated with the European enlightenment and Western modernity) are no guarantee of genuine tolerance and equality, even as the novel creates, I argue, an opportunity for readers to reflect on how the Oankali arrangement might facilitate such desirable outcomes. That reflection depends upon readers' abilities to recognize the ambivalences and paradoxes Butler's novels explore, instead of reducing these texts to a set of conflicts derived from a simplistic reading of fugitive slave narratives.[14]

Literary Politics and Black Cultural Nationalism

I want to be clear that my comments earlier about Butler's critiques of nationalism and bounded identities in the Xenogenesis trilogy are not meant to present Butler as an "antirace race woman."[15] Let me emphasize this point by briefly defining Butler's complex relation to some touchstones in African American literature, specifically post-civil rights narratives that respond to the emergence of black cultural nationalism and its revaluation of black/white color lines. The emphasis on themes of co-implication, coexistence, and mutuality in my readings of "Amnesty" and the Xenogenesis novels, rather than on the thematics of captivity and cooptation, might suggest that Butler is engaged in a critique of nationalist assumptions. Butler's focus on hybridization and the mediating status of black characters like Lilith and Noah seems to stand in contrast to Addison Gayle's definition of black cultural nationalism or the Black Aesthetic as "a corrective—a means of helping black people out of the *polluted* mainstream of Americanism" (1971, xxiii; my emphasis).[16]

John Williams's *Sons of Darkness, Sons of Light* exemplifies the connection between the Black Arts and Black Power movements that Larry Neal defined as characteristic of the nationalist period in recent African American history (1971, 272). Williams's novel makes an especially useful comparison for Butler, since it represents a relatively unrecognized subgenre of black speculative fiction, or what Kali Tal calls "black militant near-future fiction."[17] *Sons of Darkness*, published in 1969 and set in 1974, explores the possibility of a violent black uprising in that year as a result of a disillusioned civil rights worker who takes out a Mafia contract on a white policeman who shot and killed a black teenager. At one point, the main character articulates his justification for the use of violence: "It would always be open season on blacks until blacks opened the season on whites" (23). The key question then is "How to begin again," to put race relations on a new footing of mutual respect for basic rights to survival (23). What is the role of armed resistance in this process? Williams's language echoes Lilith's assertion that humanity can only be reborn or "begin again" if the Oankali "let us alone" (*Dawn* 41).

Despite the nationalistic overtones of Lilith's assertion, Butler's writing suggests discomfort with the position Williams's novel explores. Butler was even more explicit in an interview in which she recounts an anecdote about her college years in the late 1960s. She remembers a friend of hers saying "I wish I could kill all these old Black people that have been holding us back for so long, but I can't because I have to start with my own parents" (Butler 2000, 4). Butler criticizes this man for taking a "cerebral" rather than emotional perspective on Black history: "He was the kind that would have killed and died, as opposed to surviving and hanging on and hoping and working for change" (ibid.). Butler cites this anecdote to explain the origins of her neo-slave narrative/time travel novel *Kindred*, but her discomfort with violent resistance remains relevant to both "Amnesty" and the Xenogenesis trilogy.

The ambivalence Butler expresses in her work toward nationalist projects of violent resistance makes her work more comparable to a novel like Alice Walker's *Meridian* than to Williams's. Walker's novel focuses on the title character, a black woman attending college during the transition from non-violent strategies to black nationalism. The most illuminating scene in this novel with respect to Butler's writing comes when a group of black women require Meridian to "answer the question 'Will you kill for the Revolution' with a positive Yes" (1976, 27). Her inability to do so, her sense that she is "being *held* by something in the past" (ibid.) and that "it is death not to love one's mother" (30), is interpreted by the other women as an inability to decolonize her mind and to identify the real agents of her oppression: "You hate yourself instead of hating them," Meridian is told (28; this statement finds an echo in "Amnesty" in Thera Collier's demand that Noah explain why she defends the Communities [Butler, 161]).

Butler's rejection of nationalist violence, however, should not necessarily be read as a rejection of black nationalism entirely (in the same way that Meridian ultimately resolves her crisis when she observes how a black church responds to and incorporates nationalist politics, rather than black nationalism requiring a wholesale rejection of black history and institutions; 199-200). Conclusions about Butler's relationship to black political projects are complicated by her insistence on a literal reading of the science-fictional thematics of alien contact, and her rejection of any reductive or purely allegorical reading of either the Oankali or the Communities as slavers or colonialists.[18] A more persuasive reading of Butler's relation to black nationalism might note the continuities between Butler's emphasis on survival and coexistence and Williams's formulation: "It would always be open season on blacks until blacks opened the season on whites" (23). Nationalist violence is here imagined as a means to reverse relations of dominance, to render them more mutual, in fact as a way of creating a kind of mutual amnesty by committing a crime against whites, which allows blacks to live with the history of white crimes against blacks. In this sense, Butler's writing about alien contact might be understood as converging with the project of black nationalism, as one long attempt to answer Williams's question: "How to begin again" (230).[19]

"Amnesty" as Revisionist Narrative

In "Amnesty," Noah confronts the historical residue of this African American history, which informs James Adio's analysis of and orientation toward the alien Communities. Although we are told that "Noah was black herself and yet James Adio had apparently decided the moment they met that he didn't like her" (159), he later explains that "I'm angry because I have to be here!" rather than angry at either the Communities or Noah (160). Especially in relation to the Xenogenesis trilogy, my reading of "Amnesty" suggests that this statement is grounded in an accurate analysis of the consequences of coexistence with the Communities. The terms of Adio's presence, what it means to "be here," indeed, what it means to "be," are no longer in his control. One of the questions the story implicitly raises is to what extent that was ever true. The presence of the aliens, their "invasion," makes explicit the consequence of any situation of coexistence, any participation in a community: the most basic ontological categories defining "our" existence, including words like "our," are negotiated, not given.

This challenge to being itself recalls Paul Gilroy's argument that "the call of racial being has been weakened" by our current "technological and communicative revolution" and its disruption of "the old visual signatures of 'race'" (2000 36, 43). Butler uses the theme of coexistence with aliens to explore similar transformations. This basic challenge to the characters' sense of themselves is only tolerable, however, if it is reciprocal, if it feeds back into the Communities' sense of their own identities. Noah suggests this is the case when she points out that, prior to their encounter with humans, the Communities had no concept of "altered consciousness," nothing "like hypnosis or mood-altering drugs" or even sleep and dreaming: "a whole Community never goes unconscious even though several of its entities might" ("Amnesty: 163). The result is that the Communities "have no history of drug taking, no resistance to it, and apparently no moral problems with it," so that "all of a sudden they're hooked. On us" (181). In other words, the relation of humans and Communities is one of mutual, though asymmetric, vulnerability, and this vulnerability is both literal or physical and more symbolic or metaphysical: what I am describing as a kind of ontological dependence or co-implication.[20] That co-implication puts the question of Noah's (or Lilith's) cooptation by the aliens in a different light.

From this point of view, the real area of intersection (rather than analogy) between speculative alien contact scenarios and the history of slavery, between future and past, is the ambivalent space of cultural exchange they both produce, and the way in which Butler represents alien contact as neither clearly utopian nor dystopian.[21] Noah's statement that she wouldn't know how to forgive the Communities for the treatment she suffered at their hands as an abductee, even if she wished (168), exemplifies the problems with simplifying this relationship in purely positive or negative terms. As with the Oankali practice of "trade," the interaction between Noah and the Communities is reciprocal but uneven, still structured by histories of inequality. For example, the communicative practice of "enfolding," which began as a "convenient" way of "restraining, examining," and experimenting on human captives, quickly developed into something more (172).[22] "Amnesty" begins with a scene in which Noah is enfolded by her new, temporary employer. She is drawn "upward and in among its many selves," so thoroughly surrounded by the individual components of the Community's body that "she couldn't see at all" (151). In fact, she is described as closing her eyes in order "to avoid the distraction of trying to see or imagining that she saw"—that is, interpreting her experience in more purely human terms.

During her early years of captivity, before communication protocols were established, enfolding was Noah's "only dependable comfort" (151). When she tells the story of this captivity later she recalls her bewilderment at the beatings she sometimes received from her fellow human captives "for daring to ask her alien captors for comfort" (173). This passage echoes the scene at the end of *Dawn* in which Lilith lies down with Nikanj on a battlefield (231-232). In both cases, a symbiotic exchange between an alien and a black woman is interpreted by other humans as a treasonous act of sexual intimacy and racial miscegenation.

The symbiotic aspect of enfolding emerges as Noah reflects on the way in which the Communities also take an unexpected pleasure in enfolding humans, learning to enjoy first "the broad expanse of skin that the human back offered" as a canvas for signing and later the "large gestures" of the unenfolded human body (152). Noah goes on to claim that the Communities have become at least as dependent upon enfolding as humans have, though in a different and asymmetric way. For the Communities, humans constitute an "addictive drug" (179). Communities having difficulty adjusting to the terrestrial environment find that enfolding a human "calms them and eases what translates as a kind of intense biological homesickness" (180). On the human side, Noah describes enfolding oxymoronically, as a "comfortable straitjacket" (163). This paradoxical combination of comfort and confinement again encodes the complexities of interdependence, community, and intimacy with others as Butler represents them, since that interdependence always involves both pleasures and dangers, benefits and constraints.

As is typical of Butler's writing, these pleasures and dangers elicit anxiety from the human characters (and often from readers), because they are defined in contrast to the human characters' desires for autonomy, possessive individualism, and clear boundaries between self and other. The story clearly poses coexistence (with all its possibilities for inequality as well as productive exchange) against territoriality as responses to the alien presence. The most militantly anti-alien character in the story, Thera Collier, argues that we shouldn't allow the Communities to occupy even deserts or barren territory that we don't need, since they are still ours (181). At this point, Noah reminds Thera that the aliens can't simply leave (182), so the choice is between learning to live together or turning the human/alien relationship into a life and death struggle.

Noah's story unfolds indirectly during her interactions with this group and especially her polemical exchanges with Thera Collier and James Adio. "They're here," Noah points out over and over again (167), arguing for acceptance of a situation in which "we get to live, and so do they" (181).[23] The syntax of this formulation is noteworthy, since the arrangement of clauses and the use of the phrase "and so" suggest that their survival is dependent on ours, in a reversal of the expected power relations and an assertion of the continued agency of the apparently weaker party.

The danger of Noah's position is made explicit through the way she is challenged by her audience, who suggest she is helping to reproduce a relation of subordination and mystifying the power relations that underlie the "fact" of the aliens' presence by presenting that presence as a neutral "fact." In effect, the two more militant characters accuse Noah of having given the Communities an amnesty for their crimes against humanity, especially once they learn that Noah herself was originally abducted by them. In the course of the story Noah reveals that she was persecuted as a collaborator and tortured by human military authorities after her release by the Communities. Noah's reading of her history is that the human authorities who interrogate her, using techniques that drive her to commit suicide (in what seems like an allusion to US responses to 9/11, including the practice of rendition and conditions at Guantanamo Bay), assume survival under conditions of captivity is necessarily an act of treason (171).

When her audience expresses resistance to learning about the aliens and hostility toward Noah, they imply a similar reading of her, if not as a traitor, than at least as having been co-opted. At one point in the discussions, after Noah has described the sexual abuse she experienced at the hands of other human prisoners, Thera Collier tries to insist that the Communities deserve the blame for this treatment: "You were intelligent. You could see what the weeds were doing to you. You didn't have to—" (167). Noah interrupts to ask "I didn't have to what?," and Thera "backpedals," instead of going on to explicitly accuse Noah of selling out merely by surviving. Noah's interruption emphasizes how Thera's advocacy of violence toward the Communities also functions to excuse violent acts committed between humans, and specifically violence against women that reproduces gender stereotypes. This theme of literal rape is important, since an earlier passage strongly implies that human suspicion of the Communities expresses itself through rumors that the aliens' desire to enfold humans should be interpreted as sexual abuse. The result is to legitimate masculine control of women's sexuality, as suggested when Noah notes that the evidence of a recent beating of one of the potential women employees in the group could probably be explained in terms of "the rumors that were sometimes spread about the Communities and why they hired human beings" (158).

Just as Noah's relatively compromised position as an alien mediator and translator is deliberately reminiscent of Lilith's status in the Xenogenesis novels, so is the resurgence of bias and social stereotyping under the flag of fighting to preserve the truth and purity of human nature. Noah's mistreatment by both the Communities and her human "rescuers" indicates that the "amnesty" of the title works in at least two directions.

Noah's allegiance is not naturally pro-human and anti-alien, since to survive she has to forgive the human community as well as the alien ones.

Noah's debate with James Adio, the other black character in the story, is especially interesting for my argument, since I read the subtext of that debate as the question of how analogous the human/alien relationship is to the history of the relation between African persons and their European occupiers and slavers. Like Lilith's, Noah's story is clearly a kind of captivity narrative. In fact, while the main basis for that allegorical reading of *Dawn* is Lilith's race, the symbolic echoes of her waking to find she is being held captive in a ship and Lilith's own suggestion that the Oankali trade in themselves is a kind of slave trade, "Amnesty" actually intensifies the slavery analogies by imagining a history of human/alien interaction in which the aliens treated their human captors "like human scientists experimenting with lab animals" (161). But as in Xenogenesis, Butler is clearly reluctant to simply collapse this story of alien contact into the history of slavery. James does this when he asks "what will we be, then?… Whores or house pets? (179). This passage directly echoes Lilith's concern, early in *Dawn*, that the trade makes her a "nearly extinct animal, part of a captive breeding program" (58). Noah reinterprets James's language by going on to explain how the Communities are dependent on humans in ways comparable to addictive drugs (179) or, indeed, pets understood not as property but as companion species or symbiotic partners; Noah notes that "petting a cat lowers our blood pressure" in the same way that enfolding a human physically and emotionally affects the Communities (180).[24]

Still, James and Thera, like many readers, find it difficult to associate coexistence with the negotiation of inequalities and instead insist on formulating their choices as either formal equality or division into armed camps. For example, James cannot see how Noah can work for the Communities without forgiving them. When Noah begins to explain what it meant to be an early captive of the Communities, James returns to the question of what amnesty means in this context: "And what? You forgive them for what they did do?" (160). Later, Thera returns to her main point about the need for armed resistance to the "invading" alien presence. When Noah rejects the idea that "They're here" only "until we find a way to drive them away," for Thera the only alternative is letting them off the hook for all their crimes against us; she then asks Noah "do you forgive them for what they've done?" (167). Coexistence or forgiveness for Thera involves a forcible erasure of histories of conflict, not a negotiation of them. Noah, however, is clear on the fact that she doesn't forgive the Communities: "They haven't asked for my forgiveness and I wouldn't know how to give it if they did. And that doesn't matter. It doesn't stop me from doing my job. It doesn't stop them from employing me" (168). Noah's audience tends to interpret these statements as submission to the Communities, as reproducing fixed positions of power and powerlessness, rather than as participation in a process of mutual change, as indicated by James's response that Noah ought to be working "to find a way to kill them" (168). Noah replies by asking him if that is his goal, and he acknowledges that he's actually "here to work for them" (168). As in Walker's *Meridian*, the desire to kill is here presented as a desire to escape a historical relationship, rather than change it.

Both James and Thera find it hard to believe that Noah prefers accepting an ongoing and open-ended relation to the Communities to the closure provided by life-and-death struggle. James even tries to re-narrate Noah's account as such a struggle. He suggests that Noah's happiness with the idea that the Communities have become dependent on humans is "some kind of payback" for her. Noah returns to her central theme, arguing that she desires "No payback. Just what I said earlier.... We get to live, and so do they. I don't need payback" (181). Getting to live is not enough for James, or for Thera, who goes on to argue that, if the aliens cannot leave, then they can still die (182). The story suggests that the choices are not so stark, that coexistence is possible, though difficult. At the same time, violent resistance is not so much critiqued in itself, but to the extent that it forecloses on a relation to either the past (which is rejected as a state of pure victimization) or the future (which is reduced to the options of unconstrained self-assertion or death).

"Amnesty" therefore spells out more explicitly and didactically than does the Xenogenesis trilogy the political stakes of Butler's rethinking of human-alien contact scenarios. At the same time, the story remains relatively open-ended in staging this debate between a nationalist or separatist response to "invasion" and the alternative that Noah tries to articulate. In other words, the value of reading "Amnesty" back into Butler's earlier writing resides in the story's power to complicate responses that dismissively characterize the Oankali as invaders or slave traders by legitimating the Oankali as having a side that needs to be considered. This power is obtained in part by making Noah a more persuasive and less conflicted spokesperson for coexistence with the aliens than Lilith is. But the story very deliberately does not prevent readers from sympathizing with James Adio or Thera Collier, even if it does try to spell out the consequences of such sympathy. "Amnesty" then helps to restore a dimension of complexity to the Xenogenesis trilogy while remaining true to its own ambivalent representation of coexistence and symbiosis by refusing to combat oversimplified narratives of "us" against "them" with its own easy answer to the difficulties of achieving exchange and reciprocity within a framework of historical inequity. Reading "Amnesty" has helped my students generate more nuanced discussion of the Xenogenesis novels and become more self-conscious about how they deploy the rhetoric of the "human" against its others. Even when students remain unpersuaded by my arguments about how Butler's stories express a preference for xenophilia and necessary interdependence over the desire to remain (purely) human, they have to admit that remaining human is a desire, a struggle, a political project, not just common sense, and this shift is for me one of the great triumphs of Butler's writing.

Works Cited

Alarcon, Norma. 1989. "Traddutora, Traditora: A Paradigmatic Figure of Chicana Feminism." *Cultural Critique* 13: 57-87.

Allison, Dorothy. 1990. "The Future of Female: Octavia Butler's Mother Lode." In *Reading Black, Reading Feminist* edited by Henry Louis Gates Jr., 471-478. New York: Meridian.

Bonner, Frances. 1990. "Difference and Desire, Slavery and Seduction: Octavia Butler's *Xenogenesis*." *Foundation: The Review of Science Fiction* 48: 50-62.

Butler, Judith. 2004. *Precarious Life: The Powers of Mourning and Violence*. New York: Verso.

Butler, Octavia E. 1988. *Adulthood Rites*. New York: Warner.

———. 2005. "Amnesty." In *Bloodchild and Other Stories*. 2nd edition. New York: Seven Stories Press.

———. 1987. *Dawn*. New York: Warner.

———. 1989. *Imago*. New York: Warner.

——. 2000. "Octavia E. Butler: Persistence." *Locus* #473 (June): 4, 75-78.

Cherniavsky, Eva. 2006. *Incorporations: Race, Nation, and the Body Politics of Capital*. Minneapolis, MN: University of Minnesota Press.

Fuss, Diana. 1989. *Essentially Speaking: Feminism, Nature, and Difference*. New York: Routledge.

Gayle, Addison, ed. 1971. *The Black Aesthetic*. Garden City, NY: Doubleday.

Gilroy, Paul. 2000. *Against Race: Imagining Political Culture Beyond the Color Line*. Cambridge, MA: Harvard University Press.

——. 1993. *The Black Atlantic: Modernity and Double Consciousness*. Cambridge, MA: Harvard University Press.

Hairston, Andrea. 2006. "Octavia Butler—Praise Song to a Prophetic Artist." In *Daughters of the Earth: Feminist Science Fiction in the Twentieth Century*, edited by Justine Larbalestier, 287-304. Middletown, CT: Wesleyan University Press.

Haraway, Donna. 2003. *The Companion Species Manifesto: Dogs, People and Significant Otherness*. Chicago, IL: Prickly Paradigm.

——. 1991. *Simians, Cyborgs, and Women: The Reinvention of Nature*. New York: Routledge.

Hayles, N. Katherine. 1999. *How We Became Posthuman: Virtual Bodies in Cybernetics, Literature, and Informatics*. Chicago, IL University of Chicago Press.

Harper, Phillip Brian. 1996. *Are We Not Men? Masculine Anxiety and the Problem of African-American Identity*. New York: Oxford University Press.

Jacobs, Naomi. 2003. "Posthuman Bodies and Agency in Octavia Butler's *Xenogenesis*." In *Dark Horizons: Science Fiction and the Dystopian Imagination*, edited by Raffaella Baccolini and Tom Moylan, 91-112. New York: Routledge.

Jones, Gwyneth. 1994. *North Wind*. New York: Tor.

Melzer, Patricia. 2006. *Alien Constructions: Science Fiction and Feminist Thought*. Austin, TX: University of Texas Press.

Michaels, Walter Benn. 2000. "Political Science Fictions." *New Literary History* 31.4: 649-664.

Miller, Jim. 1998. "Post-Apocalyptic Hoping: Octavia Butler's Dystopian/Utopian Vision." *Science-Fiction Studies* 25.2(July): 336-360.

Neal, Larry. 1971. "The Black Arts Movement." In *The Black Aesthetic* edited by Addison Gayle, 272-290. Garden City, NY: Doubleday.

Paz, Octavio. 1985. *The Labyrinth of Solitude*. New York: Grove (orig. published 1950).

Peppers, Cathy M. 1995. "Dialogic Origins and Alien Identities in Butler's *Xenogenesis*." *Science-Fiction Studies* 22.1 (March): 47-62.

Pfeil, Fred. 1990. *Another Tale to Tell: Politics and Narrative in Postmodern Culture*. New York: Verso.

Posnock, Ross. 1998. *Color and Culture: Black Writers and the Making of the Modern Intellectual*. Cambridge, MA: Harvard University Press.

Potts, Stephen. 1996. "'We Keep Playing the Same Record': A Conversation with Octavia E. Butler." *Science-Fiction Studies* 23.3 (November): 331-338.

Pratt, Mary Louise. 1992. *Imperial Eyes: Travel Writing and Transculturation*. New York: Routledge.

———. 1987. "Linguistic Utopias." In *The Linguistics of Writing: Arguments between Language and Literature*, edited by Nigel Fisk, 48-66. New York: Methuen.

Reagon, Bernice Johnson. 1983. "Coalition Politics: Turning the Century." In *Home Girls: A Black Feminist Anthology*, edited by Barbara Smith, 356-368. New York: Kitchen Table/Women of Color Press.

Shaviro, Steven. 2003. *Connected, or What It Means to Live in the Network Society*. Minneapolis, MN: University of Minnesota Press.

Shunn, Thelma J. 1985. "The Wise Witches: Black Women Mentors in the Fiction of Octavia E. Butler." In *Conjuring: Black Women, Fiction, and Literary Tradition*, edited by Marjorie Pryse and Hortense J. Spillers. Bloomington, IN: Indiana University Press.

Smith, Stephanie. 1993. "Morphing, Materialism, and the Marketing of *Xenogenesis*." *Genders* #18 (Winter): 67-86.

Tal, Kali. 2002. "'That Just Kills Me': Black Militant Near-Future Fiction." *Social Text* #71 (Summer): 65-91.

Tucker, Jeffrey Allen. 2004. *A Sense of Wonder: Samuel R. Delany, Race, Identity, and Difference*. Middletown, CT: Wesleyan University Press.

Walker, Alice. 1976. *Meridian*. New York: Pocket Books.

Williams, John. 1969. *Sons of Darkness, Sons of Light*. Boston, MA: Northeastern University Press.

Wolmark, Jenny. 1994. *Aliens and Others: Science Fiction, Feminism, and Postmodernism*. Iowa City, IA: University of Iowa Press.

Zaki, Hoda M. 1990. "Utopia, Dystopia, and Ideology in the Science Fiction of Octavia Butler." *Science-Fiction Studies* 17: 239-251.

Endnotes

1   For other comparisons of Butler and cyberpunk or its precursors, see Smith (1993) and Haraway (1991, 173-179).

2   On loss of origin, see Peppers (1995, 56), who draws on Haraway (1991, 150, 179).

3   Allison critiques the Oankali as both rapists and masters (1990 472, 475). Butler herself rejected the idea that the Oankali are "the ultimate users" (Potts 1996, 332).

4   Compare to Hayles's definition of posthumanism as a critique of the ideology of possessive individualism and its self/other distinctions (1999, 4; see also Jacobs 2003). Fuss defines a similar paradox in the definition of "woman" (1989, 71-72).

5   See Cherniavsky (2006, 20). Harper (1996, ch. 2) critiques black cultural nationalism's rhetorics of racial and sexual purity.

6   Paz (1985) offers the classic reading of the figure of La Malinche; see Alarcon's feminist critique (1989).

7   Jones seems influenced by Butler in her use of alien biology to make a similar point about interdependence (1994, 8). Wolmark compares Jones and Butler (1994, 44-45).

8   Cherniavsky uses post-colonial theory to read Butler's story "Bloodchild" as a post-national narrative, in which the "assimilative project" of bourgeois nationalism is replaced by a more heterogeneous space of coexistence (2006, 40, 41-47).

9   The markers of Lilith Iyapo's racial background, including her last name and her skin color, are carefully revealed only in casual asides that many readers, accustomed to thinking of white protagonists as the norm, might miss; the original mass-market paperback edition of *Dawn* famously depicts Lilith as a white woman.

10   Butler has also asserted that "the only places I am writing about slavery is where I actually say so" (Potts 1996, 332), specifically *Kindred* and the Patternmaster series. For readings of the Xenogenesis trilogy in relation to histories of slavery, see Pfeil (1990, 93); Bonner (1990); Hairston (2006, 294-295); Cherniavsky (2006, 18); and Peppers, on the ways in which the analogy is both invoked and refused in these novels (1995, 51-56).

11   See Haraway (1991, 228) and Pfeil on Butler's theme of "the self mutating toward Otherness" who "becomes Other to itself" (1990, 91). For applications of such general analyses to gender and race, see Wolmark (1994, ch. 2, especially 28-29) and Melzer (2006, chs. 1 and 2, especially 45, 47-48, and 67-68).

12   Haraway analyzes these anthropological references (1991, 229-230). Cherniavsky argues that the Oankali's "expansionist 'drive'" paradoxically functions as an "abdication of sovereignty" (2006, 22).

13   Such statements are the basis for Zaki's charges of essentialism. For the opposite reading, see Wolmark (1994, 45), Melzer, specifically on race (2006, 80-83), and Hairston's critique of rhetorics of authenticity (2006, 290-291). Smith usefully argues that Butler is both attracted to the denaturalization of social categories and resists the dissolution of race or gender into nothing but a manipulable image (1993, 72-76).

14   Pratt theorizes this kind of ambivalence when she defines the "contact zone" in terms of both "copresence" and "conditions of coercion, radical inequality, and intractable conflict" (1992, 6-7). In this model "colonial

encounters" are dynamic, relationally defined, "interactive" and "improvisa-
tional," as well as structured in dominance (7).

15   I here paraphrase Tucker on the racial politics of critics' responses to
black sf writer Samuel Delany and his appropriation of poststructuralist
critiques of identity (2004, 13; see Posnock 1998, 260, for an example of
treating Delany as an "anti-race race man). This is how Michaels reads
Butler (2000, 650).

16   This critique of pollution moves beyond the focus on "self-determination
and nationhood" that critics like Neal stressed (1971, 272; see Harper
1996, 48).

17   Tal (2002) offers a longer analysis of Williams's novel.

18   See Shaviro on the literal reading of Butler's aliens (2003, 18).

19   This understanding of nationalism is closer to Reagon's, who argues that
separate "nurturing" or "home" spaces are necessary but not sufficient,
since the creation of such spaces allows differences between women or
blacks to emerge. Separatism therefore shifts toward coalition politics
and the negotiation of differences, which do not remain external (1983,
358-360). Compare to Harper (1996, 44, 53). In his work on the black
diaspora, Gilroy both critiques nationalism (1993, 2, 3) and attempts to
rethink its relation to alternative logics of identity (2000, 188) like those
embodied by Butler's aliens.

20   Judith Butler theorizes mutual vulnerability as a "normative reorienta-
tion for politics" (2004, 28, 31) and as "the precondition of the 'human'"
(43). On Octavia Butler's representations of interdependence, see Shunn
(1985, 214), Shaviro (2003, 17), and Cherniavsky (2006, 41).

21   In contrast, Miller (1998) and Jacobs (2003) analyze Butler's work in
terms of the utopian/dystopian distinction.

22   Pratt borrows the term "contact" from linguistics, where it refers to "improvised languages" developed "usually in context of trade" (1992, 6).
Enfolding is a speculative example.

23   Miller reads Xenogenesis as privileging "survival" over the more traditionally science-fictional emphasis on "transcendence" (1998, 343); see
also Allison (1990, 478). For Shunn, this message constitutes the main
connection between Butler's SF and the figure of the African American
mother (1985, 203).

24   See Haraway on companion species and interdependence (2003, 12).

A delighted Octavia peers down from a bridge at Washington's Deception Falls.

❧ Photo by Leslie Howle

Part Three

The Parables:

Approaching the Millennium with Butler

Excerpt 4 from "A Conversation with Octavia E. Butler"

Nisi Shawl

(Interview Conducted at the "Black to the Future Conference: A Black Science Fiction Festival," Seattle, June 12, 2004)

Nisi: Another area as far as your writing goes: your characters. They're vivid, they're memorable...

Octavia: Thank you.

Nisi: ...they stay with your readers, and from what I've heard you say, they stay with you as well. You get to know them and you spend more time with them, you've said, than with your real friends.

Octavia: Sometimes they want me to write about them more, yes.

Nisi: So they stick around with you after the book is finished. Are you spending time with any characters that you'd like to tell us about today?

Octavia: Well that's my new book...

Nisi: Okay, so no leftovers.

Octavia: Well, I do want to write the Trickster book, the follow-up to the two *Parable* books. That should be at least two books, but they're not ready. I mentioned the medicine, and it just seemed easier to do a vampire book. Mainly because in my *Parable* books, I try to save the world. In my Xenogenesis books—I keep saying I—my characters are trying to save the world. And okay, five books of world saving in a row, I kind of needed to get away from that and do something fun, you know. Because the world doesn't want to be saved, for goodness sake.

Nisi: Hmm, that's an interesting idea. The world doesn't want to be saved.

Octavia: Well let's put it this way,... George Bush is President.

[AUD: laughter]

Nisi: Point taken.

❦

Audience: How long does it take you to put a book together from concept to publication? And do you typically write or do you have more than one book to write about at one time—

Octavia: I don't. Some people do have more than one book going on at one time. How long it takes changes. But basically it takes how long you're alive up until the time you start writing and then some. There's no formula. When I got going with my first three novels that I talked about earlier, I had those ideas in my head for a long time. I got the idea for *Patternmaster* when I was twelve. I got the idea for *Mind of My Mind* when I was fifteen. I actually wrote a version of *Survivor* when I was nineteen. And when things have been living in your head for that long, there are developed characters. There are developed conflicts. And really what you're trying to do is figure out a way to write them down that actually works, and then you can finish. Now when I wrote these it was—I went through two and a half novels in one year. I never did that again. But it took a lot longer than that to get to the point of being able to do that. And the two *Parable* books, I think in the case of *Parable of the Sower*, I was working at it in one way or another for a couple of years before I could even get started writing it. I had some problems with my character; my character was a power-seeking character. I've had powerful characters, I've had characters upon whom power devolved, but I've never had a character who sought power. And this was a character who sought power, and the politicians have taught me not to trust power-seekers, so I was not having a good time with that character. I had to get to the point of understanding at gut level that power was a tool like anything else. And that the people who didn't want to use it would have it used on them. So that helped, but like I said, it was a couple of years before I could even begin to write the book.

Audience: The *Parable* books, would you say that those books for you are just a story that you decided to tell?

Octavia: Of course not.

Audience: Or that you actually had a goal like you wanted to send a specific message that you wanted people to get an idea, or inspire something, or maybe cause…

Octavia: Well, I've already said that I've written five world-saving novels, and the *Parable* books were of course the last two of those five. I am a news junkie, and this means that I absorb a lot of stuff that you really have to find some outlet for or it festers. And these novels were kind of my outlet. They are my cautionary tales. If we are not careful, we are liable to be living in this world.

Nisi: If this goes on.

Audience: You don't think you jinx stuff.

Octavia: No, we've been going to the dogs for a long time. I heard someone say, umm…I guess it was the panel before me, that there had been a song about pushing the button, the nuclear button. And I was at a college not too long ago where I talked about Ronald Reagan and the idea of "Beware of a nuclear war," and all that. And a young woman told me that stuff was not real. In a way, isn't it lovely that people have forgotten? But on the other hand, isn't it scary that they've forgotten. We are busy destroying ourselves in so many ways that for me to grab a soapbox and shout about a few of them probably doesn't do an awful lot of good. But, have most of you read my *Parable* books, just out of curiosity? Oh most of you have, okay, so you know what I'm talking about; if we're not careful, we're going to wind up in some very bad places. Now these are not dystopic books. These are books that take a look at what we're doing and where we're liable to wind up and how we're liable to…what way we can climb out of it. Actually several ways but only one of them works.

Fun, Fun, Fun

Merrilee Heifetz

My relationship with Octavia Butler began over 20 years ago when I sat next to her at the Hugo Awards the year "Bloodchild" won for Best Short Story. When she subsequently learned that her current Writers House agent was leaving, she wrote to me: "…you're the logical person for me to ask. Besides, you're good luck!"

For someone who led a solitary writerly life, Octavia was emotional, passionate, and romantic. For someone so steeped in science and in the starkly honest, gritty and often dark side of humanity, Octavia was a great believer in luck and really a terrific optimist. She had to be, because success did not come quickly.

The first book I sold for Octavia was actually one that had gone out of print. *Kindred* was originally published by Doubleday in 1979, but back then there was no market for a feminist novel about an African-American woman who travels through time to a slave plantation. However, in 1988 Beacon Press bought trade paperback rights for a modest sum and put it in a new line they were doing of women's science fiction. (It has since sold over half a million copies, is in film production as of this writing, and is taught in colleges throughout the country.) Also at that time, the set of novels known as the Xenogenesis series (which are now collected in the single title *Lilith's Brood*) were under contract but were not yet published. They came out over the next few years but sold even fewer copies than *Kindred* had. (At this point the only kind of luck I was bringing Octavia was not the kind she presumably had hired me for…)

But Octavia was a writer. And while she believed in luck, she also believed in hard work fueled by passion and ideas—and the ideas driving her to create at this time were based in her deep concerns about such issues as global warming, poverty, and the ruthlessness of the greedy and powerful.

This is from a letter she wrote me in July 1990 when she was working on a novel called Gods of Clay which later became *Parable of the Sower*:

The novel, as I started to tell you on the phone, is the story of Lauren Olamina: Her obsession, the religion she creates, her struggles with enemies, followers and Gage, the foster son who may become her Joshua, her Judas, or her Paul. The novel takes place on a twenty-first century Earth made somewhat grimmer by the greenhouse effect and altered by social change and technological advancement. Yet Lauren Olamina knows that human beings can still be captured, succored, motivated by religion. The religion she creates and uses, she also believes she sees as their destiny. ("The destiny of Earthseed is to take root among the stars.") What else in a time of decreased affluence, decreased freedom, and (among the world's ruling businesses) increased concern for profit and power could motivate people to reach for the stars? Interstellar travel would be fantastically expensive, difficult, uncertain, and for generations if not forever, profitless. Most people living when the starships leave Earth will not survive long enough to know whether they land safely on some extrasolar world. Such travel gives none of the quick rewards that businesses and politicians need. It offers nothing to ease the lives of the common people. It is so long-term that it isn't even good circus.

Thus religion is the ancient tool that Olamina must use to push some small fraction of humanity into the future. It is a dangerous too, easily perverted, and heavily dependent on Olamina's survival. It does not depend on logic. It does not depend on Olamina's being good or right. It depends on her survival.

Both Olamina and Gage are well aware of this.

That's the story. The form has been shifting about on me, but that's the story.

Wish me luck.

Sincerely,

Octavia E. Butler

She finished the novel about a year and half later and I began to send it out. Her sales on the previous three books had been so bad that no one offered—remember, this was before Oprah, before Terry MacMillan, well before Alice Walker was a bestselling author. One publisher actually told me, "Black people don't buy books…"

But finally, her editor at Warner (now Hachette) said that if I could find someone else to publish the hardcover he would buy paperback rights. Thus I found Dan Simon who was then co-owner of the small press Four Walls, Eight Windows—and the publishing team that would take Octavia through the next 16 years went to work.

Parable of the Sower was published in 1993 and in 1995 Octavia was awarded her MacArthur Foundation "genius" grant. I am happy to say that her book sales increased and finally, ten years after she hired me, success found Octavia.

⇒ ⇐

A perfectionist, Octavia was capable of seeing the negative side when the writing was not going well. Here is a letter she wrote me in 1997:

> Dear Merrilee,
>
> This is going to be something of a bare-bones letter because nothing I can think of to say will make it any more pleasant to write or to read. I won't be finishing PARABLE OF THE TALENTS. I believed I could finish it but I was wrong. I am sorry to let you, Dan, and myself down, but I see no alternative.
>
> Please let me know the procedure for returning Dan's money.
>
> Apologies and best wishes, Octavia E. Butler.

That book went on to win the Nebula Award in 1999.

But even when things were dark, her passion for her art was greater than any romance. This letter describes a series of books that didn't quite work out the way she planned. But this is the Octavia I will always remember and always miss:

Dear Merrilee,

Enclosed is the May '89 L.A. Style you couldn't find. I'm on page 89. "Sci-fi femme" for God's sake. But what the hell. They spelled my name right....

About the *Essence* picture, it may be my natural contrariness showing through, but I *hate* that picture. It's me under about an eighth of an inch of makeup (which kept trying to melt off under those bloody lights!) and weirdly bleached out. Me with most of the me removed. I wouldn't want to see it anywhere else.

Finally, to the most important matter this letter covers, please take the outline and chapters of JUSTICE that I sent you and *toss them out!* I'm keeping the characters' names and the concept of contagious empathy but probably nothing else. The story was beginning to feel the way an earlier novel called BLINDSIGHT used to — always just a little out of reach, and never very interesting. Ask Felicia how many times I rewrote BLINDSIGHT. No, don't ask her. Even she doesn't really know. Thoroughly bad business. Anyhow, I feel so much better about what I'm working on now that I can't even describe it. It's based on the Gaia Hypothesis — the notion that the Earth itself is a living organism. Unhappily, Dave Brin has just had a book published or will have it published soon, on his notions of Gaia. We met at LAX on our way to the same convention and he told me about it. I managed not to kill him. I've been fascinated by Gaia for years, and scared to tackle it because it's so massive, but Dave and others who worked with Gaia have stayed close to home with it. Earth only. My idea has much in common with the problems of transplant surgery and blindly responsive immune systems. The transplants are people who go to settle on living worlds of other solar systems — five shiploads of people, five other solar systems. These people can expect no help from Earth in their lifetimes — no new colonists and no useful communication. They have all the material goods they need, all the technological help they need to deal with problems they expect. What they don't expect is to be treated as organs, transplanted to blindly and persistently rejecting planetary organisms. I'm *not* talking about savage wild animals or warlike local people. I'm definitely *not* talking about intelligent plants. I'm talking about nasty little things — microorganisms that find the human body intolerable and that damage human eyes when they're blown or otherwise transferred into those eyes. The organisms die. The eyes are eventually blinded. Hearing and balance may be distroyed [*sic*]. Coloring may be changed as skin is damaged and forced to fight its own battles. People who go to sleep in apparently convenient places might awake to find themselves encapsulated in a kind of plant gall — rather like the way oysters encapsulate offending material in pearls. All local plant and animal material is inert or actively poisonous to humans, and the living world resists being killed and reincarnated — that is, terraformed. And of course, the people have brought all their human problems from Earth to complicate the ways in which they deal with the many problems the planets give them.

I plan to play with every immune response I can find a use for. I feel so good now that I'm digging around in biology again. I should have known better than to try to ignore it.

By the way, that huge paragraph above is talking not about one book, but (probably) five. At least three. They will deal with worlds with and without their own intelligent species — and under the circumstances, intelligent species, with their own particular biologies, sociologies and psychologies, are likely to be the worse [*sic*] possible complications. A world doing all it can to be rid of humanity is bad enough. Fun fun fun!

I'm researching now and playing with ideas, but I know by the way this feels that I've got something good. It will probably have to be offered book by book because it will have no onstage characters in common. Oh but speaking of characters, have I got some juicy ones demanding to be heard. Like I said, fun, fun, fun.

I'll get you an outline and chapters for the first book in perhaps the next two months of so. I've a convention and a week of Clarion coming up, so I can't quite hide out with thirty or forty books and my typewriter. That's what I feel like doing. You see, this is what I'm like when I'm in love.

Best, Octavia

Post Office Box 61293
Pasadena, CA 91116
January 11, 1997

Merrilee Heifetz
Writers House Inc.
21 West 26th Street
New York, NY 10010

Dear Merrilee,

This is going to be something of a bare-bones letter
because nothing I can think of to say will make it any
more pleasant to write or to read.

I won't be finishing PARABLE OF THE TALENTS. I believed
I could finish it, but I was wrong. I'm sorry to let you,
Dan, and myself down, but I see no alternative.

Please let me know the proceedure for returning Dan's
money.

Apologies and best wishes,

Octavia E. Butler

Letter from Octavia E. Butler to Merrilee Heifetz, Jan. 11, 1997

Post Office Box 6604
Los Angeles, CA 90055
May 30, 1989

Merrilee Heifetz
Writers House Inc.
21 West 26th Street
New York, NY 10010

Dear Merrilee:

Enclosed is the May '89 L.A. STYLE you couldn't find.
I'm on page 89--"Sci-Fi Femme" for godsake! But what
the hell. They spelled my name right. Poor Bill Glass,
who wrote the article, was so embarrassed about that
title and other editorial silliness that he called me to
apologize.

About the ESSENSE picture, it may be my natural contrariness
showing through, but I hate that picture. It's me under
about an eighth of an inch of makeup (which kept trying to
melt off under those bloody lights!) and weirdly bleached
out. Me with most of the me removed. I wouldn't want to
see it anywhere else.

Finally to the most important matter this letter covers:
Please take the outline and chapters of JUSTICE that I
sent you and toss them out! I'm keeping the characters'
names and the concept of contageous empathy, but probably
nothing else. The story was beginning to feel the way
an earlier novel called BLINDSIGHT used to--always just a
little out of reach and never very interesting. Ask
Felicia how many times I rewrote BLINDSIGHT. No, don't ask
her. Even she doesn't really know. Thoroughly bad business.
Anyhow, I feel so much better about what I'm working on now
that I can't even describe it. It's based on the Gaia hypothesis
--the notion that the earth itself is a living organism.
Unhappily, Dave Brin has just had a book published (or will
have it published soon) on his notions of Gaia. We met at
LAX on our way to the same convention and he told me about it.
I managed not to kill him. I've been fascinated by Gaia for
years and scared to tackle it because it's so massive. But
Dave and others who've worked with Gaia have stayed close to
home with it. Earth only. My idea has much in common with

Letter from Octavia E. Butler to Merrilee Heifetz, May 30, 1989., Page 1.

2

the problems of transplant surgurey and blindly responsive
immune systems. The transplants are people who go to settle
on living worlds of other solar systems--five shiploads of
people, five other solar systems. These people can expect
no help from Earth in their lifetimes--no new colonists and
no useful communication. They have all the material goods
they need, all the technological help they need to deal
with problems they expect. What they don't expect is to
be treated as organs transplanted to blindly and persistantly
rejecting planetary organism. I'm not talking about
savage wild animals or warlike local people. I'm definitely
not talking about intelligent planets. I'm talking about
nasty little things--microorganisms that find the human body
intolerable and that damage human eyes when they're blown or
otherwise transferred into those eyes. The organisms die.
The eyes are eventually blinded. Hearing and balance may
be distroyed. Coloring may be changed as skin is damaged
and forced to fight its own battles. People who go to sleep
in apparently convenient places might awake to find themselves
encapsulated in a kind of plant gall--rather like the way
oysters encapsulate offending material in pearls. All local
plant and animal material is inert or actively poisonous to humans,
and the living world resists being killed and reincarnated--
that is, terraformed. And of course, the people have brought
all their human problems from Earth to complicate the ways
in which they deal with the many problems the planets give
them.

I plan to play with every immune response I can find a use
for. I feel so good now that I'm digging around in biology
again. I should have known better than to try to ignore it.

By the way, that huge paragraph above is talking not about
one book but (probably) five. At least three. They will
deal with worlds with and without their own intelligent
species--and under the circumatances, intelligent species
with their own particular biologies, sociologies and
psychologies are likely to be the worse possible complications.
A world doing all it can to be rid of humanity is bad enough.
Fun, fun, fun!

I'm researching now and playing with ideas, but I know by the
way this feels that I've got something good. It will probably
have to be offered book by book because it will have no onstage characters in common. Oh but speaking of characters,
have I got some jucy ones demanding to be heard. Like I said,
fun, fun, fun.

I'll get you an outline and chapters for the first book in
perhaps the next two or three months. I've a convention and
a week of Clarion coming up plus a few more book signings and
a spot on the Black Entertainment Network, so I can't quite
hide out with 30 or 40 books and my typewriter. That's what
I feel like doing.

You see, this is what I'm like when I'm in love!   Best,

                                                      Octavia

(cont.) Page 2.

On Re-reading *Parable of the Sower*[1]

Kate Schaefer

Potlatch is a small literary science fiction convention aimed at foster-ing the conversation between writers and readers and closely connected with the Clarion West Writers Workshop. Most sf conventions feature a guest of honor; Potlatch has instead a Book of Honor, with panels exploring the influence of that single book on the field, dramatizations based on the Book of Honor, and informal discussions of the book out-side the formal program track.

Octavia E. Butler's Nebula-award winning 1993 novel *Parable of the Sower* was the Book of Honor at Potlatch 17 in Seattle over Leap Day weekend 2008. Butler lived in Seattle for several years and used to attend and participate in Potlatch. We miss her. The formal panel on Sower in-cluded Eileen Gunn, Nisi Shawl, Rachel Holmen, and, drafted from the audience, JT Stewart.

Although I was not on that panel, in preparation for the convention, I re-read and reconsidered *Parable of the Sower*.

In *Parable of the Sower*, Lauren Olamina travels from youth to ma-turity, from the failing traditional God-centered religious community of her father to the vibrant new human-centered spiritual community she establishes around herself, from a society founded on violence and mu-tual fear to a society founded on trust and work (backed up with working guns and a good supply of ammo). The book can be read as a utopian manifesto or as a realistic look at what might be involved in building a better way of living, and how much that better way might cost to gain, as a mystical founding document for a future religion or as a hardass rejec-tion of any religion that depends on the invisible or the irrational.

What I remembered about *Parable of the Sower*, months or years after first reading it, was the journey, narrated step by step up California from the burnt-out suburbs of LA to rural Humboldt County, sometimes on the coast, sometimes inland, following freeways without cars. It's an ex-cruciating journey, full of pain, dirt, hunger, and violence. Chance companions come and go; the ones who go probably die, and some of the ones who stay with Lauren Oya Olamina die as well.

Those who join Olamina have a chance to go on living. A chance: a better chance than if they go it alone, but still just a chance. It's a grim, sober, slender hope—a hope that lifts its head against high odds, a hope that suffers loss after loss, a hope that should have been beaten out of existence, but there it still is, hanging on.

That hope made me think about how much post-apocalyptic fiction, including *Parable of the Sower*, is more hopeful than the definition of the genre would suggest. There's that convention of sweeping away all the mistakes of the past, allowing the survivors to build a new, better society in the ruins, avoiding said mistakes. There is a magnificent, tragic optimism that somehow human beings will be able to find a way to live without enslaving and killing each other. *Parable of the Sower* doesn't show a future without slavery and murder; it shows a horrific future, with appalling slavery, violence, and injustice, while still holding out hope that it doesn't have to be that way.

And then, in preparation for Potlatch 17, I looked at the book again and was reminded that the book does not start with the journey. The journey is only the second half of the book. In that second half, the sower casts her seed onto rocky ground and barren ground and windy ground and ground that's on fire, and all of it soaked in blood. It's a harder task than that pursued by the sower in Jesus's parable, but then so was the task Jesus gave to his apostles through that parable: a sower of literal seed can examine the ground beneath that sower's real feet and decide whether to sow the seed. In Jesus's parable, the sower acts as no sane farmer would ever act, exactly as nature does act in the plant world, casting seeds all over without regard for the ground, in much greater number than could grow there if they all sprouted.

Butler's Olamina, like the apostles, goes out into the world and tells her message to everyone she meets without regard for whether that person is a good prospect or not. She does self-censor if it's clear her auditors might respond by killing, imprisoning, or enslaving her; Butler requires her characters to have a sense of self-preservation, but she doesn't hold back just for scoffing.

It works, in the novel. It works more by example than by preaching, which makes sense. "That lady looks like a survivor, and she'll help us survive, too," is more convincing than, "That lady has a deep understanding of the laws of thermodynamics as applied to social situations."

Butler doesn't cheat at all in sending her apostle out into post-apocalyptic America. Granted, Olamina is a teenage girl with a backpack, an odd psychic gift, and a few friends, out to start a new religion and change the world, but unlike accidental post-apocalyptic heroes, she's been packing that backpack and her skill set for years, all through the first half of the book.

The first half of the book, the half my memory shortened, is like the book of Job in slow but accelerating motion, a connection Butler invokes explicitly. During Olamina's adolescence, she loses everything—her best friend, her family, her house, her community—killed, burned, broken, everything but her self and those few things she had successfully hidden. As she loses each thing, each connection, she learns another painful lesson, preparing to lose and leave it all.

Unlike Job, Olamina does not have false comforters, people who suggest that she give up, give in, curse God and die.

Curse God? By this point, Olamina has ceased to believe in a personified god, and believes only in the force of change as omnipotent. Curse change? Olamina embraces change instead and takes on the task of shaping change, of shaping but not worshipping god. There will be change, but she's going to make some of that change happen her way, not by forcing it, but by altering its course just a bit, just enough.

Instead of Job's false comforters, Olamina has fellow survivors who are ready to do whatever they need to do to survive. They aren't as prepared as she is, but they're prepared enough that they're able to try, and that's the beginning that Olamina's philosophy requires.

When I look at the book this way, the journey becomes a coda. The journey I remembered as the most important part of the book is just the unfolding that follows the preparation of the first part of the book. People join Olamina, or don't; the individuals, engaging though they are, don't particularly matter. The journey is successful because the preparation was thorough and the characters lucky. They are lucky, Butler seems to tell us, because of that preparation, and because hope, persistence, and care are better tools for survival than despair.

Parable of the Sower is filled with Christian and Buddhist imagery, built on religious metaphor, parable, and story. It deconstructs the religion on which it is built and uses the basic elements to build a new religion without any gods, with change and chance at its center, and human determination and hope shaping the whole.

I step back from this re-consideration and re-reading of *Parable of the Sower* and realize that this time through, I've seen the novel almost entirely through a religious lens. The first time, I read it for story. Another time, the lens might be one of race, class, political structures; another time, I might be back to seeing the journey as more important than the preparation. I know that additional trips through *Parable of the Sower* will repay my effort.

Endnote

1   A slightly different version of this essay first appeared in the program book of Potlatch 17. My thanks to Paul M Carpentier, Debbie Notkin, Liz Copeland, and Nisi Shawl for inspirational assistance with this essay.

"A New Fashion in Faith": The Parable Novels in Conversation with Actual Intentional Communities

Lisbeth Gant-Britton

> I must create not only a dedicated little group of followers, not only a collection of communities as I once imagined, but a movement. I must create a new fashion in faith.

> Protagonist Olamina, *Parable of the Talents*

> I'm profoundly grateful to Octavia Butler for opening the possibility that I could find the people who would work with me to do what I want to do...talk about human values and how to work for a better world, even though we have different values about "God" and where we go from here."

> Brandon C.S. Sanders, Founder, The SolSeed Movement (inspired by the Parable novels' Earthseed philosophy)

During her all too brief literary lifetime, Octavia Butler created a memorable array of fictional intentional alliances and communities, each of which envisioned morality or justice in its own way. Intentional alliances or communities are groups with a mutual purpose whose members may interact in lived or virtual reality. At times, Butler created shockingly predatory communities that arrogantly used their power for domination; at other times alliances that were well-meaning and positive.[1] But whichever she portrayed, these spiritual, sociocultural, or multi-racial, groups crossed lines of class and gender to illustrate one of Butler's primary concerns: that the future does not necessarily mean progress unless a transformed and much more morally engaged citizenry makes it so.[2] All of Butler's intentional communities contributed to her overall project: narratives that prod readers to engage the often painful present and imagine a more moral, egalitarian, and productive relation to the future.

Jim Miller and others place Butler's work squarely within the tradition of "contemporary utopian/dystopian postmodern science-fiction

narratives" (1998, 337).[3] Miller notes that such narratives are "profoundly intertextual," operating at literary "intersections" that cross genres to
present alternatives that "force us to confront the dystopian elements of
postmodern culture so that we can work through them and begin again"
(337). I argue that in addition to their intertextual work on a literary
level, Butler's novels function on an "extratextual" level outside of the
works themselves. As parables of the need for renewed moral enterprise,
they have already struck a chord with a tiny but growing assortment of
readers throughout the US who are activists in real, lived society.

We may say that Butler's Parable duology is in conversation with
three kinds of audiences. First, with her general audience, one that is
content to consume her works primarily for entertainment or personal
edification. Second, as noted, she is just starting to make inroads with a
new generation of activist readers. These concerned citizens in nascent
groups are starting to use her Earthseed philosophy as a call to arms to
make change in lived reality. Third, for twenty five years, cultural critics
have been studying Butler's sociocultural thematics for the subterranean
message of social change in her work. As Miller posits, "Butler's fictions
are…a site of extremely important political activity [and]…an imaginative site of experimentation where new notions of identity and community are under construction" (338).

Examples of new "communities under construction" inspired by Butler can be found on the Internet: on low-budget individual websites that
periodically appear and disappear, in newly minted Internet chat groups
and occasional blogs, on listservs, in small book clubs and reading groups,
workshops, conferences, and retreats.[4] The assortment of fledgling intentional communities that count Butler as one of, if not their major
inspiration, is small and very loose at this time. One recently developed
online intentional community is devoted to Butler and others in "black
science fiction."[5] The website is called The Invisible Universe: A History
of Blackness in Speculative Fiction. Its creator, M. Asli Dukan, has also
created The Invisible Universe Foundation, which is producing a docu-
mentary about "the relationship between the Black body and popular
fantasy, horror and science fiction literature and film."[6] Dukan's 2007
online tribute to the late Butler reads in part: "Octavia Estelle Butler
was really more than a science fiction writer. She was a soothsayer, a wise
woman and a sage.… She is now one of our ancestors."[7]

Another intentional community, the SolSeed Movement, is a completely Butler-inspired online alliance.[8] It takes its name from her Earthseed philosophy, developed in the Parable novels. The embryonic SolSeed group defines itself as "working out what it means to live our shared truth, beauty, and values" (Sanders, Telephone Interview). Composed of a tiny eclectic group of primarily youthful adherents, SolSeed is concerned with ontological and epistemological as well as communal issues. The members ask questions such as "What gives life to the communities you care about? How can we notice this life-giving in our daily lives and create the conditions for more of that to happen?" (Telephone interview). SolSeed's founder, Brandon C.S. Sanders, is a computer programmer who lives in Portland, Oregon, with his wife and family. He describes the core group as "very small, just ten members and growing slowly" (Telephone interview).

Sanders is not a person of color nor from a traditionally marginalized group. He was "attracted by Butler's Earthseed books and their message of peace" (Telephone interview). He continues, "some books seem to help us connect with our humanity and inspire us to do something we didn't think we could do before. I'm profoundly grateful to Octavia Butler for opening the possibility that I could find the people who would work with me to do what I want to do.... I started out to mold SolSeed as a religion like Earthseed but that didn't allow me to talk with my family members, who already have a religion." (Sanders' wife and parents became his first SolSeed adherents.) "Now we call SolSeed a 'movement.' The word allows us to talk about human values and how to work for a better world, even though we have different values about 'God' and where we go from here" (Telephone interview).

Following the lead of the Parable novels, Sanders also urges his group to consider the Earthseed Destiny "to take root amongst the stars" (*Talents* 325). Like Butler, Sanders argues, "we need something to collect around that transcends some of the minor squabbles we tend to have as people. If we want to become the kind of people who can spread life throughout the galaxy, we have to become powerful enough to make a positive contribution to society right now" (Telephone interview). SolSeed's first retreat took place in January 2009 on Mt. Hood in Oregon, just one state above the northern California region where in *Sower*, Acorn develops as the first Earthseed commune of a dozen fictional characters. Eighteen people attended the fledgling SolSeed enclave.[9]

Theorists as well as activists have called for thought-experiments like Butler's to help conceptualize new, mutually empowering forms of social interaction and to reconceptualize currently divisive notions such as race, class, and gender. In *Methodologies of the Oppressed*, Chela Sandoval urges "a redefined 'decolonizing theory and method' that can better prepare us for a radical turn during the new millennium, when the utopian dreams inherent in an internationalist, egalitarian, non-oppressive, socialist-feminist democracy can take their place in the real" (5). Butler's tough, no-nonsense futuristic fiction does just that. In her Parable novels in particular, she attempts to visualize what it would take to move a frightened, apathetic citizenry towards a more egalitarian, non-oppressive future.

The Parable Novels

As Butler suggests in the Parable works, moral reform is rarely straightforward. If that were so, we would not have the kind of failed future she projects. *Parable of the Sower* and *Parable of the Talents* describe the US in the mid- to late-twenty-first century, which, after generations of seeming prosperity, is at the brink of moral and economic bankruptcy. The future generation in these works must pay the price for its predecessors' excesses. Against this existential and economic backdrop of indefatigable commodification, the dystopian Parable novels provide a discursive formula with which to examine the challenge of formerly middle-class citizens to refashion themselves as more moral agents. Butler opens *Parable of the Sower* with a mixed race group who have been forced to rig up walls around their formerly middle-class neighborhood of Robledo in order to escape from the increasingly predatory and homeless outside world (what Mike Davis characterizes in *City of Quartz* as "Fortress L. A." [221]). The neighbors are completely unprepared for basic survival in the grim future U.S. Butler portrays.

To deal with the rapidly disintegrating economic situation and environmental meltdown, Butler creates a stalwart female protagonist, Lauren Olamina, who develops an alternative community, first—in *Sower*—just to survive and later, in *Talents*, to make change in society. Butler uses the vehicle of Earthseed, a new religion, to convince the adherents in the texts, and by extension, her readers outside of them, that they really can make productive inroads in the midst of dystopian destruction. In an interview, Butler comments on recreating community in new mutually empowering ways: "Lauren uses religion as a tool.... I had in mind how certain historical populations have used religion to focus a group toward long-term goals—such as building cathedrals or pyramids. I wanted Lauren to envision, but then also to focus the Earthseed group toward, the goal of changing human attitudes about and treatment of the Earth and of each other. And a big part of that vision was to formulate not a *national* government but, instead, *multiple* communities, self-governing and -supporting, but also interactive with each other" (Mehaffy 62, 74-75).[10]

Butler's main character Olamina builds motivation within the text as her followers become inspired by the Earthseed parables' call to action. At the same time, some of Butler's activist readers outside the text are also being motivated. In fact, Butler's careful exposition of the Earthseed vision may be one reason why the concept seems to be gaining some small degree of traction among real-world activist readers. At times, the Earthseed aphorisms operate almost like a training manual for social change:

> Embrace diversity.
> Unite—
> Or be divided,
> robbed,
> ruled,
> killed
> By those who see you as prey.
> Embrace diversity
> Or be destroyed. (*Sower* 181)

By developing the *Earthseed Books of the Living* as a text within a text, Butler creates a double-layered didactic project.

The exhorting voice in the proverbs is that of the protagonist but also that of the author. Butler employs this kind of ventriloquism to maintain the Parable novels' delicate balance between overt and covert social theorizing. In so doing, readers can glimpse utopian flashes against the strong pull of the dystopian sociocultural, economic, and political downturn that the Parable novels forecast. They potentially become more invested in the idea of social change. General readers can imagine vicariously what it would be like to participate in an activist movement. And social activists in real intentional communities can potentially be further motivated by the novels' call to arms.[11] Almost as if Butler wanted to train actual activists, she puts her protagonist into situations drawn from a lived reality that community-organizing readers can relate to. Readers observe Olamina explaining her ideas to potential converts, working odd jobs to get enough money to formalize her ideas into an organization, and coaching new leaders. In this way Butler's work attempts, as Michelle Erica Green argues: "to bridge the gap between fictional discourse and everyday life" (1994, 169). Butler demonstrates to both general and activist audiences that tremendous undertakings start with ordinary people taking the smallest steps. She notes: "My characters typically don't get new powers. They stay human, and aliens don't come and give them new technology; magic doesn't suddenly work to get them out of their predicament" (McHenry and Fleming 1999, 18).

The population struggling to make change in Butler's Parable novels springs from an alienated citizenry that finds it harder and harder to survive in the false morality created by transnational capitalism.[12] Olamina's young brother Keith epitomizes youth turning to popular culture for validation and crafting value systems that mirror it. A 2008 CNN online article refers to a real young man who declared that not education nor religion, but *Star Trek* is "responsible for everything good in his life" ("John Cho" 2008).[13] Another online article from the BBC describes the kind of potential amoral future that Butler warns about. In this article, a real major game manufacturer announces research on microscopic computers that by 2033 may be injected into people's bloodstreams to induce a completely "lived" virtual experience (Waters 2008). As Butler argues via her Parable novels, without ethical oversight, there is nothing to deter developments such as these, which might seem minor today, from becoming instruments of severe social dysfunction and even oppression tomorrow. With the intersection of science fiction and lived reality coming closer than ever before, the Parable novels remind us that ethics and morality are not isolated or monolithic constructs. They're part of a complex, constantly changing network of relationships that although difficult, indeed sometimes almost impossible to sustain, must be negotiated by those who wish to create societies able to surmount the limitations of difference and dysfunction.[14]

In Conversation with Intentional Communities

Not only do the Parable texts and the alternative communities within them communicate in a dynamic multi-layered fashion to armchair as well as activist readers, they are also in conversation with intentional communities, historical and contemporary, fictional and real, inside and outside of the works. In both Parable books, the main character's small intentional communities develop slowly, step by step, by necessity as the protagonist Olamina and her cohort attempt to make sense of and eventually master the deteriorating US society. As Olamina vows, "I must create not only a dedicated little group of followers, not only a collection of communities as I once imagined, but a movement, I must create a new fashion in faith" (*Talents* 297).

Intentional communities have existed in the US since its inception and can be found throughout the world today. Alternative intentional alliances and communities vary greatly in size, goals, and direction. Intentional "alliances" are groupings of people with a shared goal, while "communes" generally, although not always, refer to those who embrace some form of collective living space. Communal living is not always a prerequisite to their goal of "preserving a unique collective purpose" (Freisen 2004, 264). Butler contends, "we've forgotten that a nation is a community of communities. If we forget that, then we start tearing things apart that make the communities work" (McHenry 18). As Yaacov Oved asserts, "there was not a single decade in the history of the US in which no new commune has been founded" (1988, xiii). During periods of uncertainty (what could be considered dystopic periods in U.S. history), utopic intentional communities surfaced in America. They briefly flourished during the rise of the 1820s Second Great Awakening, the 1840s prior to the Civil War, the twentieth century after WWI and WWII, and in the midst of the anti-Vietnam era. A wide variety of such entities exist today, with estimates ranging from up to 3,000 alternative intentional communities around the world (Fisher 2000).

Early groups included Emerson's nineteenth-century Transcendentalists and their four-year experiment in utopian communal living at Brook Farm in Massachusetts. The Transcendentalists, inspired by Romanticism, believed that God and godlike qualities were immanent throughout nature. Although Emerson did not actually move to the farm and Thoreau only briefly tried the experiment on his own at Walden Pond, some Transcendentalists tried to live and work as close to nature as possible at Brook Farm, away from the materiality of their increasingly urbanized world. Contemporary intentional communities range from The Farm in Tennessee to controversial urban religious alliances like the Scientologists in Los Angeles. Internationally, Maria Montessori's educational philosophy resulted in the development of the Montessori school movement. In Japan, the large Yamagishi Association agricultural commune survives and thrives. Also in Japan, the US, and some 193 other countries, the Nichiren Buddhist Soka Gakkai organization (SGI) is an international religious and peace movement, and a United Nations Non-Governmental Organization (NGO) with an array of ongoing peace projects including the Soka School System. These are examples of localized visions that grew into extended intentional organizations. As Ruth Levitas notes: "The alternative space of the intentional community is not empty, but has rules, structures, constraints, expectations of its own, and it is the positive presence of these, rather than simply the absence of the usual ones, that enables change" (2003, 19). The Parable novels shed light on how seemingly marginalized groups such as these may gradually gain currency and eventually influence power dynamics.

The Parable novels also gesture to history and to the strong, charismatic women like Olamina who crossed racial and class barriers in their social and moral uplift endeavors as part of the nineteenth-century reform movement. The micro-communities these women created often remained tiny themselves, but inspired larger alliances later on. After her abolition efforts, Harriet Tubman cared for disadvantaged freedmen in her own New York home, which was paid for by sympathetic white former abolitionists. Still standing, it is now immortalized as the Harriet Tubman House and is still an inspiration to social activists. In Chicago, Jane Addams's Hull House is still a monument to the moral and intellectual education she attempted to provide for disadvantaged immigrants from various ethnicities.[15]

Butler's alternative Acorn and Earthseed communities remind readers of the kind of courageous challenge found in nineteenth century "vigilance" committees and mutual self-help groups among newly freed slaves, who, thanks to the Fugitive Slave Act of 1850, might be snatched back into captivity at any time. In the Parable novels, Butler demonstrates how easily her characters can be snatched into new variations on traditional slavery, as economic conditions deteriorate. This historical resonance reminds readers of the constant potential for dystopia in the present and the future. But within that dystopian impulse, Butler interweaves reminiscences of ways in which early activists interposed a utopian impetus to inspire them to fight on. This historical layer implicitly encourages contemporary activist readers with the hope that, although they too may be beset with problems, they may eventually prevail. As Tom Moylan notes, "Indeed, if read in the spirit of the powerful traditions of strategic separatism in African American or feminist political culture (positions that enable both a refuge and a place of recuperation for renewed action), the separatist agenda of Earthseed in *Talents*, at least in the iconic register, makes a gesture of utopian resistance to the actual world in which Butler and her contemporary readers live" (Moylan *Scraps* 2000, 239).

By silently alluding to such actual figures and the intentional communities and alliances they inspired, the Parable novels serve to break down potential fear of change current readers may have. Also by recalling other groups that seemed hopelessly utopian at one time but who persevered to accomplish a great goal, the texts indirectly motivate today's readers to take action in the extra-textual world of lived reality. One Earthseed epigraph in *Talents* speaks directly to this interconnected inspiration. It precedes the very chapter that candidly describes "life at Acorn" (the first Parable intentional community) warning that it involves "a lot of hard work" (*Talents* 169). The Earthseed proverbs attempt to encourage those in the text, and by extension in the extra-textual community, who would give up and flee: "We can,/Each of us,/Do the impossible/As Long [*sic*]as we can convince ourselves/That it has been done before" (*Talents* 169). By silently reminding readers of the pathbreaking work of previous actual intentional communities ranging from the Quakers who initiated antebellum abolitionism to the 1960s counterculture ecotopias that precipitated today's environmental movement, the novels spur readers to overcome existing divides of amorality and difference.

Butler "seeds" the Parable texts with this highly diverse array of tiny oblique references to past alternative organizations and events that serve as the hidden guideposts for these thought-provoking moments. Readers may embrace or reject this trans-genre conversation between "reconstructions of the past" and our imaginative efforts to "shape our present and future" (Baccolini 2003, 119). The Parable novels suggest that a US citizenry increasingly seduced by virtual reality instead of lived reality, and living in a society where education is becoming more costly and corporate, must continually be provoked to visualize cooperative alternatives or eventually lose the ability to imagine anything different from what we already have. Lucy Sargisson observes about utopian thought-experiments: "This may not be changing the world with dramatic and easily observable impact but is, I think, what's required for sustainable and enduring transformation. This is a pluralist utopianism, and it's a utopianism of process. It's empowering in the now and isn't dependent on escapism or distant wish fulfillment, and it takes the way that we think as an essential part of social change" (Levitas and Sargisson 2003, 18).[16]

Butler's embedded historicity and overtly multiracial project may also be compared with earlier traditions of literary and social activism such as the nineteenth century "homiletic and social gospel realism" whose sermon stories and novels were composed of motivational homilies (Jackson 2006, 641). These works inspired middle and upper-class readers of the day to actually go out and participate in social reform. The Parable novels are a contemporary extension of this "popular religious pedagogy" (641). The homiletic novels were largely the product of the Reverend Charles Sheldon who, in Kansas, would write "sermon stories" that were serialized, finally appearing in novel form, among them *Robert Hardy's Seven Days: A Dream and Its Consequences* in 1898. Rather than being pedantic treatises on moral obligation, these short, practical sermonettes were closer to dime novels in their emotional appeal. Chock full of poignant moments, they described everyday churchgoers grappling with right and wrong. Week after week, Sheldon's short episodic sermons kept congregants coming back to hear what was going to happen next. As Gregory Jackson observes, "these conversations not only explored moral options but also pragmatically defined the stakes for the world around them" (642). More importantly, the novels attempted to "foster social engagement" (642). That is, listeners and readers were not expected simply to sit non-responsively. Instead, in works such as the 1896 best-selling *In His Steps* (possibly the highest selling novel in the nineteenth century), Sheldon asked readers, "what would Jesus do?" (641).

Sheldon's readers were expected to take action in their own community, in the manner they thought Jesus would have. And many did. In 1892, members of Sheldon's church organized a kindergarten for poor African American children in Topeka. That act helped generate a social movement in Kansas that facilitated what would eventually become the amalgamated cases known as Brown v. the Board of Education. As Jackson notes, the "son of one of Sheldon's kindergarten students... [Charles Sheldon Scott] would litigate the initial stages of the antisegregation case":

> Sheldon's followers worked to integrate the black community with the white congregation. They intended such

interventions not just to act on a marginalized population but also to construct an alternative, shared social reality that transcended individuation, including social markers like race and gender. (653)

Like the homiletic and abolitionist "interactive pedagogies," Butler challenges her readers to take actual ethical action. First, she names the novels *Parable of the Sower* and *Parable of the Talents* to persuade readers to contemplate how they might sow seeds of change and use their own "talents" in the construction of a rehabilitated US moral structure. Second, each book chapter is headed by an epigraph that is one of the pithy Earthseed proverbs, many of which, as noted, are themselves direct calls to action:

Shape Chaos—
Shape God.
Act.

[...]

Seize Change.
Use it.
Adapt and grow." (*Talents* 22)

The Earthseed verses intervene frequently and directly in the novelistic action to lecture the Parable series' readerly as well as activist audiences. Through Olamina, Butler employs a thinly-veiled ventriloquism to spur readers into having a greater sense of community and commitment. On the authorial level, Butler notes in an interview how she set up the Parable texts to speak to her readers: "I have people [in the novels] who are saying... 'here are some verses that can help us think in a different way'" (Goodman, 2005). On the fictional level, Olamina speaks self-reflexively about this purposeful didacticism in the texts. She declares: "I've given them a belief system to help them deal with the world as it is and the world as it can be—as people like them can make it" (*Talents* 123). The double-voiced call to community by Butler/Olamina is also reflected on the fictional level by Olamina's daughter Asha Vere's observations. When Asha writes "she," she refers both to her fictional mother, Olamina, as well as, by extension, to Butler as the authorial "mother" of the Earthseed philosophy and community. Asha comments: "she paid attention to the wider world. Politics and war mattered very much…. My mother was always noticing and mentioning things like that. Sometimes she managed to work her observations into Earthseed verses" (*Talents* 80-81). Butler also uses her main character Olamina to illustrate a determined woman going out and finding her own audience and getting them to respond. Moreover, by having the original Earthseed group consist of Olamina and twelve followers like Jesus and his disciples, Butler further establishes Olamina as a Jesus-like activist/prophet. Olamina is the everyman/everywoman who, if he or she takes sufficient action, can become "spiritually muscularized" (Jackson 657) enough to "partner with God" (*Talents* 135): "Partner one another. Partner diverse communities. Partner life. Partner any world that is your home. Partner God. Only in partnership can we thrive, grow, Change" (ibid.).[17]

Olamina becomes a transcendent figure like Jesus as she crosses lines of race, class, and gender to organize her first small multiracial intentional community. She gathers her initial group of twelve converts and establishes the secluded community called Acorn. In order to highlight Earthseed's initial mistake of trying to hide from society, Butler has Acorn raided and destroyed by marauders. Olamina must then set out to find her kidnapped daughter. But as her sense of mission grows, the search becomes more of a socio-spiritual quest to share her Earthseed religious philosophy with the world and to create a larger alternative community that can change society. Her daughter later observes: "She began to think less about Acorn and more about Earthseed—about spreading Earthseed to whole groups of new people. She wrote more than once in her journal that she hoped to use missionaries to make conversions in nearby cities and towns and to build whole new Earthseed communities" (*Talents* 170).

Furthermore, by pitting the Earthseed community against a large, extremely hierarchical and dominating organization called Christian America in *Talents*, Butler also provides a crucial reminder of the danger of an altruistic venture possibly becoming too authoritarian. Earthseed is put forth as a counter-example of less authoritarian spiritual reform. For instance, the Earthseed discussions called Gatherings suggest a somewhat egalitarian discursive structure, even though Olamina remains firmly in control. And later, after Earthseed becomes a large organization, her leadership position is reified by the title Shaper. It is not clear whether readers should critique the growing deference as the organization grows in size, or note it as a literary warning that a certain amount of hierarchy may inevitability be part of even the most open-minded intentional enterprise.

Butler's seed metaphor, as in the names Acorn and Earthseed, also recalls the figure of Johnny Appleseed, another early egalitarian social activist who would regularly forego luxury to walk among the poor and proselytize. John Chapman, as he was really known, was an itinerant and early activist who helped initiate the conservation movement. While his efforts have largely been trivialized in popular culture, Chapman actually started a series of tree nurseries across the country, using the slim proceeds to help the poor and spread the Swedenborgian religious philosophy. Its precepts of direct heavenly contact without the necessity of priestly intervention bring to mind Transcendentalism and Olamina's Earthseed proverbs that promote a direct, mutually interactive relationship with God: "We will shape God/And God will shape us/Again, Always again/Forevermore" (*Talents* 60).

Olamina's journey on foot, scattering her Earthseed message, parallels that of John Chapman and his appleseed mission. Olamina describes it thusly: "We are a beginning…one small seed" (*Talents* 177). Although formerly a member of the middle-class, Olamina, temporarily homeless, works odd jobs, sleeps in backyard sheds, and sketches portraits to survive. However, as mentioned, she turns the survival mechanism into a mission by both proselytizing for Earthseed and searching for her lost daughter. The text's depiction of her willingness to put social action with or even before the search for her own flesh and blood resonates with John Chapman's often altruistic roving missionary work and the eventual intentional communities centered on environmentalism that continue to grow in today's world.

One of Olamina's early converts is the daughter of a wealthy woman who, unable to cope with societal deterioration, spends all of her time in a "virtual room" in her mansion. The daughter, Len, has turned to drugs and is headed for suicide. Olamina encourages her convert to take moral action. In an act of double-troping, the character of Len is a stand-in for Butler's readers. Thus Butler/Olamina rehabilitates Len/ readers by providing a sense of mission regarding the Earthseed moral enterprise. Thus the line, "We'll be the ones to plant the first seeds, you and I" (*Talents* 364) can be read as an invocation both to the fictional character, Len, and to Butler's readerly and activist audiences.

Therefore, when Len agrees to participate in the moral mission to develop Earthseed, readers figuratively embark with her. General readers can imaginatively climb into Len's skin and activist readers can try things out in the real world. Through Len, Butler creates accessible examples of what it means to put oneself out to make change. Len temporarily foregoes class privilege to do odd jobs and garden work with Olamina. The text implies that as Len gives herself over to the moral endeavor, in spite of her temporary discomfort, an emotional healing takes place. The further implication is that if readers also try it, they too may be healed. Within the textual framework, Olamina notes how Len changes, in spite of what she perceives as demeaning labor: "she seemed interested in what she was doing and content to be doing it, although she complained about...the way the damp earth smelled, about getting dirty" (*Talents* 365). Thus the missionary work that Len performs is a double act of healing: reaching across class to potentially save others, while at the same time, saving herself. *Talents* effectively mimics the homiletic and abolitionist technique by calling upon contemporary readers to take up the call.

Talents also reminds readers that the process of self-challenge and self-development, painful though it may be, is the primary way thoughtful Americans have often pushed themselves to make change in preceding generations. Len's reluctance to get dirty symbolizes the challenge faced by early Transcendentalists like Nathaniel Hawthorne. Hawthorne managed to last just a month at Brook Farm doing hard manual labor before giving up on the site that was intended to actualize the Transcendentalists' Kantian unity with nature and provide an alternative to an amoral, incipient nineteenth century market-driven economy. The double-voiced Butler/Olamina warns her readerly and activist audiences of the moral as well as physical fortitude needed to forego financial incentives to counter market forces and organize alternative communities: "[A]s far as money is concerned, it's potentially so profitless, that it'll take all the strong religious faith we human beings can muster to make it happen" (*Talents* 181).

Olamina's quest to create an intentional community without thought of personal profit or societal position, like many abolitionists' and other early redemptive activists' historical efforts to do the same, further reminds us that narratives of morality must compete with the narratives of those in power who continually need to justify their position. For

example, when *Uncle Tom's Cabin* appeared in 1852, its readers were appalled by Simon Legree's justification for his oppression. Such revulsion
incited some of the morally apathetic populace to work for the abolitionist movement. We note how in *Talents*, the character Andrew Steele Jar-
ret has the potential to perform a similar mobilizing function as Legree.

The *Parable* novels further call attention to the tension between empowering and disempowering narrative voices as the books echo and extend the conversation regarding moral imperatives into the future. The
texts also highlight how much of the contemporary American populace
is unaware of the extent to which their moral decisions, both individual
and collective, are conditioned by narrative orchestrated by global corporate media: "Beware:/All too often,/We say/What we hear others say./
We think what we're told that we think.... To hear and to see/Even an
obvious lie/Again/And again and again/May be to say it,/Almost by re-
flex/then to defend it/Because we've said it" (*Talents* 307). As such, the
Parable novels participate in an international moral conversation that has
both historical and contemporary dimensions.

Parable Novels in International Moral Conversation

The year 2032 figures prominently in *Parable of the Talents*. Exactly
a century before, in 1932, an international figure started a revolutionary
intentional community composed of poor people who "voted with their
feet," walking hundreds of miles to create unprecedented social change
in their own country. That person was Mohandas Gandhi. Since Gandhi
also inspired a later generation of social activists like Martin Luther King
Jr. in the US, we may note the Parable novels' thematic debt to Gandhi's
legacy of change in a broad sense. In 1932, Gandhi embarked on the first
of his historic hunger strikes in a messianic effort to create a new moral
climate in India and relieve the Indian people from the debilitating suffering that was the hallmark of their existence under British colonialism.
Gandhi personally established an alternative intentional community (an
ashram) in India's most afflicted area where the so-called untouchables
lived. To signal his departure from the previously normative practice of
ostracizing them, he renamed the untouchables *Harijans*, "children of
God." The ashram he developed was a socio-spiritual alternative community made up largely of non-elite villagers, its adherents gathered with
a combination of moral, political, and economic determinations.

Like Gandhi's ashram of social outcasts, Olamina's first Earthseed commune, Acorn, shares a similar discredited early reputation. She notes how they are described in society: "And we are Earthseed…those crazy fools who pray to some kind of god of change" (*Talents* 20). Even Olamina's husband Bankole questions the Earthseed enterprise, as Gandhi's ashram was first criticized. But like Gandhi, Olamina does not lose hope in her undertaking: "New belief systems have been introduced. But there's no standard way of introducing them—no way can be depended on to work. What I'm trying to do is, I'm afraid, a crazy, difficult, dangerous undertaking. Best to talk about it only a little bit at a time (*Talents* 71-72). Butler's characterization is in keeping with the overall challenge of creating alternative institutions. As Tom Moylan observes: "Butler's willingness to explore the empowering force of a spiritually motivated but materially transcendent vision that is rooted in difficulty and difference allows her to posit a politicizing process that produces a vulnerable but viable utopian alternative by the end of the first book in the series" (Moylan 2000, 237).

The Parable novels engage the mutually constitutive relationship between economy and morality (or lack of it) as Butler traces the sociocultural consequences of the US as a dwindling economic and political power in the world. The novels provide a context within which to contemplate the potential repercussions of this increasingly globalizing tendency to subordinate moral concerns to market and political considerations. Thus as the Parable texts imply, socially-conscious intentional alliances and communities must constantly be on guard against encroachment by capitalism that, as we have seen in the past, is ever willing to co-opt their endeavors and try to transform them into profit-making projects. As Brandon Sanders noted earlier about his SolSeed movement, they want to talk about "human values and how to work for a better world" (Telephone interview).

At this time, Butler's activist audience may have been a miniscule portion of her general readership. But it appears as if the Parable novels' energizing socio-spiritual thematics may have begun to stimulate fresh visions of a potential moral renaissance in the US. If the tiny SolSeed Movement, Invisible Universe, and AfroFuturism websites, and other blogs, reading groups, and individual webpages are able to remain alive and active long enough, they may succeed in carrying out the humanistic principles of Earthseed and other egalitarian philosophies like it. As with Olamina's cherished Earthseed Destiny, they may spawn still more intentional alliances and communities until a critical mass, armed with hopeful visions of a new ethics, alters the moral landscape of the US and perhaps the world.

Works Cited

African American Literature Book Club. 2007. 28 November 2008. http://aalbc.com/authors/Octavia.htm.

AfroFuturism. 2003. 28 November 2008. http://www.afrofuturism.net/.

Baccolini, Raffaella. 2004. "The Persistence of Hope in Dystopian Science Fiction." *PMLA*. 119: 518-521.

Baccolini, Raffaella and Tom Moylan, eds. 2003. *Dark Horizons: Science Fiction and the Dystopian Imagination*. New York: Routledge.

Barr, Marleen. 2008. *Afro-Future Females: Black Writers Chart Science Fiction's Newest New- Wave Trajectory*. Columbus, OH: Ohio State University Press.

Barthes, Roland. 1985. *S/Z*. 1974. Trans. Richard Miller. New York: Hill and Wang.

Butler, Octavia. 2005. *Bloodchild*. New York: Seven Stories Press.

——. 1987. *Dawn: Xenogenesis*. New York: Warner Books.

——. 1993. *Parable of the Sower*. New York: Four Walls Eight Windows.

——. 2000. *Parable of the Talents*. New York: Warner Books. Seven Stories Press (1998).

——. 1976. *Patternmaster*. Garden City, NY: Doubleday.

——. 1980. *Wild Seed*. Garden City, NY: Doubleday.

Carl Brandon Society. Ed. Science Fiction Writers Association (SFWA). 2007. 28 November 2008. www.sfwa.org/members/butler.

Davis, Mike. 1990. *City of Quartz: Excavating the Future in Los Angeles*. New York: Random House.

Diaz, Junot. 2007. *The Brief Wondrous Life of Oscar Wao*. New York: Riverhead Books.

Dubey, Madhu. 1999. "Folk and Urban Communities in African-American Women's Fiction: Octavia Butler's *Parable of the Sower*." *Studies in American Fiction*. 27.1: 103-124.

Earthseed Octavia Butler Club. 2007. 28 November 2008. http://groups.yahoo.com/group/earthseedoctaviabutlerclub/.

Fisher, Jim. "Intentional Communities." *NewsHour with Jim Lehrer*. PBS. 21 Dec. 2000. Transcript. *Online NewsHour*. 10 April 2008. http://www.pbs.org/newshour/essays/december00/communities_12-21.html.

Fiske, John. 1989. *Understanding Popular Culture*. Boston, MA: Unwin Hyman.

Freisen, John W. and Virginia Lyons. 2004. *The Palgrave Companion to North American Utopias*. New York: Palgrave McMillan.

Goodman, Amy. "Octavia Butler." *Democracy Now*. National Public Radio. New York. Friday, 11 November, 2005. Audio clip. 1 February 2008. http://www.democracynow.org/article.pl?sid=05/11/11/158201.

Green, Michelle Erica. 1994. "There Goes the Neighborhood': Octavia Butler's Demand for Diversity in Utopias." In *Utopian and Science Fiction by Women: Worlds of Difference*, edited by Jane L. Donawerth and Carol A. Kolmerten, 166-189. Syracuse, NY: Syracuse University Press.

The Invisible Universe. Ed. Asli Dukan. 2007. 28 November 2008. http://www.invisibleuniversedoc.com/.

Jackson, Gregory. 2006. "What Would Jesus Do?" Practical Christianity, Social Gospel Realism, and the Homiletic Novel." *PMLA*. 121: 641- 661.

"John Cho [In Upcoming Star Trek film] Has a Cult Following," *CNN/Associated Press*. 12 March 2008. 10 April 2008. http://www.cnn.com/2008/SHOWBIZ/Movies/03/12/john.cho.ap/index.html.

Levitas, Ruth and Lucy Sargisson. 2003. "Utopia in Dark Times: Optimism/Pessimism and Utopia/Dystopia." In *Dark Horizons: Science Fiction and the Dystopian Imagination* edited by Raffaella Baccolini and Tom Moylan, 13-27. New York: Routledge.

Mark/Space Interplanetary Review. 2007. 28 November 2008. http://www.euro.net/mark-space/OctaviaButler.html.

McHenry, Susan and Mali Michelle Fleming. 1999. "Octavia's Mind Trip into the Near Future." *Black Issues Book Review.* 1.1: 14-18.

Mehaffy, Marilyn and AnaLouise Keating. 2001. "Radio Imagination": Octavia Butler on the Poetics of Narrative Embodiment." *MELUS.* 26.1: 45-76.

Miller, Jim. 1998. "Post-Apocalyptic Hoping: Octavia Butler's Dystopian/Utopian Vision." *Science Fiction Studies.* 25.2: 336-360.

Moylan, Tom. V. *Scraps of the Untainted Sky: Science Fiction, Utopia, Dystopia.* Boulder, CO: Westview Press.

Octavia Estelle Butler: An Unofficial Web Page. Ed. Sela Young. 2007. 28 November 2008. http://www.geocities.com/sela_towanda/.

OctaviaButler.net: A Fan Blog for Octavia E. Butler, writer. 2007. 28 November 2008. http://octaviabutler.net/contact.

Oved, Yaacov. 1988. *Two Hundred Years of American Communes.* New Brunswick, NJ: Transaction Books.

Rodriguez, Ralph. 2005. *Brown Gumshoes: Detective Fiction and the Search for Chicana/o Identity.* Austin, TX: University of Texas Press.

Sanders, Brandon C.S. (SolSeed founder.) Telephone interview. 26 Nov. 2008.

———. Email to Lisbeth Gant-Britton. 27 January 2009.

Sandoval, Chela. 2000. *Methodology of the Oppressed.* Minneapolis, MN: University of Minneapolis Press.

Science Fiction Writers Association (SFWA). 2003. 28 November 2008. www.sfwa.org/members/butler.

Sheldon, Charles. 1896. *In His Steps.* Chicago, IL: Advance. Nashville, TN: Broadman Press, 1983.

———. 1899. *Robert Hardy's Seven Days: A Dream and Its Consequences.* Chicago, IL: Advance.

SolSeed Movement. 2007. 28 November 208. http://solseed.org.

Stowe, Harriet Beecher. 1852. *Uncle Tom's Cabin*. London: J. Cassell.

Unofficial Octavia Butler Webpage. Ed. Kelly Bengier (Clemson University). 2007. 28 November 2008. http://hubcap.clemson.edu/~sparks/Octav2.html.

Tribute to Octavia Butler's novel YouTube. Ed. saraann28. 2007. 28 November 2008. http://www.youtube.com/watch?v=-TNgWpB3ttg.

Waters, Darren. "Virtuality and reality to merge." *BBC News website*. 2 Feb. 2008. 10 April 2008. http://news.bbc.co.uk/2/hi/technology/7258105.stm.

Endnotes

1 As part of her overall literary project, Butler has alluded to both the contributions and flaws of a range of possible alternative groups and entities that date back from the ancient past to a distant imagined future (*Wild Seed*). See also her Patternmaster series, as well as *Dawn* in her Xenogenesis trilogy.

2 My thanks to Wendy Belcher, Juanita Heredia, Rebecca Holden, and our readers for commenting on this essay.

3 For further discussions of Butler's placement within a "contemporary utopian/dystopian" narrative tradition, see Baccolini Moylan, *Dark Horizons;* Moylan, *Scraps;* Jerry Phillips, "Utopia and Catastrophe in Octavia Butler's *Parable of the Sower*," *NOVEL: A Forum on Fiction*, 35.2-3 (2002): 299-11, Hoda M. Zaki, "Utopia, Dystopia, and Ideology in the Science Fiction of Octavia Butler," *Science Fiction Studies*. 17.2 (1990): 239-251.

4 As of December 2008, these entities included the following: (1) **Book Clubs**: African American Literature Book Club, http:// aalbc.com/authors/Octavia.htm; (2) **Individual Unofficial Butler Webpages/blogs:** Kelly Bengier (Clemson University), Unofficial Octavia Butler webpage, http://hubcap.clemson.edu/~sparks/Octav2.html; Asli Dukan, The Invisible Universe (largest website to date and most organized), Sela Young, Octavia Estelle Butler: An Unofficial Web Page, http://www.geocities.com/sela_towanda/; OctaviaButler.net: A Fan Blog for Octavia E. Butler, writer, http://octaviabutler.net/contact; Mark/Space Interplanetary Review (British) http://www.euro.net/mark-space/OctaviaButler.html; (3) **Organization Webpages**: AfroFuturism, http://www.afrofuturism.net/; Science Fiction Writers Association (SFWA), including the Carl Brandon Society, www.sfwa.org/members/butler; (4) **Earthseed-Inspired Groups/Clubs/Websites:** Earthseed Octavia Butler Club, http://groups.yahoo.

com/group/earthseedoctaviabutlerclub/; SolSeed (largest website to date and most organized), http://solseed.org; (5) **Video Webpages:** YouTube, saraann28, Tribute to Octavia Butler's novel. Even Junot Diaz in his novel *The Brief and Wondrous Life of Oscar Wao* (which won the Pulitzer Prize in 2007) refers to Butler's fiction and other science fiction as one of his major subthemes.

5   AfroFuturism includes some "black" science fiction but also includes film, music, comics, and art, as well as literature. See the website located (as of this printing) at: www.AfroFuturism.net.

6   The Invisible Universe website: http://www.invisibleuniversedoc.com/. Numerous other online tributes remain posted. The largest and perhaps most serious tribute comes from the Carl Brandon Society of the Science Fiction Writers Association (SFWA), which now hosts a scholarship to the Clarion Science Fiction Writers Workshop in Butler's name. In 2008, Shweta Narayan (at Clarion) and Christopher Caldwell (at Clarion West) were presented with mementoes about Butler, as well as the first two Octavia E. Butler Memorial Scholarships. Caldwell noted, "Octavia inspired me to write science fiction… I applied to Clarion West because she wrote so highly of the experience in her book *Bloodchild*. I'm thrilled and honored. This means so much to me."

7   Another 2007 contributor to Dukan's Invisible Universe website added: "I am sad to hear that she [Butler] is no longer alive, but her books are alive to me." Patti from Vancouver, Canada. http://www.invisibleuniversedoc.com/.

8   The SolSeed Movement website is located at (http://www.aboutus.org/ SolSeedMovement). SolSeed declares themselves to be, "a practical philosophy, a praxis, a way of being in community with the body of all life. We are a coalition of diverse people brought together by the core values that we all share."

9   The event took place from January 9 through 11, 2009, at Falcons Crest Lodge on Mount Hood. According to Sanders, "Our rituals included opening each day with a ceremony during which we lit our chalice then performed a call and response version of the SolSeed Creed." (Sanders, Email).

10   Madhu Dubey meditates on the difficulty of actually creating new "models of community" that avoid simple attempts to replicate earlier agrarian "organic communities," instead taking on a "truly alternative social vision" (113).

11   To achieve her double-focused project that is both a critique of American morality and an encouragement to develop it more, Butler shows us hints of

utopian possibility ("a space of contestation and opposition") within otherwise completely dystopian texts (Baccolini and Moylan, *Dark Horizons* 7).

12 I am thinking here of Ralph Rodriguez' reference in his chapter on "Rolando Hinojosa's KCDT Series" in *Brown Gumshoes*, 15-17. Rodriguez notes that late capitalism "flattens out social relations," thus paving the way for amoral conditions under which citizens will do anything for money.

13 See also: Dave Reddick's "The Trek Life" on the webpage: StarTrek.com. http://www.startrek.com/startrek/view/index.html.

14 Butler did not get to complete her project of social critique before her untimely death. She had originally planned to write up to four more sequels in the Parable series. The next book was to have been called *Parable of the Trickster*. However, she said she had trouble completing it. I had dinner with Butler after we both spoke at USC in Los Angeles to celebrate the twenty-fifth anniversary of *Kindred*'s publication (February 19, 2004). At that time, she mentioned that she was battling an unspecified illness, and that unfortunately, it was hard for her to concentrate on her writing. She said she had shifted to the easier topic of vampires. Her final novel, *Fledgling*, is about an alternative community of vampires, but it lacks the critical dystopic and futuristic insight of previous works like the Patternmaster series that used superhuman figures as tropes of domination.

15 By calling attention to their discourse, I do not intend to imply that these intentional entities (some very large, others miniscule) are by any means all the same. I do call attention to one common feature, however, and that is, they share some kind of utopian vision of change, however small or specialized it may be. It is this quest to carve out even the smallest collaborative utopic space within elements of an increasingly contentious and competitive US society that Butler's work both celebrates and critiques.

16 Levitas's and Sargisson's co-authored chapter is written in epistolary form.

17 To signal that Butler does not mean to place Olamina or her Earthseed religion solely within a Christian tradition, Butler reminds readers that the main character's middle name "Oya" is derived from a West African Yoruba goddess (*Talents* 48).

The Third Parable[1]

Nisi Shawl

I loved Octavia. And I lied to her.

The lies themselves weren't all bad. And most of what I told her was true, of course. But those lies bother me, because Octavia prized honesty. It was, for her, a writer's essential tool.

In her books as in her life, Octavia never flinched from bringing up unpleasant realities: the ones that were, and the ones that were to be. As the situation of the world around her worsened she continued to portray it and project possible futures from it, no matter how grim the pictures thus created. Written in the '90s, *Parable of the Sower* and *Parable of the Talents* contain some of the most harrowing scenes of a near-future apocalypse and its aftermath that speculative fiction has ever produced. Her last book, 2005's *Fledgling* (which she saw as escapist fantasy), is as stark as any of her work in its portrayal of pain and loss and the flawed natures that so often lead to them.

In the ten-year gap between the publication dates of *Fledgling* and her second *Parable* book, Octavia attempted a third *Parable* book. It was to be called *Parable of the Trickster*. I want to share with you some elliptical thoughts on that unwritten book. Bear with me; the Trickster's way is a twisty one, though transcendental in the end.

I first met Octavia at a 1999 science fiction convention where she was Guest of Honor: Foolscap I. The convention took place in Tukwila, Washington. I had been living in nearby Seattle since 1994, and through various connections was known to the convention's organizers as a black female writer of science fiction. I'm sure that was why they asked me to contribute an essay about Octavia to their program.

At that time, the only fiction of Octavia's I was aware of having read was *Survivor*. Those of you with any knowledge of Octavia's oeuvre will recognize that as the title of her least favorite novel, the book she begged her publishers never to reprint. It's not awful, but it's not up to the standards Octavia usually held herself to, and it didn't, frankly, do all that much for me, either. (Footnote: I later asked Octavia to autograph my copy; she inscribed it, "Nisi, I wish you didn't have this one.") Nonetheless, I knew that the name "Octavia E. Butler" was well-respected inside and outside the field. There had to be *some* reason. I told the convention program's editor I'd be honored to contribute an essay, that writing about Octavia would be a wonderful experience for anyone. Then I read the rest of her work to figure out why.

I completed my assignment for the Foolscap I program by writing "Daughter of Necessity." It's very short. It begins by asking the reader to imagine Octavia inventing herself, goes on to briefly cover the historical facts of her genesis—her birth, upbringing, and influences—and concludes with a series of quick synopses of her work.

I went to the convention and met Octavia. I looked up at her and said the first thing that popped into my head: "Oh! You're *much* more beautiful than your pictures!"

Octavia was famously a modest woman; she rode the bus and publicly downplayed her considerable creative accomplishments. She never, in the time I knew her, seemed overwhelmed by her own good looks, but she must have recognized that I meant what I said, because she didn't treat me as a flatterer or sycophant. She invited me to sit with her in the hotel lobby and "have a chat," as she put it.

She *was* beautiful, physically compelling in an entirely unconventional way. I'm so glad I was moved by the Spirit of the Trickster to come right out and say so.

And what do I mean by "Spirit of the Trickster?"

Though in the *Parable* books she wrote with accomplished verisimilitude about the birth of "Earthseed," an imaginary religion, Octavia was not religious herself. I am. I practice a West African tradition called *Ifa*, closely related to Santeria and Vodun, to name two traditions that are better known. The Ifa pantheon includes *Exu*, one of many sacred Tricksters found in religions around the world. Exu likes candy and cigars and firecrackers and the number three. He rules surprises and epiphanies (such as my realization of Octavia's extreme beauty). Most of all he rules words and the tricks one can work with them, including telling stories. And lies.

Foolscap I took place June 11th through June 13th in 1999. Later that summer, Octavia returned to Seattle to teach for one week at the Clarion West Writers Workshop. She decided to move to Seattle. She bought a home in the Northern Seattle neighborhood of Lake City and invited me over for dinner.

Octavia was a vegetarian (I'm sure for ethical reasons). She offered me a bean casserole, if I remember correctly. I offered her a bunch of daffodils, and she revealed to me, ruefully, that a long-ago bout with the flu had robbed her of her sense of smell.

At the meal's end, Octavia administered a test I failed: she spread a piece of bread with a yellow, butter-like substance, gave it to me to eat, and asked me if it was good. I lied and said yes. It was horrible. Funky grease, that's what it was. I managed to chew and swallow one piece of this nastiness and politely refuse a second.

Octavia explained she was thinking of serving this margarine to future guests. I should have told her not to. As I later realized, having no sense of smell meant her sense of taste was impaired as well. She was relying on me to tell her how that margarine tasted, and I let her down. (I've since wondered if she served it to others, and if any of them had the guts to tell her to toss it down the garbage disposal.)

We were friends anyway. I went shopping with her for books and clothes, watched plays with her, ate at restaurants with her. Because I had no car or driver's license, I couldn't take her on expeditions to her beloved mountains or cart her around on errands. Tax cutbacks restricted bus service, so it was difficult to meet face to face sometimes. We talked a lot on the phone.

We talked about men and sex, about what we'd heard on NPR that morning, and of course about writing. Octavia was supportive of my writing, giving me advice and acting as a sounding board. I could tell her how hard I was trying to get a character to do something, and she'd understand what wasn't working and help me figure out why. She was unassuming enough to let me in on her own difficulties, allowing me to be supportive of her work in turn. But maybe not as supportive as I could have been.

Maybe I could have helped her a little bit with *Parable of the Trickster*, a book she never finished.

Parable of the Sower begins in a setting much like the one we North Americans live in now. It tells how one woman, Lauren Oya Olamina, prepares for the societal breakdown she sees as imminent, and follows her as she journeys to the site of the religious community she founds in response to that breakdown. *Parable of the Talents* continues Olamina's story, presenting it from the viewpoint of her estranged daughter. It covers Olamina's further tribulations and concludes with her death and the realization of her dream: the departure from Earth of a spaceship carrying human colonists.

At the end of each book there's an excerpt from the King James Bible giving the New Testament parable for which it was named.

In Christian lore, there is no Parable of the Trickster. That could well have been one of the many obstacles that kept Octavia from writing the third Parable book.

I've spoken with Dan Simon, her editor at Seven Stories Press, about what went on from his point of view. Dan edited the first two Parable books and says there was actually a contract for the third. According to Dan, Octavia tried several times to return the advance she'd gotten for this unwritten book. Dan would ask if it were basically dead, and she'd say no, it wasn't. "If it's something you still plan to write and still want to write," he'd tell her, "let's just wait."

Octavia herself blamed her lack of progress writing *Parable of the Trickster* on writers' block caused by blood pressure medicines. Having killed off her original heroine probably didn't help. And she was more and more discouraged by the current events her fiction was meant to reflect—9/11, the wars in Afghanistan and Iraq, the devastation of the rainforest, starvation, disease... I couldn't have done anything about those problems. But I could have told her Ifa's Trickster parable.

While Octavia was alive, I lived in a small apartment, and I invited her over on only one occasion. I asked her to attend a feast in honor of my ancestors. She accepted, which surprised me slightly, because I knew she counted herself a hearty skeptic when it came to religious matters. But in our conversations she had always been carefully respectful of my beliefs. During the ancestor feast she showed the same respect, reciting prayers and singing songs with me as the ceremony necessitated. I had asked my guests to bring flowers. She came bearing a potted pink rose (now planted outside the apartment building). I introduced her to my three Exus, statues consecrated to the Trickster's manifold aspects.

She was polite, but uninquisitive. And I didn't tell her the Yoruba teaching tale I'm going to share with you now. I've adapted it from oral tellings and from a written version compiled by a priest of the Ifa tradition (Fatunmbi 1994, 108-114):

There were two farmers who loved one another as brothers and shared in everything. The fields they cultivated lay side by side, with a footpath between them. Though they had been told to make offerings to the Spirit of the Trickster, these men saw no need to do so. They were sure that their knowledge and skill were all they needed to live well.

One day Exu himself came walking down the path. Recognizing the two farmers as men who had neglected to give him his due, Exu hid in the bushes and prepared to show them how wrong they had been. He painted one side of his face red and the other black. Then he emerged from the bushes and continued along the path.

After Exu had gone by, the farmers called out to one another, remarking on this stranger. "Did you see that man with the red face?" asked the first man. "You mean the man with the black face," said the second. "His face was black." The two could not agree on Exu's appearance, and began to quarrel about it, at last coming to blows. Their friendship and the prosperity of their farms were destroyed.

Each man was telling the truth as he saw it from his limited perspective. However, there was more going on than either of them saw. Both farmers made the same mistake: thinking that *a* truth is *the* truth, that they had no need for any knowledge beyond what they already possessed.

I didn't want to encumber Octavia with *a* truth that wasn't her own. Privately, I thought she might progress more quickly on her novel if she made an offering to Exu, but I couldn't see her doing that. So I said nothing.

Yet, one sort of lie is omitting to tell the truth. If not *the* truth, *a* truth. Any truth. The truth one knows.

There's a Yoruba proverb related to the parable above. If you want to compliment someone for her honesty you say: "She calls red 'red' and black 'black.'"

Octavia called red "red" and black "black." I didn't.

The parable's farmers came to grief not because they said what they saw, but because each insisted theirs was the one correct version. The solution to their dilemma did not lie in silence, though silence was my choice. At that time.

I heard of Octavia's death at Potlatch 15, a science fiction convention held in Seattle, on the morning of February 26, 2006. I still mourn her loss. I miss her laugh, and her voice, and her beauty. And I miss everything she was going to write, including that third Parable book.

And yet....

I have been asked by elders of my religion if I feel compelled to put on paper the stories Octavia left untold. They ask this question as if cautioning me against such an act, and my answer, truthfully, is no, I do not. Although I mourn for what might have been, I have no urge to approximate it. I have my own work, my own truth.

At the feminist science fiction convention WisCon held in May of 2007, I instigated and took part in a panel called "Genre Tokenism Today: The New Octavia." With four other African American women authors, I did my best to dispel the idea of Octavia E. Butler's life and career as a position some other black female could now be called upon to fill. We discussed tokenism, the differences between what we do and what she did, and the influences Octavia shed on us and the world at large.

Replacement is impossible. Influence is inevitable. Octavia's life and death have made it imperative for me to call red "red" and black "black."

Truth is important to me. An essential tool. It's not an absolute, though. Truth and truths change with time, with perspective, with knowledge. And so do lies. Sometimes lies become truths.

Back in 1999, when I accepted the assignment to write an essay for Foolscap I about Octavia, I spoke to the editor of the convention's program as if I admired Octavia's work much more than I actually believed I did. While researching the essay I read her short story "Bloodchild" and realized that what I was actually doing was *re-reading* it. Before, I hadn't held on to its author's name. I had only retained the impression of a bloody glory, an involved emotional landscape of intertwining needs hooked into the characters' guts in a way that twisted mine in sympathy. It was the work of a genius.

So my deep admiration for Octavia was no longer, has never been, a lie.

Is there a way to similarly redeem the parable I omitted to tell? A way to erase my silence? Perhaps in telling *this* truth, I have.

Endnote

1   A different version of this essay appeared in the program for Potlatch 16, held in Seattle, Washington February 28 through March 1, 2008. Thanks to Margaret Organ-Kean for providing me with a copy of the Foolscap I Convention Program.

Octavia stands among a few of Washington state's old-growth
forest giants.
❧ *Photo by Leslie Howle*

Part Four

New Media, New Generations,

and a New Take on Vampires:

Butler in the Twenty-First Century

butler8star@qwest.net

Nnedi Okorafor

I still keep Octavia's email address in my Outlook address book. I used to send emails to it even after she passed. How poetic would it have been if I'd gotten a reply from Octavia from the spirit world via email? The mix of the mystical and the technological would seem very much like her. Or maybe not; Octavia once told me that she didn't like using email.

Nevertheless, for a minute, she did use email. I don't recall how I got her email address, as I was not personally close to her. I may have had it after I'd interviewed her or maybe I got it after the first time I spoke with her on the phone when I was at Clarion (East) in 2000. I had it, and *of course* I used it. Octavia's email address was butler8star@qwest.net.

I kept our online exchanges like little treasures, and not only because they were emails from one of my favorite writers. It was also because of the time period within which the emails were exchanged. And the subject matter. It was right after September 11th. About a month. When there was little else on most Americans' minds.

I happened to have just read *Parable of the Sower* for the first time. This novel did *not* help with the panic I was feeling. It scared the hell out of me, solidifying my reasons to feel panicky, paranoid, and untrusting of anything the American government said or did. All I could think about was just how fast society broke down in *Parable of the Sower*. How real it was. Things fall apart.

The "war" in Afghanistan had just begun: the "war" where the richest and most powerful country in the world proceeded to bomb one of the poorest, most troubled parts of the world. Octavia and I were speculating about what would come next.

Subject: Re: CNN Questions for bin Laden
Date: Thu, 18 Oct 2001
From: butler8star@qwest.net
To: nokora1@uic.edu

I think Bush will declare victory, pin medals on a few people and try to put war in the past just as soon as he begins to suffer politically—which may be this winter if what I've heard about Afghan winters is true and if Bush really does send in ground troops.

Meanwhile, the bombs and bin Laden will have brought forth a whole new generation of much-deceived young men eager to die for Islam—or just eager to get revenge against the people who bombed their relatives.

Octavia

Subject: Re: CNN Questions for bin Laden
Date: Thu, 18 Oct 2001
From: nokora1@uic.edu
To: butler8star@qwest.net

Yeah, you're right. They are both maniacs and they seem to understand each other as if they were identical twins. However, I think hearing Osama bin Laden speak will be a benefit for the "people." I don't see this war as a war between "good" and "evil." I don't believe in that concept. I think it's a war of conditions, madness, and power.

This is off the subject but I hear that now the Taliban are teaching women how to fire guns. The same women that they wouldn't allow to move about without a male escort. Hypocrisy abounds.

Nnedi

Octavia was still seeing our president as smarter than he was. If President Bush had only done it the way she'd predicted. Nevertheless, Octavia was right about one thing, Osama bin Laden has received his legion of angry disgruntled maltreated followers.

In another email, we discussed some of the vibrations around the world caused by the September 11th attacks.

Subject: Re: CNN Questions for bin Laden
Date: Sun, 21 Oct 2001
From: nokora1@uic.edu
To: butler8star@qwest.net

Speaking of people who have been deceived, have you heard about what's happening in Nigeria? There has been tension between Christian and Muslims for decades there. But a few days ago the Hausas (who tend to be Muslim) went on a rampage and massacred Christians (mostly Igbos). They are saying all the killing was because of this jihad that's been called in the Middle East.

My family is still waiting to hear from some relatives we have in the city where all this took place. In a world where there has been such evolution in communication technology (at least in the "second" and "first" world), it's amazing how misinformed we still all are. I think the technology has only made it easier to manipulate and brainwash people.

Nnedi

Subject: Re: CNN Questions for bin Laden
Date: Sun, 21 Oct 2001
From: butler8star@qwest.net
To: nokora1@uic.edu

I'm so sorry to hear about this renewed trouble in Nigeria. I hadn't heard at all, and I pay attention to the news. I suppose a great deal is being ignored in favor of the "war." I hope your relatives are safe and well. One of my favorite quotes—so sadly true—is from Steve Biko: "The most potent weapon in the hands of the oppressor is the mind of the oppressed."

There is also the sad reality that it takes very little to set off young men who want to feel powerful and important, but who are either unwilling or unable to find constructive outlets for their energies. Testosterone poisoning. And men have the nerve to complain about women's hormonal mood swings.

Octavia

There are many things I loved about Octavia, but her unflinching political views remain my favorite. She had a way of maintaining them outside of politics. Many know the famous quote where Octavia describes herself as "a pessimist, a feminist always, a Black, a quiet egoist, a former Baptist, and an oil-and-water combination of ambition, laziness, insecurity, certainty, and drive." Each of these things is fundamental, not political. Like her writing, her statements were uncluttered, sparse, and always so so clear.

Years later, when I interviewed Octavia about her latest novel, *Fledgling*, for *Black Issues Book Reviews*, she said:

> I wanted to get away from the daily news, which was drearier and drearier and more and more awful each day. I'd read it and listen to it mainly on NPR. There isn't really much you can do about most of what's going on.
>
> You can support causes or shoot off your mouth but there really isn't a big difference you can make. With the most recent presidential elections, I was depressed for a long time; this was way before the hurricanes. I'd think about the war and watch as corruption became a more normal thing—so I wrote a vampire story.

I remember sputtering and stammering. I wanted so badly to assure Octavia that she *had* made an enormous difference in many lives. I recited to her all the ways in which her books and her existence had changed me. I told her that because of her I now knew that it was okay to write strange disturbing African characters. And that she changed the way I viewed gender and relationships. I stressed that she had shown me so many possibilities and variations in life. I wanted her to know that she had stretched my mind and it would never return to its former shape. Lastly, I told her that she had inspired, informed and energized legions of us. She just laughed and said that all this was encouraging.

On the night of September 11th, 2001, I wrote these paragraphs:

> The black pigeon with white speckles was an overachiever. She
> had the blood of the archaeopteryx from millions of years ago
> coursing through her veins. She'd taken one look at the tall
> skyscrapers and known she would nest close to the top.
>
> She sat on her eggs as she always did, gazing down at the world
> below. She cooed a sigh of contentment. Then something pricked
> her small mind. She knew she should fly but she did not. She
> had eggs. Babies. When she saw the giant metal bird careening
> toward her, she only stared, chanting a soothing mantra to her
> creator to do its will: Coo coo, coo, cooo cooo. Coo coo, coo, cooo
> cooo. It calmed her and she accepted her fate and became part of
> the blazing inferno of the World Trade Center.

That day, I had been thinking of that same powerlessness, the same
futility that Octavia would later articulate during my interview with her.
I sent the paragraphs above to Octavia September 11th, 2007, and asked
her what she thought. I was curious. But I'll never know, because for the
first time my email bounced back. Her address had been officially shut
down for good.

Though she's gone, Octavia left us with so much to chew on. This
is the beauty of the written word. It lives on when you are gone. It's as
close to immortal as you can get. The written word continues to have the
power to affect and change long after its creator has moved on.

> To survive,
> Know the past.
> Let it touch you.
> Then let
> The past
> Go.
>
> From "Earthseed: The Book of the Living," by Lauren Oya
> Olamina, *Parable of the Talents*

Exceeding the Human: Power and Vulnerability in Octavia Butler's Fiction

Steven Shaviro

The beginning is not a beginning, but a resumption: a return to life, and therefore to need, pain, and dependency. It has all happened before. Someone has been reborn. Yet this is not a fresh beginning, since that someone is haunted by all the things that he or she used to know, and used to do, and that he or she will have to learn—and suffer—all over again. Many of Octavia Butler's novels start this way:

> *Dawn*: "Alive! Still alive. Alive…again. Awakening was hard, as always. The ultimate disappointment. It was a struggle to take in enough air to drive off nightmare sensations of asphyxiation." (*Lilith's Brood* 5)[1]

> *Fledgling*: "I awoke to darkness. I was hungry—starving!—and I was in pain. There was nothing in my world but hunger and pain, no other people, no other time, no other feelings." (7)

At the beginning of *Dawn*, Lilith Iyapo awakens—in fact, goes through a whole series of Awakenings—only to find herself each time "confined…kept helpless, alone, and ignorant" (5). Being alive is literally a sort of captivity. There seems to be no possibility of communion, or companionship, or even simple communication, with whatever is keeping her captive. She cannot reach out and touch this smothering presence, from which, nonetheless, she is unable to extricate herself. There can be no dialog, and no true encounter, when one of the partners controls all the terms of the exchange.

Fledgling, similarly, begins with a narrator who cannot remember who or what she is; she doesn't even know her own name. She has language, but many of her words lack referents. She knows there are others, and therefore she feels alone, but she doesn't know who those others are. She is wounded, in great pain, but gradually she heals and finds that she knows how to do what she needs to do: hunt, kill, and feed. There is no blank slate, no pure origination; even as the narrator comes into the world afresh, entirely alone, and seemingly new, there are webs of meaning and obligation and history that surround and affect her—although she is ignorant of these things, and must discover them as if for the first time.

No wonder Butler described herself, in an Author's Note that appears in many of her volumes, as (among other things) "a pessimist if I'm not careful." These books begin with hunger, or asphyxiation, or a blind unidentified craving. They begin with amnesia and hurt, and they do not end with anything more than (at best) a tentative, slight modification of these conditions. In Butler's novels, being is not a plenitude; or better, the plenitude of being is not felt as an exuberance, not experienced as a power to act and to create. It is rather felt as an oppressive, crushing weight, like a burden from which one can never free oneself. And yet, at the heart of being, there is always also a sense of isolation, or exclusion, or separation.

Dawn, the first novel in the *Lilith's Brood* trilogy, is a book of catastrophe and encounter. Lilith Iyapo and a number of other human beings are the sole survivors of a war of nuclear annihilation that has ravaged the Earth. They have been rescued by an alien race, the Oankali, who have thus preserved the human species from extinction—at a price. For the Oankali have captured Lilith (and the other remnants of humanity, people like ourselves) because they want to trade genes with her (with them, with "us"), to mate with her (with them, with "us"). They didn't save humanity for nothing; like all merchants, they want to make an exchange and be fully paid for the services they have rendered. The Oankali's aim is to interbreed with us, in order to create a new, hybrid entity: an intelligent species that will "moderate [humanity's] hierarchical problems" and at the same time "lessen [the Oankali's] physical limitations," and will therefore be "better than either of us" (247).

Lilith only learns about this project gradually. At the beginning, she is a prisoner. From the very first, she demands answers, or an explanation. But she quickly learns that "her captors spoke when they were ready and not before," according to a timetable over which she has no control (7). They are the ones with the power to ask the questions. If Lilith were to refuse to give one of her captors the answer that it is looking for, "it would not speak to her again until she did what it wished" (12). Eventually, Lilith is released from solitary confinement. As she learns more about her situation, she is gradually granted greater degrees of freedom—or at least of movement, and of choice among alternatives. However, she is never really allowed to be an autonomous agent. Her freedom is a function of her dependency; it really only concerns the manner in which she will fulfill the demands that the Oankali place upon her.

There is a fatal logic at work here. Freedom and power, as Michel Foucault reminded us, are really two sides of the same coin. Absolute physical coercion is an extreme limit, one that is almost never reached in actuality. Total power over other people is nothing more (or less) than the power to kill them. If you want them, rather, to stay alive to do something—to work as your slaves, for instance, and to obey your orders—then you have to extort from them some minimal degree of consent. You have to accord them at least a tiny bit of freedom—enough that they agree to do what you want of them, rather than simply die. You have to instill in them a measure of complicity, which continues to exist alongside their continual acts of resistance. Such was the case with Nazism and Stalinism—and even with slavery in the antebellum American South. And such is also the case with the Oankali, in regard to Lilith and the other human beings whom they have rescued but also captured. *Dawn* is the story of Lilith's complicity, of the way that she unavoidably agrees, in spite of herself, to do the Oankali's bidding. It's always a matter, for Lilith, of "choosing" under conditions of extreme constraint, and of doing what her captors want of her, because the alternatives are even worse. At best, she is only capable of finding "a comfortable, mindless activity that gave her something to do when there was nothing she could do about her situation" (146).

This is a painfully ambivalent situation. For on the one hand, the Oankali's genetic project is a transhumanist dream: a vision of metamorphosis, of hybridity, of human improvement, of transition to something better. In *Dawn* as in many of her books Butler writes harshly about how humanity's hierarchical propensities—together with our frighteningly capacious pragmatic intelligence—create ever-more-powerful forms of destruction and oppression. Our lust for domination, so intelligently instrumentalized as it is, is the source of a long history of intolerance, xenophobia, genocide, enslavement, and other sorts of institutionalized cruelty. And this history is something that Butler never ceases to recall to us—whether in the vision of actual black slavery in nineteenth-century America (*Kindred*), or in that of a fundamentalist-Christian-imposed high-tech slavery in an all-too-likely twenty-first-century America (*Parable of the Talents*). Would it not be a good thing if the hierarchical violence that drives us could be modified, or alleviated, in some way? Isn't any sort of social hope, any progressive politics, motivated by the project of making of human life something more than a Hobbesian war of all against all?

Yet at the same time, the Oankali's project is, precisely, a form of eugenics and therefore of the very horrors that it is supposed to alleviate or abolish. It echoes some of the most hateful hierarchical projects of our own recent history, like Nazism and slavery in the American South—even if the Oankali are doing it out of entirely different motives. This enforced breeding project is a way of controlling our destiny—of making sure that we do not have any say in what happens to ourselves (and even more, to our children). It denies us basic autonomy. So, even if the result of the Oankali's project is something that we have dreamed of for so long, the means of accomplishing it amount to a violent negation of that dream—precisely because the agency is no longer ours. The dream has been stolen from us. We can only become "free" to the extent that we cease to exist as the beings we are, desiring freedom in the first place.

The result is an astonishing emotional deadlock that consumes the pages of *Dawn*. Lilith suffers the horror both of having to accommodate herself to her inhuman captors' desires, and of finding herself a victim of other human beings' murderous rage and resentment, since they see her as a collaborator with those captors. The genuinely shocking thing about *Dawn* is that it offers us a perspective (an inhuman one? an Oankali one? or simply a sufficiently objective one?) from which there is almost no way to distinguish between a group of brave humanist fighters making a last stand for freedom and a band of Ku Klux Klansmen orchestrating a lynching. The fellow human beings who wish to kill Lilith at one point are both of these. But the overwhelming fact of the matter, however we interpret it, is that there is no possibility of escape. The Oankali are simply too powerful to be stopped, not only from doing what they want to do to us, but even from coercing our consent to their demands. There is no way out: no possibility of either compromise or catharsis.

All of Butler's novels deal, as *Dawn* does, with issues of otherness, pain, and dependency, as well as, obviously, with race and gender, and racism and misogyny. But what can we make of the fact that such issues, which are largely existential, social, historical, and political, are nearly always portrayed by Butler in *biological* terms? The background for this must surely be the fact that biological reductionism and genetic determinism are in fact the predominant, hegemonic intellectual obfuscations of our age, used both to simplify issues of ethics and aesthetics into irrelevance, and to portray capitalism, racism, and gender inequality as "natural" and unalterable conditions. I think that Butler's recourse to the biological register—which provides the "science" for her novels, even though they do not fit into the category of "hard" science fiction—is precisely a response to this hegemony. If something like human beings' investment in hierarchy is ultimately genetically determined, then it is in fact quite intractable. Yet genetics is about mutation as well as preservation; Butler's biological references, from the genetic breeding programs in the Patternist novels, through the gene trading of *Dawn* and the other novels of the *Lilith's Brood* trilogy, and on to the genetic experimentation that forms the backdrop for *Fledgling*, all point to the ways that the biological realm is subject to revision and transformation as much as (or perhaps even more than) the social realm is. In a certain sense, therefore, biological changes in the worlds of Butler's fiction stand in for the social changes that occur in our actual world. And by figuring social dilemmas in biological terms, Butler in fact deconstructs the whole nature/culture binary and the way in which we misleadingly cast one of these as a realm of necessity (biology) in order to cast the other as a realm of freedom (culture). For Butler, social constraints are as oppressive as biological ones and conversely, biology is at least as mutable as is society.

Yet, at the same time that the biological power relationships in Butler's novels must be read as allegories of the social, or of gender oppression and racial oppression, I think that we also must take them quite *literally* as meditations upon human capacities and human limitations. These limitations are apparent when as human beings we are faced with ethical demands by others, as well as by forces of radical otherness, forces we cannot master and control. In all her books, Butler focuses on relationships between different groups, different species (often human and non-human), or even different orders of being. And these relationships generally take on the structure of the biological relationship between host and parasite. Think not just of the hybridization of human and Oankali genes in *Dawn* and its sequels, but also of the way that telepaths are in effect parasitic on "mutes" ("normal" human beings) in the Patternist novels, of the spreading parasitic infection that is the major focus of *Clay's*

Ark, of the way that human males serve as receptacles or wombs for the parasitic offspring of an alien species in the short story "Bloodchild," and of the ways that vampires prey upon human beings in *Fledgling.* These are all relationships in which both parties are dependent upon one another, even though they have different identities and different interests. They are also all relationships in which power is held unequally, and which therefore involve different degrees of domination and submission. So these relationships are always somewhere in between the extremes of pure parasitism, on the one hand, and pure symbiotic mutualism, on the other.

Our debates about "genetic determinism" and "social construction" are therefore almost entirely irrelevant. In Butler's world, we are bound and limited both by our genes and by our cultural inheritance: both are constraints that we cannot ignore, and yet both are susceptible (under certain conditions) to alteration. So the question is never whether something is "in our genes" or merely a "cultural construction;" everything is both, and there is no reason to see either "nature" or "culture" as more restricting than the other. We need to reject the Hobbesian reductionism and genetic determinism that are purveyed by the academic discipline of "evolutionary psychology," popularized by writers like Harvard Professor Steven Pinker and widely disseminated in the popular press. But this doesn't mean that human beings are "socially constructed" instead of innately preprogrammed. Both alternatives are wrong. With regard to biology as well as culture, the real question is how, and to what extent, we are constrained, and how, and to what extent we are free. What are our limits? And what powers can we exercise within (and despite) those limits? In nature as in culture, everything is up for grabs and alterable to suit altered circumstances: that is part of the meaning of evolution. But in culture as in nature, the forces of inertia (viral repetition on the one hand, and tradition, convention, etc. on the other) are so strong that changing them is quite difficult. We are never free from our histories and their entanglements, for their dead weight is the largest part of what constitutes "us" in the first place. Butler imagines alternative genetic and cultural histories, reminding us that life can always be otherwise. Still these alternatives aren't "utopian"; each of them represents a different set of constraints and possibilities than we are used to, though in each remain both constraints and possibilities. In depicting power relationships as host/parasite interactions, Butler looks as much to the future—with its prospects of biotechnologies that will alter what we think of as "human" quite profoundly—as she does to the past—when the "human" was defined restrictively and abusively, in an age of slavery and colonialism. In short, through her provocative use of biology, Butler refigures and rethinks oppositions (between nature and culture, between freedom and constraint, between desire and pain) that we too often and too readily take for granted.

Butler's last novel, *Fledgling*, takes up all these concerns in the context of a vampire story. Its dynamics are far different from other vampire tales I know. Vampires are usually disruptive forces from the unconscious. They give body to our least avowable desires and fears. However, there is nothing atavistic about Butler's Ina (as her vampires call themselves); they have a culture, with laws and customs, kinship groups, a religion and an ethics and a politics, and disputes and power struggles about all these things—just as any group of human beings does. Butler is after something subtler than our usual (and far too familiar, and commodified, at this point) romances with what white people, at least, are all too ready to think of as the "dark side."

The vampire narrator of *Fledgling* begins the book not even knowing her own name. This name, we learn as she eventually learns, is Shori Matthews. She looks like a 10-year-old black girl. But actually, she is a 53-year-old vampire, though 53 years old is still pre-pubescent, in vampire terms. Shori is almost completely amnesiac as a result of trauma. Her entire (extended) family has been murdered, both the female and the male family line. Shori alone has survived. She will never regain the memories she has lost; she cannot even really mourn her mothers and fathers, her sisters and brothers, and all their loved ones, because they have been so entirely erased from her memory. Her new beginning is the result of loss beyond loss, a loss even of the possibility of feeling loss. She must learn afresh, as if from the outside, all that she previously knew through the experience of growing up. She must learn about both the human world and the vampire world. She must reacquire, at second hand, all the referents and contexts that go along with the only things she still possesses: her language and her sensory-motor skills.

Reading *Fledgling*, we learn about Ina society as Shori does. Butler invents a whole biology and culture of vampire life. The Ina live for 500 years or more. When injured, they can self-repair (as Shori does) on a diet of red meat. When they are well, they live exclusively off human blood. They possess an extraordinary sense of smell, together with more acute sight and hearing than human beings have; all these senses come into play in their relationships with one another, as well as with human beings. Ina society is more or less matriarchal—female Ina are more powerful than male—and is organized around gender-segregated extended families. They mate and reproduce in family-based groups (a group of brothers mates with a group of sisters from another family). The male young live with the family of their fathers, the female with the family of their mothers. The Ina also have complex relationships with their "symbionts," the human beings upon whom they feed. In *Fledgling*, vampires almost never kill their human prey; they live together with them, and have sex with them, in extended families of seven or eight human symbionts for each vampire. Whether male or female, vampires generally have symbionts of both genders, and the symbionts often develop sexual relationships with one another. So all in all, Ina society is constituted of both vampires and human beings, involved in complex webs of polyamory. (Vampires seem to be strictly heterosexual with one another, but human/human relationships, as well as cross-species vampire/human relationships, involve all sorts of gender pairings and sexual play.)

What does it mean to be the human symbiont of a vampire? Since Shori is a vampire, and we only see human thoughts and feelings through her narration, it's difficult to know precisely. Vampire saliva is both addictive and antiseptic for human beings; the human beings experience an immense sexual pleasure from being bitten and quickly become dependent upon—no, in love with—their vampire captors. It's sort of like a biological Stockholm Syndrome. Vampire saliva also results in the human victims leading long and healthy lives: they never get sick, and they live much longer than ordinary human beings (though not quite as long as the vampires themselves do). But symbionts must give up their autonomy—just as Lilith and the other human beings in *Dawn* have to do—in return for love, pleasure, health, and long life. Those who have been bitten cannot disobey their vampire's orders. Their lives are ultimately ones of servitude. Most vampires are ethical enough to give their human prey some modicum of choice, allowing them to leave at some early stage in the relationship, before they have become so addicted to their vampire's bites that departure would be physically impossible. However, emotional dependency precedes physiological dependency, and so the symbionts almost never choose to leave. In general, symbionts are chosen by their vampires, and almost never the reverse (though rarely, human beings who have grown up in Ina culture, with symbiont human parents, do make the decision to become symbionts themselves).

I've described Ina culture in almost too much detail here, giving a flat, reductive, and schematic sketch of things that gradually become clear in the course of the novel. (And learning these things gradually, as Shori herself relearns them, is one of the pleasures of reading *Fledgling*.) Still, I hope this summary gives a sense both of the richness of the novel and of some of the things that are at stake in the narrative. Butler writes of how love involves dependency, loss of autonomy, and unequal power relations; even when both sides in the relationship have given themselves over unconditionally to an Other, they are never equal in (self-)abandonment. This leads to paradoxes and impasses that are perhaps more intimate than the ones explored in *Dawn*—but that are equally ambivalent and intractable, in a way that is almost too painful to contemplate. More often than not, as is the case in *Dawn*, Butler conveys this painful sense of dependency from the point of view of the dominated partner. Presumably the Oankali loved Lilith and the other human beings whom they rescued, even though those human beings could only experience this love traumatically. In *Fledgling*, however, Butler approaches this same knot of dependency and inequality—which is yet love—from the point of view of the dominating partner. The way that we are moved into this experience and come to share it as readers is itself not the least of the disturbances aroused by the novel.

Fledgling is also, like most of Butler's work, a story about race. The Ina are of European origin (though the novel takes place entirely in the contemporary United States); they are a separate species from human beings, but they have lived in the human world for thousands of years, like a hidden elite, with a certain ability to manipulate human opinion in their own favor, but also with a well-grounded fear of human prejudice and hatred. No matter how ethical they try to be, after all, they are still ultimately predators (or parasites), living in their own society in secret, while feeding upon the surrounding human community. This makes the Ina seem a lot like the Jews (I mean, both like the Jews as they actually were in European society for so many centuries, and like the images of "Jews" as anti-Semitic Christian bigotry portrayed them). In addition, the Ina are nocturnal, in ways that correspond to traditional vampire lore. They aren't afraid of crosses or of mirrors; but they *are* allergic to the sun—they burn in it if they go outside, and they are physiologically unable to stay awake during the daytime—and their physical appearance is almost grotesquely albino. Shori is a minority within this minority, as she is the world's only black vampire. She learns that she is the result of genetic experiments performed by her mothers: genes from black human beings have been mixed into her otherwise-Ina genome, giving her skin enhanced melanin expression and thereby allowing her to stay awake during the day, and even to endure some limited exposure to sunlight. Eventually, it emerges that racism among the Ina is the reason her family has been murdered. Shori remains a target. The Ina cling to their unique heritage, and this leads some of them to a fanatical belief in their racial purity and superiority. They hate Shori because she is "part human" (though from a biological point of view this is a meaningless statement), and their hate is amplified by the fact that the "human" part of her is black.

All this, too, is revealed only gradually in the course of the novel, and it leads to some extraordinary conceptual and emotional tangles. Things do get at least provisionally resolved by the end of the book, though the resolution is emphatically not accomplished by the recourse to action/adventure that does this work in most genre fiction. Rather, it comes about strictly within the anthropological (vampirological?) framework that the novel has constructed for itself. The last quarter of the book depicts (in great detail) a legal proceeding in which questions of guilt and responsibility are adjudicated entirely in accordance with the Ina's own social norms. This formal resolution grounds the narrative. It also forces us to think about cultural differences and to ask how "universal" our ideas about guilt and responsibility really are. While the Ina's social norms, as revealed in their legal proceedings, are largely recognizable to twenty-first century Americans, they are not altogether identical to the norms of mainstream society. These differences weigh upon any attempt at judgment.

Fledgling, like *Dawn*, is an emotionally resonant text at the same time that it is also a powerful novel of ideas. That is to say, Butler's novels are simultaneously affective (oriented toward feeling) and cognitive (oriented toward knowledge and comprehension). Emotion and understanding simply cannot be separated in Butler's world. Butler's writing tends toward the spare and descriptive, rather than towards the stylistically elaborate and rhetorically self-reflexive. Yet there is something about it that gives it an incredible intensity and poignancy when it evokes states of hunger and grief, doubt and hope, craving and lust and love, longing and anger and bitterness and rage and hatred. Both *Dawn* and *Fledgling* traffic in currents of emotional turmoil that are almost too overwhelming to be borne and that push us to the limits of who and what we are (no matter whether "we" are black or white, male or female, or for that matter, human or vampire or Oankali or hybrid).

Butler's novels produce feelings that exceed the human and that therefore imply new, different forms of subjectivity than are recognized in ordinary life (or in ordinary, "mimetic" fiction). They offer little hope of release, transcendence, or liberation. They sometimes flirt with religio-ethical responses to the traumas they depict (this is most notable in the two *Parables*); but they always also emphasize the fictiveness of such responses. Butler's novels often envision the posthuman, the transhuman, and the hybrid-no-longer-quite-human; but they never portray these in the salvational terms that white technogeeks are so prone to. Above all, Butler's novels never pretend to alleviate the pain that they so eloquently describe and evoke: in this sense, they are utterly, shockingly clear as to the forms of domination and oppression that are so often taken for granted in our (post)modern, highly technologized, and supposedly enlightened world. They bear witness to the intolerable, to how much of our social life today remains intolerable. This makes them indispensable, both aesthetically and politically. I think that we still have a lot to learn from Butler's texts: about how to understand human limits and constraints without turning such an understanding into an apologia for the current ruling order; about how to construct a politics of the Other; and about how to think about the posthuman, the no-longer-merely-human. And above all, Butler's novels teach us about a politics of affect—not a politics of emotions against reason, but one that rejects such binary alternatives altogether.

Butler's fictions, through their emotional intensities, both suggest the need (and the possibility) for metamorphosis (and the hope that comes through this possibility), and suggest that trauma and social antagonism are unelimitable and not subject to rational adjudication. This is the case with their endings, no less than with their beginnings. At the end of the *Lilith's Brood* trilogy, we are offered the prospect of a new life, a new generation, that we can hope will be better able to cope than the generations we have previously seen. But the novel declines to step across this threshold. And at the end of *Fledgling*, Shori has been freed from the death sentence with which she had been threatened—if not forever, then at least for 300 years (though that is a shorter stretch in vampire time than it would be in human time), and the way has been cleared for her to create her own Ina extended family. Still, she will never regain all that she has lost, nor even regain the memory of having lost it.

Works Cited

Butler, Octavia. 2005. "Bloodchild." In *Bloodchild and Other Stories*, second edition. New York: Seven Stories Press, 1-32.

———. 2007. *Clay's Ark*. In *Seed To Harvest*. New York: Warner Books, 453-624.

———. 2000. *Dawn*. In *Lilith's Brood*. New York: Warner Books, 1-248.

———. 2005. *Fledgling*. New York: Seven Stories Press.

———. 1988. *Kindred*. Boston, MA: Beacon Press.

———. 2001. *Parable of the Talents*. New York: Warner Books.

Endnote

1   The quotations in this essay from *Dawn* come from the *Lilith's Brood* 2000 edition.

On Octavia E. Butler

Tananarive Due

The way I remember it, the email was waiting for me as soon as I sat at my desk that morning. A writer and reporter for *Black Issues Book Review* had written to tell me that she had a friend who lived in Octavia's neighborhood in Seattle, and her friend was saying that Octavia had collapsed and died outside of her home.

One part of my world is still frozen in that moment. With a pounding heart, I dialed Octavia's number, preparing an apology for the early-morning call, hoping to share a laugh with her about the false rumor.

Her voice answered the phone, but it was only a recording. I left an incoherent message, realizing for the first time that the rumor might be true. My husband, Steve, and I phoned Harlan Ellison, Octavia's mentor and friend, who calls her "Estelle" because he knew her before she was Octavia E. Butler. Harlan hadn't heard anything yet, but he called us back with the final word all too quickly: Octavia was gone.

The next two days were a blur of ringing telephones, questions from the media, and requests for quotes. Steve and I tried to give voice to what the science fiction community had lost.

For what I lost, I still don't have the words.

⇒ ⇐

Unlike my husband, Steven Barnes—who knew her for decades—I only met Octavia Butler in 1997, at that same momentous Clark Atlanta University black speculative fiction conference where I met Steve. Having published only one novel at the time, I was more than honored simply to be invited.

In the years to follow, Steve and I appeared on panels with Octavia and visited her at her home, and I found her private but gracious. I have since learned from people who knew her very well that I should have felt free to call her more often. I was always nervous that I was interrupting her genius in progress, so I hesitated to pick up the phone.

Octavia's Christmas cards were always among the first to arrive, like clockwork. Whenever I saw that familiar handwriting on the envelope, I knew it was time to start preparing for the holidays. Even in the small ways, Octavia led by example.

Memory becomes distorted with time, but I have a vision of Octavia's house outside of Seattle with a long walkway. One day, when Steve and I visited to interview her, we heard muffled but still loud Motown music through the window as we walked the path toward her door. She almost didn't hear us knock, and she was apologetic. Sometimes, she said, she listened to music when she was working.

Octavia had been struggling with writer's block caused by her medication, so she was glad to be writing again. She spoke about her writing at length that day—a novel about a girl with a very special gift, and the price of that gift. The familiar twinge of guilt came about interrupting her, but she was clearly happy to be hosting us. Isolation has both virtues and limitations. I remember her smiling a lot while we were there. She enjoyed our company.

The three of us stood in her kitchen for animated conversation about everything under the sun. She was a vegetarian, and she served us French bread and lentil soup. On her living room wall I saw a framed photograph from Clark Atlanta University, a group portrait from the conference where I first met her in 1997. It was a photo I treasured, too. I have carried my own copy with me through three moves: me, Steve, Octavia, Jewelle Gomez, Samuel R. Delany. All of us grinning, almost giddy.

"My other family," Octavia told us.

I was moved because we felt the same way. Since that conference in Atlanta, Steve and I had appeared together on the "black speculative fiction" circuit a few times, comfortable in the knowledge that we could count on occasional family reunions when we took our show on the road. In 2004, Steve and I were in a similar photo with Octavia and Nalo Hopkinson in Seattle.

Octavia appeared at one of my favorite bookstores, Eso Won Books in Los Angeles, in October of 2005. Her signing was on Halloween night, and because my son, Jason, was just old enough to trick-or-treat for the first time, I decided not to go. I wanted to see Octavia, but book signings are a notoriously bad place for socializing with authors because they're busily at work, signing books. I told myself we would see her the next time we went up to Seattle.

By February 2006, a blink later, she was dead.

My naiveté still stuns me. I hadn't ever imagined a world without Octavia. Without our matriarch, it felt like our family was gone.

≫ ≪

My last email from *butler8star* arrived at 10:24 a.m. on June 11, 2004, as innocuous as it is now precious:

> Dear Tanana,
> Thank you so much.
> Hello to the family.
> Octavia.

I had just sent her a blurb for her newest novel, *Fledgling*. (I never knew what happened to the pages about the girl with a gift; I never asked.) Soon before that email, in my last telephone conversation with Octavia, we had discussed the novel. Originally, she had seemed almost bashful about asking me to read an advance copy. She was always the harshest critic of her own work. But I assured her that it was wonderful, and that her readers would not be disappointed. "It's an Octavia E. Butler novel," I said, paying her my highest compliment.

I can only imagine how terrifying and triumphant it must have felt to have another novel ready for the world, especially when expectations were so high. *Fledgling* is Octavia's interpretation of a vampire novel, written as only Octavia could write it. Her protagonist, Shori, naturally is not a typical vampire: She feeds only reluctantly, giving great care to nurturing the family of mortals who are drawn to her powerful allure.

That day, during that last phone conversation, I made a joke, sort of. "Shori is too *nice*," I said.

Octavia didn't laugh at my joke. "Too *nice*?" she said. When I replay that exchange in my imagination, she sounds more and more aghast.

Those were not Octavia's last words to me. We probably spoke of Steve and our son, Jason, and lamented how long it had been since we had been able to visit. But only two words have been ringing in my ear since I learned of her death: "*Too NICE?*"

Whenever we lose people we care about, we wish we could go back and refine, clarify or outright erase the careless words that have passed from our lips. I want to take that back.

Shori is not too nice, Octavia. She is uncompromising, and she has a heart deeper and kinder than we are accustomed to; one that does not easily fit into her world. Just like the woman who brought her to life.

Thank you for sharing your spirit with us, Octavia. You left a great gift behind for us, but we were greedy. We wanted more. We thought we had more time.

How could I have forgotten what you taught us? You tried to warn us all along.

You distilled it into words in *Parable of the Sower.*

The only lasting truth is Change.

From "Hierarchical Behavior" to Strategic Amnesia: Structures of Memory and Forgetting in Octavia Butler's *Fledgling*

Shari Evans

Situating *Fledgling*: Vampire Fantasies and "Serious Work"

Unnerved by the knowledge she had gained through the research on global warming and religious fundamentalism that is at the heart of the late '90s Parable novels and exhausted from the task of imagining that near-future dystopic world, Octavia Butler stopped writing. She struggled with an eight-year long writer's block that was both physical and mental: health problems and the side effects of high blood pressure medication, which left her drowsy and depressed, compounded the despair brought on by her Parable research. Understandably, to break free of her writer's block, she turned to something new. It is no accident that the main character of her final novel, like Butler herself, recovers from both physical and mental devastation. In interviews following *Fledgling*'s release, Butler indicated that she took on the fantasy vampire genre "for fun" after writer's block caused her to give up on writing the planned final Parable book. In a *Democracy Now!* interview, she said that *Fledgling* "…was kind of an effort to do something that was more lightweight than what I had been doing. […] [T]he two Parable books […] were what I call cautionary tales: […] And I found that I was kind of overwhelmed by what I had done, what I had to comb through to do it. So eventually I wound up writing a fantasy, a vampire novel" (2005, "Science Fiction Writer"). Similarly, in an interview in *Essence* magazine in October of the same year, Butler said that "*Fledgling* was a chance to play" (2005, "Having Her Say").

Despite Butler's caveats, *Fledgling* in fact serves to consolidate and extend some of the important questions of her work: Why and how do we form social groups? How are these groups tied to biological imperatives?

What are the roles of race and gender in a particular society, and how are they connected to power or identity? What is the role of power in keeping social groups functioning? How can leadership use its power ethically? And, finally, how do the injustices of the past hinder and define social groups?

I would suggest that the novel, while playful, continues Butler's prior examinations of humanity's (biological) tendency towards what she terms "hierarchical behavior" in the Xenogenesis series and can be seen as a further extension of her interrogation of biological and social determinism and power. Also, and perhaps more importantly, the novel serves to continue her meditation on the role of individual and communal memory that we see in the 1979 *Kindred* and in the late '90s Parable series.[1] In *Fledgling*, as in those earlier novels, we see Butler wrestling with issues of hierarchy and community, of power and oppression. However, it is in *Fledgling*'s consideration that a strategic amnesia might provide the ethical space for a reconstruction of social hierarchy that we can see how *Fledgling* fits into the trajectory of Butler's work.[2] By reading trauma theory into Butler's last, "playful" vampire novel, we see that Butler uses strategies of memory and forgetting to forge a means of ethical survival that makes room for new mediations of power.

Early criticism on Butler notes her interrogation of power and its relationship to gender and race. Frances Smith Foster notes that Butler's "major characters are black women, and through her characters and through the structure of her imagined social order, Butler consciously explores the impact of race and sex upon future society" (1982, 37). Similarly, Ruth Salvaggio argues that the Patternist books "are about survival and power, about black women who must face tremendous societal constraints" (1984, 81). Yet Salvaggio makes clear that Butler's books are also about the ethical choice power can offer: "Though Butler's heroines are dangerous and powerful women, their goal is not power. They are heroines not because they conquer the world, but because they conquer the very notion of tyranny" (ibid.). Sandra Govan ties this ethics to Butler's focus on difference itself. She notes that "Difference, adaptability, change and survival are thematic threads connecting Butler's books," and further suggests that the novels are designed in a way that

> subtly illustrates differences in feminine / masculine values,
> differences in approaches to or conceptions of power, dif-

ferences in the capacity to recognize and exercise social or personal responsibility. In each story, a physical, psychic, or attitudinal difference associated with the heroine sets her apart from society and often places her in jeopardy; each survives because her "difference" brings with it a greater faculty for constructive change (1984, 84).

Difference, then, becomes a catalyst through which power structures can be revised and new ethics imagined, and this difference often begins with the physical and mental characteristics of her protagonists: strong, capable, and compelling black women. While Butler identifies her final novel as "play," *Fledgling* takes on the provocative and weighty questions posed in her previous work and continues her examination of power and difference.

In her Xenogenesis series, Butler defines the "human contradiction," our "fatal flaw," as the combination of hierarchical behavior and intelligence. The problem, Butler has noted, is that although we are intelligent, "we are also hierarchical, and our hierarchical tendencies are older and all too often, they drive our intelligence—that is, they drive us to use our intelligence to try to dominate one another" (2001, "Essay on Racism"). This "human contradiction," then, leads to some of the central questions of Butler's work: if hierarchical behavior is a fundamental driving force—and Butler certainly indicates that she believes its *tendency* is—does it have to also be violent and oppressive? Are we ultimately prisoners of our biology and the biological memory of instinct, with our intelligence only rationalizing our instinct for hierarchy? In other words, are human social groups thinly disguised packs, flocks, or herds? These questions have surfaced in criticism on Butler's work as well, particularly through the evaluation of what some see as Butler's emphasis on biological determinacy, which tends to essentialize identity. Hoda M. Zaki, for example, sees in the human response to the Oankali in the Xenogenesis series a pessimism tied to the biological essentializing of human nature she considers to be pervasive in Butler's work. Zaki contends that

> Butler believes that human nature is fundamentally violent and therefore flawed. The origin of violence, she suggests, lies in the human genetic structure, which is responsible for the contradictory impulses towards intelligence and hierarchy. [...] For

Butler, there is a pervasive human need to alienate from one-self those who appear to be different—i.e., to create Others. Even when she describes the diminution of racial antagonisms among humans upon encountering a new extraterrestrial Other, she foregrounds how we seize upon biological differences between the two species (i.e., human and Oankali) to reassert, yet again, notions of inferiority and discrimination. For her, the human propensity to create the Other can never be transcended. (1990, 241)

For Zaki, Butler's interrogations of difference and social hierarchies are linked to a pessimistic essentializing that ties humans to their biology and so limits them. In Zaki's reading, the subsuming of the racialized Other by an alien Other simply works to reemphasize biological difference rather than to subvert it, and so prevents the possibility of real change. Yet Butler's work tends to focus on characters who are different, who are already Othered in their own worlds, and who see things differently because of their subject positions. In this way, the texts themselves suggest an alternative to biological determinism as end game. Thus, Jeffrey Tucker argues that in Butler, "A critique of race as biological essence removes an impediment to embracing difference among humanity; and in order for difference to be embraced it must be cultivated, articulated, and valued. Butler's Xenogenesis trilogy performs both of these, only apparently contradictory, functions" (2007, 175). For critics like Tucker, Butler's focus on bodies and biological difference opens up rather than shuts down new avenues for change.[3] This is particularly noticeable in the first of the Parable novels, in which Butler articulates the need to "Embrace diversity. / Unite— / Or be divided, / robbed, / ruled, / killed / By those who see you as prey. / Embrace diversity / Or be destroyed" (1993, 196). For Butler, while diversity and Othering may both be biological tendencies that can lead to hierarchizing, they also offer the only possibility of survival, and so the means to an ethical negotiation of power.

Butler finds a solution to these problems in *Fledgling*. Butler was in some way freed from her writer's block by what she described as her "escape" into a "fantasy, a vampire novel" (2005, "Science Fiction Writer"). As she noted in the *Democracy Now!* interview, "writers [...] who write novels about vampires make up their own [vampires]. [...] You make up the rules and then you follow them" (2005, "Science Fiction Writer"). As much fun as vampire novels might offer, critics have long noted that they offer a critique of the world out of which they are produced, presenting a lens into the anxieties of their time. The genre itself allows for play within its seemingly limited parameters of blood-sucking (parasitic) human-like creatures. Nina Auerbach notes in her seminal critical examination of vampires, *Our Vampires, Ourselves*, "To the jaded eye, all vampires seem alike, but they are wonderful in their versatility. [...] The alacrity with which vampires shape themselves to personal and national moods is an adaptive trait their apparent uniformity masks. [...] There is no such creature as 'The Vampire'; there are only vampires" (1995, 5). Further, Auerbach asserts that vampires "can be everything we are, while at the same time, they are fearful reminders of the infinite things we are not" (6).

In imagining vampires, then, Butler has engaged anew the questions of power and hierarchy. The parasitical nature of vampires in itself mirrors her questioning of humanity's power-obsessed tendencies as well as echoes the parasitical creatures in some of her early fiction, from the patternists who feed on human minds, to the Oankali who need to join with humans to survive, to the slave-holders in the Americas whose economic survival is dependent on the bodies of the enslaved. Indeed, Butler has always questioned hierarchy and power by creating societies that clearly echo our own, and thereby calling into relief the way the powerful can choose to become parasites or to recognize their own needs and move towards symbiosis instead.

Because her main character and narrator, Shori, suffers from amnesia, she has to learn who she is, and so, because she drinks blood, Shori investigates ideas and images of vampires that appear in literature, film, anthropology, and folklore. In a kind of selective remembering, Butler dismisses most of the accumulated "knowledge" about vampires, while maintaining just enough of previous ideas about the biological specificity of the vampire's body—vampires are "allergic" to the sun, drink human blood, and are stronger than humans—to position the novel within the genre. However, to further counter and challenge vampire lore, while vampires have traditionally been depicted as tall and pale, Butler's vampiric narrator appears as a pre-pubescent black girl.[4]

In Butler's version of the vampire story, the Ina are an ancient species, separate from humans, and with better memories, more acute senses, and greater strength.[5] They are not humans "infected" with vampirism, as in the lore mentioned above, and so people can't "catch" vampirism. Instead, the Ina are biologically distinct from humans, yet dependent on both human blood and human companionship for survival. Rather than being completely parasitic, they exist in a symbiotic relationship with humans: they take blood from and have sex with adult humans, even as children, but they only reproduce with others of their kind. The symbiosis we see here—as potentially beneficial or destructive—is a theme repeated in Butler's work, from the Patternist dichotomy presented by the parasitic Doro and the more mutualistic Anyanwu, to the Oankali's merging with humans, and finally to the sentiment expressed by the *Parable of the Talents* verse: "Partnership is giving, taking, learning, teaching, offering the greatest possible benefit while doing the least possible harm. Partnership is mutualistic symbiosis. Partnership is life. // Any entity, any process that cannot or should not be resisted or / avoided must somehow be partnered…" (2000, 125). In each of these we see Butler negotiating the play between those with power and those without as she attempts to discover a possible ethical space of beneficial symbiosis rather than oppression. Critics have tied Butler's examination of symbiosis to Donna Haraway's cyborg and Gloria Anzaldúa's mestiza consciousness, suggesting that in her novels, symbiosis—and the changes it necessitates—can provide a new, alternative path.[6] Thelma Richard, for example, argues that Butler's work reveals the "hope that miscegenation can metamorphose into symbiosis if humans use their intelligence to cultivate compassion rather than to perpetuate hierarchical structures" (2005/2006, 123). At the same time, it should be noted that Butler is not exactly rejecting hierarchy here, but suggesting a beneficial symbiosis that can alter it and so lead to a more ethical structure, a conscious move to reject dominance and subjugation as the ultimate end of hierarchy.

Symbiosis in Butler's work is often tied to biological demands and changes, whether through Doro's need for human minds in the Patternist series, or the Oankali-human hybrid in the Xenogenesis books. Similarly, the Ina are notable for their biological distinctions. The Ina are long-lived, self-healing, regenerative, and slow-aging, with acute memories: our narrator and protagonist is a vampire child at fifty-three; the oldest Ina we see is almost five hundred. Further, Ina are perfectly set up to rule humankind, to exist at the top of the hierarchical ladder. However, they have at least one fatal flaw that they recognize (and that readers recognize from most vampire lore): the sun destroys them and leaves them vulnerable to human attack. It is this vulnerability, we learn, that has led to the genetic engineering that creates our narrator, Shori: she has been altered with an increase of human melanin from an African American "mother," making her skin brown and more resistant to the sun, and marking her body as the site of hybridity and permeability. Unlike other Ina, who as in vampire lore, burn up in the sun and sleep during the day, Shori can maintain alertness during the day and can survive sun exposure.

Shori's genetic alteration inserts the issue of race into the idea of purity and corruption typical to vampire literature, drawing the reader both to an examination of human systems of discrimination and to the ideas of the "natural" that underlie ideologies of racism. In this revision, Butler's vampire-human hybridity fits into vampire literature because, as Donna Haraway argues, the vampire is "[a] figure that both promises and threatens racial and sexual mixing, [and so] the vampire feeds off the normalized human" while it also "insists on the nightmare of racial violence behind the fantasy of purity in the rituals of kinship" (1997, 214). The signifiers that Butler chooses for her central vampire—female, black, orphan, child—play with Haraway's ideas of permeability, mixing, and racial- and sexual-violence. Butler's interrogation of hierarchies ultimately calls into question the very category—human "nature," particularly as it is gendered or raced—that she uses to raise the question of hierarchy in the first place. In addition, the result of this biological difference is interestingly tied to memory: the Ina are witnesses to human history. With the insertion of racial difference, the history the Ina remember and the ways they bear witness to that history suggest that institutional and cultural history are potential sites of contestation.

Hierarchy and Ethical Structures

While the Ina's longevity and powerful memories suggest their tie to history and the maintenance of a unified culture, Butler narrates her novel from a more peripheral location. The narrative is constructed so that the reader learns about the Ina, their history, and their culture along with the narrator, Shori, as she awakens in a feral state: blind, battered, hungry, and focused on survival. *Fledgling* begins, then, with sensation and discovery, two biological tendencies that also structure the novel. Shori, as yet unnamed, feels pain and desperate hunger, and so acts—and kills—to survive. Initially, she has no self-knowledge, and no knowledge of the world, only the need to survive. This reduction to biological need draws our attention to "natural" impulses and instincts. As Shori moves beyond pain and hunger, she begins to see a world around her, to recognize that she has lived in and knows something of that world, but the structures of language—the names of things—and morality come to her slowly. As in Plato's cave, Shori comes out of the darkness of unreason—of only sensation and the will to survive—into the light of reason and her own "humanity." The novel begins in Shori's coming to self-knowledge, but the second half of the novel takes place inside an Ina community and includes a legal trial, so that we learn of the Ina's social, moral, and legal structures.

Shori is the quintessential "out kid," a term Butler used to describe herself and her own feelings of being an outsider.[7] Shori is disconnected, particularly when she awakens, from both human and Ina communities. Despite her appearance, she is clearly not human. This is evident in her physical strength and bodily needs (along with drinking human blood, she runs down and kills two deer and eats their flesh raw); in the sophistication of her intellect and emotion; and in her sexuality (although she appears to be a pre-adolescent human child, Shori gives and receives sexual pleasure with multiple partners, both male and female, and is, in fact, the dominant sexual partner in these relationships). At the same time, her blackness makes her suspect to other Ina, who question whether or not she is "really Ina." Indeed, her racial otherness leads to a brutal attempt on her life—an attempt to destroy and end the genetic tampering that created her and that sparked the racial animus that annihilated her entire community—that causes her memory loss. Through Shori's remembrance, Butler imagines a solution to the dilemma of culture that has haunted her: painful histories and memories (many of which result from the human need for hierarchy that Butler posits) both threaten and strengthen communal life, as bearing witness and healing from trauma compete with one another for the resource of memory.

Shori's memory loss becomes another mark of her difference. Once she encounters other Ina, she discovers that such memory loss is unusual for Ina, who pride themselves on their ability to remember. Along with her physical markings of difference, her amnesia makes her a cultural outsider with no knowledge of family, community, or society, human or Ina. It also makes possible a selective remembering that allows Shori to see her role in the hierarchy from a new angle, in the same way that Butler's choice of genre allowed her a new kind of freedom to imagine new solutions to the dilemma of memory.

Shori's memory loss, while further distancing her from the Ina, also reduces her belief in the underlying and seemingly "natural" structures that form their society. Although her memory is wiped out, she retains the structures of language and a particular morality and ethical behavior—she senses what is right or wrong both for her small community of human symbionts and for herself as an Ina. At the same time, she is open to examining the structures she sees in Ina communities. The Ina-human relationship is termed "mutual symbiosis" by Shori's Ina father, but it is also particularly hierarchical, with the Ina biologically dominant over the human symbionts (and all other humans) while dependent on them for survival. The Ina have a number of advantages over humans: they are physically stronger and faster; they have better memories and longevity; their senses are more powerful; and most importantly, they addict people to their venom, binding them, and also making them susceptible to mind control. Humans are biologically altered through this addiction; indeed, their bodies become so dependant on their particular Ina's saliva that they will die without it. They are also rationally led to tie themselves to the Ina because of their desire for longevity and health. The Ina bite alone—and the saliva that is transferred in the process—would support their dominance over humans: it provides intense physical pleasure, as well as longevity and health to humans. That is, the Ina bite excites both sensuality and rationality, joining body and mind. Yet, ultimately, these positives come at a price—the saliva is also a form of mind-control, binding the humans to their Ina completely and overpowering any individual will. Shori's father explains that Ina saliva is "a powerful hypnotic drug. It makes [humans] highly suggestible and deeply attached to the source of the substance. They come to need it" (79). Because of this, human symbionts are dominated by and dependent on the ethical beliefs and behavior of their Ina.

Shori's initial taking over of humans is driven by her physical need for human blood and unconscious desire for human companionship, but without the conscious understanding or ethical practice of what that assertion of superiority means to either the people whose blood she takes or herself. A symbiont tells Shori that, "You don't forget something your Ina tells you to do. You can't. That's one of the first things you learn as a symbiont" (267), and neither can a symbiont refuse a command, even if it is to murder or commit suicide. In other words the symbiotic relationship removes some aspect of a human's free will. Because of these mind-controlling powers, humans are susceptible to being used as weapons by the Ina, and have been so used in the Ina's historical past. Here biology creates the framework for a hierarchy that defines both Ina-human relationships and community, but at the same time, the considered response to that biology creates the possibility for ethical structures and behavior.

As the symbionts depend on their Ina, so the Ina need the blood and companionship of their symbionts. The Ina respond to this need-based hierarchy in disparate ways: some Ina "resent [their] need of them, [see] it as a weakness, and yet…[love] them" (276). Others see humans as their "less gifted cousins" (ibid.), as apes seem to humans. Still others see this interaction as a weaving of relationship and care. While they are able to mentally control their symbionts, most Ina "would not order them to harm themselves or one another. And […] would never harm one of them" (ibid.) because the loss would be too much to bear. Yet, despite this caveat, Ina history is full of just such violent use of symbionts. Joan Braithwaite, one of Shori's relatives, explains that Ina are unable to kill the humans with which they have bonded:

> I think it's an instinct for self-preservation on our part. […] We need not only their blood, but physical contact with them and emotional reassurance from them. Companionship. I've never known one of us to survive without symbionts. We should be able to do it—survive through casual hunting. But the truth is that that only works for short periods. Then we sicken. We either weave ourselves a family of symbionts, or we die. (ibid.)

This paradox of biological and emotional need and dominance is also the ethical point of departure, the question Butler continually returns to in her work—what can or will we do with our tendency toward hierarchy? The physical symbiosis suggests something beyond biology as well. The Ina need a "family of symbionts" in order to live; they need more than the sustenance of blood. This suggests the importance of both ethical response and relationship, and the danger of their loss. Like the hyper-empathy syndrome that might create a biological conscience in Butler's Parable series, here Butler is imagining a biological need for care and empathy in contrast to power and control. Humans are only protected against their own Ina, and only once they are bound to them; this protection does not transfer to other Ina. Instead, as Joan explains to Shori, "human beings who are not bound to us, who are bound to other Ina, or not bound at all…they have no protection against us except whatever decency, whatever morality we choose to live up to" (ibid.). Ina are free either to live ethically, treating the humans they can control with respect and restraint, or to follow their hierarchical impulse to dominate. The voluntary practice of morality keeps the Ina's dominance in check.

Ina-human relationships offer new familial and communal structures, compounds in which Ina families live with each Ina's group of human symbionts and whatever human families they create. The symbionts sexually share the Ina with others in their group—not always comfortably—and create community based on their shared position; yet they ultimately have to sever their ties to humans outside the Ina-human communities and admit to their loss of free will. The symbiont Martin notes that when he was first introduced to his Ina and asked to become a symbiont, he thought it "sounded more like slavery than symbiosis" (210). Yet, not only does he choose to join his Ina, he raises a son who chooses to join Shori as one of her symbionts. In these choices we see physical desire and self-interested reason up against the idea of "free will." The conflict suggests the compromises that we all necessarily enter into in order to live in our hierarchized societies—the surrender of individual will to the social contract.

During the trial over the attacks on Shori, we are shown the various forms the human-Ina hierarchy can take. In some families, the symbionts retain some control over their own lives: they have careers and human relationships, and work out their own problems. Indeed, Shori's father cautions her to

> treat your people well. Let them see that you trust them and let them solve their own problems, make their own decisions. Do that and they will willingly commit their lives to you. Bully them, control them out of fear or malice or just for your own convenience, and after a while, you'll have to spend all your time thinking for them, controlling them, and stifling their resentment. (79)

Enforcement of Ina dominance, Shori's father points out, is its own prison. Still other Ina play with their control over their symbionts, using
them for entertainment—like a personal soap opera—and pitting them
against one another. The Ina vary in their choices of ethical codes, but
each must choose some code, some kind of structured society, in order
to survive.

As in the Ina-human relationship, Ina have an internal hierarchy,
based on their own biological imperatives. They are, in some ways, both
more human (in emotion and reason) and more animal (in instinct and
biological imperative) than their symbionts. For example, Ina's sense of
smell is so acute that they can differentiate species, genders, and individuals by smell alone. Further, Shori's father tells her that "Ina are sexually territorial" (85) and that because their senses are so acute, the scent
of sexually mature members of the opposite sex makes Ina extremely
uncomfortable, potentially out of control. But Shori's father assures her,
"your brothers and I have our sexual predispositions—our instincts—but
we are also intelligent. We are aware of our urges. We can stand still
even when the instinct to move is powerful" (86). This knowledge of the
power of instinct has structured their society; because of their biology,
they live in same-sex intergenerational familial units (several generations of eldermothers, mothers, and daughters or elderfathers, fathers,
and sons) and mate in groups (a group of daughters with a group of
sons) so that families are multiply tied to one another, creating a moral
restraint through familial connections. Controlling instinct means intri-
cate kinship structures that limit risk. This form of mating is both biological adaptation and moral choice. This interconnection makes the loss
of family that Shori experiences—both her female and male families and
all their generations are annihilated—almost apocalyptic. At the same
time, males and females are not equal. Mating for the Ina includes the
same bonding through bite that takes place with symbionts, yet it is the
Ina female's venom that offers the more powerful bonds—indeed, Ina
females learn very young to watch what they say, because they can exert
such powerful sway over both Ina and humans. An elderfather tells Shori
that outside of mating, "The only other reason for you to take blood from
an Ina male would be to kill him" (201). Butler's inversion of stereotypical
gender hierarchies leaves hierarchy itself intact, as even a pre-adolescent
girl is potentially stronger than elder males. Ina-symbiont families that
include male and female symbionts in sexual relationships with their Ina,

and with the Ina clearly leader of the unit, leads to the re-evaluation of human hierarchies based on notions of gender or sexuality.

The Ina insist that human hierarchies and bigotries are absent from their heritage, that they are distinct from humans in that they are both more sensual and more rational, driven by their need to bind with all humans for survival rather than to distinguish *between* humans. After Shori's families are killed and her symbiont suggests race as the motive, another Ina counters that, "the Ina weren't racists […]. Human racism meant nothing to the Ina because human races meant nothing to them. They looked for congenial human symbionts wherever they happened to be, without regard for anything but personal appeal" (154). Yet, it is Shori's blackness that marks her as Other to the Ina—who, as in traditional vampire lore, are pale, tall and spidery. Her dark skin, and some Ina's response to it, sets the Ina's whiteness into relief and makes visible the racial underpinnings of their society and its beliefs. Rather than existing outside of human history, they are implicated in it. Marking Shori as the bioengineered, genetically-altered vampire who can survive the sun, her dark skin is the symbolic mark of Ina vulnerability, identifying a strength (melanin) that only humans have.

At the same time, her skin color and the Ina response to it also forces the Ina to acknowledge a return to their bodies, to become embodied and also re-connected to the humans they are tied to by the biological need for their blood. This re-embodiment reconnects them to human history, human bigotry, and human passion, despite their claims to the contrary. Indeed, the Silk family (the family that has been trying to kill Shori and is on trial for her families' murders) curses Shori at the trial with racial slurs that belie all their attempts to distinguish themselves in this way. As in Butler's other novels, the self-serving ideology apparent in the Ina's naturalization of their characteristics (height, skin color, acute memory, health, etc.) and the hierarchy and Ina-supremacist practice that result from it echo Western and particularly American racism and the hierarchies of white supremacy. Shori's being marked as a raced body draws attention to the Ina's equation of their biological position with superiority. The eldest elderfather of the Silk family begins his opening statement in this way:

> "May we remember always that we are Ina […] We are an ancient and honorable people with more than ten thousand years

of recorded history. We are a proud and powerful people, well aware of our duty to our families, to our kind, and to the truths that make us who we are. […] May we remember always that our strength flows from our uniqueness and our unity. We are Ina! That is what this Council must protect." (238-239)

The Silks fear disintegration—that with genetic engineering, Ina will lose the essence of what makes them Ina, and that they will therefore not survive intact (or, importantly, not as they remember—and the eldest Ina is 541 years old).

In a sense, because of their long memory, their ideological beliefs are even more invisible and they have an even more urgent need to halt change. The "uniqueness" the Silks wanted to protect by killing Shori and her family is not only their belief in an unchanging essential identity, but also their fundamental belief in their difference from and superiority over humankind, echoing much of the racist ideology espoused in antebellum and segregationist America. At the beginning of the trial against the Silks, their advocate, the Ina relative assigned to represent them, tells Shori, "I challenge your right to represent the interests of families who are unfortunately dead. You are their descendant, but because of their error, because of their great error, you are not Ina" (277). Shori's racialized—and humanized—body and her power, as the only Ina who can walk in the day, challenges the Silks and their advocate's belief in Ina superiority, in Ina "uniqueness." It also makes the Ina need for humans that much stronger—they need symbionts, and the human genes for melanin may be the thing that can ensure their survival.[8]

Each of the structures Butler presents is based in a response to biological imperative and hierarchical tendencies, and ultimately, a response to the question of survival as one's ultimate motivation. The uneven relationship between humans and Ina, but particularly the fact that humans are physically and mentally tied to their Ina for survival, put the Ina in the ultimate position of dominance. Yet the choice to maintain a code of ethics, to exert will and intelligence beyond the desire or ability to dominate and towards a sense of all our morality, is somehow tied to our biology. When the powerful submit themselves to a code of ethics, there may be a biological motivation as well: moral behavior ensures a *better* survival.

The Strategic use of Memory and Forgetting

That better survival—one that clearly depends on intellectual and willful moral choice—may also include a strategic amnesia. The hierarchies that our nature seems to force on us, according to Butler, may need strategic amnesia and ethical remembering in order to overcome the brutalities and injustices of history, the kind of history that reinforces the Silks' violent racism. Of Butler's novels, only *Fledgling* suggests that we have to choose not to remember everything in order to proceed. I began with Butler's comments on *Fledgling* as a playful move away from the serious questions her work has raised and a way out of her writer's block. Through this approach, the novel itself allowed Butler to "forget" the serious questions and concerns of her "save-the-world fiction" long enough to imagine a future in a world that she knows is full of people who begin displaying their tendency towards hierarchical behavior on the schoolyard. These hierarchies become the "racism, sexism, ethnocentrism, classism, and all the other 'isms' that cause so much suffering in the world" (2001, "Essay on Racism"). Yet, as I have shown, Butler has not left the critical questions of her work behind and has not abandoned her belief that despite these tendencies, there is also hope for resistance and change:

> Too many people will not, perhaps cannot, [resist their hierarchical tendencies]. There is, unfortunately, satisfaction to be enjoyed in feeling superior to other people. […] [D]oes tolerance have a chance? Only if we want it to. Only when we want it to. Tolerance, like any aspect of peace, is forever a work in progress, never completed, and, if we're as intelligent as we like to think we are, never abandoned. (2001, "Essay on Racism")

This "work in progress" continues in *Fledgling*'s examination of both hierarchical tendencies and the critical roles of memory and forgetting. In many ways, the strategic forgetting of the novel serves as a negotiation of space for Butler—a momentary creation of room to move through the erasure of memory and also a way back to the fundamental issues left behind. In the same way, Shori's amnesia serves a strategic purpose—for the reader, who gets to piece together her past and to discover the Ina world with her; for Shori, who is able to survive the traumatic loss of her families by this emotional distancing; and within the text, which is structured through the process of forgetting and remembering. Shori's coming to consciousness in the beginning of the novel is violent—it is an abrupt and painful reintegration of a broken self, what trauma theorist Robert Jay Lifton terms the "numbing" that leads to a "second self," the re-integration of which is part of the healing and re-unification of identity.[9] Lifton's work focuses on "survival, rather than on trauma," suggesting that the post-traumatic experience and its integration into the self is as important as the trauma itself. *Fledgling* highlights this post-traumatic survival in Shori's amnesia and in her coming to self through the re-integration into and re-learning—even altering—of her community.

Yet, although Shori's body painfully regenerates itself, her memory remains lost. It is this loss that further identifies her as Other to the Ina, who value their exceptional memories as essential characteristics; it is this loss, along with her racial marking, that ties her to humanity. Like humans, Shori is left to reassemble the past through written records and written and oral narratives, through the pieces of the past that leave their tracks today. Although distant from the past by definition, individuals are normally situated within and in relation to cultural memory. In *Feminism and Cultural Memory,* Marianne Hirsch and Valerie Smith define the relationship between the individual and cultural memory:

> Individuals and groups constitute their identities by recalling a shared past on the basis of common, and therefore often contested, norms, conventions, and practices. These transactions emerge out of a complex dynamic between past and present, individual and collective, public and private, recall and forgetting, power and powerlessness, history and nostalgia, conscious and unconscious fears or desires. Always mediated, cultural memory is the product of fragmentary personal and collective experiences articulated through technologies and media that shape even as they transmit memory. Acts of memory are thus acts of performance, representation, and interpretation. They require agents and specific contexts. They can be conscious and deliberate; at the same time, and this is certainly true in the case of trauma, they can be involuntary, repetitious, obsessive. (2007, 225)

This negotiation between the individual and culture is noticeable in *Fledgling* because of its absence. Shori, because of her amnesia, must reconstruct her relationship to herself and her culture, must re-create an identity, and must re-learn cultural memory and how to perform it. Embedded in this, however, is the implication that she can choose what she wants to remember and enact. That is, she is not controlled by cultural memory, but instead is in the position of inscribing that memory onto herself. Removed from culture by her traumatic memory loss, Shori may choose her own integration into and participation in Ina society according to her own ethical principles. Further, Hirsch and Smith argue that "Cultural memory is most forcefully transmitted through the individual voice and body—through the testimony of a witness" (ibid.). Shori is indeed called to testify, to bear witness to the loss of her families, yet in her inability to recall her own loss, she both signifies the depth of that loss and finds her voice. So, rather than channeling the unacknowledged or invisible voice of cultural memory, Shori points to the desire to control that memory by narrating it.

Shori's re-integration into a new self is the conscious re-education of herself as Ina and re-connection of herself to her families' histories. Lifton suggests that

> In trauma one moves forward into a situation that one has little capacity to imagine; and that's why it shatters whatever one had that was prospective or experiential in the past. [...] And being shattered, one struggles to put together the pieces, so to speak, of the psyche, and to balance that need to reconstitute oneself with the capacity to take in the experience. Something tells one, or one becomes partly aware, that if one doesn't take in some of it one is immobilized by the numbing, that the numbing is so extreme, in that kind of situation. But this is not a logical process, and it's not a conscious process primarily. (in Caruth 1995, 137)

The immobilization, this numbing, in trauma is like being caught in an echo chamber—only the trauma is repeated, yet it is also repeated as an out-of-body experience, a distancing from the self. The Ina who murdered Shori's families counted on the traumatic disintegration of the self that should have marked and altered Shori; instead, her amnesia protects her. One of her advocates tells her that this loss is to her advantage during the trial: "If your memory were intact, you wouldn't have been in control of yourself, you couldn't have been so calm as you sat in the same room with the people who probably had your families killed.[...] [They expected you] not only to look unusual with your dark skin, but to be out of your mind with pain, grief, and anger, to be a pitiable, dangerous, crazed thing" (271). If she remembered her loss, it would disable her, eclipse her present, keep her locked in the "involuntary, repetitious, obsessive" moment of trauma Hirsch and Smith identify. Instead, Shori's amnesia provides her with a critical distance and therefore the chance for both survival and an ethical future practice.

Once Shori has won her initial struggle for her basic survival, recovering from her injuries and then protecting herself from further attacks, she can also struggle for the justice that would ensure her survival. The emotion of personal memory would lead her, at most, to seek vengeance rather than justice, as it does in the more recent and remembered loss of her symbiont Theodora. But vengeance is the stopping of time, another way to be frozen in trauma, as the traumatic experience dictates one's behavior, alters one's ethical practice. As in the immobilization and numbing Lifton discusses, the memory of traumatic events is often described as the emotional repetition and reliving of the past trauma. Thus, the strategic forgetting that Butler offers allows Shori to ethically remember (but not relive) her past, and so to imagine a future.

This can be seen as a return to and reappraisal of the embodied cultural memory evident in Butler's 1979 *Kindred*, in which Dana is literally disfigured by the past; slavery is physically represented on her through her lost arm and battered body, which together signify the trauma of her individual and cultural past. *Kindred* ends with Dana's search for a historical record of the slave past and her discovery that it is rife with gaps and ambiguity. In some ways, *Fledgling* picks up where *Kindred* left off: Dana's disfigurement and her search for the past become the trauma of Shori's battered body and her loss of history. Unlike Dana, Shori is able to heal herself physically, to regenerate her body, however painfully, and to negotiate a new relationship to both the personal and cultural past. Dana's traumatic loss is symbolic of the painful mark of history, of the lasting wound the slave past has left. Unable to regenerate, forced to make her way despite her structuring loss, Dana must learn to live with both the painful knowledge of her lost past and the trauma of her experience. Shori, hero of Butler's vampire tale, is unmarked by her initial trauma—her body completely heals and she loses all memory of the experience or who she was before. Instead, her racial marking and her biological superiority (as Ina and as female) are joined to a conscious ethical remembering to suggest a future outside of trauma.[10]

In *Fledgling* Butler circles back to the question of how individuals and societies can confront the past and still survive, or even better, thrive.[11] Here, Shori is protected from the enormity of her loss by her amnesia, but also committed both to a just retribution and an ethical remembering of her lost family—she plans to continue her mothers' family line, to relearn her personal and societal history, and to establish a future for herself, her symbionts, and her descendants. She is not crippled by the past. And Ina justice ensures that while Shori will thrive, the Silks will be dissolved—their unmated sons will be dispersed, adopted into other families, and their line will be swallowed by history just as Shori's fathers were. The difference lies in ethical practice: instead of the slaves being forgotten and the slave-owners writing history, here the perpetrators of the violence are consciously forgotten while the survivor of the violence is remembered. The novel suggests that part of the restraint of the ethical system Shori discovers is the simultaneous threat of being forgotten and being remembered, of having one's past reduced to one's final actions.

However, Butler also makes sure that we can see the difference that distance from trauma makes. Shori's amnesia protects her from experiencing the loss of her families, and so it enables her to seek justice. At the same time, her amnesia does not protect her from the emotional trauma caused by the murder of her symbiont, Theodora, by Katharine Dahlman, the Silk's advocate; instead of justice, Shori repeatedly asserts to herself that she will have Katharine's life in exchange for her symbiont's. In Shori's understandable rage and emotional desire for vengeance, Butler acknowledges the natural response to loss, the need to lash out. However, instead of acting on this need for vengeance, Shori waits for and accepts the Council's verdict against Katharine. Shori's ethical choice to contain her desire for vengeance and follow the community's social contract (the Law) is in direct contrast to Katherine's enraged response. Rather than accept the verdict, or subsume her own rage, Katherine attempts to kill Shori. This violence provokes Shori's defensive violent response, and ends in Katherine's death, suggesting that the choice of rage is itself self-destructive. Shori is able to negotiate a critical distance from her individual and cultural past and so find another way to behave apart from sheer domination.

Part of the hope of the ethical survival that Butler suggests is the simultaneous forgetting of the things that would cripple us and the ethical remembering of the past. Strategic amnesia gives us the critical distance to remember ethically rather than vengefully. This strategic amnesia in which Butler's final novel situates us, then, leads, past forgetting, to the justice of remembering on a historic and cultural scale. Although Butler spoke of this novel as a "fantasy," as "play," this play is serious, like all of Butler's work. The fantasy of *Fledgling* offers more than another vampire novel; it offers us the hope that through a considered relationship to memory, we can use our intellect to navigate cultural and individual trauma, control the natural urge towards hierarchy and dominance, and create an ethical society.

Works Cited

Auerbach, Nina. 1995. *Our Vampires, Ourselves*. Chicago and London: The University of Chicago Press.

Bollinger, Laurel. 2007. "Placental Economy: Octavia Butler, Luce Irigaray, and Speculative Subjectivity." *Lit: Literature Interpretation Theory* 18.4 (Oct.): 325-352.

Butler, Octavia. 2004. "Amnesty." *Callaloo*. (Summer) 27.3: 597-616.

——. "Essay on Racism: A Science-Fiction Writer Shares her View of Intolerance." September 1, 2001. NPR Weekend Edition Saturday. March 15, 2008. <http://www.npr.org>.

——. 2004. *Kindred*. 1979. Boston, MA: Beacon Press.

——. 2005. *Fledgling*. New York: Seven Stories Press.

——. 1994. *Parable of the Sower*. New York: Seven Stories Press

——. 2000. *Parable of the Talents*. 1998. New York: Aspect-Warner Books.

——. 2005. "Having her say: Octavia Butler talks with Evette Porter about *Fledgling*." *Essence* 35.6 (Oct): 96.

——. "Science Fiction Writer Octavia Butler on Race, Global Warming and Religion." Democracy Now! Interview. November 11, 2005. http://www.democracynow.org.

Caruth, Cathy. 1995. "An Interview with Robert Jay Lifton." In *Trauma: Explorations in Memory*, edited by Cathy Caruth, 128-147. Baltimore, MD: The Johns Hopkins University Press.

Foster, Frances Smith. 1982. "Octavia Butler's Black Female Future Fiction." *Extrapolation* 23.1: 37-49.

Gateward, Frances. 2004. "Daywalkin' Night Stalkin' Bloodsuckas: Black Vampires in Contemporary Film." *Genders* 40.

Gomez, Jewelle. 1997. "Recasting the Mythology: Writing Vampire Fiction." In *Blood Read: The Vampire Metaphor in Contemporary Culture*, edited by Joan Gordon and Veronica Hollinger, 85-92. Philadelphia, PA: University of Pennsylvania Press.

Govan, Sandra. 1984. "Connections, Links, and Extended Networks: Patterns in Octavia Butler's Science Fiction." *Black American Literature Forum* 18.2 (Summer): 82-87.

Green, Michelle Erica. 1994. "'There Goes the Neighborhood': Octavia Butler's Demand for Diversity in Utopias." In *Utopian and Science Fiction by Women: Worlds of Difference*, edited by Jane L. Donawerth and Carol A. Kolmerten, 166-189. Syracuse, NY: Syracuse University Press.

Haraway, Donna. 1991. "A Cyborg Manifesto: Science, Technology, and Socialist-Feminism in the Late Twentieth Century" 149-181, and "The Biopolitics of Postmodern Bodies: Constitutions of Self in Immune System Discourse" 203-230. In Simians, Cyborgs and Women: The Reinvention of Nature. New York: Routledge.

——. 1997. *Modest_Witness @ Second_Millennium. FemaleMan_Meets_ OncoMouse*. New York: Routledge.

Hirsch, Marianne and Valerie Smith. 2007. "From Feminism and Cultural Memory." In *Theories of Memory: A Reader*, edited by Michael Rossington and Anne Whitehead, 223-229. Baltimore, MD: The Johns Hopkins University Press.

Holden, Rebecca J. 1998. "The High Costs of Cyborg Survival: Octavia Butler's Xenogenesis Trilogy." *Foundation: the International Review of Science Fiction* 72(Spring): 49–56.

Jacobs, Naomi. 2003, "Posthuman Bodies and Agency in Octavia Butler's Xenogenesis." In *Dark Horizons: Science Fiction and the Dystopian Imagination,* edited by Raffaella Baccolini and Tom Moylan, 91–111 New York: Routledge.

Luckhurst, Roger. 1996. "'Horror and Beauty in Rare Combination': The Miscegenate Fictions of Octavia Butler." *Women: A Cultural Review* 7.1: 28–38.

Mehaffy, Marilyn and AnaLouise Keating. 2001. "'Radio Imagination': Octavia Butler on the Poetics of Narrative Embodiment." *MELUS* 26.1 (Spring): 45-76.

Michaels, Walter Benn. 2004. "Political Science Fiction." *New Literary History* 31.4: 649-664.

Miller, Jim. 1998. "Post-Apocalyptic Hoping: Octavia Butler's Dystopian/Utopian Vision." *Science Fiction Studies* 25:2(75): 336–360.

Patterson, Kathy Davis. ""HAUNTING BACK": VAMPIRE SUBJECTIVITY IN THE GILDA STORIES." *Femspec* 1 Jun 2005: 35. *GenderWatch (GW)*. ProQuest. Claire T. Carney Library, University of Massachusetts Dartmouth, Dartmouth, MA. 10 Jan. 2009. http://www.proquest.com/.

Peterson, Nancy J. 2001. *Against Amnesia: Contemporary Women Writers and the Crises of Historical Memory.* Philadelphia, PA: University of Pennsylvania Press.

Ramirez, Catherine S. 2002. "Cyborg Feminism: The Science Fiction of Octavia Butler and Gloria Anzaldúa." In *Reload: Rethinking Women and Cyberculture,* edited by Mary Flanagan and Austin Booth, 374-402. Cambridge, MA: MIT Press.

Rowell, Charles H. 1997. "An Interview with Octavia Butler." *Callaloo* 20.1: 47-66.

Richard, Thelma Shinn. 2005/2006. "Defining Kindred: Octavia Butler's Postcolonial Perspective." *Obsidian III: Literature in the African Diaspora* 6-7.2-1: 118-134.

Salvaggio, Ruth. 1984. "Octavia Butler and the Black Science-Fiction Heroine." *Black American Literature Forum* 18.2(Summer): 78-81.

Sands, Peter. 2003. "Octavia Butler's Chiastic Cannibalistics." *Utopian Studies: Journal of the Society for Utopian Studies* 14.1: 1-14.

Tucker, Jeffrey A. 2007. "'The Human Contradiction': Identity and/as Essence in Octavia Butler's Xenogenesis Trilogy." *Yearbook of English Studies* 37.2: 164-181.

Warfield, Angela. 2005/2006. "Reassessing the Utopian Novel: Octavia Butler, Jacques Derrida, and the Impossible Future of Utopia." *Obsidian III: Literature in the African Diaspora* 6-7.2-1: 61-71.

Winnubst, Shannon. 2003. "Vampires, Anxieties, and Dreams: Race and Sex in the Contemporary United States." *Hypatia: A Journal of Feminist Philosophy* 18.3 (Fall): 1-20.

Zaki, Hoda M. 1990. "Utopia, Dystopia, and Ideology in the Science Fiction of Octavia Butler." *Science Fiction Studies* 17: 239-251.

Endnotes

1   For discussions of the debate about utopic and dystopic elements of Butler's work, see: Hoda M. Zaki, "Utopia, Dystopia, and Ideology in the Science Fiction of Octavia Butler" (1990); Michelle Erica Green, "'There Goes the Neighborhood': Octavia Butler's Demand for Diversity in Utopias" (1994); Angela Warfield, "Reassessing the Utopian Novel: Octavia Butler, Jacques Derrida, and the Impossible Future of Utopia" (2005/2006); and Peter Sands, "Octavia Butler's Chiastic Cannibalistics" (2003, among others.

2   Alternately, Nancy J. Peterson suggests in *Against Amnesia: Contemporary Women Writers and the Crises of Historical Memory* (2001) that contemporary multicultural women writers have written works that challenge and confront American society's seeming refusal to address its own history by their own focus on traumatic moments in our history. While I agree with much of what Peterson argues, I would suggest that in *Fledgling* Butler considers an appropriation of amnesia that is strategic in its positioning of its practitioners in a conscious, ethical relationship to memory, forgetting, and remembering.

3   For an interesting reevaluation of this debate, see Walter Benn Michaels'
    "Political Science Fiction," in which he argues that essentialist and anti-
    essentialist (or physical and cultural, fixed and mobile) claims about iden-
    tity have already agreed that identity itself matters:

> What they agree on is the value of difference itself, a value
> created by turning disagreement into otherness. [...] [The
> dispute] is primarily the expression of a consensus about the
> desirability of maintaining difference, or making sure that
> differences survive. If difference is physical, then what must
> survive are different species; if difference is cultural then it is
> cultural survival that matters. (2004, 656)

He suggests that, for Butler, in the Xenogenesis series, "it is not difference
itself but one's attitude toward difference that is the source of conflict. [...]
Insofar as identity and difference are complementary rather than oppositional
terms, the human desire to stay human is simultaneously (and without contradiction) the desire to stay the same and the desire to be different" (ibid.).

4   Critics have recently noted the appearance of black vampires in con-
    temporary film and literature. See Frances Gateward, "Daywalkin' Night
    Stalkin' Bloodsuckas: Black Vampires in Contemporary Film" (2004). See
    also Jewelle Gomez's essay, "Recasting the Mythology: Writing Vampire
    Fiction" (1997). Kathy Patterson's essay, "'HAUNTING BACK': VAM-
    PIRE SUBJECTIVITY IN THE GILDA STORIES" (2005), does a nice
    job of interrogating Gomez's recasting of racial- and gender-based power
    structures. Shannon Winnubst's "Vampires, Anxieties, and Dreams: Race
    and Sex in the Contemporary United States" (2003) examines race, gender,
    and sexual hierarchies and Others through the vampire, also in the Gilda
    Stories.

5   Butler revamps and interrogates the mythological and pop-culture "un-
    dead" worlds of Dracula, Lestat, Buffy, and Angel into a complete historic
    culture, that of the Ina, that has developed alongside that of humans.
    Although *Fledgling* is all her own, in writing her vampire novel Butler joins
    a fairly recent spate of African American writers of vampire stories, includ-
    ing Tananarive Due, Jewelle Gomez, Zane, and Leslie Banks, who all add
    race to the issues of gender, power and control, and permeability tradition-
    ally raised in vampire literature.

6   For discussion on hybridity, see Tucker (2007), Jacobs (2003), Bollinger
    (2007), Ramirez (2002), Luckhurst (1996), and Holden (1998).

7 See, for example, Mehaffy and Keating's interview, "Radio Imagination" (2001); Charles H. Rowell's 1997 *Callaloo* interview; or Butler's NPR essay, "Essay on Racism" (2001).

8 During this trial, the Ina Council of Judgment and the extended Ina families have to reconsider their beliefs about the value of both Ina and human life. The Silks are on trial for wiping out two extended Ina families and their human symbionts. At the same time, Shori's families are under scrutiny for their genetic experimentation—for the creation of Shori herself. The Council is made up of the elders of seven Ina families who are all related to Shori and to the Silks. This family tree both aligns with and reveals the Ina social structure and its underlying beliefs. What Shori's symbiont Wright says earlier becomes ever more apparent: "[the Ina] seem to be made up as much of individuals as [people are]. Some people are ethical, some aren't" (154). When some Ina reject what they know to be true and choose to accept lies, we see this ethical division.

9 Lifton's work in psychoanalysis and trauma is grounded in an analysis of the major traumatic events and threats of modern society: Hiroshima, Vietnam, the Holocaust, the threat of nuclear war, and other apocalyptic violence. Lifton's work in psychoanalytic theory and trauma studies is much more complex than I've indicated here, including reexamination and revision of Freud's theories and the "death-life" continuum, and particular examination of human survival and apocalyptic tendencies, issues that Butler's work is also closely engaged with. See "An Interview with Jay Lifton" in Caruth (1995, 128-147).

10 Although I'm not discussing it here, Butler's 2004 short story "Amnesty" also deals with the issues of both hierarchical control and negotiating memory and communities in such a way as to imagine and create a more positive future.

11 Butler's *Parable* series offer other confrontations with the personal and cultural past. First, in *Parable of the Sower*, the black adolescent heroine Lauren is set against a world frozen in a repetition of trauma—in the seeming repetition of America's history of racial enslavement, gender oppression, and class struggle. This traumatic repetition is further emphasized through Lauren's positioning next to an older generation blinded by their own nostalgia for a fabricated past (of racial harmony and plenty) and a youth obsessed with a denial of either past or future in their pursuit of pleasure. Lauren's ethical practice—through her religion Earthseed and the community she builds—provides an alternative future. While *Sower* is narrated in the first person, with a wholly integrated voice, *Parable of the Talents*

breaks up this unity as Lauren's stolen daughter Larkin pieces together her and her mother's past through the interrogation of textual reminders—her mother's journals and other documents. Stolen from her mother as a child, Larkin's trauma is her separation from her mother, her mother's traumatic experiences, and her own history. Although Larkin's scars aren't physical, she remains disfigured by the past and estranged from it. Left at a distance from the past and her mother as its symbolic representation, Larkin is unable to reintegrate herself with her mother's world or any other.

Excerpt 5 from "A Conversation with Octavia E. Butler"

Nisi Shawl

(Interview Conducted at the "Black to the Future Conference: A Black Science Fiction Festival," Seattle, June 12, 2004)

Audience: Yeah, so you started reading, and you were writing science fiction; it was action, but how did you start selling? What did you do? You said it was really lousy but you kept trying.

Octavia: I went to Clarion; that helped a lot. I think I'm the one who started calling Clarion the writer's boot camp. It works very much as a writer's boot camp.

Audience: How did you hear of Clarion?

Octavia: You're trying to get me to tell stories that you already know. I do realize this.

Audience: They're good stories.

Octavia: I was taking a workshop in California that was being given by the writers who donated their time to teaching minority students how to write screenplays, and Harlan Ellison was impressed by my writing—but not by my screenwriting. He thought I should go to Clarion, where he was also going to be teaching. He told me about it and said, "Oh Chip Delany [Samuel R. Delany] is going to be there." And I said, "Oh, is he black?" I had nothing to do with fandom. I knew nothing. I mean I was just this little island person, writing and reading science fiction and not even having anyone to talk to, talk to about the books I was writing… I was reading and I said I'd go. And the problem was of course it cost money, still does.

Nisi: But there are scholarships now.

Octavia: Uh-huh, and Harlan was sort of a partial scholarship for me. I mean he put something like $100 on me you know, to see whether I was going to run or not. And I had to come up with the rest of the money, which was, I don't know, at that time about $600. And that was a lot of money in 1970. And I could come up with it except that all of a sudden my job disappeared. These things happen. And I was so relieved. All of a sudden I didn't have to go to Clarion. And it wasn't my fault.

Well my mother got tired of hearing me whining. I was doing a lot of fake whining: "Oh gee I can't go. It's such a shame." And she came up and knocked on my door and said, "Here's the money. Go. I want you to go." And then she said, "By the way, I was saving that money to get my teeth fixed so I want you to pay it back to me when you come back. No pressure." And there it was. I had to go. And I got to Clarion, and I was terrified; I went on the Greyhound bus. That was my first experience crossing the country on Greyhound, and as I always say, don't do that. Got there. Was scared to death. Didn't have any idea what I was getting into. And there I was in a little town with maybe three black people in the whole town. Little children ran screaming. They had never seen a black person before, and such a big one. [AUD: laughter]

And I did what I always do when I'm really frightened and don't know what to do—I slept a lot. And when I couldn't sleep anymore, I did the other thing that I always do, I got up and wrote. And I wrote a letter to my mother. "Oh God I hate this place. I wish I hadn't come. I'm going to be the worst writer here. I'm going to disgrace my race because I'm going to be only black person here, and I'm going to be the worst writer here. I'm going to disgrace my sex because there aren't going to be very many women. I'm going to be the worst writer here. I'm going to disgrace myself intellectually because everybody else will come here knowing a lot of science and all I know is where the library is, and now that I'm here, I don't even know that. And they've got one radio station and they keep playing these Perry Como records. [AUD: laughter] They've got one TV station and I can't even get to that." At that point, I hadn't figured out how to navigate the grounds and get to the TV station—the TV, I mean. And finally, you know, I'd written myself out this long letter, single-spaced, to my poor mother who lent me the money to go to Clarion. And I did what you should do with letters like that; I mailed it to my bottom drawer and forgot about it. No doubt someone later found this thing in the bottom drawer and opened it and wondered and threw it out, because I never saw it again. But I had more energy after that, and I wrote a story. And I wrote this story about a woman who is upset, frightened, and scared and shy and doesn't know what to do with herself. Gee, where'd I get an idea like that? And that was my first sale. So, see, you got your story. And I sold one more story while I was in Clarion. So Clarion is a good place to get going.

Goodbye, My Hero

Benjamin Rosenbaum

I was a student of Octavia Butler's at the Clarion West Writers Workshop held the summer of 2001. I chose that workshop largely because of her.

I wrote about getting in, on what was then my "online journal" (blogs were still a year or two in the future), shortly after the birth of my daughter Aviva:

Monday, February 26, 2001

Yep, I got into Clarion East. I will be spending six weeks this summer (most of them away from Aviva, which sounds like sheer hell at the moment;-<) being pounded and fired like a Ploughshare of Longing beaten into a Sword of Truth. Or something. Either in Michigan or in Seattle, as I am still waiting for a response from Clarion West. Clarion West is actually my preference, as it would be easier timing-wise for Esther and Aviva to visit in the middle of my stay, I have friends in Seattle, and Octavia Butler is teaching and I think her work is fascinating.

"Fascinating" was an understatement: discovering her work as a teenager in the 1980s (I'd read *Wild Seed* first, and the stories in the digests, and years later the Patternist books, the *Parable of the Sower*, "Bloodchild"…) had been a revelation.

Some sf writers you read for their breathtaking ideas, ignoring awkward prose and thin characters. Others take the wild ideas of these innovators and flesh them out into worlds peopled by characters you love or hate, dread or miss long after you've closed their pages. Others yet are brilliant stylists, so that even if the ideas are borrowed or the characters remote, you read on because every word is right.

Octavia managed to do all of these things at once: the ideas thrilling, the people real and nuanced, the prose unerring. She married, too, sf's

266

sometimes incompatible traditions of thrilling adventure and deeply engaged meditation on the world. Octavia never paused her stories to lecture: her books are full of ideas and arguments, but they are the ideas and arguments of particular characters in the midst of events and conflicts, with their own overwhelming and conflicting personal stakes in the matter. Reading her work, you never have the luxury of simple agreement or disagreement—rather, you are plunged into an uncomfortable, compromised *intimacy*—with her characters, with her startling ideas, and with the mechanics of power, history, brutality, love, and implacable change. It is this state of compromise and being complicit, this constant denial of any place of smug security from which the reader can sit and judge, that gives her work its shocking moral power. And this is connected intimately with what was maybe her most salient characteristic—her honesty; her inability to lie, to say the easy thing, or to turn away.

This, I knew a few pages into *Wild Seed*, was the real thing. This was what I wanted to write. I wanted to emulate her ruthless honesty, her ability to grapple with a morally messy world, her amazing catholicity of interest, her taking it *all* seriously—language, ideas, the physical world, and the world of the heart.

So, when I did get into Clarion West (CW), I leapt at the chance. We met Octavia the first night, and she gave us an assignment—to freewrite on an unpleasant real experience from our past, and then, without stopping, to turn the page and begin a new story steeped in that same emotion, without naming it. Challenged by the administrators to come up with a story for critiques the first week, I wrote "Embracing-the-New" in two all-nighters, after which I stumbled to a computer to record my impressions of CW for the journal:

Wednesday, June 20, 2001

Hello from Clarion West.

If you really want to know what life is like here on a regular basis, you'll need to check out the journals of Sam/Ling and Allan. They are much more organized than I am and somehow manage to post about every day [...]

It's six a.m. and I have been up since five or so finishing up my critiques of other people's stories for class. I'm still on

European time in a way, and I may keep it that way. Early morning is a good time to write.

I am daily astounded that I found this place.

I expected Clarion to feel like college—and in a way it does, the giddiness of a new adventure, the wonderful craziness of dorm life (last night several of us were sitting in a circle on the long hallway floor running between all the rooms, playing the Surrealist Oracle game and exploding intermittently with laughter, with the sound of someone's stereo drifting through an open door and people drifting by to watch). But it's also not like college. In college we didn't know what we wanted to do—we were crazy young animals, jumping around, trying things out, wondering what our passions were. At Clarion we are older—and what a wealth of life experience is here, the struggles and triumphs of seventeen utterly different, examined lives!— and we know what our passions are. And in at least one of those passions—the writing of speculative fiction—we are all united. So where in college there was this crazy restless puppy energy going all over the place, chasing its tail, here there is the focused power of a pack of greyhounds racing.

For pretty much everyone here, this is the fulfillment of a long-held dream. (Some people just started writing a few years ago, granted—but I think the writing bug, or some bug to write one's name deeply into the surface of the world, must have been there before.) So there isn't much of the wasted energy of college (though, for those who recognize the Surrealist Oracle game above, it should be clear that I am a ringleader of procrastination—ahem, I mean recharging our mental batteries).

I am astonished at the high level of the critiques and the diversity of ways of seeing the same story—some people dreaming their way through its symbolism, some rigorously interrogating its plot and worldbuilding, some reaching with great empathy into the hearts of its characters, some digging into the social and political contexts it creates and challenges—and how uniformly everyone brings something of value. I am also amazed at the difference and richness of the stories. Many are rough, and as we get more tired, they're bound to get even rougher—it's not like reading *Asimov's*—but at the same time, that roughness lets you see the richness of seventeen different souls, with their jagged edges not yet filed off. It's a privilege.

So I wrote a story Sunday night/Monday morning, revised it Tuesday morning (adding a scene and bringing it to 3700 words) and then handed it in. The critique is today. I'm excited!

The story, "Embracing-The-New," is from the mra/Uoo/Tring/symbiont universe you've heard me grumbling about for months on months. Amra herself is not in it. I had done a lot of worldbuilding but could never fit a story into it until now [....] I used Octavia's one-sentence summary system (the sentence must contain character, conflict, and conclusion), and before writing the story I had this sentence written down (which, of course, gives the story's end away, so don't read it if you hate spoilers and expect to read the story). It made a big difference, writing the story, to know ahead of time, in a very specific and measurable way, where I was going.

Octavia is kind and full of useful tales and ideas about writing, besides being, you know, Octavia Butler (which is to say, one of the best science fiction writers alive).

Everyone (the administrators, the instructors—including those not yet here, and so on) keeps warning us to stay nice to each other and not let the pressure-cooker atmosphere create scapegoating. They seem overly worried to us—but of course, they speak from bitter experience (though probably the classes with problems stick in memory more vividly than those who do fine). I appreciate their warnings—it's good to be on our guard. I also appreciate the structures they've established to keep hostilities from arising, like the critiquing format with its strict three-minute time limit (a lifesaver for me in particular, as I would likely otherwise ramble). But I'm not too worried, now that I've met the group. We're just not going to let scapegoating happen. Period.

It was Nalo Hopkinson, I believe—our third-week instructor—who had written us, pre-Clarion West, an impassioned letter on the danger of cliques, scapegoats, and schisms in the fragile, ego-abrading, pressure-cooker atmosphere of a Clarion-style workshop. It was our able administrators, Leslie Howle and Neile Graham, who fretted and fussed over our social cohesion. But it was also surely no accident that they'd picked Octavia as the first-week instructor, to set the tone.

Nor was all this concern without cause; I may have been sanguine in that first-week blog entry, but by the infamous week four we had had plenty of tears, frayed tempers, and narrowly averted splits. We held together, though—all seventeen of us keeping in touch for years afterwards—and surely the tone Octavia set that first week was a crucial anchor.

You could not imagine Octavia being cruel or glib or selfish or self-righteous. Nor, as shy as she was, could you imagine her being intimidated by anyone or anything. Octavia took every one of us seriously, every story, every comment seriously. She knew what it was to be slighted and ignored. She'd been informed early on, she told us, that the idea of a working-class black girl growing up to make a living as a writer was comically absurd. Octavia knew how to look beneath the surface. Though she was resolutely this-worldly and deeply suspicious of fuzzy mysticism, the message we got was that this work was holy. We wanted to be worthy of her expectations of us.

Octavia finished her week on Friday, June 23 (we took her out for her birthday dinner at an Ethiopian restaurant, where her usual reserve diminished and she smiled a lot). It wasn't until some time later, after Bradley Denton's and Nalo's weeks, that I managed to drag myself back to the online journal:

Thursday, July 12, 2001

To bring you up to date… "Embracing-The-New" got a generally good reaction. I put the climax scene off-stage, and employed a deus ex machina to save the hero, and there were some info dumps and unclear bits, but mostly people liked it. Octavia said basically "don't screw with it too much." In conference, she told me "Baby Love" is a little implausible, "The Death Trap of Dr. Freezo" is publishable as is, and that I should try a novel soon, set in a world I've dwelt in and played around with in my mind for a while. (I have several of those.) Octavia was wonderful, of course: a star of the SF firmament descended to walk among us, with an absolutely clear literary compass, and a sweet person to boot.

I never saw Octavia again. Her words, though, lent me courage. Life teemed with distractions, I spent five years on a novel that died on me, and writing often seemed like an emotionally grueling slog. But Octavia Butler, who was the real thing, had told me to keep going.

"Embracing-the-New" was eventually nominated for a Nebula Award, and some of my other stories got nominated for other things, and I went to conventions and ceremonies and hobnobbed with others of my heroes. Sf is a small world; I was hoping I would meet her again there sometime. But I didn't. She died, only 59 years old, four and a half years after that summer at Clarion West. A final blog entry:

Tuesday, February 28, 2006

Octavia Butler, June 22, 1947–February 24, 2006, zikhronah livrakhah[1]

She was one of my heroes. She wrote the real stuff, the stuff that shakes you, gently but deeply, leaves you different than you were going in.

I came to CW 2001 largely because she would be teaching (the first week!) and I was not disappointed. She had an enormous grace and dignity and power. It wasn't the power of personality—you could tell that, as a personality, she'd just as well say nothing. You could tell how quiet and intro-verted she was, but she spoke, for us. She wasn't like me—I talk your ear off, out of a sense of entitlement—it occurs to me only belatedly, upon reflection, that you might have something else to do than listen. Octavia spoke, as far as I could tell, out of a sense of honor and courage—she could see that no one else was going to be able to say what she had to say the way she could, and she was too much of a mensch to turn away from her duty.

She was wickedly funny in a dry way that you could miss if you weren't paying attention. She was unfailingly courteous and kind. I think Brad Denton (2nd week) found us a little wild at times, Nalo (3rd week) found us almost sufficiently wild, and Connie Willis (4th week) would holler at us, in her fifth-grade-teacher voice, to "Settle down!"—but we didn't pull anything with Octavia, I can tell you. Not because we imagined that she would chide us (she wouldn't have) nor because we thought she might be wounded (ha! like we could wound her!), but because her dignity filled the room. You had the sense of what a crime it was to waste this life, to waste whatever God had given you.

In critique, she was both unfailingly gentle and principledly ruthless. Again you got the sense of two Octavias speaking—the ordinary one, who knew acutely what it was to feel pain, and wished you not an ounce—and the extraordinary one, the outsized courage and wisdom and skill that had grown in her by virtue of her being unwilling to refuse it, unwilling to shut up about it, and which would speak.

She said things that were short and true. About my first story, "Embracing-the-New," she said, "I wouldn't change this too much," and she was right—I did change it too much, and eventually had to change it back. About my career, she said, "it's time for you to write novels," and she's still right, and I'm still trying to get there. I could use your courage, Octavia.

I'm so sorry I'll never see her again. I was always hoping I would.

Goodbye, my hero.

Endnote

1   "*Zikhronah Livrakah*" means in Hebrew "may her memory be for a bless-ing." There are several traditional Jewish honorifics, sort of equivalent to "rest in peace," when speaking of the dead; this is the one used for great teachers and for *tzaddikim*, "the just"; it's appropriate in both senses.

Annotated Bibliography of Butler's Fiction

1. "Crossover" (in *Clarion* 1971).

   This is Butler's first published work, written while a student at the Clarion Science Fiction and Fantasy Writer's Workshop. In the story, a woman who works on an assembly line in a factory hallucinates the return of her boyfriend, who she believes is in prison. To avoid her hallucinations, she turns to alcohol and the company of a "wino."

2. *Patternmaster* (Doubleday 1976; Avon 1979; Warner 1995; in *Seed to Harvest*, Grand Central Publishing 2007).

   Patternmaster is set far in the future of the Patternists, a group of genetically engineered humans who have various psionic (mental) abilities. The Patternmaster is at the top of the Patternist hierarchy; he controls the Pattern—the psychic web that links the Patternists together. The Patternists wage constant battle against the "Clayarks," humans who have been mutated by the Clayark disease into super-fast, super-strong, animal-like creatures. *Patternmaster* centers on Teray, a strong young Patternist, who is one of the sons of the current Patternmaster, and his struggle with his brother Coransee, an extremely powerful Housemaster who hopes to take over the Pattern. In Coransee's house, where Teray has been forced to become an outsider, he meets the healer Amber and the two of them run away together from Coransee's house. In a final showdown against Coransee, Amber helps Teray defeat Coransee but refuses to become Teray's wife so that she can head her own House. At the end of the story, Teray learns from his father, the current Patternmaster, that now that he has defeated Coransee, the Patternmaster is content to die and pass the Pattern onto Teray.

3. *Mind of My Mind* (Doubleday 1977; Warner 1994; in *Seed to Harvest*, Grand Central Publishing 2007).

   Set in Los Angeles in the 1970s, *Mind of My Mind* goes back in time in the Patternist chronology to tell the story of the genesis of the Patternist society. We learn that Doro, a four-thousand-year-old immortal originally from Africa, is the literal and figurative father of the telepathic group of humans who become the Patternists. Doro's body is not immortal, but he moves his essence from one body to the next as necessary for his survival. He mates with and breeds telepathically sensitive people, often his own descendants, in an attempt to create a superhuman race of telepaths. This novel focuses on his daughter Mary, a young, poor, mixed-race African American woman who Doro hopes will become a special telepath able to link with other telepaths. During her transition from "latent" to "active" telepath, Mary creates the first Pattern by mentally latching onto six active telepaths. After two years, during which Mary adds fifteen hundred people to her Patternist community, Doro thinks that she has too much power and orders her to stop acquiring telepaths. However, Mary cannot stop adding to her Patternists without destroying herself and thus all the Patternists. Drawing on the strength of her people, Mary fights and kills Doro. Many Patternists die in the fight, but Mary is free to continue building and protecting her Patternist society.

4.   *Survivor* (Doubleday 1978).

Only loosely connected to the other Patternist books, *Survivor* tells the story of the "Missionaries," a group of religious Christians who establish a colony on another planet in order to maintain what they see as God's chosen form of humanity, one free of the Clayark disease or Patternist mental interference. The story begins with the rescue of Alanna from the Tehkohn (one of the competing tribes of the native intelligent inhabitants of the planet—the humanoid, blue-furred, and clawed Kohn). Prior to the opening of the novel, Alanna, the protagonist of the story, had been adopted by the Missionaries on Earth after several years of living as an orphaned feral child. When the Missionaries arrive on the planet, they are befriended by the local Kohn tribe, the Garkohn, who help them set up their colony. Captured by the Tehkohn, Alanna has adapted herself once again to a new society, eventually marrying the Tehkohn leader and bearing his child. Through her relationship with the leader of the Tehkohn, Alanna learns that the Garkohn have addicted the Missionaries to a local plant, hoping to assimilate the humans and use human technology against the Tehkohn. After she has been "rescued" by the Missionaries, Alanna leads them to ally themselves temporarily with the Tehkohn so that they can break away from the Garkohn and establish a colony of their own. However, her adoptive human father cannot accept Alanna's romantic relationship with the Tehkohn leader, and Alanna leaves the human group for life with her new people, the Tehkohn.

5. *Kindred* (Doubleday, 1979; Beacon Press, 1988; reprint Beacon Press, 2004).

Dana, an African American woman, is mysteriously transported back and forth from 1976 Los Angeles—where she has just moved into a new home with her white husband Kevin—to a nineteenth-century slave plantation in Maryland. She is repeatedly called back to this past to save the life of her white, slave-owning ancestor Rufus—beginning when he is five—and is returned to her present only when her own life is in danger. As a black woman without the proper papers in this pre-Civil War past, she is treated as—and thus takes on the role of—a slave. She is nearly raped twice and is brutally beaten several times. On one occasion her white husband is transported with her, but he cannot protect her. She is forced to aid her ancestor Rufus in the rape of the slave woman Alice—who eventually will bear Dana's ancestress—and must continue saving Rufus's life in order to ensure her own survival in the future. Eventually, Dana kills Rufus rather than submit to being raped by him; she is returned to her present for good but loses an arm in her final transportation home.

6. "Near of Kin" (in *Chrysalis 4* 1979; in *Bloodchild and Other Stories*, Four Walls Eight Windows 1995, Seven Stories Press 1996, 2005).

In this story, a young college-aged woman is going through her mother's things after her mother's death, in the company of her beloved uncle. We learn that she never lived with her mother and had been raised by her grandmother. The daughter resented her mother for not keeping her. The daughter had guessed years before that her uncle was not simply her uncle, but her biological father. She gets her uncle to admit the truth, a truth that no one else, not even her grandmother, knew.

7. *Wild Seed* (Doubleday, 1980; Warner Books, 1988, 2001; in *Seed to Harvest*, Grand Central Publishing, 2007).

    The fourth Patternist book to be published, *Wild Seed* goes back to seventeenth-century Africa to trace the origins of the Patternists and narrates the relationship between the two immortals, Doro and Anyanwu. Doro—the immortal telepath introduced in *Mind of My Mind*—is drawn to Anyanwu, an immortal shape-shifter and healer living in an Onitsha Igbo village. Now three-hundred-years old, Anyanwu exercises complete control over the biological processes of her body. Her ability to understand and manipulate her own body makes her an effective healer and enables her take on alternate shapes, both animal and human. Doro convinces Anyanwu to come with him to America as his wife. However, once they arrive in the New World, Doro marries her off to one of his white sons. From this time onward, Anyanwu and Doro become adversaries; he uses her children to enforce her loyalty, and she continues to resist him. After her husband's death, Anyanwu escapes Doro by taking on various animal forms. In the guise of a white man, she becomes the owner of a Louisiana plantation, where Doro finds her in 1840. Tired of fighting with Doro for the lives and rights of her children and herself, Anyanwu decides to die. Doro finally realizes the worth of his only long-lived companion and makes a reconciliation with her that convinces her to go on living.

8. "Speech Sounds" (in *Isaac Asimov's Science Fiction Magazine*, 1983; in *Bloodchild and Other Stories*, Four Walls Eight Windows, 1995, Seven Stories Press, 1996, 2005); Winner of Hugo Award for Best Short Story (1984).

    Set in Los Angeles at some indeterminate point in the near future, this story documents the effects of a stroke-like, civilization-wide illness that attacks the language centers of the brain. Those who survive the illness often can no longer talk or read or understand spoken or written language. Those less impaired by the illness might retain one or more language ability. In the opening scene of the story, Valerie Rye is traveling on a bus when a wordless fight breaks out among the passengers. The bus driver stops the bus and a man, wearing the uniform of the obsolete LAPD, breaks up the fight, and then with gestures asks Rye to come with him in his car. She discovers that he can read, and he discovers that she can speak. He shows her the token for his name, a piece of obsidian; in her mind, she calls him Obsidian. They make love, and he agrees to come home with her, though he indicates that he will continue trying to keep the peace in the now mostly lawless world. On their way to her home, they encounter a man attacking a woman. Obsidian is killed in his attempt to save the woman, who also dies. Two young children come out to find their mother, who has been killed. Rye discovers that the children can talk fluidly and takes them home, resolving to teach and protect them.

9. *Clay's Ark* (St. Martin's Press 1984; Ace Books 1985; Warner 1996, in *Seed to Harvest*, Grand Central Publishing 2007).

This book, the last published in the Patternist series, narrates the beginnings of the Clay Ark disease that mutated normal humans into the sphinx-like Clayarks of *Patternmaster*. A physician living in a gated enclave in Southern California, Blake Maslin, and his sixteen-year-old twin daughters, Rane and Keira (the latter dying of leukemia), attempt to travel through a dysfunctional society. They are kidnapped by Eli Doyle, the only survivor of Clay's Ark, the first manned spaceship to reach another planet, and Eli's "family"—those whom he has infected with the alien virus he brought back to Earth. The virus genetically mutates its victims, giving them strength, speed, a possibly invulnerable immune system, unknown healing abilities, and an uncontrollable desire to pass on the virus. The children of those infected are extremely fast and strong sphinx-like creatures. Despite being infected by the virus, Blake and his daughters escape from Eli's group only to be captured by a "car family." Blake and Rane, drawn uncontrollably to both food and sex due to the virus, are killed in their attempts to escape from the car family. Before he dies, Blake passes the disease to a long-haul truck driver, and within a short time, the virus has spread all over the world. Riots and fires rage in many of the major US cities. Keira, whose cancer is cured by the virus, joins Eli's family, pregnant with her own sphinx-like child.

10. "Bloodchild" (in *Isaac Asimov's Science Fiction Magazine*, 1984, in *Bloodchild and Other Stories*, Four Walls Eight Windows, 1995, Seven Stories Press, 1996, 2005); Winner of Nebula Award for

Best Novelette (1984); Winner of Hugo Award for Best Novelette (1985); Winner of Locus Award for Best Novelette (1985); Winner of *Science Fiction Chronicle* Award for Best Novelette (1985).

Sometimes referred to as Butler's "pregnant man" story, "Bloodchild" tells of the relationship between the insect-like alien Tlic and the humans who have traveled to the Tlic planet in order to escape death and enslavement on Earth. The humans attempt, but fail, to colonize the Tlic. The Tlic discover that humans provide ideal hosts for Tlic eggs and establish a human preserve where human families are protected but required to make one child per family available for egg implantation. Tlic usually choose boys and men to carry Tlic young, so that human women can bear their own young. Gan, the story's narrator, lives with T'Gatoi, the Tlic who had chosen him at his birth to carry her eggs. T'Gatoi regularly brings Gan's family sterile eggs to eat; for humans, eating these eggs gives them long life and an enjoyable "high." When Gan and T'Gatoi are visiting Gan's family in the Preserve, a N'Tlic—a human implanted with Tlic eggs—collapses outside their home because the eggs he carries have hatched early. T'Gatoi has to remove the grubs immediately, or they will eat their way out of the N'Tlic and kill him. Gan helps T'Gatoi as she cuts the N'Tlic open and removes the grubs, placing them inside a slaughtered animal so that the grubs will have fresh meat to eat. The man's Tlic arrives and is able to save the man. Gan, however, is horrified by what he has seen. In spite of his love for T'Gatoi, he is not sure that he still wants to carry her eggs. T'Gatoi must begin laying her eggs that night and asks Gan to choose whether or not she should use Gan's sister instead. Gan agrees to host T'Gatoi's eggs, because he wants to protect his sister and also because he wants to keep T'Gatoi's love for himself.

11. *Dawn* (Warner Books 1987, 1989, 1997; in *Xenogenesis*, Guild America Books 1989; in *Lilith's Brood*, Warner 2000).

In *Dawn*, the first book in the Xenogenesis trilogy, Lilith Iyapo awakens in a living space ship some two hundred fifty years after a nuclear war has destroyed Earth. She learns that her "rescuers," the tentacled Oankali aliens, have collected the human survivors, placed them in animated suspension aboard their ship, and restored the Earth so that the Oankali can enter into a "gene trade" with the humans. In this gene trade, the Oankali will mix their DNA with human DNA in order to create a new hybrid species and thus modify what they see as the human genetic flaw, the fatal combination of intelligence and hierarchical tendencies. At the same time, the Oankali believe that by modifying human cancers they will learn how to regrow limbs and reshape themselves. They have chosen Lilith to lead the first group of humans who will enter into this gene trade. Humans will no longer be allowed to produce human children with the lethal genetic flaw or without the participation of an ooloi, the third sex of the Oankali—the gene mixers. After awakening, Lilith lives among the Oankali and is bonded to Nikanj, an ooloi. She then awakens a group of humans and begins to train them for their return to Earth, hoping that once they reach Earth they will be able to escape the Oankali. However, the humans Lilith awaken rebel against her and the proposed gene trade. They kill Lilith's new human mate Joseph, and the first group of humans is sent to Earth without her. Using Joseph's DNA, Nikanj makes Lilith pregnant with the very first human-Oankali construct child.

12. "The Evening and the Morning and the Night" (Omni Publications International 1987; in *Bloodchild and Other Stories*, Four Walls Eight Windows 1995, Seven Stories Press 1996, 2005); Winner of *Science Fiction Chronicle* Reader Award; Nominated for Nebula Award for Best Novelette (1987).

The protagonist of this novelette, Lynn, is a young woman who is a double DGD—a child of parents who both had the Duryea-Gode disease, an unintended side-effect of a cancer cure. In a later stage of the disease, DGDs mutilate themselves and stop responding to their surroundings. At age fifteen, Lynn attempts suicide, and just before she leaves home for college, her father kills and mutilates her mother, and then himself. At college, Lynn shares a house with four other DGDs, becomes the unofficial house mother, and gets engaged to housemate Alan Chi, another double DGD. Lynn accompanies him on a visit to his mother at Dilg, a special DGD "retreat." They discover that at Dilg, uncontrolled DGDs are not restrained and do not mutilate themselves, but instead produce artwork, research, and new technologies. Alan's mother, who is blind because of the damage she did to herself before she came to Dilg, has become a sculptor and can even converse with them once Beatrice, the director of Dilg, gets her attention. Beatrice explains that female double DGDs produce a pheromone that allows them to communicate with out-of-control DGDs and can help keep the patients from hurting themselves. Lynn learns that she could head a DGD retreat like Dilg and Alan could work as a doctor with her. Lynn knows that she has to take up this work, but Alan is conflicted about being married to someone who "controls" him. Beatrice sends them home to think about it and lets Lynn know that she has the power to keep Alan or drive him away.

13. *Adulthood Rites* (Warner, 1988, 1997; in *Xenogenesis*, Guild America Books, 1989; in *Lilith's Brood*, Warner 2000).

The second book of the Xenogenesis trilogy begins thirty years after humans have been returned to the Earth's surface. One of Lilith's human-Oankali hybrid children, Akin, is kidnapped when he is a little over a year old by one of the human-only groups that have run away from the Oankali. Unable to have children without Oankali gene mixing, these humans kidnap or buy the more human-looking hybrid children. Akin is bought by a resister village where two of the humans first wakened by Lilith live. The Oankali decide to leave Akin with the resisters as long as he is safe, hoping that he will be able to learn about the resisters in a way not available to the Oankali themselves. Construct children develop intellectually much faster than human children (Akin begins to put together sentences when he is two months old), and Akin hopes to use this time to learn about his human side. His family recovers him when he is three, but as an adolescent, he continues to contact various resister villages, trying to learn more about the humans. When he is twenty, Akin and his sibling are sent to the Oankali parent ship so that he can learn more about his Oankali side. Among those aboard the ship is the Akjai group of the Oankali who do not participate in the Oankali-human gene trade. The existence of an Akjai group guarantees the survival of the Oankali if the trade fails. With the help of an Akjai ooloi—the gene manipulators of the species—Akin argues that there should be a human Akjai group, a purely human group not altered by the trade. He makes it his life's work to help prepare

Mars as a human-only colony and teach human volunteers how to
live there.

14. *Imago* (Warner 1989, 1997; in *Xenogenesis*, Guild America Books
    1989; in *Lilith's Brood,* Warner 2000).

    Set some fifty years after *Adulthood Rites*, the third book of the Xe-
    nogenesis trilogy centers on another of Lilith's children, Jodahs, the
    first human-Oankali ooloi. Jodahs and its family live in exile in the
    wilderness because of Jodahs's instability. There, Jodahs discovers a
    human brother and sister, who have descended from a small group
    of fertile, though diseased, resister humans. Members of this group,
    bred out of necessity with close relatives for multiple generations,
    have numerous birth defects, and many die. Cut off from all others,
    this group does not know about the Mars colony and sees them-
    selves as humanity's only chance to breed without alien interfer-
    ence. Jodahs bonds with this brother and sister and heals them; in
    doing so, Jodahs becomes stable, no longer a threat to its own kind.
    When Jodahs's sibling Aaor also develops as an ooloi, Jodahs knows
    it must find Aaor mates among these young diseased humans as
    well, or it will be fated to life on the Oankali ship with no mates. Jo-
    dahs's human mates lead Jodahs and Aaor to their village, and Aaor
    finds willing mates among them. However, this group of lifelong
    resisters insists on keeping the two ooloi as hostages, knowing that
    the Oankali will eventually come to take over the village. Over the
    course of several months, Jodahs and Aaor heal and bond with many
    members of the village so that when the Oankali finally arrive, the
    humans do not panic. The villagers know that they will have a choice
    to either stay on Earth and mate with the Oankali or immigrate to
    Mars and have healthy human children. Won over by Jodahs and
    Aaor, many choose to stay on Earth and find Oankali mates. Jodahs
    and Aaor are allowed to start a village at the base of the mountains
    where new hybrid human-Oankali ooloi like themselves can come,
    find willing human mates, and learn how to become stable.

15. *Parable of the Sower* (Four Walls, Eight Windows 1993, Women's
    Press Ltd. 1995, Warner 1995, 2000). Nominated for a Nebula
    Award for Best Novel (1994); *New York Times* Notable Book of the
    Year (1994).

The first in the Earthseed series, *Parable of the Sower* is set in California in the years 2024 to 2027 and narrated by Lauren Oya Olamina, who is fifteen years old when the story starts and lives about twenty miles from Los Angeles in the walled enclave of Robledo. Global warming, the increasing gap between the rich and poor, illiteracy, rampant crime, drug addiction, and corporate greed have led to the general breakdown of society. Essential goods are expensive and scarce. The government is nominal at best, and few people bother to vote. Some towns also have been "bought" by multinational corporations and operate like the "company towns" of the early twentieth century in which the workers and their families were essentially owned by the coal or lumber companies. Because of her late mother's drug addiction, Lauren is a "sharer," someone who suffers from a hyperempathy syndrome in which she literally feels the physical pain she witnesses. Aware of the limited protection provided by Robledo's walls, Lauren prepares a survival pack and plans on traveling north as soon as she is eighteen. Also, in opposition to the traditional beliefs of her Baptist minister father, she develops a new belief system, which she calls "Earthseed," based on the premise that "God is Change." When Robledo is destroyed by roving bands of arsonists and all of Lauren's family is killed, she heads north with the other two survivors of the attacks: Zahra, a black woman a few year older than herself; and Harry, a white boy Lauren's age. Along the way, they are joined by others they encounter. The new members of the group include Bankole, an older African American doctor who becomes Lauren's lover, two young white women rescued from prostitution, a mixed race family, a three-year-old orphan, as well as four other "sharers." Lauren believes that Earthseed will help prepare the human race for its destiny of life on another planet—a life that will force humanity into its adulthood—and decides to found the first Earthseed community with this mixed group. Eventually, the group reaches land owned by Bankole in Northern California and decides to settle there. The members of the group plant acorns in memory of their dead families and name their community "Acorn."

16. *Bloodchild and Other Stories* (Four Walls, Eight Windows, 1995, Seven Stories Press, 1996, 2005).

The first versions of this short story collection include the stories "Bloodchild," "The Evening and the Morning and the Night," "Near of Kin," "Speech Sounds," and "Crossover," as well as two nonfiction pieces about writing titled "Positive Obsession" and "Furor Scribendi." Each story and essay is accompanied by a brief afterword. The revised edition published in 2005 includes two new stories: "Amnesty" and "The Book of Martha."

17. *The Parable of the Talents* (Seven Stories Press, 1998; Quality Paperback Book Club, 1999; Women's Press Ltd., 2000, 2001; Warner, 2000, 2001); Winner of Nebula Award for Best Novel (1999).

A continuation of the Earthseed story, this novel starts in the viewpoint of Lauren's daughter Larkin, in the aftermath of Lauren's death. Larkin has been separated from Lauren for most of her life and has little love for her. She's compiling a book using entries from her mother's journals. We learn from these texts that in 2032, Acorn had 64 inhabitants; that Lauren bought the freedom of her younger brother Marcus, who had been enslaved as a prostitute; that after Marcus failed to convert Acorn's members to his version of Christianity he left and became a preacher in the right-wing Christian America (CA) Church. Larkin was born in 2033, two months before Acorn was destroyed by a group of right-wing vigilantes. Larkin and the other children were adopted by CA families, and the surviving adults put into slave collars to be "reeducated." When a landslide shut down the slave collar control unit, they killed their captors and escaped. Marcus first contacted Larkin when she was nineteen. He told her that her biological parents were dead and took her to live with him. At thirty-four, Larkin discovered that Lauren, now a famous cult leader, was her mother. They met, but Larkin believed Earthseed was her mother's preferred child. Lauren died at the age of eighty-one, shortly after the first Earthseed shuttles left Earth.

18. *Lilith's Brood* (Warner, 2000).

The Xenogenesis trilogy of the *Dawn, Adulthood Rites*, and *Imago* are collected in this volume.

19. "Amnesty" (SciFi.com 2003, in *Bloodchild and Other Stories*, Seven Stories Press 2005).

A black woman named Noah Cannon works as a translator for alien entities called "Communities," who have colonized Earth. The aliens communicate with humans by "enfolding" a human within their many selves and using a system of touches. In the beginning of the story, Noah is running an orientation for a multi-ethnic group of potential human employees, six people ranging from a woman who worships the aliens to another who wants to learn how to fight them. As Noah answers the applicants' questions, we learn about the history of the aliens on Earth and Noah's own history with them. The Communities, each of which consists of a multitude of individual entities and physically resembles a large bush, came to Earth on a one-way ship and settled in uninhabited deserts. Their arrival led to a depression in the human economy, and the Communities proceeded to abduct humans, killing most of the early abductees in their experiments. Noah was abducted at age eleven in the second wave of abductions. Treated like lab animals, the abductees were often hurt and the women, included Noah, were raped by their fellow captives. In order to communicate with their captors, Noah and the other surviving prisoners put together a code that led to the language now used to communicate with the Communities. Twelve years after her abduction, Noah was released by the aliens and immediately captured and tortured by the human military, which for her was worse than anything the aliens had done. The military released her only when someone leaked her story. After recovering from her torture, Noah went to school and returned to the Communities to work for them. Now, she explains to the prospective employees, her family is well provided for because the Communities pay her well. Noah describes the enfolding process as something that can be pleasant for the humans and addictive for the aliens—which means good jobs for many humans who wouldn't otherwise have them. The story ends as Noah leads the group to their final interview, an enfolding with their prospective employers.

20. "The Book of Martha" (SciFi.com 2005; in *Bloodchild and Other Stories*, Seven Stories Press, 2005).

In this story, God appears to Martha Bes, a forty-three-year-old African American novelist, and tells her that she must make a single important change to creation to help humans mend their self-destructive ways. Martha worries about inadvertently hurting people, especially since God tells her that he won't fix her mistakes or allow her to fix any problems that occur once she has made her decision. First Martha wonders about allowing people to have only two children, no matter what. God points out problems with her solution, including the fact that given natural disasters, diseases, and wars, humanity would eventually go extinct, unable to replace themselves. She eventually asks about giving people vivid, satisfying dreams each night that would allow them to vent their aggression and greed, but not prevent them from caring for their families. Martha knows that as she asks this, people will no longer be interested in reading novels and she will have to find a new profession. God agrees that Martha's plan will probably do more good than harm, and she tells him to make it happen. She then asks to return to her life with no memory of her encounter with God.

21. *Fledgling* (Seven Stories Press, 2005; Grand Central Publishing, 2007).

Fledgling begins with the novel's narrator, Shori Matthews, waking up with intense hunger, pain, and complete amnesia. Shori learns that although she appears to be a ten-year-old African American girl, she is an Ina, a fifty-three-year-old vampire child, a member of the long-lived Ina species who have co-existed with humanity for thousands of years. Ina saliva gives pleasure to humans, helps them heal and stay healthy. The Ina develop relationships with their human symbionts, who provide the Ina with both blood for nourishment and companionship. Shori finds her Ina father and learns that she is the only survivor of an attack on her entire female family; her mothers, sisters, and eldermothers as well as all their human symbionts were killed. (Ina live in same-sex households with their human symbionts, separate from their Ina mates.) Shori is different from other Ina, who are generally tall, thin, and very pale. Her mothers mixed her Ina genes with that of an African American woman in order to make an Ina who would not be completely vulnerable during the day. Unlike other Ina, Shori can stay awake during the day and function in the sun, as long as her skin, head, and eyes are protected. One of the Ina families, the Silks, repulsed by Shori's "human" genes, seek to annihilate Shori and her families. Her allies call a Council of Judgment, a three day "trial" in which seven Ina families come together, hear testimony regarding the attacks, and decide on the fate of the family accused. The evidence against the Silks is damning. Also, the Silks' advocate has one of Shori's symbionts killed during the trial. Still, despite the fact that the majority of the Council finds in favor of Shori, the judgment against them is not unanimous. Thus, the Silks will not be executed; instead, all of their unmated children will be adopted into other families and the Silks will cease to exist as a family. Shori, along with her symbionts, will spend time with various Ina relations in order to relearn Ina life and will eventually mate with the sons of her allies, hopefully passing on the protection her human genes have given her to her children.

22. *Seed to Harvest* (Grand Central Publishing, 2007).

This volume includes the novels *Wild Seed, Mind of My Mind, Clay's Ark,* and *Patternmaster.*

Octavia E. Butler Biographical Timeline[1]

1947	Octavia Estelle Butler is born to Laurice and Octavia M. (Guy) Butler on June 22 in Pasadena, CA. Her father dies when she is very young. She is raised by her mother and her grandmother.
1957-59	Butler begins writing science fiction stories.
1960-61	With the help of her science teacher, Butler submits her first story to a science fiction magazine.
1965	Butler graduates from John Muir High School in Pasadena.
1967	Butler wins Fifth Prize in *Writer's Digest* Short Story Contest.
1968	Butler earns an associate degree from Pasadena City College and enters California State University, Los Angeles.
1969-1970	Butler leaves Cal State and takes UCLA extension writing courses. She attends the Open Door Workshop of the Screen Writers Guild of America, a program designed to mentor Latino and African American writers. Butler meets Harlan Ellison at the Open Door Workshop.
1970	At the behest of Ellison, Butler attends the Clarion Science Fiction Writers Workshop, a six-week program for aspiring science fiction writers in Clarion, PA. Butler meets Samuel R. Delany at the Clarion Workshop. Butler sells her first two stories: "Crossover" to Robin Scott Wilson, the current director of Clarion, and "Child Finder" to Harlan Ellison.
1971	"Crossover" is published in Clarion's 1971 anthology.

1974	Butler begins work on what is to become her first published novel, *Patternmaster*.
1976	Butler's first novel, *Patternmaster*, is published by Doubleday.
1977	*Mind of My Mind*, prequel to *Patternmaster*, is published by Doubleday.
1978	The third book in the Patternist series, *Survivor*, is published by Doubleday. Butler will later refer to this novel as her "Star Trek" novel and will not allow it to be reprinted with the rest of the Patternist novels.
1979	Butler's stand-alone novel *Kindred* is published by Doubleday. Her short story "Near of Kin" is published in *Chrysalis 4*. Butler becomes a full-time writer.
1980	The fourth book of the Patternist series, *Wild Seed*, is published by Doubleday. Butler is the Guest of Honor at WisCon 4, the feminist science fiction convention in Madison, WI. She wins the Creative Arts Achievement award from the Los Angeles YWCA.
1983	Butler's short story "Speech Sounds" is published in *Isaac Asimov's Science Fiction Magazine*.
1984	The fifth and final book of the Patternist series, *Clay's Ark*, is published by St. Martin's Press. "Speech Sounds" wins the Hugo Award for Short Story. Butler's "Bloodchild" is published in *Isaac Asimov's Science Fiction Magazine* and wins the Nebula Award for a novelette.
1985	"Bloodchild" wins the Hugo Award, the *Locus* Award, and the *Science Fiction Chronicle* Reader Award for Best Novelette.
1987	The first book of the Xenogenesis trilogy, *Dawn*, is published by Warner Books. "The Evening and the Morning and the Night" is published in *Omni Magazine* and is nominated for the Nebula novelette award.

1988	*Adulthood Rites*, the second book of the Xenogenesis trilogy, is published by Warner Books. *Kindred* is reissued by Beacon Press. "The Evening and the Morning and the Night" wins the *Science Fiction Chronicle* Reader Award. Butler is the Guest of Honor at InConJuntion VIII, a SF and fantasy convention in Indianapolis, IN.
1989	*Imago*, the final book of the Xenogenesis trilogy, is published by Warner Books.
1993	*Parable of the Sower* is published by Warner Books. Butler is the Guest of Honor at the first ConDor, an SF convention sponsored by California Association for the Advancement of Speculative Media in San Diego, CA.
1994	*Parable of the Sower* is nominated for a Nebula Award.
1995	Butler is awarded a John D and Catherine T. MacArthur Foundation fellowship, commonly called a "genius" grant. She is the first science fiction writer to receive this grant. Butler's collection of short stories, *Bloodchild and Other Stories*, is published by Seven Stories Press.
1997	Butler is the Guest of Honor at Intervention, the 1997 U.K. National SF Convention (Eastercon), a SF convention in Liverpool, UK.
1998	The second Earthseed book, *Parable of the Talents*, is published by Warner Books. Butler is the Guest of Honor at LunaCon 98, an SF/fantasy convention organized by the New York Science Fiction Society, better known as "The Lunarians."
1999	*Parable of the Talents* wins the Nebula Award for Best Novel. Butler moves from Pasadena, CA, to Seattle, WA. Butler is the Guest of Honor at MiniCon 34, an SF convention in Minneapolis, MN, and at the first FoolsCap convention, a convention dedicated to written SF and fantasy held in Bellevue, WA.

2000   The Xenogenesis trilogy, *Dawn, Adulthood Rites*, and *Imago*, is republished by Warner Books as *Lilith's Brood*. Butler receives a Lifetime Achievement Award in Writing from the PEN American Center. Butler is the Guest of Honor at Balticon 34, an SF convention in Baltimore, MD.

2002   Butler is the Guest of Honor at ReaderCon 14, a convention that focuses on SF books in Burlington, MA, and EerieCon Four, an SF, fantasy, and horror convention in Niagara Falls, NY.

2003   Butler publishes the short stories "Amnesty" and "The Book of Martha" online at SciFi.com. Butler is the Guest of Honor at DemiCon 14, an SF convention in Des Moines, IA.

2005   Seven Stories Press publishes Butler's final novel *Fledgling*. Butler is awarded the Langston Hughes Medal of The City College. Seven Stories releases an expanded version of *Bloodchild and Other Stories*, which includes the new stories, "Amnesty" and "The Book of Martha."

2006   On February 24, Butler dies outside her home at the age of 58.

Endnote

1   The information in this timeline has come from a number of sources, mostly web pages. These include the following:
"Octavia Estelle Butler Biography," *Contemporary Novelists Vol. 3*, 31 Jan. 2008, <http://biography.jrank.org/pages/4197/Butler-Octavia-Estelle.html;

"Octavia Butler," *Black Women in America*, ed. Darlene Clark Hine, 2006, 9 Jan. 2008,<http://blog.oup.com/2006/02/octavia_butler/.>

"Octavia Estelle Butler," *Voices from the Gap: Women Artists and Writers of Color, an International Website*, ed. Laura Curtright, Aug. 2004, 30 Jan 2008, <http://voices.cla.umn.edu/vg/Bios/entries/butler_octavia_estelle.html>.

Octavia Butler, "'Devil Girl from Mars': Why I Write Science Fiction," *MIT Communications Forum* (1998), 6 Sept. 2007, <http://web.mit.edu/comm-forum/papers/butler.html>.

"The Hugo Awards: Hugo Award History," 7 Feb. 2008, <http://www.thehugoawards.org/?page_id=6>.

"SFWA Nebula Awards," 7 Feb. 2008, <http://dpsinfo.com/awardweb/nebulas/>.

Shawl, "Daughter of Necessity" *Foolscap I Program*, Seattle, WA, 1999

The web pages for the SF/fantasy conventions that are noted in the timeline.

We have included the dates for Butler's Guest of Honor appearances that we were able to discover. The list of such appearances is by no means complete.

Bibliography

African American Literature Book Club. 2007. 28 November 2008. http://aalbc.com/authors/Octavia.htm.

AfroFuturism. 2003. 28 November 2008. http://www.afrofuturism.net/.

Alarcon, Norma. "Traddutora, Traditora: A Paradigmatic Figure of Chicana Feminism." *Cultural Critique* 13 (1989): 57-87.

Allison, Dorothy. "The Future of Female: Octavia Butler's Mother Lode." In *Reading Black, Reading Feminist.* Edited by Henry Louis Gates, Jr. New York: Meridian, 1990.

Attebery, Brian. *Decoding Gender in Science Fiction.* New York: Routledge, 2002.

Auerbach, Nina. *Our Vampires, Ourselves.* Chicago and London: The University of Chicago Press, 1995.

Baccolini, Raffaella. "The Persistence of Hope in Dystopian Science Fiction." *PMLA.* 119 (2004): 518-521.

Baccolini, Raffaella, and Tom Moylan, eds. *Dark Horizons: Science Fiction and the Dystopian Imagination.* New York: Routledge, 2003.

Barr, Marleen. *Afro-Future Females: Black Writers Chart Science Fiction's Newest New-Wave Trajectory.* Columbus: Ohio State UP, 2008.

Barthes, Roland. *S/Z.* 1974. Trans. Richard Miller. New York: Hill and Wang, 1985.

Bennett, Drake. "X'ed Out: What happened to the anti-porn feminists?" The Boston Globe 6 March 2005. 6 March 2008. http://www.boston.com/news/globe/ideas/articles/2005/03/06/x_ed_out?pg=full.

Bollinger, Laurel. "Placental Economy: Octavia Butler, Luce Irigaray, and Speculative Subjectivity." *Lit: Literature Interpretation Theory* 18.4 (Oct. 2007): 325-352.

Bonner, Frances. "Difference and Desire, Slavery and Seduction: Octavia Butler's *Xenogenesis*." *Foundation: The Review of Science Fiction* 48 (1990): 50-62.

Brand, Chad, Charles Draper, and Archie England eds. *Holman's Illustrate Bible Dictionary*. Nashville, TN: Holman Bible Publishers, 2003.

Butler, Judith. *Precarious Life: The Powers of Mourning and Violence*. New York: Verso, 2004.

Butler, Octavia E. *Adulthood Rites*. New York: Warner, 1988.

——. "A Few Rules for Predicting the Future." *Essence* (May 2000): 165-166; 264.

——. "Amnesty." *Callaloo*. (Summer 2004) 27.3: 597-616.

——. "*Black Scholar* Interview with Octavia Butler: Black Women and the Science Fiction Genre." Interviewed by Frances Beal. *The Black Scholar* 17.2 (March/April 1986): 14-18.

——. *Bloodchild and Other Stories*. New York: Four Walls Eight Windows, 1995. New York: Seven Stories Press, 1996, 2005.

——. *Clay's Ark*. New York: St. Martin's Press,1984; in *Seed to Harvest*. New York Grand Central Publishing, Hachette Book Group, 2007.

——. *Dawn*. 1987. New York: Warner Books; in *Xenogenesis*. Guild America Books, 2000; in *Lilith's Brood*. New York: Warner Books, 2000.

——. "'Devil Girl from Mars': Why I Write Science Fiction." *MIT Communications Forum* 1998. 6 Sept. 2007 http://web.mit.edu/comm-forum/papers/butler.html.

——. "Essay on Racism: A Science-Fiction Writer Shares her View of Intolerance." September 1, 2001. NPR Weekend Edition Saturday. March 15, 2008. http://www.npr.org.

——. *Fledgling*. New York: Seven Stories Press, 2005.

——. "Futurist Woman: Octavia Butler." Interviewed by Veronica Mixon. *Essence* 9 (April 1979): 12, 15.

———. "Having her say: Octavia Butler talks with Evette Porter about *Fledgling*." *Essence* 35.6 (Oct 2005): 96.

———. *Imago*. New York: Warner, 1989.

———. "An Interview with Octavia E. Butler." In *Across the Wounded Galaxies: Interviews with Contemporary American Science Fiction Writers*. Edited by Larry McCaffery. Urbana, IL: University of Illinois Press, 1990.

———. "An Interview with Octavia E. Butler." Interview with Randall Kenan. *Callaloo* 14.2 (1991): 495-504.

———. *Kindred*. 1979. New York: Pocket Books, 1981; Boston, MA: Beacon Press, 1988, 2004.

———. *Lilith's Brood*. New York: Warner Books, 2000.

———. *Mind of My Mind*. New York: Avon Books, 1978.

———. "Octavia E. Butler: Persistence." *Locus* #473 (June 2000): 4, 75-78.

———. "Octavia Butler Presents Her Novel *Kindred*." Videotape of Shults Center Forum recorded March 3, 2003. Nazareth College, Rochester, New York.

———. *Parable of the Sower*. New York: Four Walls Eight Windows, 1993; New York: Aspect-Warner Books, 2000.

———. *Parable of the Talents*. New York: Seven Stories Press, 1998; New York: Warner Books, 2001

———. *Patternmaster*. 1976. New York: Warner Books, 1995.

———. Reading and Interview. Vertigo Books, College Park, MD. March 27, 2003.

———. "Science Fiction Writer Octavia Butler on Race, Global Warming and Religion." Interview. November 11, 2005. http://www.democracynow.org.

———. *Seed To Harvest*. New York: Warner Books, 2007.

———. *Survivor*. New York: Signet, New American Library, 1978.

———. Telephone interview with Sandra Y. Govan. May 18, 1990.

———. "'We Keep Playing the Same Record': A Conversation with Octavia E. Butler." Interviewed by Stephen W. Potts. *Science Fiction Studies* 23.3 (November 1996): 331-38.

———. *Wild Seed.* 1980. New York: Warner, 1988, 1999.

Carl Brandon Society. Ed. Science Fiction Writers Association (SFWA). 2007. 28 November 2008. www.sfwa.org/members/butler.

Caruth, Cathy. "An Interview with Robert Jay Lifton." In *Trauma: Explorations in Memory.* Edited by Nigel Fisk. Baltimore and London: The Johns Hopkins University Press, 1995.

Cherniavsky, Eva. *Incorporations: Race, Nation, and the Body Politics of Capital.* Minneapolis, MN: University of Minnesota Press, 2006.

Clute, John, "Butler, Octavia E(stelle)." *The Encyclopedia of Science Fiction.* Eds. John Clute and Peter Nicholls. New York: St. Martin's, 1995. 180.

Crosby, Christina. "Commentary: Allies and Enemies." In *Coming to Terms: Feminism, Theory, Politics,* edited by Elizabeth Weed. New York: Routledge. 1989. 207-8.

Davis, Angela. "Reflections on the Black Woman's Role in the Community of Slaves." *The Black Scholar* 3 (December 1971): 3-15.

Davis, Joel. *Mapping the Mind: The Secrets of the Human Brain and How it Works.* Secaucus, NJ: Carol Publishing Group, 1997.

Davis, Mike. *City of Quartz: Excavating the Future in Los Angeles.* New York: Random House, 1990.

De Beauvoir, Simone. *The Second Sex.* Trans. H.M. Parshley. New York: Knopf, 1971.

Delany, Samuel R. *About Writing: Seven Essays, Four Letters, and Five Interviews.* Middletown, CT: Wesleyan University Press, 2005.

Diaz, Junot. *The Brief Wondrous Life of Oscar Wao.* New York: Riverhead Books, 2007.

Dick, Philip K. *Do Androids Dream of Electric Sheep?* New York; Doubleday `968; New York: New American Library, 1969.

Doane, Mary Ann. "Commentary: Cyborgs, Origins, and Subjectivity." In *Coming to Terms: Feminism, Theory, Politics*, edited by Elizabeth Weed, New York: Routledge. 1989: 209-14.

Dubey, Madhu. "Folk and Urban Communities in African-American Women's Fiction: Octavia Butler's *Parable of the Sower*." *Studies in American Fiction*. 27.1 (1999): 103-124.

Dworkin, Andrea and Catherine A. MacKinnon. "Statement by Catherine A. MacKinnon and Andrea Dworkin Regarding Canadian Customs and Legal Approaches to Pornography." Press Release. 26 August, 1994. 6 March 2008 http://www.nostatusquo. com/ACLU/dworkin/OrdinanceCanada.html.

Earthseed Octavia Butler Club. 2007. 28 November 2008. http://groups. yahoo.com/group/earthseedoctaviabutlerclub/.

Falk, Dean. *Braindance*. New York: Henry Holt and Company, 1992.

Fatunmbi, Awo Fa'lokun. *Iba'se Orisa*. Bronx, NY: Original Publications, 1994. 108–114.

Federmayer, Éva "Octavia Butler's Maternal Cyborgs: The Black Female World of the Xenogenesis Trilogy." In *Anatomy of Science Fiction*, Edited by Donald E. Morse. Newcastle upon Tyne, England: Cambridge Scholars, 2006.

Fisher, Jim. "Intentional Communities." *NewsHour with Jim Lehrer*. PBS. 21 Dec. 2000. Transcript. *Online NewsHour*. 10 April 2008. http://www.pbs.org/newshour/essays/december00/ communities_12-21.html.

Fiske, John. *Understanding Popular Culture*. Boston, MA: Unwin Hyman, 1989.

Foster, Frances Smith. "Octavia Butler's Black Female Future Fiction." *Extrapolation* 23.1 (1982): 37-49.

Freisen, John W. and Virginia Lyons. *The Palgrave Companion to North American Utopias*. New York: Palgrave McMillan, 2004.

Fuss, Diana. *Essentially Speaking: Feminism, Nature, and Difference*. New York: Routledge, 1989.

Gane, Nicholas. "When We Have Never Been Human, What Is to Be Done? Interview with Donna Haraway." *Theory, Culture & Society* 23.7-8 (2006): 135-158.

Gateward, Frances. "Daywalkin' Night Stalkin' Bloodsuckas: Black Vampires in Contemporary Film." *Genders* 40 (2004).

Gayle, Addison, ed. *The Black Aesthetic.* Garden City, NY: Doubleday, 1971.

Gearhart, Sally Miller. 1979. *The Wanderground: Stories of the Hill Women.* Boston, MA: Alyson Publications, Inc.

Giddings, Paula. When and Where I Enter: The Impact of Black Woman on Race and Sex in America. New York: Bantam, 1984.

Gilroy, Paul. Against Race: Imagining Political Culture Beyond the Color Line. Cambridge, MA: Harvard University Press, 2000.

———. *The Black Atlantic: Modernity and Double Consciousness.* Cambridge, MA: Harvard University Press, 1993.

Gomez, Jewelle, "Recasting the Mythology: Writing Vampire Fiction." in *Blood Read: The Vampire Metaphor in Contemporary Culture.* Philadelphia, PA: University of Pennsylvania Press, 1997. 85-92.

Goodman, Amy. "Octavia Butler." *Democracy Now.* National Public Radio. New York. Friday, 11 November, 2005. Audio clip. 1 February, 2008. http://www.democracynow.org/article.pl?sid=05/11/11/158201.

Govan, Sandra Y. "Connections, Links, and Extended Networks: Patterns in Octavia Butler's Science Fiction." *Black American Literature Forum* 18 (1984): 82-87.

———. "Going to See the Woman: A Visit with Octavia E. Butler," *Obsidian III* V.6 no.2/V.7 #1 (Fall/Winter 2005–Spring/Summer 2006): 5-31.

Green, Michelle Erica. "'There Goes the Neighborhood': Octavia Butler's Demand for Diversity in Utopias." In *Utopian and Science Fiction by Women: Worlds of Difference.* Edited by Jane L. Donawerth and Carol A. Kolmerten. Syracuse, NY: Syracuse University Press, 1994.

Hairston, Andrea. "Octavia Butler—Praise Song to a Prophetic Artist." In *Daughters of the Earth: Feminist Science Fiction in the Twentieth Century*. Edited by Justine Larbalestier. Middletown, CT: Wesleyan University Press, 2006.

Haraway, Donna. *The Companion Species Manifesto: Dogs, People and Significant Otherness*. Chicago, IL Prickly Paradigm, 2003.

———. *Modest_Witness @ Second_Millennium. FemaleMan_Meets_ OncoMouse*. New York: Routledge, 1997.

———. *Simians, Cyborgs, and Women: The Reinvention of Nature*. New York: Routledge, 1991.

Harper, Phillip Brian. *Are We Not Men? Masculine Anxiety and the Problem of African-American Identity*. New York: Oxford University Press, 1996.

Hayles, N. Katherine. *How We Became Posthuman: Virtual Bodies in Cybernetics, Literature, and Informatics*. Chicago, IL University of Chicago Press, 1999.

Hirsch, Marianne and Valerie Smith. "From *Feminism and Cultural Memory*." In *Theories of Memory: A Reader*. Edited by Michael Rossington and Anne Whitehead. Baltimore, MD: The Johns Hopkins University Press, 2007.

Holden, Rebecca J. "The High Costs of Cyborg Survival: Octavia Butler's Xenogenesis Trilogy." *Foundation: the International Review of Science Fiction* 72 (Spring 1998): 49–56.

Holloway, Karla FC. *BookMarks: Reading in Black and White* New Brunswick, NJ: Rutgers University Press, 2006.

"The Hugo Awards: Hugo Award History." 7 Feb. 2008 http://www.thehugoawards.org/?page_id=6.

Hull, Gloria T., ed. *All the Women Are White, All the Blacks Are Men, But Some of Us Are Brave*. Old Westbury, NY: The Feminist Press, 1981.

Hurston, Zora. *Dust Tracks on a Road*. 1942. Edited by Robert Hemenway. 2nd ed. Urbana, IL: University of Illinois Press, 1984.

The Invisible Universe. Edited by Asli Dukan. 2007. 28 November 2008. http://www.invisibleuniversedoc.com/.

Jackson, Gregory. "What Would Jesus Do?" Practical Christianity, Social Gospel Realism, and the Homiletic Novel." *PMLA*. 121 (2006): 641- 661.

Jacobs, Naomi. "Posthuman Bodies and Agency in Octavia Butler's *Xenogenesis.*" In *Dark Horizons: Science Fiction and the Dystopian Imagination.* Eds. Raffaella Baccolini and Tom Moylan. New York: Routledge, 2003.

"John Cho [In Upcoming Star Trek film] Has A Cult Following," *CNN/Associated Press*. 12 March 2008. 10 April 2008. http://www.cnn.com/2008/SHOWBIZ/Movies/03/12/john.cho.ap/index.html.

Jones, Gwyneth. *North Wind*. New York: Tor, 1994.

Kenan, Randall. "An Interview with Octavia Butler." *Callaloo* 14.2 (1991): 495-504.

Larbalestier, Justine. *The Battle of the Sexes in Science Fiction.* Middletown. CT: Wesleyan UP, 2002.

Lefanu, Sarah. *Feminism and Science Fiction*. Bloomington, IN: Indiana UP, 1989.

Levitas, Ruth and Lucy Sargisson. "Utopia in Dark Times: Optimism/Pessimism and Utopia/Dystopia." In Raffaella Baccolini and Tom Moylan (Eds) *Dark Horizons: Science Fiction and the Dystopian Imagination.* London: Routledge. 2003. 13-28.

Littleton, Therese. "Octavia E. Butler Plants and Earthseed." *Amazon. com*. http://www.amazon.com/exec/obidos/tg/feature/-/11664/.

Long, Lisa A. "A Relative Pain: The Rape of History in Octavia Butler's *Kindred* and Phyllis Alesia Perry's *Stigmata.*" *College English* 64.4 (March 2002): 459-83.

Luckhurst, Roger. "'Horror and Beauty in Rare Combination': The Miscegenate Fictions of Octavia Butler." *Women: A Cultural Review* 7.1 (1996): 28–38.

Mark/Space Interplanetary Review. 2007. 28 November 2008. http://www.euro.net/mark-space/OctaviaButler.html.

Maryland Historical Society. "A History of the Maryland Historical Society, 1844-2006." *Maryland Historical Magazine*. Special Issue. 101.4 (Winter 2006).

McCaffery, Larry. "Interview with Octavia E. Butler." In *Across the Wounded Galaxies*. Edited by Larry McCaffery. Urbana, IL: University of Illinois Press, 1990.

McHenry, Susan and Mali Michelle Fleming. "Octavia's Mind Trip into the Near Future." *Black Issues Book Review*. 1.1 (1999): 14-18.

McKay, Nellie. "Remembering Anita Hill and Clarence Thomas: What Really Happened When One Black Woman Spoke Out." In *Race-ing Justice, En-gendering Power: Essays on Anita Hill, Clarence Thomas, and the Construction of Social Reality*. Edited by Toni Morrison. New York: Pantheon Books, 1992.

Mehaffy, Marilyn and AnaLouise Keating. "'Radio Imagination': Octavia Butler on the Poetics of Narrative Embodiment." *MELUS* 26.1 (Spring 2001): 45-76.

Melzer, Patricia. *Alien Constructions: Science Fiction and Feminist Thought*. Austin, TX: University of Texas Press, 2006.

Merrick, Helen. *The Secret Feminist Cabal: A Cultural History of Science Fiction Feminisms*. Seattle, WA: Aqueduct Press, 2009.

Michaels, Walter Benn. "Political Science Fictions." *New Literary History* 31.4 (2000): 649-664.

Miller, Jim. "Post-Apocalyptic Hoping: Octavia Butler's Dystopian/ Utopian Vision." *Science-Fiction Studies* 25.2 (July 1998): 336-360.

Mitchell, Margaret. *Gone with the Wind*. New York: Macmillan, 1936.

Moraga, Cherríe, and Gloria Anzaldúa, eds. *This Bridge Called My Back: Writings by Radical Women of Color*. Watertown, MA: Persephone, 1981.

Morris, Richard. "Left Brain, Right Brain, Whole Brain: an examination into theory of brain lateralization, learning styles and the implications for education." (March 2005) *Random Thoughts from a Random Fellow*. http://www.singsurf.org/brain/rightbrain.php.

———. Email to Sandra Y. Govan. 9 July 2007.

Morrison, Toni, ed. *Race-ing Justice, En-gendering Power: Essays on Anita Hill, Clarence Thomas, and the Construction of Social Reality.* New York: Pantheon Books. 1992.

Moylan, Tom. *Scraps of the Untainted Sky: Science Fiction, Utopia, Dystopia.* Boulder, CO: Westview Press, 2000.

Neal, Larry. "The Black Arts Movement." In *The Black Aesthetic.* Edited by Gayle Addison. Garden City, NY: Doubleday. 1971.

Norman, Brian, "'We' in Redux: The Combahee River Collective's *Black Feminist Statement*," *differences* 18,2 (2007): 103-132.

"Octavia Butler." *Black Women in America.* Edited by Darlene Clark Hine. 2006. 9 Jan. 2008, http://blog.oup.com/2006/02/octavia_butler/.

OctaviaButler.net: A Fan Blog for Octavia E. Butler, writer. 2007. 28 November 2008. http://octaviabutler.net/contact.

"Octavia Estelle Butler." *Voices from the Gap: Women Artists and Writers of Color, an International Website.* Edited by Laura Curtright. Aug. 2004, 30 Jan 2008 http://voices.cla.umn.edu/vg/Bios/entries/butler_octavia_estelle.html.

"Octavia Estelle Butler Biography." *Contemporary Novelists Vol. 3,* 31 Jan. 2008, http://biography.jrank.org/pages/4197/Butler-Octavia-Estelle.html.

Octavia Estelle Butler: An Unofficial Web Page. Edited by Sela Young. 2007. 28 November 2008. http://www.geocities.com/sela_towanda/.

Oved, Yaacov. *Two Hundred Years of American Communes.* New Brunswick, NJ: Transaction Books, 1988.

Patterson, Kathy Davis. "'HAUNTING BACK': VAMPIRE SUBJECTIVITY IN THE GILDA STORIES." *Femspec* 1 Jun 2005: 35. *GenderWatch (GW).* ProQuest. Claire T. Carney Library, University of Massachusetts Dartmouth, Dartmouth, MA. 10 Jan. 2009. http://www.proquest.com/.

Paz, Octavio. *The Labyrinth of Solitude.* New York: Grove, 1985 (orig. published 1950).

Peppers, Cathy M. "Dialogic Origins and Alien Identities in Butler's *Xenogenesis.*" *Science-Fiction Studies* 22.1 (March 1995): 47-62.

Peterson, Nancy J. *Against Amnesia: Contemporary Women Writers and the Crises of Historical Memory.* Philadelphia, PA: University of Pennsylvania Press, 2001.

Pfeil, Fred. *Another Tale to Tell: Politics and Narrative in Postmodern Culture.* New York: Verso, 1990.

Piercy, Marge. *Woman on the Edge of Time.* New York: Knopf, 1976.

Posnock, Ross. *Color and Culture: Black Writers and the Making of the Modern Intellectual.* Cambridge, MA: Harvard University Press, 1998.

Potts, Stephen. "'We Keep Playing the Same Record': A Conversation with Octavia E. Butler." *Science-Fiction Studies* 23.3 (November 1996): 331-338.

Pratt, Mary Louise. *Imperial Eyes: Travel Writing and Transculturation.* New York: Routledge, 1992.

———. "Linguistic Utopias." In *The Linguistics of Writing: Arguments between Language and Literature.* Edited by Nigel Fisk. New York: Methuen, 1987.

Ramirez, Catherine S. "Cyborg Feminism: The Science Fiction of Octavia Butler and Gloria Anzaldúa." In *Reload: Rethinking Women and Cyberculture.* Edited by Mary Flanagan and Austin Booth. Cambridge, MA: MIT Press, 2002.

Reagon, Bernice Johnson. "Coalition Politics: Turning the Century." In *Home Girls: A Black Feminist Anthology.* Edited by Barbara Smith. New York: Kitchen Table/Women of Color Press, 1983.

Richard, Thelma Shinn. "Defining Kindred: Octavia Butler's Postcolonial Perspective." *Obsidian III: Literature in the African Diaspora* 6-7.2-1 (2005 Fall-2006 Summer 2005): 118-134.

Rodriguez, Ralph. *Brown Gumshoes: Detective Fiction and the Search for Chicana/o Identity.* Austin, TX: University of Texas Press, 2005.

Rowell, Charles H. "An Interview with Octavia Butler." *Callaloo* 20.1 (1997): 47-66.

Russ, Joanna. *The Female Man*. In *Radical Utopias*. 1990. New York: Quality Paperback Book Club. 1975.

Sacks, Oliver. "A Neurologist's Notebook: A Bolt from the Blue." *The New Yorker* 23 July 2007: 38-42.

Salvaggio, Ruth. "Octavia Butler and the Black Science-Fiction Heroine." *Black American Literature Forum* 18 (1984): 78-81.

Sanders, Brandon C.S. (SolSeed founder.) Telephone interview. 26 Nov. 2008.

———. Email to Lisbeth Gant-Britton. 27 January 2009.

Sandoval, Chela. *Methodology of the Oppressed*. Minneapolis, MN: University of Minnesota Press, 2000.

Sands, Peter. "Octavia Butler's Chiastic Cannibalistics." *Utopian Studies: Journal of the Society for Utopian Studies* 14.1 (2003): 1-14.

Schlitz, Marilyn Mandala, Tina Amorok, and Cassandra Vieten, eds. *Living Deeply: The Art & Science of Transformation in Everyday Life.* Oakland, CA: New Harbinger Press, 2008.

Science Fiction Writers Association (SFWA). 2003. 28 November 2008. www.sfwa.org/members/butler.

Scott, Joan. "Commentary: Cyborgian Socialists." In *Coming to Terms: Feminism, Theory, Politics.* Edited by Elizabeth Weed. New York: Routledge. 1989.

"SFWA Nebula Awards." 7 Feb. 2008 http://dpsinfo.com/awardweb/nebulas/.

Shaviro, Steven. *Connected, or What It Means to Live in the Network Society.* Minneapolis, MN: University of Minnesota Press, 2003.

Shawl, Nisi. "Daughter of Necessity," *Foolscap I Program*, Seattle, WA, 1999.

Sheldon, Charles. *In His Steps*. 1977. Nashville, TN: Broadman Press, 1983.

———. *Robert Hardy's Seven Days: A Dream and Its Consequences*. Chicago, IL: Advance, 1898.

Shunn, Thelma J. "The Wise Witches: Black Women Mentors in the Fiction of Octavia E. Butler." In *Conjuring: Black Women, Fiction, and Literary Tradition.* Edited by Marjorie Pryse and Hortense J. Spillers. Bloomington, IN: Indiana University Press, 1985.

Siegel, Deborah. *Sisterhood Interrupted: From Radical Women to Grrls Gone Wild.* New York: Palgrave Macmillian. 2007.

Simon, Dan. Personal conversation with Nisi Shawl, 2008.

Smith, Shirlee. "Octavia Butler: Writing is finding out that you can." *Pasadena Star News* 2 February 1994: A-14.

Smith, Stephanie. "Morphing, Materialism, and the Marketing of Xenogenesis." *Genders* #18 (Winter 1993): 67-86.

SolSeed Movement. 2007. 28 November 208. http://solseed.org.

Stowe, Harriet Beecher. *Uncle Tom's Cabin.* London: J. Cassell, 1852.

Tal, Kali. "'That Just Kills Me': Black Militant Near-Future Fiction." *Social Text* #71 (Summer 2002): 65-91.

Talbot County Visitor's Guide & Map. Easton, MD: Talbot County Chamber of Commerce, 2006-2007.

Thompson, John. *The Life of John Thompson, A Fugitive Slave.* 1856. New York: Negro Universities Press, 1968.

Teish, Luisah. *Carnival of the Spirit: Seasonal Celebrations and Rites of Passage.* New York: Harper Collins, 1994.

———. *Jambalaya: The Natural Woman's Book of Personal Charms and Practical Rituals.* San Francisco, CA: 1985.

Tribute to Octavia Butler's novel. YouTube. Ed. saraann28. 2007. 28 November 2008. http://www.youtube.com/watch?v=-TNgWpB3ttg.

Tucker, Jeffrey A. "'The Human Contradiction': Identity and/as Essence in Octavia Butler's Xenogenesis Trilogy." *Yearbook of English Studies* 37.2 (2007): 164-181.

United States Federal Writers' Project of the Works Project Administration. *Slave Narratives: A Folk History of Slavery in the United States from Interviews with Former Slaves.* Vol.

VIII: Maryland Narratives. Washington, DC: Works Project Administration, 1941.

Unofficial Octavia Butler Webpage. Edited by Kelly Bengier (Clemson University). 2007. 28 November 2008. http://hubcap.clemson.edu/~sparks/Octav2.html.

Van Thompson, Carlyle. "Moving Past the Present: Racialized Sexual Violence and Miscegenous Consumption in Octavia Butler's Kindred." In *Eating the Black Body: Miscegenation as Sexual Consumption in African American Literature and Culture.* Edited by Carlyle Van Thompson. New York: Peter Lang. 2006.

Vint, Sherryl. *Bodies of Tomorrow: Technology, Subjectivity, and Science Fiction.* Toronto, ON: University of Toronto Press, 2007.

——. "'Only by Experience': Embodiment and the Limitations of Realism in Neo-Slave Narratives." *Science Fiction Studies* 34.2 (July 2007): 241-61.

Walker, Alice. *Meridian.* New York: Pocket Books, 1976.

Walker, Hazel R. Personal interview with Sandra Y. Govan. 5 March 2007.

Warfield, Angela. "Reassessing the Utopian Novel: Octavia Butler, Jacques Derrida, and the Impossible Future of Utopia." *Obsidian III: Literature in the African Diaspora* 6-7.2-1 (2005 Fall-2006 Summer 2005): 61-71.

Waters, Darren. "Virtuality and reality to merge." *BBC News website.* 2 Feb. 2008. 10 April 2008. http://news.bbc.co.uk/2/hi/technology/7258105.stm.

Weed, Elizabeth, ed. *Coming to Terms: Feminism, Theory, Politics.* New York: Routledge. 1989.

Weeks, Christopher. *Where Land and Water Intertwine: An Architectural History of Talbot County, Maryland.* Baltimore, MD: The Johns Hopkins University Press, 1984.

West, C. S'Thembile. "The Competing Demands of Community Survival and Self-Preservation in Octavia Butler's *Kindred.*" *Femspec* 7.2 (2006): 72-86.

Williams, John. *Sons of Darkness, Sons of Light.* Boston, MA: Northeastern University Press, 1969.

Williams, Sheila. Editor, *Asimov's Science Fiction Magazine.* Unpublished interview with Sandra Y. Govan. 7 May 2007.

Winnubst, Shannon. "Vampires, Anxieties, and Dreams: Race and Sex in the Contemporary United States." *Hypatia: A Journal of Feminist Philosophy* 18.3 (Fall 2003): 1-20.

Wolmark, Jenny. *Aliens and Others: Science Fiction, Feminism, and Postmodernism.* Iowa City, IA: University of Iowa Press, 1994.

Yaszek, Lisa. "'A grim fantasy': Remaking American History in Octavia Butler's *Kindred.*" *Signs* 28.4 (Summer 2003): 1053-66.

Zaki, Hoda M. "Utopia, Dystopia, and Ideology in the Science Fiction of Octavia Butler." *Science-Fiction Studies* 17 (1990): 239-51.

Zerilli, Linda M. G. *Feminism and the Abyss of Freedom.* Chicago, IL: University of Chicago Press, 2005.

Contributor Biographies

Steven Barnes writes novels, short stories, screenplays, and teleplays, and lectures on writing, psychology, and creativity. His more than twenty-five published books include *The Descent of Anansi* (with Larry Niven, 1982, Tor Books), *Lion's Blood* (2002, Warner), *Zulu Heart* (2003, Warner), and *Shadow Valley* (2009, Random House). The *Twilight Zone*, the *Outer Limits*, and *Baywatch* have broadcast his teleplays. Barnes currently resides in Atlanta, Georgia, with his wife, Tananarive Due, daughter Lauren Nicole, and son Jason Kai. He is a martial artist, with a black belt in Karate and proficiency in many other martial arts disciplines. A Hugo and Nebula Award nominee and winner of the Endeavour Award, Barnes is also a respected film industry consultant.

doris davenport is a Performance Poet, Educator, and Writer, from Cornelia, Georgia, in the Appalachian foothills, a locus of fantasy and parallel/alternate realities. She has earned degrees from Paine College (BA English), SUNY Buffalo (MA English), and the University of Southern California (PhD Literature). doris appears regularly at workshops, conferences and performances (including the Science Fiction Research Association's Annual Conference in June 2009, which is how she got in this anthology!). She has published reviews, essays, and eight books of poetry. The most recent is *ascent: poems* (2011). Currently she is an Associate Professor of English at Stillman College in Tuscaloosa, AL, where she also works—surreptitiously—to eliminate all the -isms including "stupidism" and to include a bit of "alternative" into mundane daily realities. More information: http://redroom.com/member/doris-diosa-davenport.

L. Timmel Duchamp is the author of the five-volume Marq'ssan Cycle (which won special recognition from the James Tiptree Award jury), consisting of *Alanya to Alanya* (2005), *Renegade* (2006), *Tsunami* (2007), *Blood in the Fruit* (2007), and *Stretto* (2008); *The Red Rose Rages (Bleeding)*; two collections of short fiction, *Love's Body, Dancing in Time* (2004), which was shortlisted for the Tiptree, and *Never at Home* (2011); numerous reviews and essays; and co-author, with Maureen McHugh, of a mini-collection, *Plugged In* (2008, published in conjunction with the authors' being GoHs at WisCon). She is also the founder and publisher of Aqueduct Press. Some of her short fiction and essays are available at http://ltimmel.home.mindspring.com/.

Tananarive Due is the American Book Award-winning author of more than a dozen books, ranging from supernatural thrillers to a mystery to a civil rights memoir. Her novel *The Living Blood* (2001) received a 2002 American Book Award, and *The Good House* (2003) was nominated as Best Novel by the International Horror Guild. *The Black Rose* (2000), based on the life of business pioneer Madam C.J. Walker, was nominated for an NAACP Image Award. She received the NAACP Image Award for *In the Heat of the Night*, which she co-wrote with Blair Underwood and her husband, author Steven Barnes. Due has a BS in journalism from Northwestern University and an MA in English literature from the University of Leeds, England. She has taught creative writing in the MFA program at Antioch University Los Angeles and is currently the Cosby Chair in the Humanities at Spelman College. She lives in Georgia with Barnes, their son Jason, and her stepdaughter Nicki.

Shari Evans is Associate Professor of English at the University of Massachusetts—Dartmouth, affiliate faculty for both Women's Studies and African and African American Studies, and Director of the Liberal Arts Program. She earned her PhD at the University of New Mexico in 2005, and her work has centered on space, gender, and feminist concepts of "home" in contemporary multiethnic women writers. Her essays on Toni Morrison, Margaret Atwood, experimental writer Elaine Kraf, and pedagogy have appeared in journals like *African American Review*, *Critique*, and *Femspec*, as well as in essay collections. A scholar, teacher, and fan of feminist science and speculative fiction, she has chaired and presented papers at numerous panels on feminist science fiction and Octavia Butler at national conferences. Her most recent work examines the strategies of forgetting and remembering in multiethnic contemporary authors such as Louise Erdrich, Brenda Marie Osbey, and Octavia Butler.

Thomas Foster is Professor of English at University of Washington, Seattle. His book *The Souls of Cyberfolk: Posthumanism as Vernacular Theory* was published by the University of Minnesota Press in 2005. He has published a number of essays on science fiction and technoculture studies, including "The Postproduction of the Human Heart: Desire, Identification, and Virtual Embodiment in Feminist Narratives of Cyberspace," which appeared in *Reload: Rethinking Women + Cyberculture* (MIT, 2002), as well as contributions to the *Routledge Companion to Science Fiction* and the forthcoming *Oxford Companion to Science Fiction*. His current work-in-progress is tentatively titled "Ethnicity and Technicity: Nature, Culture, and Race in the Cyberpunk Archive."

Lisbeth Gant-Britton is the author of *Holt African American History* (2007). Formerly the Marlene Crandell Francis Professor of the Humanities in the English Department at Kalamazoo College, she has also taught courses at the USC Film School in African American Literature and Culture. She currently teaches at UCLA and Los Angeles City College, as well as serving as the Student Affairs Officer for the UCLA Interdepartmental Program in Afro-American Studies. Her previous work, *African-American History: Heroes in Hardship*, won the Los Angeles Mayor's Office Special Commendation for its contribution to racial understanding through education in 1992. An Americanist focusing primarily on narrative, Dr. Gant-Britton is the former Modern Language Association (MLA) Science Fiction and Fantasy Discussion Group Chair. She is currently at work on a book on AfroFuturism. Her published essays and articles include "Our Fate or Our Future: The Hip Hop Nation and Alternative Intentional Communities for Social Justice" (in *Africana Studies: A Review of Social Science Research*, 2013), "Mexican Women and Chicanas Enter Futuristic Fiction" (in *Future Females: The Next Generation*, 2000), "Octavia Butler's *Parable of the Sower*: One Alternative to a Futureless Future" (in *Women of Other Worlds: Excursions Through Science Fiction and Feminism*, University of Western Australia Press, 1999) and "Exploring Color-Coding at the Beginning and End of the Twentieth Century in Ursula Le Guin's *The Left Hand of Darkness* and Joseph Conrad's *Heart of Darkness*" (in *Peering Into Darkness: Race and Color in the Fantastic, 1997*). She is also a frequent television commentator regarding African American issues.

Candra K. Gill is a lifelong speculative fiction fan. She serves on the editorial board of *Watcher Junior: The Undergraduate Journal of Whedon Studies*; she is also a cofounder of the Carl Brandon Society and serves on the organization's Steering Committee. She has presented at conferences including PCA/ACA, WisCon, and Slayage. Her controversial essay "Cuz the Black Chick Always Gets It First: Dynamics of Race in Buffy the Vampire Slayer" appeared in the anthology *Girls Who Bite Back* (Sumach Press, 2004). A former teacher and student affairs professional, she currently works as a user experience designer.

Sandra Y. Govan is Professor Emerita, English Department, at the University of North Carolina, Charlotte. Writing about African American participation in science fiction has been a major component of her professional life. She wrote the "Afterword" to Warner's 2001 edition of Butler's *Wild Seed*. Among other essays, Govan's publications include "Going to See the Woman: A Visit with Octavia E. Butler" (*Obsidian III*, 2005–2006); "Silent Interviews: On Language, Race, Sex, Science Fiction, and Some Comics" (*African American Review*, 1997); "Homage to Tradition: Octavia Butler Renovates the Historical Novel," (*MELUS*, 1986); "Connections, Links, and Extended Networks: Patterns in Octavia Butler's Science Fiction" *Black American Literature Forum*, 1984); and "The Insistent Presence of Black Folk in the Novels of Samuel R. Delany" (also *Black American Literature Forum*, 1984). Govan has also written on the Harlem Renaissance and Black American writers from the 1960s onward. She remains professionally active, lecturing for the North Carolina Humanities Council; she is also a founding member of the Wintergreen Women Writers Collective.

Merrilee Heifetz is senior vice president of Writers House literary agency in New York, where she has been a representative for twenty-five years. Her current clients include Neil Gaiman, Laurell K. Hamilton, Melissa Marr, Cynthia Voigt, and many others. She was Octavia E. Butler's agent for twenty years. A member of the Association of Authors Representatives, she chaired that organization's Contracts Committee for five years. She was instrumental in the creation of the Octavia E. Butler Memorial Scholarship Fund. Heifetz is now Butler's literary executor.

Rebecca J. Holden is an adjunct writing professor in the Professional Writing Program at the University of Maryland, College Park, as well as a scholar of feminist science fiction. She received her PhD in English from the University of Wisconsin–Madison. Her published essays include

"The High Costs of Cyborg Survival: Octavia Butler's Xenogenesis Trilogy" (in *Foundation*, 1998) and "Of Synners and Brainworms: Feminism on the Wire" (in *Women of Other Worlds: Excursions through Science Fiction and Feminism*, University of Western Australia Press, 1999). She coordinated the academic track of programming at WisCon, the world's largest feminist science fiction convention, for several years and continues to attend and present at WisCon, as well as at other sf conferences.

Leslie Howle, Workshop Director of the Clarion West Writers Workshop, is also the founder and administrator of Northwest Media Arts, a nonprofit literary events organization. She was the Senior Education and Outreach Manager for the Science Fiction Museum and Hall of Fame for several years, served on the jury of the James Tiptree, Jr. Award in 2008, and in 2007 was nominated for a World Fantasy Award in the Special Award: Non-Professional category. Howle was a longtime friend of Octavia E. Butler.

Nnedi Okorafor is a speculative fiction novelist of Nigerian descent. Her novels include *Who Fears Death* (winner of the 2011 World Fantasy Award for Best Novel), *Akata Witch* (an Andrea Norton Award nominee), *Zahrah the Windseeker* (winner of the Wole Soyinka Prize for African Literature), and *The Shadow Speaker* (winner of the Carl Brandon Parallax Award). Her children's book *Long Juju Man* won the Macmillan Writer's Prize for Africa. Nnedi holds a PhD in Literature and is a professor of creative writing at Chicago State University. Visit Nnedi at nnedi.com.

Benjamin Rosenbaum is an American science fiction, fantasy, and literary fiction writer and computer programmer, whose stories have been finalists for the Hugo, Nebula, Theodore Sturgeon, BSFA, and World Fantasy awards. His work has been published in *The Magazine of Fantasy & Science Fiction*, *Asimov's Science Fiction*, *Harper's*, *Nature*, and *McSweeney's Quarterly Concern*. It has also appeared on the websites *Strange Horizons* and *Infinite Matrix*, in various year's best anthologies, and in his 2008 collection *The Ant King and Other Stories* (Small Beer Press). Born in New York but raised in Arlington, Virginia, he received degrees in computer science and religious studies from Brown University. He currently lives in Basel, Switzerland, with his wife Esther and children Aviva and Noah.

Kate Schaefer has volunteered to help put on science fiction conventions since 1976. She served as Chair of the Potlatch Science Fiction Convention in 1992, 2002, and 2008. She was a longtime member of the Board of Directors of the Clarion West Writers Workshop and currently works for the organization as a key volunteer. Schaefer served as Jury Chair for the James Tiptree, Jr. Award in 1998, and helped create the Carl Brandon Society's Octavia E. Butler Memorial Scholarship Fund. She designs and sews art-to-wear vests, jackets, hats, evening wraps, and handbags. Schaefer once turned down Octavia Butler's offer to pitch in for gas money.

Steven Shaviro is the DeRoy Professor of English at Wayne State University. He is the author of *Doom Patrols: A Theoretical Fiction about Postmodernism* (Serpent's Tail, 1997), *Connected, or, What It Means to Live in the Network Society* (University of Minnesota Press, 2003), *Without Criteria: Kant, Whitehead, Deleuze, and Aesthetics* (MIT Press, 2009), *Post-Cinematic Affect* (Zero Books, 2010), as well as numerous essays about film, video and new media, science fiction, cultural theory, and contemporary American popular culture.

Nisi Shawl's collection *Filter House* (Aqueduct Press, 2008) won the James Tiptree, Jr. Award in 2008. Her story "Cruel Sistah" was included in *The Year's Best Fantasy & Horror #19* (St. Martin's, 2006). Her work has also appeared in *So Long Been Dreaming: Postcolonial Science Fiction and Fantasy*, both volumes of the groundbreaking Dark Matter anthology series, several other notable anthologies, and leading science fiction print and web magazines. With Cynthia Ward she teaches "Writing the Other: Bridging Cultural Differences for Successful Fiction;" the workshop's companion book came out from Aqueduct Press in Summer 2005. She edited the 2011 nonfiction anthology *The WisCon Chronicles 5: Writing and Racial Identity*, and the 2013 fiction anthology *Bloodchildren: Stories from the Octavia E. Butler Scholars*. In 2011 she was WisCon 35's Guest of Honor. A board member for the Clarion West Writers Workshop and a cofounder of the Carl Brandon Society, Shawl has appeared as a guest speaker at Stanford University, Duke University, and Smith College.

JT Stewart—writer, poet, playwright, editor—has taught Cross-Cultural Humanities and writing at the University of Washington, Seattle Central Community College, Fairhaven College (Western Washington University), and Richard Hugo House. By including Octavia Butler's *Kindred* in her curricula, she exposed hundreds of students to this literary example of an empowered black woman. Stewart, an alumna of the Hedgebrook writing retreat, has been the featured poet for the online journal *Stone Telling*. Her work also appears in *The Moment of Change* (Aqueduct Press, 2012). She began her professional affiliation with science fiction in 1973 as a member of Vonda N. McIntyre's Clarion West Writers' Workshop at the University of Washington, and later co-founded the current iteration of Clarion West's yearly summer workshop, where Octavia Butler often taught.

Luisah Teish is a writer, performer, and priestess. Her published books include *Jambalaya: The Natural Woman's Book of Personal Charms and Practical Rituals* (1985), *Carnival of the Spirit: Seasonal Celebrations and Rites of Passage* (1994), *Jump Up: Good Times Throughout the Seasons with Celebrations from Around the World* (2000), and *The Stained Glass Whore & Other Virgins* (2006). Her essays have appeared in *Shaman Drum*, *Essence Magazine*, and more than one dozen anthologies. Teish is an initiated elder in the Ifa/Orisha tradition of the West African Diaspora, and Olori (director) of Ile Orunmila Oshun and the School of Ancient Mysteries/Sacred Arts Center. She holds a chieftaincy from the Fatunmise Compound in Ile Ife, Nigeria, and is Chair of the World Orisha Congress Committee on Women's Issues. Teish is also a devotee of Damballah Hwedo, the Haitian Rainbow Serpent, under the guidance of Moma Lola. A resident of the San Francisco Bay Area, Teish has been actively involved in peacekeeping, teaching transformation, and working to insure justice for over thirty years.

◆■ *Photo by Leslie Howle*